DESERT SUNDAYS

A NOVEL

William T. Goodman

Oak Lee Publishing *APRIL 2020*

www.oakleepublishing.com

DESERT SUNDAYS

Copyright © 2014 by William T. Goodman

All rights reserved. No part of this publication may be reproduced, distributed, or transmitted in any form or by any means, including photocopying, recording, or other electronic or mechanical methods, without the prior written permission of the publisher, except in the case of brief quotations embodied in critical reviews and certain other noncommercial uses permitted by copyright law. For permission requests, write to the publisher, addressed "Attention: Permissions Coordinator," at the address below.

Oak Lee Publishing
P.O. Box 10532
Bozeman, MT 59719

www.williamtgoodman.com

Ordering Information: Quantity sales. Special discounts are available on quantity purchases by corporations, associations, and others. For details, contact the publisher at the address above.

Printed in the United States of America

Cover Design by Oak Lee Publishing, Design Department
Editing by Oak Lee Publishing, Editing Department

First Edition, First Printing, 2014

*To the singers and musicians performing
in remote backwater bars and restaurants across
America from whom the initial inspiration for
Desert Sundays originated.*

ONE

LUNDEN, ARIZONA

Continuing quietly, they made their way along a narrow game trail that gently ascended to a sandy ridge. Long shadows streaked the ground as the first rays of morning turned the rocks from gray to dull shades of yellow and red. He pointed to a distant coyote trotting away from view. Light and quick, the coyote glanced over his shoulder at them until he disappeared behind a rocky rise.

Had anyone been there to observe them, they would have appeared an odd and unlikely couple walking in the Arizona desert while the sun was beginning its rise from the eastern horizon. She – with her thick strawberry blonde hair hanging straight and half way down her back, bundled in a Woolrich Alaskan shirt under a down vest, jeans and oddly, wearing ankle high moccasins – seemed chilled as she walked. He – naked but for a red bandana headband, cutoff gray sweatpants and the same style mocs, wearing only a small suede pouch suspended by a leather thong which hung high on his bare chest between two symmetrical scars – ambled at her side in seeming comfort. They did not speak, but when a small bird fluttered from a prickly pear cactus, both instantly turned in unison at the disturbance and focused for a moment on the sparrow before returning their gaze ahead. It was a Sunday in January and the temperature was slowly rising from the morning low of 42 degrees.

Standing just over five-foot-seven, she was about an inch taller than he. She was also nearly ten years older. In the early morning light their breath was mist that puffed then dissolved in the cool dry air. On these weekly jaunts she always felt a little out of place compared to him. He walked so naturally and with an easy sure-footed quietness. His bronze skin appeared always smooth without any of the goose bumps she usually had in the colder temperatures. He was short and fit and tight, but she thought at 28 he should be. His straight dark brown hair hung just past his shoulders and parted in the middle. The rolled, red bandana kept it from blowing into his face and eyes. Twin scars on each pectoral muscle were still relatively new and pink. Later, she knew, they'd turn a more fleshy hue and blend in better. Each scar consisted of two parallel vertical lines a few inches long connected by jagged tissue in the middle. When she looked at them she couldn't help but shudder slightly. The first time he caught her staring at the scars he just smiled with his perfect white teeth and told her it was nothing to be concerned about and that he'd explain some time. That was almost two years ago. Eventually he did explain them and she tried to understand, which at the time was very difficult. Now she took his ideas and explanations without the nervous apprehension she experienced in the beginning of their friendship. Being a transplanted Crow Indian from Montana and she a singer from Tennessee, they were both strangers to the Arizona desert. Still, he blended easier and faster than she. They had blended together in friendship almost immediately.

They walked in near silence. Joseph had introduced her to the moccasin experience. He said shoes and boots confined and dulled the foot senses. Moccasins set them free. He was right. She could actually determine the ground under her feet and feel each rock, pebble or sandy patch as they walked. There was just enough thickness in the double-soled smooth leather bottoms to protect her feet, but not so much that they "blinded the feet," as Joseph put it. It was a strange sensation at first, but once gotten used to, somehow added a new dimension to walking. Moccasins were also quiet. The stiff lug soles of hiking boots crunched over rocks and seemed to grind in sand. Mocs conformed to the ground. Joseph said mocs allowed you to walk *with* the land instead of trampling on the land. It was a simple concept like so many of his truisms and ideas. Mocs over boots, not exactly a major revelation, but still another small part of dealing with the world in a slightly different manner which she found appealing. Little things, like wearing mocs in the desert, combined with other similar little things to change preconceived notions and habits that were previously adhered to without thought or question. It was these small things, Joseph said, that together determined how people dealt with each day. You could walk upon the land feeling its texture or you could crush the ground leaving heavy, sharp-edged foot prints. You could be silent and observant of nature or be loud and oblivious to your surroundings. Mae knew

Joseph wasn't necessarily criticizing as much as he was just finding his own way.

All week Mae looked forward to these *Secret Sundays,* as she called them, with Joseph. It seemed any stresses and concerns that built up during the week were somehow released on these Sunday mornings. Or, if not completely released, then at least mellowed and put into a better perspective. The desert seemed the great releasing ground for worry.

Joseph's kiva was situated about a mile from his small and secluded rented home. He'd found it soon after he'd moved in while exploring his new surroundings. It was simply a ring of rocks in the dirt about eight feet across. At first it looked like an oversized campfire ring. Later, Joseph would dig out the middle to expose a round stone-lined chamber about six feet deep. Ceremonial kivas could be many sizes. This was a small, personal one probably used by an individual or maybe a family. From the style of a few pottery shards Joseph uncovered while digging out the structure, his online research indicated the kiva was probably in use around 1200 AD. Further reading revealed this was fairly typical for the area. There were probably hundreds of kivas in the surrounding desert hills that were now filled in and covered with layers of sand and dirt, invisible to the present world. Joseph was fortunate to have found this one. In another decade or two the top ring of stones he discovered might have been reclaimed by the ever shifting desert sands.

When they reached the kiva the sun was well above the horizon and burning the night chill from the new day. From under a heavy tarp Joseph pulled out two folding camp chairs. He slid each from its zippered case, pushed them open and placed them facing the east. Before sitting, Mae removed her down vest and unbuttoned her long-sleeved gray wool shirt. "You're still dressing too warm," Joseph taunted.

Mae smiled, "I know. You tell me that every time we come here. It doesn't make sense to walk around half naked pretending you're not cold."

He chuckled for a moment and replied, "You'll never know unless you try it. I swear it's the truth. If you fight the cold you feel it more. I don't know how it works, but it does. This isn't some ancient Indian crap, maybe I even discovered it myself, but it really is true. I think I told you how I learned about this when I got a touch of food poisoning in Montana."

"Yeah, I've heard this before."

"Well, it's a good story and obviously you didn't pay much attention the first time, so I'll tell it again." He glanced at Mae for some reaction, but getting none he continued; "It was late spring, but still pretty cold. Hit me in the middle of the night. Came on so fast I didn't have time to put a jacket on. I was camped along the Milk River and barely made it out of my tent. The runs came on quick and stayed a while. I was out in the cold with only a T-shirt on and my boxers around my ankles. There was no wind fortunately – wind changes everything – but after a while I realized I was cool, but not cold. I relaxed between bouts of emptying and actually enjoyed the cold. Hard to explain. I let the cold become me and I became the cold. It was like a truce between us. It's as much a mental thing as a physical thing. I finally went back to the tent and slept for a while before the next series of scoots hit me. This time it wasn't as much of an emergency and I put a jacket on before leaving the tent. I put it on without thinking and after being outside again I started feeling really chilled. Remembering my earlier experience which seemed kind of like a dream by then, I took my jacket off, tried to relax and presto, I wasn't cold. Now, I'm not saying I'd try this in a blizzard, but it does seem to work when the air is calm and above freezing. Like this morning. "That was perfect."

"Yes, you've told me that lovely story before. It leaves me with such a delightful mental image of you. Maybe you should change the story to something about a grizzly bear ripping your tent to shreds while you escape into the cold night wearing only your boxers. That image I find more attractive. The whole diarrhea thing just doesn't work for me."

"Actually Mae, it was a mountain lion and I had to kill it with my bare hands. But I somehow always thought you were more into human suffering at its basest level, so I made up the diarrhea stuff for your benefit. I guess this was another time when the truth would have served me better."

"I never really believed your story anyway. Saw right through it. I knew you were downplaying your true heroic self."

"Yeah right, I'm quite the hero."

They sat for a while feeling the increasing warmth take over the land with the rising of the morning sun. A few ravens flew circles overhead and a desert cottontail broke cover to feed on some nearby grass. "Did you want to use the kiva today?" Joseph asked.

"I'm pretty happy to just be here. I'm fine like this unless you want to."

"Nope, suits me. I like mornings like this."

A few minutes went by before Mae spoke. "Today's my anniversary... our anniversary."

"Really, how so?"

"Exactly two years ago today I arrived here in Lunden and exactly two years ago today I met you."

"And you know for sure it was *exactly* on this date?"

"Yes, because that's the day I started keeping my journal."

Joseph smiled at Mae, "Let me guess. I'd say your first entry went like this:" and he spoke in a whimsical girlish voice, 'Dear Diary, today I met the most handsome and erudite man! I didn't know anyone so wonderful could actually exist! I think I'm in love!'"

"You're such a jerk." Mae turned to Joseph and lightly punched his upper arm.

"Actually it was more like this: 'Today I met the most pathetic half-breed, starving Indian. I felt so sorry for him that I pulled a dollar bill from my purse which he snatched from my hand and ran off into the desert. Poor creature ... I only hope he survives."

"All this time I thought I'd made a good first impression. At least now I know. Probably something I need to work on."

"Actually, the first impression wasn't so bad; it was the second one that needed improvement."

"I'm not real proud of our second meeting, now that you mention it. We don't need to talk about that one."

"Probably best," Mae said and started quietly laughing. Joseph laughed too. He got out of his chair and stood behind her. He gave her shoulders and neck a firm massage for a couple minutes, kissed the top of her head and said, "Happy anniversary," before returning to his chair next to her.

Mae asked, "I didn't hear from you this week. Busy?"

"Kind of. The parts I ordered for the Jeep finally came in and it took me longer than I thought it would to install correctly. Turns out I needed some other parts too which I was able to get, but had to drive all the way to the Jeep dealer. I also tutored more kids than usual this week."

"Good kids?"

"Yeah, nice bunch of kids. Mostly I tutored math and two of them had English papers I helped them write. A lot of the kids on the reservation aren't doing as well as they should. It's their damn attitude that keeps them down. At least some of the kids and their parents take education seriously."

"You sure you wouldn't consider teaching in a classroom again?"

"Been there, done that, Mae. Besides, with my, shall we say, less than stellar past performance, I probably wouldn't get hired anyway. Just as well. I like helping the kids who actually want to do better. As you know, my last teaching gig didn't turn out so well."

"You're too hard on yourself. You have so much to give. Maybe you gave up too soon."

"Maybe. We'll see, but I don't think so. How 'bout you? Singing go okay?"

"Yeah, it's been good. As I've said, sometimes I can really lose myself singing. It's been like that lately. Usually on the slow nights when everyone seems more interested in their dinners or drinks than the music. That's fine with me. Sometimes it can be nice to just sing the songs I like and not worry about what anyone listening thinks."

Joseph silently nodded with closed eyes letting the morning sun engulf his face.

A short time later Mae continued, "I did have a funny thing happen the other night. This guy I'd never seen before, probably an out of towner passing through, asked me to play anything by the Allman Brothers. I told him I would when the rest of my band arrived later. He said that would be great and he went back eating. He left about ten minutes later."

Joseph chuckled. "Did he really think there was room for a band in your little corner of Chuck's Desert Oasis?"

"I guess he did. He seemed happy enough when he left though. Maybe that's what I need – a full band to make me sound better."

"You don't need anything to make you sound better. This place is damn lucky to have you. Chuck should pay you more too. You're the only real bright spot around here." Joseph folded his arms over his chest and slid a bit further down in his chair.

"I did meet someone kind of interesting a couple nights ago."

"Male or female?"

"A guy. New here. Just moving in from out of town."

Joseph sat up straighter in his chair and looked at Mae sitting next to him. "Is this something I need to be worried about? If he even comes close to you I'll tear him limb from limb."

"Would you stop being such an idiot? Seriously, he seemed nice. Smart too. I think he's either separated or divorced or maybe going through a divorce or something. Anyway, it was strange how we got talking."

"How so?"

"Well, you know I like to end for the night by saying how I enjoyed playing for everyone and taking requests, but that I always reserve the last song for me. I then sing something by Megan McDonough."

"She's the one your father played on his old phonograph when you were a kid, right?"

"See you do listen."

"Nothing escapes me," and he sent an ingratiating smile at Mae.

"Except when you've had a few too many."

"Getting back to your new mystery man..."

"So. I'm finishing up the evening and I say the usual thing about this last song being for me. I sang a song called 'Daddy Always Liked a Lady' and ended for the night. There weren't many people left in Chuck's by this time. Dinner was over and the last stragglers were finishing their drinks as I put my guitar back in the case. I've been singing here for a couple years now and usually end with a Megan McDonough song which nobody has ever heard of. Well, the other night as I said, this guy comes up to me and says he thought *he* was the only Megan McDonough fan left in the world."

Joseph stared at Mae. "Sounds intriguing. You know how I think about things like this. Sometimes they mean nothing, but really unusual things usually mean something. Tell me more."

"There's not much to tell, really. He said he taught at some college back East. English department, I think. He said a friend who taught in the music department liked to listen to Megan McDonough and turned him on to her."

"How old's this guy?"

"About my age, I'd say. Maybe a little older, maybe not."

"So he's in his mid-twenties, huh?"

"Maybe late twenties," Mae laughed. "No, seriously he's probably early forties."

"And then he left?"

"No, we sat for a while and had a drink. Actually he ordered white wine. Not exactly making an effort to blend around here. Nice guy though."

"Interested in you? Let's see, new in town, smart college professor from the East, drinks Chablis, impeccable taste in folk music," Joseph pondered, "probably drives a sports car. Sounds irresistible."

Mae giggled. "He does drive a sports car."

"This could be big trouble if you ask me," Joseph said feigning concern. "What's he doing here?"

"I'm not sure and I'm not sure he even knows. He seemed a little sad actually. He told me things weren't going well where he came from and that he needed a break. He said he needed someplace completely new. He said something about wanting to write. We really didn't talk that long. I was tired and wanted to get home. And no, before you ask, he didn't offer to take me home. I think he was lonely and just wanted someone to talk to. He's rented a small house in town." Mae looked at Joseph for a moment, "I have the feeling he might be worth getting to know.'

"We could double date sometime."

"That's an idea. I can just picture cultured me escorted by Mr. Eastern Aristocrat doubling with interesting, philosophical you and some local floozy on your arm."

"Not fair!" Joseph declared in mock outrage. "You judge too harshly."

"C'mon Joseph, when was the last girl you went out with who had read a book in the last two years?"

"I seek inner intelligence and individual worth in people, unlike someone I know."

"Honestly, you're so full of crap. How can you keep a straight face and say that? You look for skin deep qualities in women, present company excluded, of course, and your track record proves that out. You don't have a little black book, you have a scratch pad titled 'Honky-Tonk Hotties.'"

"It's not like the single female population in Lunden has a lot of depth. I make do with what's offered. And thinking about it, aren't you in that pool?"

"No, I'm not in that pool. I'm off limits to the likes of you. I'm too old for you anyway. Besides, I wouldn't go out with an Indian," Mae looked at Joseph trying unsuccessfully not to laugh.

"I'm a half-breed or at least some part non-Indian, so it would probably be okay, but you're right, you are too old for me." Joseph too tried not to laugh.

Neither Joseph nor Mae could completely conceal their smiles as they sat facing the rising sun. Joseph always seemed to like this kind of semi-insulting, yet benign banter. Mae was adept at these easy, non-serious conversations too. It allowed them a license to say in jest what would normally be unacceptable. Both understood the unspoken rules and played by them to a point. There was also a line that couldn't be crossed and this too was wordlessly understood. Damage could easily be done by either with a thoughtless word or suggestion, though their mutual understanding of each other made this unlikely.

More than anything they were simply comfortable in each other's company.

Joseph asked, "What's this guy's name?"

"Tom. I didn't get his last name."

"Seeing him again?"

"I told him I only sang at Chuck's on Friday and Saturday nights. He said he'd be back Friday. You should come. You haven't been by in a while. It might be fun." Then nudging Joseph with her elbow she added, "so long as you don't bring one of your little air-headed girlfriends."

"I might just do that."

"Which? Show up or bring one of your sleazy girlfriends?"

Joseph just smiled, recrossed his arms and closed his eyes again knowing Mae was looking at him and waiting for an answer that was not going to come.

There was an understood feeling of contentment between them. The short, humorous verbal jousting events almost always ended in a draw leaving both sides lighthearted and at ease. Time slid through the cloudless sky behind a rising sun and the rising temperature. Mae was reduced to a thin T-shirt and jeans when Joseph asked if she was ready to head back.

"Yup, this was wonderful, as always," Mae replied, brushing absently at a loose strand of hair that tickled her cheek.

"C'mon, let's stash the chairs and have some lunch. I've got a good one waiting for us that should be about done by the time we get there."

Joseph tied Mae's Woolrich shirt around his waist and draped her down vest over his arm. Mae tried to stop him, but he insisted it was the only gentlemanly thing to do.

The walk back to Joseph's small house was uneventful. The morning's small wildlife now hid in shaded and protected areas, out of sight from winged predators who circled lazily in the dizzying heights above.

Joseph's home was a compact two bedroom single-story of typical desert stucco with a red tile roof. Mae was always surprised at how cool it stayed inside even during hot afternoons. Living room furniture was sparse – a sofa and two upholstered chairs – none of which matched and all of which needed replacing. The kitchen too was basic with a square dull yellow painted eating table and three matching chairs. Where the fourth chair went was a mystery about which Mae didn't even bother to inquire. A narrow doorway from the kitchen led to a single car garage that extended in length to accommodate a work bench, cabinets and an assortment of hand and power tools. The two small bedrooms were located opposite the front door behind the living room. Joseph used one as an office. It was lined with overflowing book shelves and an out of date oak teacher's school desk. A half bathroom containing a simple sink and toilet lay just off the kitchen with a full bathroom connected to the master bedroom. All walls were painted a sand beige and showed light and dark areas where framed art or photographs had once hung and later been removed. A vintage Bear-Archery laminated fiberglass and exotic wood recurve target bow and scuffed black leather quiver of aluminum arrows hung over an arched stone fireplace in the middle of one wall in the living room. A narrow pine rifle cabinet with glass door held two rifles and a pump shotgun. There was a sophisticated Harman Kardon stereo with two large speakers positioned on either side of the fireplace, but no TV. A scratched coffee table and end table finished the furnishings.

"I'm always taken with what you've done with this place," Mae jested. "Have you heard from the Better Homes and Gardens people about that photo shoot they were anxious to do?"

"Just because I've moved beyond materialism, is no reason for ridicule, Mae," he postured.

"You're not beyond materialism; for a man of means, you're just too damn cheap to buy some decent furniture. This place has some potential, you know."

Joseph smiled, but didn't reply. He hung Mae's wool shirt and down vest on two wooden pegs by the front door. Slipping on a Denver Broncos T-shirt, he turned to Mae and said, "As you know, I always like to dress for luncheon. And speaking of which, how's it smell to you?"

"Smells great. What are we having?"

"Stewed rabbit with some extras thrown in for good measure."

"Like what's thrown in for good measure? Wait, don't tell me. I'll guess after we eat."

Joseph brought a steaming covered iron cook pot to the table. Removing the lid, he ladled out two full bowls of the aromatic mixture.

"Seriously, Joseph, this looks and smells terrific. I think I detect sage and something else," Mae said as she pondered the aroma.

"Don't worry about that, just eat. I think you'll like this."

Mae blew on a spoonful of the stew and tasted her first sample.

"God, this is good. In fact it's amazing. Okay, where did you get the recipe?"

"Just made it up as I went along. No big deal really."

"Bullshit! I know if I went in that office of yours I'd find a dozen wild game cookbooks and this recipe is probably the first one in the rabbit chapter of every one of those books."

"Just eat and enjoy, Mae. I promise you won't find this recipe in any book. At least not exactly with the same ingredients I used."

They ate intently with little conversation. Joseph refilled his bowl and Mae managed an additional half bowl before pushing her chair back from the table. "Chef Joe, that was superb, simply superb."

"Why, thank you madam. Your seal of approval is most appreciated. There's plenty left in the pot if you'd like to take some home with you."

"Sure. The rabbit was really tender and no gamey flavor either. Really delicious. What about the chicken strips in there? Was that a gift-hen from one of your tutored kid's parents?"

Because Joseph refused to take money for his tutoring sessions on the reservation, most of the parents gave him presents of food or crafts. These items he gratefully accepted. Aside from canned goods, dairy products and some baking supplies, he bought very little at the Lunden Safeway store.

Joseph tried to hide an almost secretive smirk, "To what chicken were you referring, Mae?"

"Oh, no! What exactly was in that stew aside from rabbit?"

"Let's see now," he paused as if pondering some complicated question, "some veggies and spices. Most of it's privileged information and I'm not at liberty to tell."

"Alright, Chef Joe, what was the meat I just ate?"

"Well let me think a minute," he paused again before continuing, "You just dined on cottontail rabbit and rattlesnake."

"Jeez, gag me with a spoon!" Mae grimaced and clutched her throat theatrically.

"Gag me with a spoon, Mae? *Gag me with a spoon?*" he repeated. "And you criticize me for the lack of eloquence in the girls I go out with? It did taste good, didn't it?" Joseph taunted.

"Yeah, but that's not the point – "

"Actually Mae that truly is the point," Joseph cut her off curtly.

For a moment she wasn't sure just how serious he was. Sometimes it was hard to tell. They looked at each other searchingly. For a moment neither spoke. Mae finally broke the awkwardness, "If you have any Tupperware around, I'd love to take some with me for tomorrow."

Joseph returned to the kitchen and found a plastic container in a cabinet under the sink. While he spooned stew into it, Joseph asked if she wanted to listen to some music, but Mae said she needed to get back home. Then, thinking she didn't want to leave with things possibly unsettled, she changed her mind.

"Maybe I can stay a little longer," she said. "How about I make some tea and you put on a CD. Something light and fun perhaps."

"That sounds good. I'll be back in a flash," he said and left the house to return a few moments later.

Pouring some boiling water into two matching but chipped cups, Mae heard the first notes of the 1970s Megan McDonough album she kept in her car. It was not an easy CD to acquire and had to be ordered online. Mae smiled to herself knowing this was a symbolic peace offering, maybe even an apology from Joseph. It was a simple gesture that brought a simple relief to Mae. She needed to be a little more sensitive to and less critical of his way of living. Over time she'd grown accustomed to his basic, even minimalist home. At least it was always kept clean if a bit cluttered in the office. His desire to feed himself off *the grocery shelves of the desert,* as Joseph put it was as much a difficult and challenging learning experience as it was a day to day exercise. Finding edible plants wasn't always easy, but once located, usually offered a constant source of food. Meat, on the other hand, had to be hunted. When game was scarce or the shot missed its mark, a great deal of time could be expended for no benefit. A rabbit and a rattlesnake could be an all day quest, maybe two. She needed to remember the effort that went into his food gathering. Sunday was his special meal prepared with Mae in mind. Her childish outburst concerning the rattlesnake meat was immature and selfish. For a moment she felt a little ashamed, but she was learning too. After all, how many people, women especially, would immediately accept trudging around in the desert during the cold hour before sunrise and eating rabbits and snakes? This was a friendship built on patience and compromise. She had put a lot of effort into this relationship too. She knew Joseph was just as aware of the balance between them as she. This was his turf and while she learned from him in subtle ways, and some not so subtle, he also benefited from her empathy and sincere caring for him. Mae knew she was the grounding wire that brought some of his past guilt and sense of failure to neutral. She was his connection to a less idealistic and possibly, more realistic world. At times their friendship seemed both so simple and yet so deeply complex that Mae felt a little overwhelmed and baffled. It was best, she'd long ago realized, to just enjoy their time together and not try to *fight the direction of the wind that blows our lives,* as Joseph once said. Usually that was pretty good advice.

Mae brought the two cups of tea to the living room and put them on the rectangular table in front of the sofa. Joseph was sitting sideways with his back against the arm rest. Mae sat at the other end and put his feet in her lap. She untied his moccasins and placed them on the floor.

"Looks like these are going to need re-soling before too long. You're almost through them."

"I'll send them in soon. They're still okay, but I don't want to wear through to the inner sole."

Mae began to massage his feet with long strokes of her thumbs. "Thanks Mae, that feels great."

"Just be glad you wore socks today. There's no way I'd even consider touching your stinky, bare feet."

They both laughed and any previous tension belonged to the past. "And I'm sorry for my behavior about the rattlesnake. That was really stupid of me."

Joseph answered, "That's understandable, Mae. I know you southern girls don't eat rattlesnake. I should have sent away for some Louisiana water moccasin meat. Maybe next time I'll cook some 'possum so you can feel more at home."

Mae tickled the bottom of his feet with her nails making him shout and pull his knees to his chest. "Are you going to behave and get a foot rub or act like a jerk and be tortured? You decide."

"Okay, I'll behave,' he said and stretched his legs out again with his feet once more in Mae's lap. He closed his eyes enjoying the attention and listened to the music.

A short time later Mae said, "Gotta go. That's all you get." She stooped and removed her own mocs. "I'll put these away," she said placing both mocs behind the front door and retrieving her sneakers. She quickly stepped into each, tied them and stood looking at Joseph. "This was a great morning and lunch. Thank you."

Joseph walked over to her and wrapped his arms around her waist. He briefly shook her back and forth, lifted her off the ground and made a growling sound before putting her back down. "This *was* a great morning. Thanks for coming out. It wouldn't be the same without you." He gave her one last hug, kissed her forehead and said, "Now get out of here. Civilization's calling."

She looked into his eyes for a moment, smiled and walked out the door.

TWO

MAE'S JOURNAL: TWO YEARS PREVIOUS

It is going to be good to write again. I haven't kept a journal since before it happened. God, that's nearly seventeen years! I need to get used to this, though. I mean, who am I really writing this for? I wouldn't want anyone to read it, I don't have kids to leave it to, but that's okay. It just feels good to try to think straight and write for me. Maybe sometime in the future I'll want or even need to look back on this time and read this. The last years seem such a blur it's like they are lost to me forever. Maybe that's good, maybe not. But, I feel good today. Best I've felt in a long time. I remember I always liked writing when I felt good. This might be an auspicious time, so here goes!

I left Tucson this morning. My apartment lease was up, job was boring – boss was an ass, just time to move on again. Wow, I could have written that last line a bunch of times in the past number of years! Probably not a good habit. Anyway, I loaded up the old Ford and hit the back roads heading north. Thought I'd take the scenic, less traveled route. No real destination beyond checking out the Grand Canyon. Never made it that far. By afternoon I was on a two lane highway in the middle of nowhere – desert on all sides. Suddenly the small red engine light came on and a few minutes later I found myself pulled over on the side of the road. The day was hot by this time and there wasn't any cell phone service. I admit feeling a little vulnerable and afraid – old feelings die hard. Before I had time to work myself up into a real state of fear, an old yellow open-sided Jeep pulls up. This guy jumps out and asks if he can help.

Normally I'd have been wary considering the situation and location, but this guy put me at total ease instantly. It was like something out of a movie. He was in his twenties, I'd guess, and gave off an aura of being completely confident, yet in a good way. He wasn't some macho guy trying to show off for the lady in distress. The first thing I noticed after seeing he was some kind of Indian, was his smile. Like a picture off the cover of a dental brochure you'd find in the waiting room of an orthodontist's office. Straight, perfect white teeth. Second thing I noticed were his eyes. Startlingly blue! His hair parted in the middle, thick dark brown with a very slight wave that hung to his shoulders. He wore a light blue chambray shirt with the sleeves rolled to the elbow and a pair of faded jeans. And he wore moccasins. I didn't think anyone really wore moccasins! His skin looked more deeply tanned than naturally dark. He couldn't be a full-blood Indian, but I'm not exactly an expert on these things.

Anyway, as I said, something about his persona just put me at ease. He asked if he could help and I told him something was wrong with the car and that I couldn't drive it. He looked under the hood for a minute and said it was too high tech for him to figure out, but offered me a ride to town where I could get someone to tow it in and fix it. Something about this guy made me feel it was okay to get in his Jeep. Actually, I didn't have a lot of choice. With no cell phone service I could wait forever before a cop drove by. Besides, if I didn't accept help from this guy, who would I get help from?

When I got in his Jeep he turned to me from the driver's seat, extended his hand and introduced himself as Joseph Curley. I shook his hand and told him my name. Just before pulling out onto the highway he must have noticed my guitar in the back seat of my car, because he told me it wouldn't be smart to leave it in plain view. Made sense to me, so I returned to the car, got the guitar and tossed it in the back seat of the Jeep.

As we drove down the highway – we passed almost no cars and I realized how lucky I was that Joseph stopped to help me. I felt the warm sun on my face, the wind whipped my hair around – I didn't have a rubber band to put it in a pony tail – and for the first time in a long while I felt really free and, yes, even happy. Joseph didn't say much at first and I found myself looking at him as he drove. I have to admit I found him attractive. His profile was magnificent. Aquiline nose, clear smooth skin, strong chin, wonderful smile. And those eyes! I also noticed his forearms because they were almost hairless and *looked really defined. Joseph isn't very tall – maybe five foot six or seven, but he appears lean and strong without being bulky. I have to admit to feeling a kind of sexual rush (I don't know how else to explain it!) riding in this open Jeep with the sun and wind and sitting next to this... exotic? young man who I didn't even know! I'm not used to such feelings and I liked it. It made me feel like I did back in high school. Pretty awful to think I have to go back eighteen years to remember feeling this way.*

Town turned out to be Lunden, Arizona about a dozen miles up the road. We talked a little. It turns out Joseph came down from Montana a year or so before. He said he was looking for a new, simpler life and had rented a small house on the edge of an Indian reservation a few miles from town. I didn't know what he meant by a simpler life, especially coming from Montana! I don't think Montana living is exactly Los Angeles, but I shouldn't pass judgment as I've never been there. I was surprised at how smart and educated he sounded, but maybe I'm just showing my prejudicial bias, my pre-conceived notions that Indians aren't educated or well-spoken. I'm almost ashamed to have thought such things. I still have a lot to learn about the West!

We drove into town and Joseph first stopped at the only service station in town – a place called Roger's Garage and Towing. Roger was in. I explained my problem and gave him the car keys. He said he'd get my car right away and tow it in for repairs which he assured me he could handle. He seemed okay, but I didn't like the way he looked me up and down in his greasy little office. I know I'm too conscious of this, but I can't help it. That was one thing I noticed Joseph didn't do, or at least, not so I could see.

We left the garage and Joseph told me to grab my guitar case – can't leave it in an open Jeep. He then walked me across the street to a place called Chuck's Desert Oasis. An okay place with one large room partially divided in half. Had a full bar and tables on one side and dining tables on the other. Not much in the décor department. Chuck probably did the decorating himself without the benefit of any female input! Couple deer heads on the wall, some mirrors behind the bar, a few old framed prints of desert scenery and some Indian teepee pictures too. Not exactly the Ritz, but kind of homey and comfortable. Definitely a place for the locals to drink and eat.

We sat at a little table on the bar side of the room. Chuck came over and Joseph introduced me. Nice enough late middle aged fellow with a balding head and stained apron around his waist. I ordered a Diet Coke and Joseph said he'd have the same. When Chuck returned with the drinks he mentioned the guitar case I'd brought in and asked if I was a singer. I told him I'd sung in a few places before and he asked if I'd like to try singing in the Oasis. He added that I'd have to audition, of course (like I might not come up to his standards!). I don't know what got into me and I said, "Sure, what the hell." (Who is this person?) I unpacked the Gibson, tuned it and sang "Desperado" for him – Eagles or Linda Ronstadt, take your pick. I was feeling good and full of fun and I think it showed. If I do say so myself, I did a pretty impressive job. Chuck and Joseph both applauded – they were the only ones in the place. Chuck said if I played Friday and Saturday nights from 6:00 to 10:00 he'd pay me $20 an hour plus I'd make tips. This was all moving a little too fast. I'd only been in the Oasis for fifteen minutes! I said something like, "Hold on a minute. I just stopped here to get my car fixed. It's not like I'm planning on moving here permanently." Then Chuck asked where I was headed and I replied, "Nowhere really." Now that sounded intelligent! So he said, "Then it's settled. There's an empty room upstairs with its own bath. Keep it clean and it's yours for as long as you sing here." What could I say? "Done!" (Is this really me?) Chuck went back to the kitchen saying over his shoulder that the room was just up the staircase and to the left, adding that I could move in anytime.

A little while later Roger walked in and said my car was now in his garage. It's got some kind of alternator problems and he'd have to order some parts. He thought he'd have them in a day or two. It's Thursday, I've got a place to stay and a glamorous job singing in Chuck's Desert Oasis. What more could a girl want? Joseph asked if I needed any help moving stuff to my new digs. I refused his offer (stupid me) and went into my purse for a twenty to give him for his trouble. He just laughed and told me to keep my money. He said the song was worth twice that! What a charmer! I thanked him for the coke and took my guitar upstairs to the room – not bad. Decent bed, desk, TV, Internet, couple chairs, okay bathroom with a shower. When I came downstairs Joseph was gone and so was his Jeep.

I'm writing this at the desk in my new room. It's strange how things happen. It's like a plot cliché in a B-movie: Girl's car breaks down, meets dark stranger, arrives in little town, is offered job and a room and lives happily ever after. Well, while I might feel happy tonight, I don't think there's going to be a lot of "ever afters" for me in Lunden, Arizona!

THREE

Mae's two bedroom home was a short walk from Chuck's Desert Oasis. The outside of the house was the attraction for her. Situated on a quiet street it was a white painted single story with blue tinted shutters and front door. A small outside yard was framed by a low matching blue picket fence. Mae thought it looked like an oversized doll house. Having been built in the 1920s, the floors were wide plank oak and the walls were accented in heavy base board and crown molding. The wood gave the place an old fashioned lived-in feel that Mae found appealing. It reminded her of her grandparents' home in Tennessee. She thought she could even detect the same smells she remembered so fondly as a child – accumulated years of bread baking, bacon simmering and turkeys roasting, her grandfather's occasional pipe tobacco. This home had been occupied by an elderly couple who had recently moved to an assisted living center in Flagstaff. Their daughter was anxious to rent the place to offset the high cost of their new arrangement. As they had moved all their furniture to Flagstaff, the house stood empty except for a surprisingly in tune upright piano. After living in Chuck's upstairs room for a couple months, this was paradise.

Mae spent her spare time picking out furniture. The only new item was a simple full size bed and mattress set. Everything else came from antique shops and used furniture stores in the larger surrounding towns. Until the house was furnished to Mae's satisfaction, she stayed in Chuck's upstairs room. She took her time and the result was comfortable and pleasing.

Yards were styled in what Arizonans called "desert landscaping." This amounted to local pebble ground covering planted with cactus and other vegetation that needed little water or maintenance. Mae had tried some flowers around the house, but had to give up. Besides, the cactus bloomed. She'd have to be patient if she wanted flowers.

At first, singing two nights a week was fun, just a temporary lark. She'd planned to move on when this became another boring routine, but that was not the case. The locals were starved for music in a town too small to attract much in the way of entertainment. Within a week or two everyone knew of the new singer at the Oasis and tables were filled Friday and Saturday nights. Chuck was accommodating and a genuinely honest man to work for. At the beginning of Mae's third week he told her he was giving her a raise to twenty-five dollars an hour and asked her to sing from 5:30 until 7:30 – dinner time, and again from 9:00 until 11:00 – bar time, with breaks as she needed, of course. Reflecting the town's appreciation for Mae's singing and guitar playing, tips were unexpectedly good. More importantly to Mae, the people of Lunden embraced her with kindness. The dinner set tips were usually cash, but it wasn't unusual for a diner to leave a jar of home made preserves, a small gift certificate, or some useful hand made craft for Mae. Bar set tips were always cash. The single men could be annoying as the night wore on, but nothing that would be considered troublesome. After a few drinks some men lost their inhibitions and made mostly innocent suggestions of getting together with Mae, but so far that was expected and not a problem, and besides, Chuck was always there should things get out of hand.

A little after 10:00 Tom entered the Oasis and found a corner table at the front of the bar. Mae acknowledged him with a smile as she sang an old Patsy Cline number. He ordered a glass of white wine and lifted his glass to Mae when it arrived. She smiled again and gave him an almost imperceptible nod.

If anyone looked out of place in the Oasis, it was Tom. At forty-one he was in good shape physically. At an even six feet tall and 170 pounds he was not a robust man, but with straight posture he carried himself well. Years of being respected by students in the classroom at Laurel College outside Kingston, New York had bestowed on him an air of slight intellectual superiority that wasn't always apparent, but could be at times. When it was apparent most people found it annoying. In his usual gruff and straightforward manner, Tom's former neighbor and friend in New York, Jake, had first brought it to his attention and Tom was working on this. Tonight he wore a pinstriped long sleeve white shirt under a pale green sweater vest and a pair of kaki Levi Dockers. Tan socks in brown loafers completed his outfit. Tom had dark hair with a touch of gray on the sides that he wore a little longer than most men his age. But he was a college professor; he could do what he liked. In fact, it was expected. Sue, his estranged wife and colleague in the English department at Laurel, liked his hair short. Time to let it grow out a bit, Tom figured. He was handsome enough, but lacked the kind of masculine energy women found attractive – this also according to Jake. Tom would see what he could do about this situation too. He was the only patron of the Oasis not wearing either cowboy or work boots or maybe sneakers and certainly the only person drinking white wine.

At 10:20 Mae began her final break before starting her last set for the evening and took a seat with Tom. Without having to ask, Chuck brought her a Diet Coke.

"I was wondering if you'd show up," Mae said, taking her first swallow of her soft drink.

"Where else would I have a chance of hearing a Megan McDonough song?" Tom replied with a smile.

"Yes, that's right. I forgot you're a big Megan fan," Mae lied. She'd been thinking about this coincidence since she'd briefly talked to Tom before. Mae remembered a short quote from a book Joseph said he read years ago which he shared with her: *If you believe in coincidences, you're not paying attention.* That stuck in her mind every time something would happen that seemed oddly timed or coincidental. On this topic, it seemed crazy how she ended up in Lunden a couple years ago. If her car hadn't died who knows where she'd be now? If she'd packed her guitar case out of sight in the trunk of her car, she wouldn't have brought it in where Chuck saw it and asked her to audition for the Oasis. And if Joseph hadn't chanced to drive by in his old yellow Jeep, God only knows what might have happened. Probably best not to think too deeply into all this. Better to just be aware of odd occurrences or situations and let it go at that. Any more and things get complicated and philosophical and metaphysical. All that is fine to occasionally talk about abstractly, but too much isn't good. Sometimes, Mae thought, Joseph was too heavily involved in this kind of thinking and she saw little purpose in it. Such ideas seem real at times, but you can never prove it or harness it for use. Mae long ago concluded that it's best to make your own way and let the things that are out of your control happen as they will. That's what makes life unpredictable and interesting. Still, what were the chances of someone familiar with Megan McDonough's music coming into Chuck's Desert Oasis and hearing Mae sing one of her songs? Aw hell, Mae had thought, the guy moved here and sooner or later he'd have come in to the Oasis and heard me sing a Megan song to end my last set. Eleven O'clock isn't exactly two A.M. and face it; this is the only game in town. Yet, Mae had also thought, I'm probably the only person in all of Arizona singing Megan songs and I'm out here in *Lunden,* not Phoenix or Tucson!

The ten minute break passed quickly. Tom and Mae didn't have much of a chance for more than small talk before she announced, "Showtime," and went back to the chair with her Gibson leaning against it at the front of the bar.

Tom ordered another glass of wine and settled in to listen to Mae's last set. Shortly before eleven o'clock Mae told those remaining, "As always, thanks for being such a fine audience. I hope you've had as good a time here tonight as I have. And," Mae added with a smirk and sidelong glance, "if you simply can't imagine a Saturday night without me in it, I'll be right here in this same chair singing again tomorrow night."

There were chuckles all around and one girl yelled back, "Hell yeah, we'll be back. Where else we gonna go?"

More good natured laughter and Mae responded loudly, "Well, I don't know how to take that exactly, but I'm just glad I don't have much competition around here for at least ten miles or I'd be out of a job!"

This brought still more laughter along with one of the regular Friday night guys who walked up to Mae, dropped a Twenty dollar bill in her tip jar and said for everyone to hear, "I for one wouldn't care who else was playing here or anywhere, I'd come to hear you, Mae."

Applause followed and Mae thanked everyone again before playing the first chords of a Megan McDonough song while softly saying, "This last one's just for me."

Mae put the Gibson in its case and stored it in a locked closet behind the bar before returning to the table were Tom patiently sat with his near empty wine glass. Chuck brought a Diet Coke for Mae and refilled Tom's glass, "On the house," he said quietly before returning to the bar.

"That was delightful," Tom said to Mae, lifting his glass to her and taking a sip.

"Have you done any recording?"

"Thank you, and no, never recorded. I don't think that's really for me. I also don't believe I'm nearly good enough. Besides, people aren't really buying the stuff I sing."

"Well, for what it's worth, I think you're good enough."

"Thanks," and changing the topic, "So, what are your plans? No wait, I think I know. I bet you came here with lofty political aspirations. You're here to run for mayor, aren't you?" Mae had a mischievous grin on her face as she brought the Coke glass to her lips.

"Saw right through me, didn't you? Amazing perception. It's a small step from mayor of Lunden to Governor of Arizona." He too smiled, but a little awkwardly.

"Seriously, Tom, what brings you here? Unless you're a rancher or with the government, there's not much going on here."

"That's why I'm here. No, I don't mean I'm a rancher or with the government."

"Could have fooled me. I spotted you for a rancher the minute I laid eyes on you," Mae said with a straight face.

"Really? I would have never thought…"

"Mae broke up laughing, 'Tom, I'm kidding. You're the furthest thing from an Arizona ranchman as I've ever seen. Although, the New York license plate on your cute sports car might have been a little bit of a giveaway. Most ranchers around here opt for pick-ups."

"You had me for a minute there. I'll have to watch myself with you. A singer with a sharp wit, dangerous combination."

"I'm the last person you need to 'watch yourself with,'" Mae answered. "So come on now, Tom, why Lunden?"

"Okay, because it's in Arizona and I've never been to Arizona and don't know a soul in this state," he thought a moment and added, "and Lunden's in the middle of nowhere," he paused again, "just like me."

"Now, that sounds a little mysterious. Go on."

"I need space and time."

"Are we talking Einstein's theories here or just Star Trek," Mae chided and took another drink of Coke.

"That was pretty quick, Mae," Tom laughed. "Sorry for sounding cryptic."

"Cryptic? I don't think I've heard that word in my two years in Lunden. Is that a rancher term or a politician's word?" Smiling again as she spoke, "Tom, forget the cryptic stuff, what's going on? I mean, you don't have to tell me if you don't want to. I'm seriously not trying to pry."

"Sorry, Mae, I must seem a little uptight. This is all pretty new to me," he stopped there for a short time. Neither spoke. Mae looked into his face and decided to wait him out. She knew he'd blink first.

"My marriage is on the rocks. Is that a pun to say that in a bar?" Mae looked at him a second before laughing easily at his dopey joke.

"Yes, that's a pun, go on."

"My marriage is over, and that's fine. I was suffocating. Teaching freshman English and British Lit to upperclassmen might be over too. I think I've made a mess of my life and didn't even know it. I was just Mr. Status Quo – Mr. Inoffensive, Go-Along Status Quo. Year after year, and I didn't even realize it." Tom thought a second and added, "Quiet desperation."

"Thoreau warned you, and you just didn't listen, did you?" Tom looked at Mae and she quickly said, "Now I'm sorry. I don't mean to make light of what you're saying. You're not exactly alone here. Most people are leading lives of 'quiet desperation.' The difference is you recognize it while few others do."

"Where'd you go to school?"

"You mean aside from Life's School of Hard Knocks? University of Tennessee. Degree in accounting, but I minored in English."

"Something tells me you're not here in Lunden as a big rancher or government worker either." They both laughed feeling comfortable in their company as if through this short conversation a kind of truce had been negotiated with friendship as the result.

"We've all got a story to tell. Or not tell."

"Did I use the word cryptic before?"

"Touché, Tom. Very good. This is refreshing." Mae downed the last of her Coke, "I'm beat. I know we'll talk again." Mae stood up and held out her hand to Tom, "It's been a pleasure."

Tom took her hand gently and said, "Thank you for a fine evening on several levels."

"Pretty cryptic again there Tom, but yes, a fine evening."

"Can I walk you to your car?"

"No need. I walk home. It's only a couple blocks from here."

"Then how 'bout you walk me to my car?"

"I'd be honored."

Tom laid a twenty on the table to cover his eight dollar bar bill which Mae noticed as they got up to leave. Only a few stragglers were left sitting at the bar. Mae waved to Chuck from across the room as Tom held the door for her to leave. The night air was cool and the clear inky sky was alight with stars. Looking up Tom spoke.

"The heavens are alive tonight."

"They're always alive; it's just us poor mortals who usually don't notice."

"I had to park around back. It was packed when I got here," he said looking at Mae. "Must be nice to be the belle of the ball," Tom said.

"Or something," Mae responded absently. In the dark Tom couldn't see if she was smiling or not.

As they walked around the side of the Oasis Tom heard faint sounds of classical music coming from around the back of the building.

"That's Beethoven's Third Symphony, *Eroica*!" he exclaimed. "I knew there was a vast cultural side to Lunden."

"Probably not the culture you're expecting," Mae responded doubtfully.

Beethoven got louder and louder as they approached Tom's car in the rear of the back lot. Parked next to him was a seemingly empty, dusty yellow open Jeep from which the lusty opus blared from what had to be an expensive stereo system. Tom said nothing as they approached, but was clearly baffled. Mae could only hide her concern.

Tom was about to press the auto door opener on his keychain when someone appeared briefly in the driver's seat of the Jeep, spoke out, "Yo, Mae," and slumped over toward the passenger seat. Tom immediately put himself protectively between Mae and the person in the Jeep.

"It's okay Tom," she said, reaching into the Jeep and turning the stereo volume lower, "allow me to introduce you to my cultured friend, Joseph." The form in the Jeep roused himself and sat back upright using the wheel for balance.

"Pleased indeed to make your acquaintance, Sir," Joseph said extending his hand.

Tom hesitated, glanced at Mae and grasped Joseph's firm handshake. "Likewise," was all he said. Mae could detect the obvious disgust in his voice.

"Joseph, are you okay?"

"Yeah sure," he slurred. "Sleeping one off a bit. How'd it go tonight?"

Joseph's face was partially concealed by his disheveled hair. His denim shirt was buttoned crookedly which Mae noticed and wondered who he might have been with tonight when he was putting it back on. His feet were bare with one moccasin behind the driver's seat and the other in the parking lot. Mae picked up the moc and put it in the Jeep with the other one and removed the mostly empty Crown Royal bottle still in its purple velour bag, only the neck sticking out. She also slid into her pocket a garish silver and turquoise earring that was lying in the crease of the back seat.

With unfocused eyes, Joseph stared at Tom for a moment, "You like Beethoven?"

"You obviously do."

"Yup, just like alcohol, it's an old Indian tradition. Did you know Sacagawea's kid Pompy went to Europe and hung out with Beethoven? Ever since, we Injuns have had a thing for classical music." Joseph closed his eyes and started to slump over again. Mae grabbed his sleeve and steadied him.

"We need to get him home," she said

"Where's home?" Tom asked

"It's a ways out. Will you help me?"

"Sure, be my civic duty."

"No, not any kind of duty. You'll just be helping out a friend."

Tom briefly wondered which of the two was *the friend* he would be helping when Mae read out loud from the back of Tom's car, "Porsche

Boxster S. Nope, not exactly a rancher's car. Can this thing handle a dirt road?"

"I imagine it will. Never driven it off the pavement. As long as I don't bottom out it should be fine."

"Good, help me move him over to the passenger seat and for God's sake make sure his seatbelt's on." Mae walked around the Jeep and got her arms around Joseph as best she could. She held her breath as soon as she smelled the booze mixed with some kind of cheap flowery perfume on him. Tom pushed from the other side saying, "good thing he's a lightweight."

"You got that right," Mae said before adding, "at least physically." In short order Joseph sat sleeping in the passenger side. "Here's the seat belt. Snap it in for me, Tom," Mae said, reaching with the belt around Joseph. "Thanks."

Mae went around the Jeep again and got into the driver's seat. She started the engine, checked the gas gauge – over half full – and turned to Tom, "I really appreciate you helping me out here. I'd take him back to my place to sleep it off, but this is a small town if you know what I mean?"

"Not a problem. So where are we going?"

"Follow me. We're going to turn right out of the parking lot and go south on Main Street. A mile or so out of town we turn left at the National Forest Access sign. After a couple miles that road turns to a dirt road, but it's kept in good shape. Stay a ways behind me or you'll get dusted out. We're gonna go several miles down the dirt road. When I turn off to another dirt road I'll go slow. Just follow and it's about ten minutes to Joseph's place. And thanks again, this means a lot."

A half hour later Tom and Mae parked in front of Joseph's house. Still sleeping in the passenger seat, only the shoulder belt holding him upright, Mae turned off the motor and walked around the side of Joseph's house. Under a heavy piece of sandstone Mae removed a front door key and brushed the dirt from it. She opened the entrance and flipped the light switch. "Good, let's get him to bed."

Showing surprising strength and agility, Tom reached around Joseph, undid the seat belt and in one smooth motion had Joseph over his shoulder. "Lead the way," he said smiling.

Carrying the two mocs, Mae turned on the bedroom light and backed out of the room pointing with her finger, "in there's fine."

Tom gently put Joseph on top of the bed. "Should we cover him?"

"He'll be fine like he is. He just needs to sleep. Besides, he doesn't feel the cold much," and she chuckled to herself. "C'mon, our work's done. Let's leave him be." Mae put the mocs by the front door and locked it before leaving. She replaced the key under the stone making sure it was in exactly the same position as before. "You're the only one who knows about this key, Tom. If anything happens to Joseph or his house, the police will come looking for you."

"Oh, I won't tell anyone about the key, Mae. I wouldn't come here anyway…"

Mae interrupted, "Relax, Tom. I'm only kidding."

A little flustered Tom said, "Do you always do this to people you don't know well?"

"No, only to friends," she looked at Tom and grinned. "Now give me a ride home in your Autobahn Cruiser."

The following afternoon May picked up her phone to hear a groggy voice say, "Jeez, I'm sorry Mae. What a night. I wish you hadn't seen me like that."

"Not the first time, you know. You okay?"

"Yeah, bit of a headache. Thanks for getting me home. But how'd you get back to town from here?"

"You don't remember?"

"Mae, if I remembered I wouldn't ask."

"Tom followed me out and drove me home."

"Tom?"

"You know the guy I told you about. New in town. From back East. College prof."

"Right, right." Joseph paused, "I'm sure he was impressed with me. I didn't say anything stupid or insulting, did I?"

This was an opening Mae couldn't resist. "Well, nothing too bad. Don't worry about it. Tom seems a pretty understanding guy."

The grogginess immediately leaving his voice, Joseph stammered, "Oh, Christ Mae. What did I say? You gotta tell me."

"You sure you want to know?"

"Mae, just tell me!"

"Okay, you told him – and I think this is a quote – that I belonged to you and he better stay the hell away or you'd kick his eastern white ass all the way back to New York."

There was silence on the line. "Oh God, Mae, No…"

"There's more, if you're sure you want me to tell you." It took all of Mae's self-control to keep a serious voice.

"Go on."

"Well, Tom's from New York and you gotta understand that. Eastern people are different, you know. Now, don't worry, because I talked him out of it, but he was going to go right to the sheriff and fill out a complaint and get a restraining order because he said you threatened him. But it's okay, like I said I talked him out of it."

There was silence on the line. Mae continued in a low, serious tone, "Joseph, you need to sit down. Are you sitting?"

"Sitting? You kidding? I'm still in bed."

"Good, because you need to listen very carefully now." She waited a few moments before continuing, "I can't ever talk to you again. I'm in love with Tom and after dropping you off last night we decided to leave Lunden together."

Long, total quiet followed by, "What the fuck…"

Again, there was silence on the line for a moment more before Joseph had to pull the phone away from his ear as Mae shrieked with laughter. She heard Joseph try to say more, but she was in hysterical fits. When she finally regained control enough to speak, the line was dead. She waited a few minutes before calling him.

"I owe you big time for that, Mae."

"You might as well have painted a big bullseye on your butt. I couldn't help myself, it was just right there for the taking. After last night you deserved it. You should have heard yourself just now. You're lucky I didn't let this go on for longer. I could have, you know. God, that was the funniest thing I ever did," and she started shrieking again. This time Joseph stayed on the line and let her laugh herself out.

"You're right, I deserved that one. But seriously, did I say or do anything really bad?"

"No, you mostly slept. Tom's a good guy. He was a big help getting you home."

"Yeah, I'd really like to thank him. How 'bout you bring him out Sunday. We'll skip the walk to the kiva and just have lunch. And don't worry, I won't make any snake or skunk stews. Do you think he'd be receptive, or isn't he, how do I put this, the kind of person you'd want to bring here, if you know what I mean?"

"I really don't know him that well, but he's smart and has at least some kind of sense of humor, though probably not like ours. He doesn't know anybody here and I think it would do him good to join us."

"Okay then. Let's do it. Noon?"

"See you then."

FOUR

Sunday mornings in Lunden were usually quiet. There was some early activity and traffic as churchgoers gathered their families after breakfast, ushered everyone into cars or pick-ups and headed for one of several churches in town. Once services began, the town settled down again as the remainder of its citizens slept in, read the Sunday newspaper or occupied themselves with at-home activities. Except for the Safeway and a couple gas station-convenience stores, just about everything in Lunden closed down on Sundays.

Mae thought of the time between church doors closing for services and church doors opening to release the believers back into society as *Lull Time.* Hardly anybody seemed about. Few cars motored down the streets. A small number of the town's kids could be seen peddling bikes which Mae always enjoyed watching, and there were the regular dog-walkers, but generally this time was like a short, second night's sleep for Lunden.

It was during this serene Lull Time that Mae normally left for Joseph's place. It's not that Mae was overly secretive, but as she'd hinted to Tom the other night in the Oasis parking lot, Lunden was a small town and people talked. Mae knew about towns where people talked. Folks who once seemed like friends could be cruel and vindictive for no good reason at all. She could never understand this apparently universal human attribute and didn't need gossip about herself circulating in Lunden. Her singing job at the Oasis was secure and easy. Chuck let Mae sing as many Friday and Saturday nights as she liked. Sometimes, Mae explained to Chuck, it's good to skip occasional nights and a few weeks so people don't take the entertainment for granted. Being absent from the Oasis also gave Mae a chance to work on some new songs, change some old ones a bit, or simply regroup to stay fresh and enthusiastic for the patrons. She was always aware of the dangers of becoming stale.

Mae's other job was also steady, if seasonal. She prepared individual income tax returns. In fact, she had to turn away business for the simple fact that most people tended to wait until a few weeks before the April 15th tax deadline to start worrying about either paying owed taxes or filing for refunds. When confusion set in, they'd head for Mae's house. When too many taxpayers showed up Mae could only apologize saying, "Sorry, but there are only so many hours in a day," before turning them away to seek assistance elsewhere. Once she'd sorted their tax returns and filed them for a reasonable fee, they typically returned the following year – often after referring friends. During the hectic weeks leading to tax time Mae usually didn't do much singing at the Oasis. She did file for a number of extensions though which kept her accounting fees coming in for several months after.

In the middle of Lull Time, Mae drove to Tom's rented house. The black Porsche Boxster was parked along the street where he lived. Mae felt certain everyone in Lunden knew of the new guy in town who drove some kind of fancy foreign sports car with New York license plates. Rumors were already circulating as to who he was and what in the world he was doing in Lunden. Yesterday in the Safeway checkout line Mae had actually overheard on elderly woman say to a man wearing cowboy boots and hat that she'd heard from a friend of hers who knew for a fact the new guy was an FBI agent from *the main office in New York City* and was here in Lunden to investigate the possibility of some local citizens giving information to terrorists. It was at this point Mae excused herself from the line saying, "Darn it, I forgot the lemons," and headed for the deserted produce section where she could laugh unseen and unheard.

At times like this she wondered why she'd remained so long in Lunden. Then she'd remember the home baked pie on her front stoop left with a note from a woman who said how much she enjoyed listening to Mae sing while she ate dinner with her family at the Oasis the night before. She'd also think how her singing helped Chuck's revenues increase and how thoughtful and helpful he'd been to her. Lastly, she'd think of her friendship with Joseph and further thoughts of leaving Lunden, at least for the present, vanished.

Obviously watching for her from the front window, Tom left the house as Mae drove up in her Ford Taurus. He quickly took the passenger seat while Mae glanced around to see if any neighbors might be watching, but saw no one. She smiled a greeting at Tom while closing her window and before he could open his, said, "Let's get some AC in here, it's getting warm." Mae was also glad she'd had her windows tinted dark while living in sunny Tucson. She pulled away from the curb as soon as Tom had fastened his seat belt.

"This is a quiet place," Tom spoke as they turned on to Main Street and headed away from town.

"Sunday church time is always like this," she replied. After a short while she continued, "You know, Joseph was very upset that you saw him," she paused to get the right words together, "in that condition Friday night. I think he was truly embarrassed, even humiliated. I hope you'll get to know him. I promise he's one of the more interesting people around here. He's also a just plain good person. If you were ever in any kind of need where he could help, he'd be right there at a moment's notice. As an English prof I'm sure you've told your students not to judge a book by its cover."

"I'll defer to your judgment, Mae."

"Defer to my judgment? C'mon Tom," and referring to the famous line in *The Wizard of Oz* finished her thought, "You're not in Kansas anymore."

"Sorry, you're right. I need to loosen up a bit. Lunden isn't exactly a college town a hundred miles from New York City. You can be my speech coach."

"I'm about ready to open your door and throw you out... before bothering to stop!" Tom looked at her behind the wheel and was relieved to see her smiling. "Tom, just be the nice guy I know you are who lurks underneath all the façades of academia. Listen, I'm no genius, but I've read a few books and got me some ed-jah-mah-kay-shun under my belt. Same with Joseph, so just relax. Nobody's judging anybody here; nobody has to prove anything. In two years of living in Lunden you're the first and only person I've taken to Joseph's house.

Take that as a supreme compliment. Be yourself. I know he's in there somewhere."

Tom didn't know what to say and was afraid if he said anything it'd come out wrong, so he stared out the window watching the desert scenery go by. Mae purposely said nothing, waiting to see his next move. She knew this was game-playing. She also knew she had the home court advantage. Tom probably wasn't kidding the other night when he intimated at being a lost soul. Mae wasn't making this easy for him, but in an unfamiliar way she was enjoying his discomfort. "I hope you're not sulking over there, Tom," she finally said, breaking his apparent pastoral concentration.

"Not in the least. In fact, I was just thinking how refreshing it is to not be on my guard all the time. I'm not really used to it. You're a good coach," catching himself too late, he quickly turned to Mae, almost expecting her to reach over, open his door and boot him out. She met his glance and laughed out loud.

"You're a good sport, Tom. I'm becoming more and more fond of you as time goes on," and she continued laughing. "By the way, ever eat snake?" and she broke up in such laughter that Tom felt the car lurch on the dirt road from her hysteria.

"Now, how do you want me to answer that without getting into trouble?"

"Private joke. That wasn't fair."

"Maybe some time you'll let me in on it," he said cautiously.

"Might be sooner than you think!" And the car swerved a second time as the laughter started all over again.

In the sunlight Tom thought Joseph's house looked smaller than he'd remembered it from two nights ago. Day allowed him to see how remote its surroundings were. Desert and hills in every direction with hazy mountains toward the horizon. Like sentries guarding the landscape, Saguaro cacti stood throughout in no particular pattern. Distance could be measured by their heights. Those close to the house towered to sixty feet or more while those in the far distance looked like twigs. Tom realized he'd never been to anyone's home even remotely similar to this. Briefly, this thought made him feel alienated and alone, but almost immediately a new kind of excitement replaced that emotion with the knowledge he really was out of New York. He really was on his own with new people in an unfamiliar, yet exotically beautiful setting.

Joseph opened the front door as Mae parked the Ford. With Tom following behind, Mae walked up to Joseph and gave him a brief hug. Tom held out his hand for Joseph to shake saying, "Good to see you up and about."

An awkward silence followed before Joseph and Mae broke out laughing in unison.

"I think I like this guy already," Joseph nearly shouted to them both. He shook Tom's hand an extra few seconds while looking into his face. "Sorry 'bout the other night, but thanks." He turned to walk back inside saying, "C'mon in where it's cool. Lunch won't take long."

Mae noticed the charcoal barbecue smoking in the back yard. "What's on the menu?" Then quietly she added so only Joseph could hear, "I'm almost afraid to ask."

"A simple and easy meal. Deer steaks."

Tom walked to the window looking at the outside grill, "Sounds interesting, I've never had venison before."

"And you're not going to have it today, Tom. *Venison* is for fancy restaurants and non-hunters. We're having good old char-grilled desert mule deer steaks." He smiled at Tom. "I did use an old family recipe I just made up for the marinade. The steaks have been soaking in it for twenty-four hours. It should take any gaminess out of the meat and make it more tender too. I think you'll like it."

"Old family recipe you just made up, huh? Getting pretty lame around here already," said Mae. Then looking toward Tom and winking she remarked, "Chef Joe's got the biggest collection of wild game cook books in Arizona. He'd be lost without them. The only old family recipe he's got is the one he uses to boil water, and even that he usually screws up."

Joseph looked at Mae while shaking his head from side to side.

"The gratitude in this house is overwhelming."

"Never mind my chauffeur," Tom answered conspiratorially, "I'm certainly grateful and damned hungry too. Is there anything I can do to help?"

Joseph looked again to Mae, "I told you I like this guy." Then to Tom, "Sure, you can pick out some music and pour the wine. I've got a pretty decent Pinot Grigio and a Merlot. The red might go best with the steaks, but I still prefer the white. Open them both."

Tom was already viewing the shelf of CDs and did not see Joseph's quick glance to Mae. In a flash she understood Joseph's outreach to Tom. Typical Joseph, she thought. Diffuse any awkwardness for Tom, make him feel at home. Make him feel accepted and welcome. Why his little acts of kindness still surprised her – she didn't know – but they did. Probably, she thought, it's just that so few people were this thoughtful. Instinctively she knew this would be a good afternoon.

With Tom occupied for the moment, Mae joined Joseph in the kitchen.

"That was sweet of you," she whispered. "Oh, and by the way," she said, reaching into her pocket and holding out the silver and turquoise earring she'd taken from the back seat of Joseph's Jeep, "You might want to return this to its rightful owner – it was in your Jeep the other night."

"I don't think I can do that."

"Why not?"

"I'm not exactly sure just who it might belong to," he said sheepishly.

"You're disgusting!" and gave his hand a light slap. "But who am I to judge?"

Joseph gave a barely perceptible grin. "It's no big deal really." He started to wash the first of three large baking potatoes. Mae took it from his hand saying, "I can handle this."

"Thanks. And I also have some Coors and Diet Coke in the fridge."

"That's no surprise."

"I'm gonna check the grill. Be right back."

The first solitary, haunting notes of Mussorgsky's *Pictures at an Exhibition* began to waft through Joseph's house. It was powerful yet soothing music and one of Tom's favorites. He was glad to have spotted it in the classical section of Joseph's CD collection.

From the kitchen Mae taunted, "You better actually like this music, 'cause if you're just showing off you'll be doing the dishes."

Joseph returned and said to Mae as she pulled silverware from a drawer, "Grill's about ready. I'll pop the potatoes in the microwave." Then he shouted to Tom who was still studying the CDs, "Good selection. I never get tired of listening to this."

"I think you're both a bunch of phonies just trying to impress me," Mae said, "Truth be told, the two of you would be listening to heavy metal or punk rock if I wasn't here."

"Are we really that transparent," came the voice by the stereo.

"See what I have to put up with, Tom? Nice to have someone on my side for once. Now the ridicule and insults can be shared."

Tom began opening the two wine bottles. "Mae, white or red?"

"I normally don't drink, but a little Merlot might be nice. Just a half glass, thanks."

Tom handed Mae her glass and put one with the Pinot Grigio on the counter for Joseph. He then poured a second of the same for himself.

Joseph busied himself arranging napkins, salt, pepper and a Navajo pottery bowl of his own recipe steak sauce on the table. "I'm gonna put the steaks on. Mae, you want yours medium I know. Tom, how do you like yours?"

"I'm new to game. However you recommend is fine by me."

"I like mine a little more on the rare side. Sound okay?"

"Sure, can I do anything else?"

"Nope, you can remain the wine steward and CD selector."

"That's easy enough," he took a sip of the Pinot, "This is nice.'

Mae glanced at Tom, "I hope you mean the company as well as the wine."

"What made you think I was referring to the wine?"

"Getting pretty thick in here," Joseph said as he carried the platter of steaks outside to the grill.

Tom picked his wine glass from the counter and followed Joseph outside, "I'll watch and learn, if that's okay."

"Right this way."

Forking the steaks, Joseph said, "I've found it best to get the grill really hot and just sear each side for a minute. Seals in the flavor and doesn't dry out the meat. We'll do Mae's just a little longer than ours."

They both stared at the steaks as they began to sizzle. Tom said, "This is a great place you have here. Do you own it?"

"Nope, but I've thought a little of making an offer for it. Land out here is pretty cheap, especially on the reservation."

"How long have you lived here?"

"'Bout three years now."

"It's really quiet and peaceful."

"It is now, but you can't believe the dust storms. Not to mention the summer monsoons. The thunder can be deafening. And then there are the flash floods too. The house is built high on this ridge, so that's not a problem. You do need to be careful if you're out and about during one of the really big downpours. People can vanish in a New York minute, if you know what I mean," and he looked up at Tom smiling.

"I never could quite figure that one out. Sixty seconds in New York is faster than sixty seconds elsewhere. Gives one pause."

"Indeed it does that." Joseph picked up the fork and said, "Time to flip 'em," which he did. "Just another minute and we're good to go."

Mae had retrieved the wooden salad bowl from the refrigerator and was placing it on the table when they came in with the steaming steaks. "Smells great," she said. "'Taters are done. Let's eat. I'm starved. Water, beer, soft drinks or more wine?" she called out as Joseph put the steak platter on the table and stood behind his chair.

"I'll have a Coors. Tom, what's your pleasure?"

"I'll stick with wine and a glass of water, if it's no trouble."

Mae reached for two glasses from a cupboard, "No trouble at all. One water coming up for the gentleman and another for the lady."

"And don't forget a beer for the Injun."

Mae responded, "You sure you're old enough to drink?"

"It's okay, I borrowed an ID."

Mae brought the drinks to the table, "Anything else needed? Speak now or forever hold your peace."

No one spoke for a second and Joseph said, "Good, let's eat," and in unison the three took their seats.

The platters of food were passed; plates filled and for a short time only the clicking sound of forks and knives was heard. Tom took a bite of the deer steak, "This is great!"

May proclaimed, "Great flavor. Your marinade really makes it."

"Thanks. Glad you like it."

Tom spoke again, "Did you catch this deer yourself?"

Joseph turned to Tom, "I tried, but just can't seem to run fast enough – so I shot him."

Tom looked a bit confused for a moment and then smiled and said, "Right, I see what you mean. I think of catching fish or catching a deer as kind of the same thing."

Joseph laughed quietly, "I'm assuming you're not a hunter."

"Not me, but I think I had an uncle who hunted a little," and there was that damn awkwardness again. Tom was so used to being in control that now in this unaccustomed environment with new people, new friends actually, an uncomfortable feeling of inadequacy replaced his usual confidence. Sensing this, Mae reached over and placed her hand on Tom's arm, "Don't worry, I went through the same thing the first time Joseph fed me some horrible thing he'd proudly collected." Smiling she turned to face Joseph and continued, "We eastern citified folk just aren't used to the uncivilized ways of certain others who will remain nameless for now. However, what we lack in, shall we say, outdoor survival skills we more than make up for in intellect, wit and affability."

"I was just thinking exactly the same thing, Mae," Tom agreed.

"Fine," Joseph said, "Next time it's corn-dogs,"

"Seriously though," Mae said, "Wild game is healthier for you than just about anything you can buy in the supermarket. Notice there's almost no fat on this meat and no chemicals or preservatives in it either."

"Inuit, or Eskimos, can live on a wild game diet almost exclusively and not have high cholesterol or other problems people have from eating domestic red meat," Joseph added.

"Are you trying to turn me into a hunter?" Tom asked in jest.

"That's up to you, but it's not a bad idea," Joseph replied.

"Mae, do you also follow in the aspirations of Diana?" referring to the Greek goddess of the hunt.

Mae looked at Tom thinking *cut the English professor crap, nobody's impressed,* but said, "Diana's sphere of influence doesn't work here, but a few times I've gone with Joseph when he hunts. I'm more in the way than any help though," she added glancing over at Joseph.

"Not at all. Mae's got good instincts actually."

"You're too kind. More than once I've spooked game Joseph had already spotted."

Tom then asked Mae, "Doesn't it bother you to kill things?"

"Sure it does. I don't like the kill. I've gone with Joseph, but never killed anything myself. I understand it's all part of nature, but somewhere in the last few centuries the carrying out of the actual act has been bred out of me."

Joseph continued his thoughts, "Look, it's simple. If you're an animal born into nature, you're going to face a nasty, unpleasant death. If you're a deer, you'll probably get sick, or if you're lucky – old, and at some point you slow down, can't keep up with the herd. That's when a predator – wolf, coyote, mountain lion, bear – will chase you down and start to devour you before you're even dead. That's the hard and sad fact of it. If I were a deer and could think rationally, I'd seek out a hunter and hope he was a good shot so I wouldn't have to face the fate nature had in store for me. A quick shot out of nowhere and an almost instantaneous death is a better option. Most of the anti-hunting crowd have never stopped to think what a natural death in the wild entails. Their intentions are good – they hate cruelty as does every hunter I've ever known – but they really don't understand nature." Joseph ate a forkful of potato before continuing thoughtfully, "I once asked a woman I knew who absolutely hated hunting if it was okay for a coyote to kill and eat a rabbit or grouse. She said that was fine. Then I asked why there was a difference if I kill and eat the same rabbit or grouse. She insisted there was a difference, but I never could get her to explain it logically. I understand it's an emotional issue. I met a doctor one time who was a hunter. He put it this way, if you eat meat and don't hunt, you're cheating. I think that's a little extreme, but I get his point."

Tom said, "It's a valid point. I don't think it's so much that people are against hunting or eating wild game. I think it's just not mainstream now. What was once a necessity isn't anymore."

Mae said, "And I think you summed it up perfectly. So, enough talk about killing and hunting or I'll lose my appetite. I still like to think of this as just food or meat, not Bambi."

Changing topics, Tom said to Joseph, "So Joseph, aside from hunting, what do you actually do for a living."

Chuckling, Joseph replied, "That actually *is* what I do for a living. But I spend my non-hunter-gatherer time reading, tutoring kids on the reservation and simply pursuing the things I enjoy. I've been doing this for a few years now, but don't know how long it'll last. For now life is good."

"But don't you have to work or make money?"

"Not really, I own a ranch in Montana that I lease. It's not a fortune, but I get by on that."

"You do more than get by. Especially living this, shall we say, Spartan lifestyle," Mae said knowingly. "Tell Tom what happened on your move from Montana."

"Okay," He took a long drink from his Coors can, "Well, I was leaving Montana in a new Chevy Suburban pulling a big U-haul trailer with my stuff in it. I had some beautiful hunting rifles, camping equipment, some good furniture, even some art. I checked into a Motel in Utah for the night. Next morning I found the U-haul in the parking lot with the padlock cut and the doors open. My Chevy was gone too. They cleaned out the trailer except for some clothes and a few boxes of books and CDs. Police never did find the Suburban or any of my stuff. Aside from that all I had was in my travel duffel. Of course, I got compensated pretty well from my insurance company, but the experience got me thinking. Did I really want to spend the insurance money to replace all the things that had been stolen? Some things, sure, but I realized I could do without a lot of what I'd lost. Obviously, the stereo is new." Joseph saw the rapt attention in the faces of his audience and continued, "So in the little Utah town I found myself in I walked to a used car lot and bought the old yellow Jeep that I still have. When I got here, I just didn't see any great need to buy all new stuff when what was already in the place seemed adequate. In the spirit of Henry David Thoreau, I declared this my Walden Pond and have been quite content ever since.

"Funny you should mention Thoreau," Tom said. "The other night Mae made mention of him regarding his observation of *quiet desperation* in peoples' lives."

"Yup, Thoreau's everywhere," Joseph said dismissively.

Lunch progressed with a relaxed and easy atmosphere. They asked Tom about his plans in Lunden. He said he might do some writing, but wasn't sure yet. Mae spoke of some funny incidents singing at the Oasis. Although Joseph did more listening than talking, he enjoyed the meal and company immensely.

Nearing the end of the main course Joseph asked, "Could I interest anyone in my homemade Safeway brownies?"

"I'm game," Tom answered and quickly said, "But don't shoot me."

"Ugh, that was really lame," Mae said, getting up from the table with hands full of empty plates. "I'll clear the table and get the preservative laden and chemically enhanced brownies. Yum!"

"Sounds good to me," Tom said, "It's what I'm used to."

Tom brought the platters to the kitchen where Mae was filling the dishwasher. "Go on, get out of here. Why don't you and Joseph relax and I'll bring the brownies into the living room as soon as I'm done with this. Just be a minute."

Joseph and Tom took the two mismatched easy chairs, leaving the sofa for Mae. Tom asked, "You really don't miss the things you lost?"

"Some, but not most. There was a painting of a teepee by a stream I miss. I miss the rifle I was given when I graduated from high school – but the deer we ate today didn't know the difference. So to really answer your question, when I think about what I lost, I miss a few things, but not enough to feel I have to replace them for now. I'm trying to make my life about what I *do* instead of what I *own*. I have no beef with wealth or even opulence. Maybe in the future I'll change priorities. If I ever get married and have kids I'm sure everything will change, but for now, well, this is it. And it suits me."

"Can I ask how old you are?"

"Sure, twenty-eight."

"Seems like you've got the world at your fingertips here. When I was twenty-eight I was going through a pretty screwed up time..." Tom paused, thinking, "and things are still screwed up which is why I'm here." Catching himself again he quickly said, "I don't mean here at your home, I mean here in a state I know little about and in a town that was no more than a dot on a map when I first heard of it."

Mae arrived with a packaged container of brownies. She peeled back the plastic wrap and offered them with a napkin to Tom and Joseph before stretching out on the sofa.

"Tom, did I hear you say that you first saw Lunden as a dot on a map? So how did you actually pick our fair community to be your landing zone?"

"A dart was thrown at the map of the U.S. and it hit Lunden, Arizona."

"Seriously, you threw a dart at a map?" Mae asked incredulously.

"Yes. Took three tries though. First dart hit somewhere in the middle of the Gulf of Mexico – I'd had a little wine before the launching of darts began – and house boating was not for me." Both Mae and Joseph laughed at this. He continued, "Second dart hit Trenton, New Jersey. Too close to home. As they say, third time lucky. A direct hit on Lunden, Arizona. An online search told me what I needed to know. A rental search pulled up a few houses, of which only one was in town and fully furnished. That was it. A phone call, a lease agreement and a check in the mail, done! It worked well because I told the administrators at Laurel College I would be taking a sabbatical to do research and write in *Lunden*. Of course, they assumed *London, England,* which was just fine with me. Let them all try to locate me there! So, here I am." Tom looked at Mae and Joseph's blank faces.

Joseph spoke first, "Good for you, Tom. That's the kind of decision making I admire. But somehow I have a sneaking feeling that preceding this little dart throwing thing there was probably some heavy shit taking place, if you'll forgive my choice of words."

All eyes were on Tom. Being put on the spot was not something he was accustomed to, at least not when it came to his personal life. "I suppose you could say that," was all he managed.

Again, Joseph looked at Mae and then back at Tom, "You ate my food and drank my wine. You owe us a story!" Tom said nothing and Joseph said, "Tom, really, I'm kidding, you don't need to explain anything. I'm glad you're here. I want you to feel at home among friends. No need to expose your past," he again looked to Mae with a bit of deviltry in his smirk before continuing, "Of course if you ever want to speak to either of us again, you better open up."

Mae said, "Shut up, Joseph. You're such an ass. Leave Tom alone. He's polite enough to not pry into your life. You should extend the same courtesy to him. Tom, ignore Joseph. If it weren't for his good cooking, I'd never come here. He's lived alone so long he doesn't understand how boorish he's become. Another brownie? No, not you, Joseph. You don't deserve one."

They all laughed at this. Joseph went to the table in front of the sofa and grabbed a brownie saying, "This is my castle and I am king."

They laughed again and Tom said, "If you really want to know, I'm here partially because of my old neighbor, Jake."

Nobody spoke a word for a moment or two. "This sounds like it might just take a while, which is good," Joseph said. Before you begin, can I get anyone anything? Don't worry Tom. You've got dibs on the Pinot Grigio. Mae?"

"Nope, I'm fine."

"Mae, turn off the stereo. I'm gonna grab another beer and be right back."

FIVE

KINGSTON, NEW YORK: APRIL – 19 MONTHS PREVIOUS

I

Over a low fence a simple handshake between neighbors started a life altering ball rolling. Professor of English at Laurel College, Thomas Sloan introduced himself to the newly arrived occupant of the house next door, high school grad and Vietnam vet Jackson "Jake" Taylor. Parked in Tom's driveway were two Toyota hybrid compacts, both different shades of green, of course. Parked in Jake's driveway was a nine-year-old Ford F-150 pick-up with a Harley-Davidson Sportster in the bed, both black, of course.

They appeared stereotypes of their respective stations in life. Tom with short hair in cuffed trousers, button down shirt and black dress shoes looked every bit Laurel College faculty. Jake with over-the-collar gray hair and matching beard, sleeveless denim vest over black Harley-Davidson T-shirt, jeans and stout boots looked every bit the part-time motorcycle mechanic. Across the fence Tom conversed with an attitude of barely detectible aloofness, maybe even slight condescension mixed with a little discomfort. Jake spoke with casual indifference and a relaxed brusque confidence.

Near the end of their brief first encounter Jake said, "I better get back to unpacking, but once I get settled a bit, you'll have to drop by for a beer."

Tom replied offhandedly, "Sure, I'd like that," and the two neighbors returned to their homes.

Tom's wife of a dozen years, Sue, had been waiting at the front door when he came in. With obvious distaste she said, "I see you made friends with our lovely neighbor."

"Seems nice enough."

"For God's sake, Tom, he's a biker. That'll do wonders for the neighborhood. I don't know why he'd move here. We're almost all Laurel people or at least white collar."

"Well, I don't know. Like I said, he seems okay.'

"Well, he's not okay by me. I only hope he's renting and not buying."

"Sorry, Sue. Bought and paid for he told me."

"Well, Shit…" she mumbled under her breath as she went to their bedroom.

On a Saturday afternoon several days later Sue walked into the living room where Tom was watching CNN. Backing up to him she asked, "Can you zip me up? I'm running late."

Tom immediately stood and raised the zipper on her formless short sleeved black dress. "Be sure to get the hook-eye at the top,' she said.

"I did." Sitting back down he asked, "When will you be back?"

"By dinner. These meetings don't usually last too long, thank goodness. You should be going too."

"Yeah, I know," he mumbled in a low voice.

"Well, we won't get into that now," she said putting on a shawl from the closet. "And Tom, I wish you'd fix the hose holder-thing. It pulled off the side of the house several days ago and I really don't want to keep asking you to do it." Without looking back she said, "I better get going."

Tom didn't reply as he heard her car back out to the street and drive away. For several minutes he sat unwatching in front of the TV. Finally he clicked off the remote and walked into the laundry room. He found a screwdriver in a drawer and advanced to the job at hand. He wasn't particularly skilled at household maintenance, but this one seemed simple enough.

He pulled a short distance of hose from the rack to lighten it and lifted it to the siding of the house. "Shit," he said more loudly than he'd intended when he realized the four mounting screws not only pulled out, but were nowhere to be found.

"Wassup, Neighbor?" came the cheerful voice from the other side of the fence.

"Oh hi. Jake, right?"

"Yup," he said looking at the situation. "What do you need?"

"It looks like this thing has pulled out and needs some screws to reattach it."

"I'll be right back." Jake went into his garage for a brief time and emerged with a small toolbox. "Hang on, Pardner, help's on the way."

Jake took a brief look where the bracket had been mounted. "Just needs four bigger screws. I've got some here oughta work. Have this thing back up in a jiff." He searched in the toolbox and said, "These will do. You lift it up and I'll screw it in." A minute later Jake said, "That should hold it. Mission accomplished!"

"Thanks for your help. I don't think we had any screws to repair this. My wife would have been annoyed if she came home and it wasn't reattached."

"Glad to help," Jake said as he put his screwdriver in the box and closed the lid. "C'mon over for that beer I promised."

Taken off guard, Tom stuttered, "Well thanks, but actually, I have to…" he paused for a couple seconds and reconsidered, "Well actually nothing. That sounds good. I haven't had a beer in ages. Let me put this thing back," he said holding up his own screwdriver, "and I'll be right over."

Walking through the open garage Tom glanced at the spotless Harley. Jake said, "I used to ride a shovelhead, but now this one's lighter and easier to handle. You ride?"

"Never been on one."

"You're missing a thrill. C'mon inside, plenty of beer in the fridge."

They walked through the simple kitchen where Jake grabbed two cans of Budweiser, through an unadorned living room and into a bedroom that had been converted to a den. Tom took an upholstered chair and accepted the Bud from Jake who sat on a leather covered sofa. Jake popped the top and took a long drink. Realizing a glass would not be forthcoming, Tom did the same.

"Budweiser," Jake said, "King of beers. Been drinking this stuff my whole life."

"It's good," Tom said stiffly taking another short sip.

Jake's den was as masculine as any room Tom had ever entered. Aside from the sofa and chair there were a couple end tables holding dog-eared motorcycle magazines, some old issues of Playboy and an ashtray on each containing thin Swisher Sweet cigar butts. A narrow bookcase held a small group of books and curios of a military nature – a German helmet, an inert – he hoped – hand grenade on a wood stand, a fired .50 caliber Browning machine gun casing and some smaller items. An oak frame with medals arranged around an American flag hung on a wall. Against another wall stood a low cabinet with a few liquor bottles and glasses on top. Some swords or bayonets – Tom didn't know which – hung on another wall above a poster of a triumphant Muhammad Ali standing over a knocked out Sonny Liston.

Tom had rarely felt so out of place, but he managed to say, "Nice room."

"Thanks. I come in here to relax. Every guy should have a room like this." Jake took another pull from his Bud can. "So, I figure you teach at the college?"

"Yes. English department."

"Yeah, I'd have guessed that," Jake said and quickly added, "No offense, of course. You just look the part. I never made it to college. Thought about going on the G I bill after 'Nam, but never made it."

"When were you in Vietnam?"

"Near the end – '72; '73."

"Pretty bad?" Tom asked, not knowing what else to say.

"It was a fucked up mess, if you'll pardon my language."

"Sure, of course." Tom took a drink from his can feeling awkward. He knew no one who'd been in the military.

"Two tours. Can't say why I signed up for the second. Maybe I was afraid to get back to the U.S. I didn't know what I'd do when I got back or if I could ever adjust to civilian life again. Saw some nasty shit over there. People who haven't been can't imagine." Jake drank more and continued, "I don't mean *you* can't understand, but most people can't."

"No, you're right. I can't imagine it. I've never been in a war. I've never even been in a uniform."

"Well, consider yourself lucky. It's no picnic."

Tom thought for something to say. "You've got some interesting artifacts in here." He knew that sounded wrong, but it was too late.

"I suppose you could call them that. Mostly just souvenirs. I've got a trunk full of stuff I haven't unpacked yet."

Changing course a little, Tom asked, "How did you end up here? I mean in Kingston."

"I lived outside of Kingston as a kid. Went through school here. After 'Nam I moved to Florida. Worked at a car dealership as a mechanic. Then got into motorcycles. Easier and more fun than working on cars. Never got into the biker lifestyle, but I do like to ride."

"Interesting," Tom said, although it was nothing to which he could relate.

"Not really. I got tired of the type of people moving into Florida. Mostly snowbirds from New York City and Philadelphia, Canadians too – retired bunch of assholes who complain about everything under the sun. I left and traveled a bit. When you can work on cars and motorcycles, jobs aren't too hard to find," he stopped and pondered for a minute. "I got tired of moving around and thought I'd make the circle complete and try Kingston. I still know a few people here and I got some family not too far away. I'm dealing with some medical issues – not a big deal, but having family around could be a help. I like the mountains and changing seasons too. A friend got me introduced to the people who own the Harley dealership. I only work there part time. I could retire, but I don't know what I'd do with myself all week. This works out pretty good."

Jake reached for a box of plastic tipped Swisher Sweets and offered one to Tom who refused saying he didn't smoke. "Smart. I smoke too many of these things." He lit one up and took a long drag. "What about you? How'd you end up here?"

"I'll give you the condensed version. I met my wife, Sue, when we were both in grad school. We were in the same weekly study group. She was one of the brightest people I'd ever met. We got our master's degrees in English together. I focused on British Literature. She was into Shakespeare. Sue and I got married while working on our Ph. Ds. We marketed ourselves as a team and got hired here at Laurel College. Been here ever since." Tom drank the last of his Budweiser.

Jake went to the kitchen and returned with two more beers. Handing one to Tom he asked, "You must like teaching then."

Tom was actually a little jolted by this remark. In all the years he'd been in the classroom he couldn't ever recall being asked whether he *liked* to teach. He and Sue never discussed it. Teaching was what they did. When not in the classroom or grading tests and papers, they read and did research. They also wrote papers for publication in academic journals few actually read. As a couple, they socialized with other faculty members. Most of their life centered around Laurel College. Did he like teaching? Like and dislike had never been part of the equation.

"It's okay. It's what I do.'

"You don't sound too thrilled about it. I always liked – and still do like – working on motorcycles. Cars you mainly fix back the way they were when they left the showroom, but bikes can be altered or modified. Hell, you can take a frame and completely rebuild a motorcycle around it any way you want. My Sportster's pretty much stock because it's almost new. I may add a few things to it, I'll see."

Tom and Jake finished their second beers. They talked about Kingston and how it had changed over the years. Jake did most of the talking. Tom, who was used to being the center of conversation with students and at least an active participant in discussions with faculty members, actually found it refreshing to be more of a sounding board. Jake talked of Vietnam, riding motorcycles and traveling the country. What could Tom throw into the conversational cauldron? Keats and Shelly were irrelevant in Jake's den. It was good to leave them in the dusty past for a while. Tom felt immersed in a new world with Jake – a guys' world – a no bullshit world devoid of political correctness or hypothetical academics. This was real. And Tom liked it. In fact, he liked it enough to have a third Budweiser.

Sue arrived home to an empty house. Tom's Toyota was in the driveway. She called his name and walked through every room. She looked in the backyard and walked around the sides of the house, noticing the hose holder had been fixed. At least that was something. In the bedroom she removed her delicate onyx earrings and matching choker, placing them in the jewelry box on her dresser. She looked at her watch, 6:12. They usually ate by six, or if they were going out for dinner, they usually left around six. Since there had been no discussion of food or anything put out defrosting on the counter, and since it was a Saturday after all, Sue assumed they'd be going out for dinner. She slipped out of her black dress and hung it neatly in the closet, exchanging it for loose fitting gray slacks and a dark blue sweater, the low-heeled pumps for simple black oxfords. If they were going out, it would be casual. At this late hour, reservations at any place decent would be impossible. She found herself getting a little past the annoyed stage as she gazed into the mirror, putting on simple gold hoop earrings.

Sue was not a vain woman. Having just turned 40, she thought she looked about right. A bit more time spent at the makeup table would certainly help, but was it really worth the time and effort? She wasn't trying to impress anyone with her looks. Her short brown hair remained free of gray, thank God, and only small lines around her eyes and the corners of her mouth indicated a push past youth. That was fine too. She was a Ph. D. She impressed with her mind. A mostly vegetarian diet kept her weight under control, yet she noticed the firm upper arms of her twenties had slowly been turning to a loose shapelessness. She should spend some time in the gym, she knew, but sweating with a bunch of moronic showy women wasn't going to happen. Sue didn't buy much in the way of sleeveless tops or dresses anymore. She was who she was, an accomplished scholar and teacher. That was enough. Now, where the hell was Tom?

Sue sat in the same chair Tom had occupied when she'd left. She picked up the remote from the side table and absently clicked on the TV – same CNN channel Tom was watching. A sportscaster recited scores and a rundown on some sort of team game or something. "Christ," she said aloud and clicked it off. She looked at her watch again. Just after 6:35.

Sue felt the anger rise and instantly fall when she thought *what if he's had an accident or heart attack. Maybe he called 911 and got taken to the hospital.* Feelings of guilt replaced her anger. She grabbed the phone and nearly ran to the kitchen where a list of emergency phone numbers was magnetically attached to the side of the refrigerator. She was beginning to dial the hospital when she heard Tom walk in the front door.

"Oh my God, are you okay?" she nearly gasped.

"Of course. Why? What's the matter," Tom replied a bit surprised and confused.

Sue just looked at him while her recent guilt and concern turned back into anger. "Do you know what time it is? You didn't leave a note or anything. I was worried half to death! Where have you been?"

Tom still looked confused, "I've been right next door, just visiting with Jake for a while."

"Jake!" Sue exclaimed. "The *biker*?" She said it like a dirty word.

"Yes, Jake. Our neighbor who generously helped me fix the hose thing," Tom said, a little anger starting to rise in him now.

Sue stared at Tom. She looked at her watch yet again. "Do you know it's almost six forty-five? I said I'd be home for dinner. Did you even consider that? Did you even consider me?"

Tom walked past Sue, "Excuse me, I have to use the bathroom."

"Is that beer I smell on you?"

"Budweiser," he said and continued with a laugh, "King of beers."

"Damn you," she muttered as the bathroom door closed. "I'll eat on campus," she said through the door.

"Sue, just wait a minute," Tom yelled back, but she was already halfway to the front door. A few seconds later he heard it slam.

II

Students for a Greener Planet meetings were held twice monthly on Saturday Afternoons. Sue had volunteered as a faculty sponsor. Tom had not. When asked to be a sponsor he'd responded with, "At the moment, I've got my hands full teaching and I'm working on a paper." This was mostly true; accept *the paper* was an ongoing excuse as most faculty were continually writing papers for publication. Sue had also urged him to take an active role in S.G.P., as it was known, saying, "As faculty we need to encourage our students to be the environmental leaders of tomorrow." To which Tom said, "I drive an ugly green hybrid electric car. I set an example which shows my support for the movement. That's about as far as I'm willing to go. All the endless talk of ideas to save the planet from some kind of manmade climatic catastrophe is mostly bunk at this point."

"Well, I certainly wouldn't agree with that."

"Look Sue, if mankind is polluting the atmosphere to the point of melting the ice caps, a relatively few people in America driving electric cars or installing solar panels or wind turbines isn't going to amount to a hill of beans if China, India and most of South America won't curb their emissions."

"I know the hybrid cars are mostly symbolic, but we have to show what side we're on. Our country will need future leaders who believe in the environmental movement if the rest of the world is going to be brought in line. S.G.P. is a good start."

"Okay fine. You go to the meetings and mould a future leader to save the world. I need my Saturdays for me.'

"I think that's a selfish attitude, but have it your way."

Sue went to S.G.P. meetings. Tom went to Jake's. She couldn't understand the allure of spending time in some kind of biker clubhouse, as she assumed it must be. She'd never been to Jake's house, had never been invited, so she really didn't know what it was like, but she imagined Tom in a seedy and maybe dangerous setting. Still, she had to admit, she'd never seen other cars or, heaven forbid, other motorcycles at Jake's when Tom was there, so maybe it wasn't so bad after all. Could this be some middle-age-crazy stage Tom was going through? Could be, but probably not worth thinking about too much. She didn't like the beer and twice he'd had cigar breath when he returned, but there were things worse than that. Dr. Morse, 52 years old and a favorite in the English department, had unexpectedly dumped his wife of twenty-six years for a recent Laurel grad. They lived together just down the street. At least Tom wasn't involved in that kind of shenanigans. She felt sure he'd outgrow this infatuation, this nonsense with Jake. The thought of the two of them *hanging out together*, there was no other term for it, nearly made her ill. At least their friends didn't know about Jake. That would be an embarrassment she definitely would not like to face. When she'd confronted Tom with why he wanted to continue visiting Jake, he'd blown her off saying, "He's an interesting guy. It's nice to just talk with someone not in academia. It's also damn refreshing in a way you probably wouldn't understand. And don't take that the wrong way; just consider it a guy thing." Well, it was hard to take any way, wrong or not. *A guy thing?* What the hell did that mean? Hadn't they moved past such antiquated ideas in their marriage? This had to be Jake's influence, and she didn't like it one bit.

Tom knocked loudly on Jake's front door and let himself in. Holding a cold six pack of Budweiser, King of Beers, in his left hand, he walked to the kitchen and was about to put them in the refrigerator when he heard, "Hey Bro. I thought I heard you. I was in the garage. I'm still unpacking some stuff from the move. Can you believe I've been here three months and I'm not done yet?" He pulled a Bud from the six pack Tom held and headed for the den.

"Looks like you unpacked that trunk of *artifacts,*" Tom said and gave Jake a wink and a smile.

Over the last months they had become relaxed with each other. Well, Jake had always seemed relaxed. It was Tom who'd settled down and *kicked back,* according to Jake's terminology. Jake was no scholar in an academic sense, but he was quick-witted and espoused a wealth of common sense. He wasn't abstract or hypothetical, but he maintained a philosophical poignancy that made Tom question his own attitudes and opinions.

While Tom had always held a passion for classical literature, Jake instilled in him some lost passion for the here and now. This living for the present had apparently been swept aside in his marriage. Tom and Sue rarely traveled away from the college, but when they did it was usually to visit historical sights germane to their respective academic fields or go to seminars or hear other professors give papers. It's not that Tom didn't enjoy these trips, he did very much, it was that he'd unconsciously convinced himself that this was all he needed to sustain his life. He didn't often ponder his own feelings of fulfillment or happiness. It was easier to simply accept his life with Sue. He was never bored exactly, not with student papers to read or tests to grade or class prep to do. He filled his time with Laurel College and an easy, uncomplicated marriage.

They'd never had children. Their careers came first and took up nearly all of their time. Sue was also adamant that the United States of America used up more than her fair share of the world's resources.

"Our consumption is totally out of balance with the rest of the world," she'd said on many occasions. In her mind the rest of the world offered up and America gobbled up. Our increasing population would only guarantee that this inequitable conundrum would continue. More people meant more mouths to feed, more schools to be built, more houses, more factories, more jobs, more destruction of wildlife habitat, more pollution… It went on and on. It was a good reason not to procreate. She was not going to add to the problem. She would at least set an example.

Coming from a more or less traditional family, Tom had always envisioned himself as a father. In the early years of his marriage, regardless of Sue's ideas on the subject, kids were out of the question from a practical standpoint. Advanced degrees and the work that went into attaining them left little time for anything else – especially something as demanding and self-sacrificing as raising children. Tom put the idea of a family temporarily out of his mind assuming it would naturally come along at a later date. Now, he realized, the later date and the time for kids had pretty well passed. No use putting too much thought into that now. Besides, he couldn't imagine Sue holding a squirming infant or changing a diaper while he warmed a formula bottle. That was for other, younger couples. They were different.

As was the norm, Jake sprawled on the leather sofa and Tom took the upholstered chair. Looking around the den, Tom said, "I see you've done some more decorating."

"Yeah, found some more things as I was unpacking. Most of this stuff has been in storage a long time. Brings back a lot of memories."

"Good or bad?"

"Some of each. Bittersweet, you might say."

"How so?"

"Some of these *artifacts,*" Jake said with emphasis on the last word, "remind me of the war – the friends I saw die. Killing. Burned-out villages. That kind of shit. But it also reminds me of being a young guy, a kid really, full of piss and vinegar. I wouldn't mind being young again – not young and stupid, just young," he drank from his can and lit a Swisher Sweet. "What I'd really like is to be young again, but know what I know now," and he laughed.

"You and me both! Things would be different now if we could turn back the clock and deal with our lives with a bit more wisdom and knowledge." Tom reached into a drawer on the table next to his chair and found one of his own cigars he kept there. He lit it, drawing in the smoke without inhaling.

Jake said, "Reminds me of a line from an old Harry Chapin song. In the song this guy meets up with an old girlfriend. Years ago they'd had a thing that didn't work out. Now the guy's wondering how his life would be different if they'd put it together instead of breaking up. So the song goes, 'one side thinking of what might have been, the other thinking just as well.'"

"Interesting how we view the past like that. Thinking we could have or should have done things differently. Yet, it's my belief that if put back in the same situations, we'd still react and follow through with our past decisions in an identical way."

"Maybe. Maybe not. I'd like to think some of the things I fucked up I'd do differently if given the chance."

"Like what?"

"Stuff I did in the war. Some things I did when I got home. Nothing worth talking about now."

They both drank from their Bud cans and smoked their cigars for a few moments in silence. Tom indicated with a nod of his head at the far wall where a poster of a mostly naked blonde sat curled on a chromed chopper hung beneath a large sheath knife, "Do you have any memories regarding that?"

Jake smiled, took another sip of his beer and said, "Yes indeed I do. I went out with a girl who looked a lot like her once. Just about as good looking as the one on that bike. She was originally from Palm Beach, I think. From a wealthy family too. Crazy broad. She always wanted me to take her riding on the back roads through the orange groves. She'd snuggle up real tight behind me and then do me with her hand while we rode," Jake laughed and looked over at Tom. He'd known for some time that Tom seemed uncomfortable talking about women in a sexual way. That was okay. Jake figured Tom was just uptight about such things. What'd he care anyway? Jake finished by saying, "Don't know how we never crashed. She was one wild chick though."

Tom surprised Jake by saying, "Yes, some women seem to have a need to mix danger and sex. It can be quite extraordinary actually." After saying that Tom realized he'd also surprised himself. He glanced awkwardly at Jake who was now looking back at him.

"But that was not what I was referring to." He pointed and said, "I meant the knife you recently hung on the wall. I haven't seen that before."

Jake looked back at the wall and laughed again realizing his mistake, "Oh, that. That's my Randall. Carried it nearly every day in 'Nam."

"Randall?"

"The Randall Made Knife is the finest fighting knife that's ever been." Jake snuffed out his Swisher Sweet and got off the sofa. Walking to the wall he stopped and just stared at the sheathed knife a while before he took it down. Turning to Tom, he drew the blade and said, "In the Randall Knife catalogue this is listed as a Model 1 All Purpose Fighting Knife. The original design. They started making them in their Orlando, Florida shop around World War II. Bo Randall's knives made their reputation from that war, for sure. You could order one with fancy extras like stag handles, stainless steel blades, brass guards and matching grip caps, but this is just the original standard model with leather washer handle and aluminum grip cap. The blade is carbon tool steel so it'll rust and stain, but holds a better edge than stainless steel and sharpens easier too."

He handed the eight inch blade knife to Tom. The scarred steel had turned a dull gray patina and the leather grip was deep brown, almost black from sweat and god only knew what else. Tom noticed the top portion of the blade was sharpened back from the tip for a couple inches. The leather sheath too was dark stained, like old saddle leather. Heavier than any kitchen knife, he'd never held a knife like this one. It felt powerful and lethal. This was a new sensation and it felt good, somehow exhilarating.

Jake said, 'That's one hell of a knife. If you ordered one like that today, you'd wait five years for delivery. After market they sell for nearly six hundred bucks. A Vietnam era one has collector value and will bring a grand or more even in that condition."

Reluctantly Tom handed the knife back to Jake who, with seeming reverence, hung it back on the wall. "Before enlisting in the Army, I read an article in Soldier of Fortune magazine about Randall Made Knives. I was just a dumb kid itching to go to war. I wrote Bo Randall a letter telling him I was going into the service and wanted to take one of his knives along. At that time the wait was about six months or more. The next week I got a package from the Randall shop. Bo himself sent me this knife with a bill for only half the catalogue price and a note that just said 'Good luck and stay safe.' My letter to Randall was one of the smartest ideas I ever had." Jake went back to his usual position on the sofa and lit another Swisher Sweet.

"I've never held a knife like that. Impressive, to say the least."

"When you can't chance the sound of a gunshot sometimes a knife is your only option. That knife saved my hide more than once. I probably should have written a letter to Bo Randall telling him that and thanking him, but I never did. Never felt right to thank a man for making a knife you used for...," Jake didn't complete the sentence. "Anyway," he said, "that shit's all in the past. Sometimes I wonder why I hang some of this stuff up. You mentioned memories. Lots of the memories in these things aren't so great. Probably best left behind.

"The past was the gateway to our future selves,' Tom reflected.

Jake guffawed, "There you go with that professor shit again."

"It's not *professor shit,* it's truth," Tom said seriously. He took another drink of beer. "We are the end result of all we have done and thought before – which is the present time and always moving forward, evolving even. You might say our lives presently are the consequences of the sum of our past actions. To put it in simplified form, what we did *then* makes us who we are *now*."

Jake said, "I suppose that makes sense."

They quietly sat for a while, both lost in their own thoughts – thoughts of the past largely unknown to each other. It was good to share this in silence. There was no need to speak. They had different pasts, different lives now, but they shared a common maleness that while often overlooked, ignored, even unrecognized, has been an essential component of mankind for millennia.

III

Sue walked into the living room where Tom was watching the Discovery channel. "Would you mind putting my overnight case in the car for me? I'm done packing."

"Sure, no problem. Got everything you need?"

"I think so. It's only two nights. If I forgot anything I can make due with what I've packed."

Tom got the latched suitcase from the bed, carried it to Sue's Toyota and placed it in the back seat. Kissing him lightly on the cheek she joked, "Now don't you go buying any motorcycles while I'm gone."

"Not a chance of that happening. Drive safely and give me a call when you get there."

"I hate driving in Manhattan. I always seem to get lost, but I'm sure I'll get there safe and sound by this evening. Don't worry, I'll call you."

She got in and Tom shut the door for her. With a quick smile and a wave she backed out of the driveway and off to a Shakespeare seminar in New York City.

At 5:00 there was a loud knocking on Tom's front door. Jake was all smiles. "Tonight's the night, Buddy!"

"What do you mean, *tonight's the night?*"

Jake reached into his back pocket and produced two tickets which he waved in front of Tom's face. "This is what I mean."

"Okay, I'm all ears. Come on in, make yourself at home. What can I get you?"

"Nothing, we only have a few minutes if we want to catch dinner first."

"Dinner first? What are you talking about?"

"Well, you told me the little woman was going to be gone for a while, so I figured it was high time we had a boys' night out. I got us two tickets for the New York State Extreme Cage Fighting Championships. Starts tonight at 7:00 and we're going. No excuses, I already paid for these tickets and they weren't cheap."

"Cage fighting? I don't even know what that is."

"Don't worry, you'll love it. There's more to life than poetry and books, Doc. I need a quick shower, pick me up in fifteen minutes. I'd drive, but I'm working on the truck and there ain't no way I want you wrapping your arms around me on the back of my Harley!"

"Go, take your shower. I need one too. I'll pick you up in fifteen minutes. Think where you want to eat. Dinner's on me."

The Empire Steakhouse in downtown Kingston was where Jake chose to eat dinner. "This ain't no high class joint," he said, putting on the New York accent he knew Tom disliked, "but they serve one mean ribeye."

"I haven't had a good steak in a while. This might be just the protein fix my metabolism has been craving."

"I'm not sure, but I think you just said that a steak sounds good to you too."

"In so many words, yes."

They were laughing like old pals when they entered the restaurant and were seated. Jake told the waitress they didn't need menus and ordered for them both. "This should be a good night," Jake said while they waited for their dinners.

"From what you've told me, this cage fighting thing sounds like it will be an interesting spectacle. I'm anxious to see it."

"It's a spectacle alright. Pretty intense stuff. Could be a lot of blood. I'm sure you'll enjoy yourself."

The service was quick, steaks tender and rare and the check total was cheaper than Tom expected. He paid with his American Express Gold Card and said, "Oh hell. I forgot my cell phone.'

"Don't worry about it. You won't need to call anybody. We're out for us tonight."

"It's not that. Sue is supposed to call me when she gets into her hotel in New York tonight."

"Let it go. You can talk to her later tonight or in the morning. C'mon man, take the leash off for just this one night."

Tom parked the Toyota in the rapidly filling arena parking lot. He'd ignored Jake's jokes about his *putt-putt-mobile* with the hamsters running on the treadmill under the hood to create the electricity to make it run. Kidding Tom, Jake even put on his dark aviator sun glasses and crouched down in the seat so anyone he knows won't recognize him driving in a rice-burner hybrid. "After all," Jake said, "I have my reputation to uphold."

Tom took the jesting with a good natured grain of salt. What could he expect from a guy who works in a Harley-Davidson shop? Jake's reputation? Seriously? Well, what about Professor Thomas Sloan's reputation? Going to a cage fight with a biker! So whose reputation was really in the most jeopardy here? Tom felt almost giddy walking with Jake. Tonight would be all in the spirit of a great deal of fun.

Walking toward the arena and looking at the other cars in the lot, Tom realized he probably drove the only eco-car. These cage fight fans obviously did not maintain an acute environmental awareness. Pick-up trucks and massive SUVs were the most common vehicles with a scattering of vintage muscle cars, new Camaros and Mustangs.

Taking their seats – best in the house, three rows from the chain link cage, close enough to see everything without getting splattered with spit or blood – Tom observed an almost entirely male audience. There were a few women escorted by their boyfriends or husbands, but not many. Tom thought they looked mostly tartish with their high heels, short skirts or shorts and layers of makeup.

At 7:00 sharp an announcer stood in the center of the cage with a microphone. He introduced the first of the heavy-weight fighters who'd arrived in each corner. Both were well over six feet tall, both weighed over two-forty and both were emblazoned with tattoos. There was not an ounce of fat on either combatant. Tom had never seen anyone as muscularly cut and bulked as these two. Their scars attested to the many fights they'd endured.

"I don't think I'd want to be in there with either of those goliaths," Tom said to Jake.

"You got that right! Jeez, look at those guys. They must spend eight hours a day in the gym. This is gonna be good."

The barefoot fighters wore only trunks – one red, the other blue – and very light boxing gloves. In the cage they moved in a slow, almost nervous fashion like tightly wound springs ready to explode into violence. Seated in rows of connected chairs around the cage, the audience waited unmoving in anticipation for the action that was sure to come. They stirred with each preliminary half kick or head faint. The fighters circled and moved, looking for an opening. Totally absorbed, Tom sat forward in this chair like everyone else waiting, waiting, not yet, not just yet... the fighters shuffling side to side, forward a little, back a little, a pulled right hook, a slight head bob... Then, seemingly out of nowhere, a roundhouse kick landed with an audible whack squarely to the side of Blue Trunk's face. A tornado of kicks and punches followed from Red Trunks and the recipient appeared too stunned to protect himself as blood began to stream from the corner of his left eye and nose. The crowd was on its feet sweeping Tom with it. A surge of yelling, red-faced humanity urging more contact, more destruction, more pain. They yearned for it like a starving dog begs for food. And Tom seemed as starved as the rest of the pack. He was transformed like all of the vicarious gladiators. They – he – wanted, no – demanded a victor and a vanquished, one to conquer and one to succumb, one to live and one to die.

Crouched and covering his face and body with his arms, the fighter, Blue Trunks, who had taken the kick and beating that followed was leaning against the steel chain link cage side. His tormentor was slow and methodical – a kick to the side of the body, wait... wait, a left hook to the head... slowly watch, anticipate, stay cautious, another kick to the body... sway to the right, now the left...two short jabs and a right upper cut... now pause, slow, look for the opening, yes!, no!, not yet, close in, now back a little, hop...hop, flatfooted now, pause, hop, hop again, patience, and there! A dropping of an arm, now land the kick! But Blue Trunks had planned the move, a sucker move, and as the bare right foot began its arc Red Trunks knew it felt wrong, but could do nothing to stop what he'd put in motion. Against the cage side the bleeding fighter ducked and raised his left forearm for a leg block. The foot seemed to stop inches from Blue Trunks' face and remain suspended. A burst of power and agility brought a right fist into the exposed kicker's stomach followed with a tremendous growl of pent up rage and frustration along with a knee sharply lifted to meet the sagging kicker's face. Red Trunks' head snapped back, the eyes lifelessly half open.

From the first contact only moments before, the outcome seemed certain, but like the ancient oak that has withstood storms for decades and seems invincible, in an instant a sudden lightning bolt can tear it asunder. Surprise didn't have time to register on the now debilitated fighter's face. Before Red Trunks could fall to the mat, Blue Trunks scooped him off his failing legs as a father would playfully lift a sleeping child and carry him to bed. Only semi-conscious, there was little movement. Smiling through the still dripping blood, the underdog, Blue Trunks slowly twirled his prey for the crowd to see. Someone yelled, "End it! End it! End it!" and the chant gained momentum. It spread like wind-blown fire and built to a crescendo until "End it! End it! End it! End it!" encircled the cage. Red Trunks, still suspended in Blue Trunks' arms, began to recover and struggle. Sensing renewed danger, his captor spun faster and faster, the crowd screaming "End it! End it!" and with a bestial roar abruptly ran at the cage side, crushing his opponent's body and face into the chain link. They hit with a metallic clatter directly in front of Tom and Jake. Droplets of sweat mixed with blood sprayed a red vapor on those in the front row standing ringside. Jake elbowed Tom, "That's why we're three rows back." But Tom heard nothing. Even after most of the audience had quieted he still bounced on the balls of his feet hoarsely chanting "End it! End it!" Jake stared uncertainly at Tom for a moment, but turned back to the cage in time to see the winning fighter drop the loser to the mat and dance around with his fists held victoriously over his head. The crowd cheered and applauded its collective approval for long minutes until the beaten fighter recovered enough to get back on his feet, stumble to the winner and with a weak and feeble smile, shake his hand.

There were several other bouts after this one. None seemed to have the ferocity of the first, and by the last match of the evening the crowd yelled less, stood less and appeared to have satisfied its bloodlust goal. The arena exited from the rear and Jake said to Tom, "Might as well sit a while and let this place empty out. There's usually a pretty long traffic jam getting out of the parking lot anyway, so we should just stay put for a bit." Continuing he asked, "So, how'd you like your first cage fight?"

Tom looked at Jake for a short time, expressionless and saying nothing. Jake noticed how ashen he looked and was about ask if he felt okay when Tom said, "Exhilarating! Absolutely the most exhilarating event I've ever attended."

A little taken aback by this reaction to the fights, Jake looked at the thinning crowd remaining in the arena and said, "C'mon, we can leave now. Are you okay? You look a little pale."

"Oh, I'm just fine. I feel exhilarated!"

"Yeah, you said that before. Sure you're okay?"

"Yes, of course. Let's go"

The halls of the arena were still fairly crowded with fight fans as they exited to the parking lot. Jake could still feel violence in the air. He knew he could sense this when others could not. It was a volatile mixture of testosterone and adrenaline that he picked up on. An unpredictable and dangerous mixture.

The Toyota was near the back of the lot. When it came into view Jake saw two men who each looked to be about twenty leaning against the car smoking cigarettes. They were talking to a couple of trashy looking late-teenage girls. Best to just ignore them and unlock the car. They'd probably apologize for leaning against it and walk off.

When they reached the car Tom shocked Jake by yelling, "Off the car, assholes!"

The two young men instantly stood up straight and faced them. Walking next to Tom, Jake grabbed his upper arm in a vice-like, painful grip that silenced him and said pleasantly, "You'll have to excuse my rude friend here. He's had a little too much to drink tonight and he just lost a big bet on that last fight."

The two men looked at each other briefly. One mumbled, "Yeah, no problem," and they put their arms around their girlfriends and slowly walked away with the other one speaking over his shoulder, "He's the asshole."

Jake said to Tom, "You need to simmer down and we need to have a little talk. I know a place nearby we can get a cold one."

Jake and Tom didn't speak on the short drive to the Horseshoe Bar. It was a small, dark place with some tables separated from the bar by two pool tables. They sat in the back and Jake ordered two draft beers.

"Look Tom, I know you're not exactly used to these kinds of things. I mean cage fights, sporting events, bars like this one." Tom sat expressionless although listening intently. "These people aren't like the students in your classes. When these guys get riled up, like at a football game or cage fights, things can get out of hand quickly. Men see violence and blood and it does something to them. Not all men, but at least some. Me, I've seen my share and I can separate sports from true death matches where I've been involved whether I like it or not. At things like this I stay polite and friendly. Someone wants to fight in a parking lot, that's fine as long as they don't want to fight me. At my age I got no reason to fight for the sake of fighting. Getting hit, or worse, ain't my idea of fun. Trust me on that one."

Tom still said nothing, but Jake knew he was digesting every word he heard. Good. He continued, "Look man, I know you didn't mean to, but you broke a few basic rules of conduct back there tonight. First, for not much of a reason you insulted two guys you didn't know. Maybe one was armed and drunk. Maybe one had a knife or brass knuckles. Suppose one or both had black belts in karate. Probably they were none of those things, but you never know. So in a nutshell, don't fuck with someone, anyone, you don't know, period. The second rule you broke was that you involved a person other than yourself – me. There were two of them. That means if trouble started I'd be involved. And I assure you, I didn't want to get involved. But know this, if there was trouble, I'd never leave you – friends don't do that. So remember, friends don't put friends in danger, not ever. And the last rule you broke was a really basic one. Don't provoke a guy who's with a girl. His honor and manhood will make him fight even when he doesn't want to if his woman's watching. I've seen guys get the holy shit kicked out of them in fights they knew they couldn't win just because some broad was with them. Believe me when I tell you a guy with a bitch is the most dangerous animal of all." Tom still said nothing. He hadn't touched the beer on the table in front of him. "And one more thing. Regarding weapons. There's only one thing more frightening than a guy with a knife. Know what that is?" Silence still. "A guy with a knife who knows how to use it."

Tom nodded thoughtfully. "Thank you, Jake. You've instructed me in some important lessons tonight. I promise to heed your advice and wisdom. I hope I didn't ruin your evening."

"Course not. I had a great time. Looked like you did too."

"I've never known anything like it!" Tom drained his beer and started to signal the bartender for another.

"One beer, Pal. You're driving and I want to get home in one piece. Seen enough blood for one night."

They arrived home a little past midnight. Tom parked the Toyota in his driveway. They both got out and faced each other. Tom said, "Thank you, Jake. That was a truly wonderful experience tonight."

"Yeah, some good fights, no doubt about it. A good time." He turned toward his house and said, "I'll see you later, Doc."

Unlocking the front door, Tom could hear his cell phone ringing. By the time he grabbed it off the coffee table where he'd left it the ringing had stopped. He noticed eleven missed calls – all from Sue. He dialed her number.

"Tom, I've been calling all night! Are you alright?"

"Yes, yes, I'm so sorry Sue – I left my phone on the table and by the time I realized it, it was too late to turn back to get it."

"What do you mean *too late to turn back*? Where were you?"

"Jake bought two tickets for an event at the arena. I had no idea he was going to. It was a surprise. We had nothing planned, but he knew you were going to be away, and I assume he didn't want me to be alone."

For a brief moment the line was silent. Tom knew Sue was collecting herself, calming herself. "What was the event?" she finally asked in a controlled voice..

"We went to the fights."

"You mean a boxing match?" She seemed incredulous.

Trying to make it sound more sporting he said, "No, not exactly. It's called cage fighting – but it's similar to a boxing match with perhaps fewer rules. Very exciting to watch actually."

Again the line went quiet. Tom waited, not knowing what to expect next.

"Cage fighting? What in the world's gotten into you, Tom? Who are you becoming? Maybe the question should be asked more specifically: who are you *trying* to become? I think things have gone way too far."

Tom could sense the rising anger in her tone. "I'm not *trying* to be anyone. Simply put, Sue, I've had my eyes opened a little wider and my horizons expanded a bit further." Without thinking he added, "And I'm a better man for it."

Yet again, no response. Tom could hear her breathing, but no words came. He realized it would be advantageous to shift topics. "So Sue, were you able to navigate Manhattan and find your hotel without difficulty?"

There was more breathing and an awkward pause. This was finally followed by an exasperated, "Being a Neanderthal is *not* being a better man!"

And the line disconnected.

IV

Sue stayed on in New York for an extra day. She said as long as she was in the city she might as well take in some galleries and a show. Tom thought this a fine idea and might give her an extra day to calm down about the situation, which Tom decided shouldn't have been any real problem to begin with.

When Sue did return – a day late – she seemed her usual self. Tom was there to greet her when she drove up, took her overnight case into the bedroom so she could unpack and asked the usual questions about the traffic on the thruway and how she'd slept in the hotel. From her answers, and tone while answering, Tom could tell all was forgiven – if there should even be anything to forgive. Better to let sleeping dogs lie and move on – which is exactly what they did for several uneventful months after the boys' night out at the cage fights – until Dr. Jonas Freeman's party.

Sue was attending a special, non-scheduled S.G.P. Meeting. Thank God he'd nipped that one in the bud long ago. As soon as her green Toyota left the driveway, Tom grabbed the six pack of Budweiser from the refrigerator, headed for Jake's house and knocked on the door.

Normally, he'd let himself in, but this was an uninvited visit on the spur of the moment.

Opening the door Jake said, "Hey Doc. I see you got a six pack there so I better put on my best manners and invite your ass in here."

They both laughed walking to the den. Jake said, 'And to what do I owe this unexpected pleasure of your company?"

"That sounded fairly authentic, Jake. For a minute I almost thought you a gentleman."

"Screw that, hand me a beer."

"Actually, Sue's at some special emergency S.G.P. Meeting – you know, Students for a Greener Planet."

"Yeah, you told me about that before, but what's the special emergency this time?"

"I suppose saving the earth from global pollution and warming wasn't enough to keep them busy. Now they've included social issues. Apparently there's a bill in the state legislature regarding some new gun control measures and the S.G.P. is trying to mobilize a phone-in movement to pressure the representatives to vote for the bill."

"And how do you feel about that?"

"If that's what the S.G.P. wants to organize, they should do it."

"No, I mean about the gun control bill?"

"I'm not entirely sure what exactly is in it, but I suppose fewer guns on the streets are a good thing – less guns, less crime, less killing. It's not really something I'm overly concerned with one way or the other."

"Well I am and I'm dead set against it. It's tough enough in this state to own a gun, much less a handgun which you gotta have a permit for. Criminals don't follow laws, only decent citizens do. Pass all the damn gun laws you want and all you'll do is make it easier for the bad guys to do as they want since fewer and fewer good guys will have the guns to stop them."

"I don't own a gun, so I never really thought much about it. This is a pretty safe community. If ever there were trouble, I'm sure the police could get here pretty fast."

"That's sounding like the victim you'll be if ever there really is a problem and the cops don't get there in time. I know you don't get out to the woods or mountains much, but if shit happens out there, you're really on your own. C'mon Doc, you're an English professor. You must have read *Deliverance* or at least seen the movie."

"Both actually."

"Well, that shit in the movie goes down in one form or another more than you might think. I'd never go into any wilderness area unarmed. And don't think bad stuff can't happen even in this nice neighborhood of ours, 'cause it can."

"Maybe, but I just don't feel threatened enough to own a gun."

"That's your choice, Tom." Jake looked him in the eyes and continued, "Now I'm a peaceful guy as you well know, but there's an old saying that I live by: it's better to have a gun and not need it than need it and not have it."

"That's certainly logical so I find it difficult to argue against."

"Open another beer and I'll tell you a true story. It might just change your mind."

Jake and Tom both opened their second Buds. Jake as usual was lying across the leather sofa with his back against the armrest facing Tom in the overstuffed chair. "This happened a lot of years ago and I haven't told this to too many people. Let's keep it between us, not that you have anyone to blab it to anyway."

"Sure, just between us."

"Okay," Jake said and raised his can. "When I got back from the war, I found a job in central Florida. I lived there for a while and had a girlfriend named Ellen. She knew I'd recently gotten back from Nam and understood there were some readjustment problems that went along with that. Anyway, Ellen was the sweetest, kindest, most gentle person I'd ever known. And believe me, she truly hated guns. Didn't matter what kind – rifles, pistols, shotguns – she hated 'em all. Just for fun one time, I tried to take her target shooting, but she wouldn't have anything to do with it. Just stood off to the side, held her ears and refused to even handle a gun. You following this, Tom?"

Popping the top of another can, Tom replied, "Yes, every word. Please continue."

"Well, some time later we decided to go on a weekend canoe trip down one of those lazy Florida rivers. It was great. We paddled and camped out each night, drank beer, cooked good food on the campfire. I was lovin' it. Brought the two of us closer too. I was starting to think maybe we had a future together. You know, after all these years, it's still not easy for me to talk about Ellen and me."

"Believe me, I understand."

Jake looked at Tom briefly. He wondered if Tom had an Ellen somewhere in his past too. Pushing away that idea, he went on with his story.

"We ended the trip at a small riverfront park with a few picnic tables and a little parking lot. It was about a mile and a half down a dirt road from the main paved one. I'd canoed this section of river a couple times before and I told Ellen as we pulled the canoe out of the river that I'd grab a paddle and jog down the dirt road where it meets the main street. Then I'd hitch hike the twenty miles back to where we'd left my car. People around there were used to hitch hikers with paddles doing just what I was doing and getting a ride wasn't usually too hard. I told her I'd be back as soon as I could.

"So, I grab the paddle and jog down the dirt road. As I was jogging, an old VW van with Texas license plates passed me heading for the little park. I remember because I had to run off the one lane road for it to pass and that's when I noticed the Texas plates. I really didn't give it much thought at the time. Once on the main road I stuck out my thumb and within about ten minutes got a ride to my car. I threw the paddle in the trunk and drove back to get Ellen and the canoe and our camping stuff. I wasn't gone more than an hour or so."

Jake took another swallow of beer and seemed to be collecting himself to finish the story. Tom thought he saw Jake's eyes water slightly, but maybe it was just the light. Tom was about to ask if he was all right, but Jake spoke again.

"When I get back to the park I don't see Ellen at first. Then I see her huddled under a picnic table. Then I see a dead dog – a pit bull lying about ten feet in front of her. I jump out of the car and run over to her not knowing what the hell is going on. She comes out from under the table sobbing and throws her arms around me. The crazy thing is she's holding my gun in her hand – the one I threw in my duffle as I always do. It was a Ruger Blackhawk Single Action in .45 Colt. Shoots a big heavy bullet without a lot of recoil. A real fight-stopper. Anyway, I calm her down as best I can and here's what she tells me.

"After I left to hitch hike back to the car, Ellen's sitting at a picnic table when that Texas van drives up and stops – the one that passed me on the dirt road. Five men get out. They're speaking Spanish and look like pretty rough guys – no doubt migrant workers who pick oranges and grapefruit. Maybe illegals, who knows? She sees them passing around a bottle and eyeing her. Ellen tries to ignore them, but they start making vulgar remarks to her in Spanish and English. She's getting scared. When they start to walk her way she reaches in my duffle and pulls out the Ruger .45. They back off a bit for a pow-wow and then one goes to the back of the van and opens the rear door. Out jumps this pit bull – a real fighter, covered with scars. They send him at Ellen, probably to see if she's serious about using the gun. For all they knew it wasn't even loaded. I'm sure the dog could smell her fear. So Ellen crawls under the table, but that's dumb and offers no protection. The dog stops a few feet away growling and drooling. So, my sweet, gentle Ellen shot him point blank right in the mouth. Took out the back of his throat and a big hunk of his spine – killed the son-of-a-bitch instantly. That's when her new friends left. Half hour later I arrive."

Now Tom is sure he sees Jake's eyes fill. Without embarrassment, he wipes them with the sleeve of his shirt. "Sorry, I wasn't kidding when I said this wasn't easy."

"Take your time. I find this remarkable."

"Okay," Jake reached into his shirt pocket for a Swisher Sweet, lit it and settled back in the sofa. "Don't mean to be so melodramatic, if that's the word."

"You're not, and that *is* the word," Tom said smiling at his friend.

"All right," Jake began again, "I put Ellen in the car, throw the canoe on top and get our stuff in the trunk. Crazy thing is that Ellen is still holding the .45 and won't give it up. She's got it clutched in both hands to her chest as if she was holding a load of school books. She screams at me that we have to call the police. I tell her no way. Cops would probably arrest her and throw her in jail for shooting a gun at a park, not to mention killing a dog. I tell her to just put it out of her mind. I say it's over and to forget it ever happened. Ellen goes quiet except for crying from time to time. She's like this the whole way back. I couldn't get her to say much. When we got to her apartment I brought her duffle to the front door for her. She got out of the car and yelled at me that this was all my fault and that she never wanted to see me again. She told me not to call her anymore," Jake wiped his eyes on the same sleeve as before and took a deep, audible breath.

"She went inside and I drove home. I thought I'd give her some time alone to sort things out and calm down, you know, get back to normal. So about a week or ten days later I tried to call her. I got a recording that the phone was not in service. I drove to her place and found she'd moved. You don't need to be a rocket scientist to understand a message like that. I could have tracked her down probably. But I wouldn't do that. Maybe I should have. Anyway, I never saw her or spoke to her again."

Jake popped another Bud and as an after thought concluded, "She did keep my Ruger though, and I'll bet anything she's still got it."

"My God, Jake. I'm so sorry!"

"It was a long time ago."

"What do you think would have happened if Ellen hadn't retrieved your gun?"

"I've been asking myself that for almost forty years. Maybe I'd have gotten back to the river and she'd have been gone. Maybe raped. Or worse. No point in thinking about that too much especially now after all these years."

Tom opened his fourth Bud. "So you think I should have a gun?"

"That's your choice. Look, what you do is your business. You and your wife don't like guns and don't want one, that's fine. It's your decision. Probably you'll never be in a situation where you'll need a gun. But if you ever are, and you don't have one, you have no one to blame but each other. It's no skin off my or anyone else's nose. But I tell you this, anyone who's the head of a household with kids – man or woman – and doesn't have a gun... well, in my opinion they're saying that in a worst case scenario, in a life or death situation, they have decided that they refuse to protect themselves or their children. They'd rather be victims than fight. And that, my friend, is no less than cowardly. Anyone who won't protect his kids shouldn't have them in the first place. You got 'em, then you damn well owe it to them to protect 'em. And I don't want to hear that crap about kids finding guns and shooting someone by accident. They sell little strong boxes with touch-button combinations. No kid can break into those, yet even in the dark you can hit your four digit combination and get your gun if you need it. It's just taking responsibility for yourself and your family. You buy insurance, don't you?" Jake asked rhetorically, "in case of accidents or sickness or floods... well, this is just another kind of life insurance."

"You've certainly given me something to think about, Jake. I've never considered life insurance in quite that way, but again, what you are saying is logical. And it's hard to argue against logic."

Tom was just finishing his beer when he heard his cell phone, "Hello."

Jake watched as Tom held the phone to his ear. "Okay. Yes I know. I didn't realize it was this late. Sorry. I'll be right home."

Tom put the cell back in his pocket and stood. "I'm late. We're supposed to go to some party or something."

Jake stood too and said, "I'm sure you'll have a good time, and listen, I didn't mean to get off on the gun thing and Ellen –"

"No, that's perfectly all right. As often seems to be the case, you've given me much to consider."

Dr. Jonas Freeman, professor of political science at Laurel College, was hosting a cheese and wine party for select faculty. Since he was also a sponsor of Students for a Greener Planet, he and Sue were well acquainted. Dr. and Mrs. Freeman lived in a contemporary four bedroom home just off campus. Large windows looked over some of Laurel's oldest ivy covered buildings. Chrome and glass tables, floor to ceiling built-in book cases, abstract art and tiled floors with hemp rugs gave the place a modern, intelligent feel. It was, after all, a professor's home.

Because of Tom's seeming indifference to time and schedules, he and Sue were a little late in arriving. In fact, they were the last to arrive. "Stop worrying," Tom said on the drive over, "we're just fashionably late." Sue did not reply.

They rang the bell and entered the Freeman home through the propped open front door. Inside was fairly crowded with people and the evening's cool air was welcome. Between Tom and Sue they knew most of the people at the party. Sue introduced Tom to the Freemans, about the only couple Tom really didn't know.

Jonas said, "Tom, it's good to finally meet you. You're wife has told me a lot about you. I wish we could get you to help us with S.G.P."

"Well first, don't believe everything Sue says. I'm really not such a bad guy." It was a stupid cliché of a remark, but it got some polite smiles and laughs from those nearby.

"Nothing of the sort! Only good reports, I assure you."

"Then you're obviously not getting the full story." While saying this last bit Tom thought, *what a bunch of bullshit. I hate this crap.*

"Not hardly, I'm sure!"

Quickly grabbing two wine bottles from the counter, Jonas said, "Red or white… I've found both of these exceptional. Which would you like to try?"

Already feeling the effects of the four Budweisers, King of Beers, Tom replied, "White," without bothering to read the label.

"Excellent choice. I'll be right back with a glass."

Sue took Tom's arm and pulled herself close, "What's gotten into you tonight? You're really not being particularly funny and Jonas is obviously going out of his way to make you welcome in their beautiful home. How much did you drink next door?"

Before he could answer, or not answer, Jonas returned with a glass of the white wine Tom had selected. Handing it to him he said, "Seriously, do you think we could count on you for some help with S.G.P.? It's a great organization with a fine bunch of students participating."

Downing the wine, a little too sweet, and holding out the glass for a refill, Tom said, "Don't think so, but thanks for asking."

Not relenting, Jonas said, "But why? Sue's doing a wonderful job, but there's so much more that needs to be done. I know you'd be a terrific asset."

Another sip of the wine, more of a gulp this time, "If you must know, Jonas, I don't think I could support all the S.G.P. positions." Tom finished his wine and added, "At least not with a clear and honest conscience."

Perhaps the beer mixing happily with the white wine made Tom speak louder than was normal for him. At first Sue looked at him askance, wondering what in the world he was up to now; but that changed quickly to worry in anticipation of what might follow. She glanced around and a number of people had stopped their conversations to listen to Jonas and Tom. Sue tried to think of something to say to diffuse the potential bomb to come, but it was too late. Jonas proceeded to ask Tom what he could find objectionable in the positions held by the Students for a Greener Planet.

"Well, if you really want to know," and it seemed everyone around them did, "their activism concerning the climate change stuff is fine... Ineffectual, but fine. If that's what they want to do with their time, no problem by me. But the gun control business..." Tom looked around seeming to take satisfaction in his new audience, "that's simply misguided at best and just plain wrong at worst – even dangerous – If you ask me."

Jonas registered surprise, even bewilderment by Tom's statements. He'd worked closely with Sue and assumed they shared the same, or at least similar, viewpoints. Sincerely curious, if incredulously so, he pressed Tom further, "Never mind climate change. That's an endless debate raging between every political faction and even within the scientific community. But you can't seriously believe America's gun culture is a positive force." Now it was Jonas's turn to glance around for approval from the many onlookers. Receiving it, he spoke directly to Tom, "My good Dr. Sloan, please explain this – can I say it? – *archaic* view of requiring guns in the 21st Century. Clearly we need a more civilized approach to society."

Tom thought a moment, which he was good at. He was in his element here – a room full of logical thinking Ph.Ds. Tom owned this cage and if they wanted a fight, well, bring it on. He could feel the wine settling in with the King of Beers. They were both getting along just swell together. It felt good. He felt good. So he didn't give a good goddamn when he said mockingly, "Well, my good Dr. Freeman, a civilized philosophy of victimization only serves evil. Just ask the Jews of Nazi Germany." From somewhere off to the side Tom actually heard a slight gasp. "I see it this way. Unless you deny the existence of good and evil, there will always be those who wish to do harm to others. The more people who allow this without putting up resistance, the more it will occur. Let me just give you an example. You're a smart fellow. This will be easy for you." Tom noticed the sour expression on Jonas's face after this remark and didn't really care.

"You're in bed with your wife. It's two o'clock in the morning. Your daughter – I believe you have a daughter – is sound asleep in her room. Life is good until two assholes break in through a window. They are going to steal whatever they can sell for drug money. Your daughter hears the racket and walks in on them ransacking the place. One of the assholes takes a real shine to her and decides to take her in the other room for a little fun."

At this point someone – Dr. Adams from the English department – interrupts, "Tom, how can you even think such a thing!"

"How can I even think such a thing? Well, I just spoke it, so I must have thought it. Just hear me out. Where was I? Oh yes, one guy takes your daughter into the other room. Now, you and your wife hear the noise and get up to investigate. At this point, your daughter starts to scream and the other asshole facing you pulls a big, sharp knife and tells you he'll carve you both like a Thanksgiving turkey if you make so much as a move to help your daughter. And now, I'll leave the ending up to you. You're a clever man. You can come up with some endings. Only trouble is, none are happy endings." Tom glared at Jonas, his wife, and anyone else caught in his view.

"But wait, all is not lost. Here's a different middle and ending to the same story and it's my preferred version. You and Mrs. Freeman hear the noise and investigate. Your daughter starts to scream. The asshole facing you pulls his big knife." Tom has everyone's shocked attention.

"So your wife pulls a .38 from her bathrobe pocket and plugs the son-of-a-bitch six times while you, my dear Dr. Freeman, pull your larger and more powerful .45 from behind your back and blast the bastard in the other room seconds before he violates your daughter." Not a sound from anyone.

"Now, the question for the night is, in which story would you rather play a part? Don't answer that; it's rhetorical, something to ponder in the dead of night when everyone else is asleep. I'll sum it up this way. Any head of a household – man or woman, doesn't matter – in which there are kids, who doesn't own a gun and know how to use it, shouldn't have kids in the first place. Choosing not to retain a firearm is making the declaration that in a worst case scenario, as unlikely as that may be, but none the less within the realm of possibility, such a person will decidedly rather be a victim, would watch his or her children be raped or abducted or killed rather than bear arms to protect them. Well, to my mind at least, this is irresponsible and, truth be told, blatant cowardice.

"Think of your gun as just a different kind of life insurance. I'm sure you all believe in insurance, don't you?"

Tom was more than the center of attention now. He was the master of ceremonies in a sea of surprised, but perhaps awakened faces. Theatrically, if more than partially intoxicated, he said, "Ladies and gentlemen of the Freeman wine and cheese party, in conclusion I submit that if the well intentioned and empathetic members of the Students for a Greener Planet wish to truly save lives they'd best be guided by us, their esteemed professors and mentors, to petition the federal government to lower the speed limit to forty-five miles per hour, to outlaw all alcohol and tobacco products – which directly or indirectly kill and maim more people on a daily basis than guns ever will – to require helmets for all motorcycle and bicycle riders, to mandate children under the age of twelve wear life jackets while swimming, and you might as well throw in overturning Roe V Wade while you're at it!" (*Where did that come from?*) "Either you really want to protect and save lives, or you're just being hypocritically political!"

Tom looked around the room at the people who until this moment thought they knew Dr. Thomas Sloan. Horrified and aghast, Sue had moved as far away from her husband as the room allowed. Eyeing her finally, Tom said loudly, "Sue, my good wife, I apologize for embarrassing you so. Another reason to ban alcohol. I believe I've made quite a spectacle of myself here tonight and for this reason I think it best we leave. Oh, and as I sincerely wish to save lives, I think it best you drive. There's been enough carnage for one night."

In a state of mortification, Sue did not speak to Tom on the drive home. Once inside she said, "You were drunk and obnoxious tonight. Sleep on the sofa."

"By that proclamation I don't know whether I'm being punished or rewarded."

Looking at him with total disgust, Sue said brusquely, "To repeat myself, you're drunk and obnoxious. Sleep it off."

Leaving him swaying in the entryway, Sue walked quickly to the bedroom and shut the door.

V

Turning forty had been a piece of cake – literally. There had been a white frosting cake with *HAPPY BIRTHDAY TOM* spelled out in slightly crooked red script with a big four and a zero underneath. A few people had been there for the slicing, a few presents given and few or no unfunny, undignified comments about being over the hill or being ready for Geritol. Most of the faculty were well past Tom's age. He was one of the younger professors. But now, a year later, turning forty-one was not a piece of cake at all. Actually, it hit him like the proverbial freight train or ton of bricks or even the more appropriate *bat out of hell.* Tom felt keenly aware of the passage of time. Ideas he'd put out of his mind in the past were trying to surface in his psyche as if *they* had a mind and will of their own. *Hey Tom, don't forget about us! What ever happened to that trip to northern California? Tommy, Old Boy, weren't you going to write a novel? Yo T., when was the last time you took in a concert – no, not a symphony, man – a fun concert, some rock n roll? Now Thomas, is it really too late for children...*

Tom and Sue weren't big celebrators when it came to most things like anniversaries, Valentines Day or birthdays. Even Christmas passed uneventfully, a small artificial tree on a stand the only indication of the holiday season. So, birthday number forty-one might include a modest gift or two, an equally modest cake afterward, maybe dinner out.

"Tom, don't forget to take your car in to Toyota today. I spoke with Sid in the service department and they want it at 3:00. They'll give you a loaner car."

"Sure, no problem. I won't forget."

"I made a dinner reservation for 6:00 at Le Tropical."

"Sounds fine."

In the months since the Freeman wine and cheese party Tom had spent more time alone preparing for his classes, reading student papers, grading tests. He also started running again – it had been years –

and began some weight training in the college gym facility. He'd forgotten how invigorating it felt to work up a sweat and feel out of breath! Just because he was past forty was no reason to let himself go. Getting back into better physical shape made him feel healthier and more energetic than he'd felt in years. Why had he neglected himself so? With his physical improvement, he also noticed a marked increase in his sex drive. On several occasions he had to re-read parts of student papers he was correcting when his mind wandered to carnal subjects. Observing heavy breathing, shorts clad co-eds on the tread mills and Stair Masters didn't help matters either, but he found himself enjoying the renewed mental and physical sensations. Sue, on the other hand, seemed indifferent to Tom's annoying revival of youth. Maybe women just age differently than men, Tom thought. Or maybe not.

Laurel was a small liberal arts college where word of anything out of the ordinary spread rapidly. Tom's outburst at Freeman's party had been witnessed by a number of professors and their spouses. For a few days it was the talk of the faculty and even spread to the students who, except for those in the S.G.P., couldn't really care less. Being held captive by The King of Beers and the Fruit of the Vine wasn't considered a legitimate excuse. So fuck them all, Tom thought to himself. Let them talk and gossip like a bunch of old hens. If that's all they have to discuss in their sanctimonious lives they can all go to hell, go directly to hell – without passing Go and without collecting two hundred dollars (he did have a sense of humor left!) for all he cared.

But Sue cared. The day after the *unfortunate event,* as she called it, she chastised him in no uncertain terms that if he wanted to make a fool of himself in front of his peers, he should do it when she was not in his presence. Fair enough, he thought. Next time he decided to make a fool of himself he'd tell her to wait in the car. But to Sue he said nothing. He just listened.

Scheduled service on the Toyota hybrid seemed like just another way for the dealership to make extra money. The car ran fine, had amazingly few miles on it and was trouble free. Yet here he went, back to the dealer to spend money to make sure things continued to run smoothly. So be it. Tom drove to the service department where he handed the keys to Sid, the Toyota service manager.

"How's everything running, Dr. Sloan," he asked taking the keys from Tom.

"No problems."

"That's good. It's only two years old so there shouldn't be any problems."

Tom wondered if that actually meant that *after* two years there *should* be problems, but he didn't bother asking, even though it was a joke. Sid wasn't the sharpest tool in the shop and he'd just end up apologizing and explaining he was only kidding. "How long do you think you'll need it, Sid?"

"Should be done tomorrow morning. Mrs. Sloan said you would need a loaner-car. I'll find you one. Give me a few minutes to do the paperwork on your car and I'll bring you the keys for a loaner."

"Sounds like a plan."

While Sid filled out whatever forms were necessary, Tom walked outside into the spring sunlight. Without any particular reason he wandered to the used car section of the lot adjacent to the service center. He was not a *car person* by anyone's definition, but he enjoyed looking at the different models. In the front of the lot facing the street one car did catch his attention. Low and wide, the top was retracted to reveal only two seats. It was Jet black in color with tan leather. On the rear Tom read Boxster S.

"I see you have an eye for quality," said an approaching salesman wearing a Toyota shirt with the name Peter embroidered over the left pocket.

"I don't know about that, but this looks like an interesting car. What is it exactly?" Tom knew he always sounded awkward dealing with less educated people who knew about things which he hadn't a clue – things like cars.

"That, my friend, is a Porsche Boxster S. It is one amazing machine. Only three years old with low miles. I got a chance to drive this one just after it got traded in, and let me tell you, this baby can fly!"

"What's the S in Boxster S stand for?"

"That just means it's even sportier and faster than the standard Boxster, as if the standard model wasn't fast enough!" He held out his hand to Tom, "Name's Peter. Can I sell you this car?" he smiled a superior, know it all smile – at least that's how Tom wrongly interpreted it.

Ignoring his question, Tom asked, "Why would someone turn in a car like this at a Toyota dealership?"

Peter slowly and dramatically shook his head saying, "Very sad situation. The guy who owned this car got married a year ago and now finds out his wife is pregnant with twins. Bye-bye Porsche, hello Toyota mini-van. I was here when he made the deal. You never saw a guy who was buying a new car look so down and out. Most people who buy a car here are all excited and shit. This guy looked like he was gonna cry. At least his wife seemed happy. That's often the way."

"So what kind of car are you looking for?"

"I wasn't actually. I just brought my car in for service."

"Well, that's too bad for me. I took one look at you and thought, this guy looks like a Porsche man – here's my big sale of the week."

He actually winked at Tom after saying this. Tom knew he was just doing his job, trying to be personable. Still, Tom took a disliking to him. A few minutes later Sid arrived with keys to a loaner car. "Here you go Dr. Sloan. I hope this car's okay for you. It should be as it's just like your own car."

Pointing to the Porsche Tom said, "How about loaning me this one instead?"

Sid laughed, "I don't think that's going to happen somehow. Only way this one leaves the lot is with a new owner."

"Well, you know my car, Sid. What would it take for me to be the new owner?"

Tom surprised himself with this question almost as much as Sid and Peter were surprised by it. Sid asked, "Seriously?"

"Today's my birthday. Why not?"

"Let me get you the keys. Take it for a spin with Peter and I'll talk to the sales manager. I'll have your answer by the time you get back. Oh, and Dr. Sloan," Sid added with a smile, "we're not responsible for any speeding tickets."

The Boxster handled like no car Tom had ever driven. It was fast too. At first he was a little hesitant with the clutch – it'd been a long time since he'd driven a stick – but after a few tentative shifts he ran smoothly through the gears. Driving home he realized this was the first car he'd ever owned that actually made him feel... what would describe it? Cool! This car actually made Dr. Thomas Sloan of Laurel College's English department feel cool. He pulled up to a stoplight and two teenage boys in the car next to him looked the Porsche over, smiled and gave him the thumbs up. Both of them! Birthday forty-one melted away. Tom was young and cool again. This Porsche wasn't just a *Boxster S* it was a time machine!

Sue would have to be dealt with, of course. But it was *his* car that got traded, not hers. She said driving the green hybrids was mostly symbolic, a way to show which side they were on. Which side they were on? Maybe she knew which side she was on. Tom sure as hell didn't know which side he was on. Was he on the side of the Students for a Greener Planet? Not hardly. Was he on Jonas Freeman's side? Don't think so. If anything, he was more on Jake's side than anyone's – whatever that even meant. Tom finally concluded he was on his own side. Tom was on Porsche's side.

Sue was putting the garden hose on the rack when Tom pulled in-to the driveway. Just for affect, he revved the engine before shutting it down. Wiping her hands on an apron, Sue said, "That's what they gave you for a loaner? When will you get your car back?"

"Never. They liked my car so much they gave me this one in trade."

"I don't understand. You're not making sense. When will you get your car?"

"Sorry for trying to be cute. This is my car now. It's a birthday present I bought for myself. How do you like it?"

"Seriously, Tom, I have to take a shower and get dressed. I don't have time for this. Just tell me when you're car will be done."

"*Seriously*, Sue, this is my car now."

"Are you nuts? What in the world has gotten in to you? I don't even know what kind of a car this is."

"No, I'm not nuts. Nothing in the world has gotten in to me. And it's a Porsche Boxster S."

"I see. And what does the S stand for?"

"It means it's sportier and faster than the standard Boxster model."

"No, it means this ridiculous thing SPEWS more vile SHIT into the STRATOSPHERE than the standard model."

"Sure Sue, whatever you say…"

"And Tom, it's *black*! I thought we agreed to only get green cars, eco-friendly cars. This doesn't look like a hybrid to me.

"That's because you wanted hybrid cars painted ugly green. You wanted eco-mobiles. You wanted to make some kind of statement. Now it's my turn. I'm making a statement. I'm free from having to own an ugly, politically correct car. I'm making a statement that there is still some fun left in life and I'm not too old to enjoy it!"

"So that's what this is all about. It's your birthday and you feel old. So you're trying to feel like a young stud in a sports car. That's pathetic and beneath you."

"Maybe you're ready to hang up the towel, but I'm not."

"I'm not going to even dignify that with a response. Come in the house. We need to talk."

Sue sat in a single chair facing the sofa. She pointed to it and said, "Sit."

Tom hesitated just long enough to show some free will and independence before he took a seat on the sofa as instructed.

"Look Tom, I don't know what's going on in that head of yours, but you need to straighten yourself out. If you were one of my confused eighteen-year-old freshman students I'd tell you to go someplace and find yourself. I thought you were light years beyond that, but I may be wrong. So whatever it is, fix it. Do what you have to do, but get it done because I can't stand the way you are anymore – the way we are anymore. You want to be Darth Vader in that hot rod, fine. You want to embarrass yourself in front of everyone we know at Laurel, fine. Just do it without me. I've had it. I'm better without you than with you. You and your infantile rebelliousness are bringing me to the brink of insanity. You have become an unpredictable surprise a minute – and the surprises are never good.

"You are an intelligent man Tom – a scholar, a gifted teacher. But you need to accept who you are and come to grips with your life – which isn't so bad if you'd take the time to examine it honestly. Here's what I think... I think you need to clear out for a while, take a sabbatical. You've certainly earned it. Do research. Get published. Just go someplace away from here, away from me, do some thinking and come back when you are the Tom I married. That's all I have to say and I don't want to discuss this further. I'm going back to campus. I'll eat later."

"I didn't realize we just had a discussion," Tom began, but Sue was already headed for the door.

VI

With warmer weather Tom heard Jake's Harley pull in to his gar-age more frequently. He also heard it pull out and noticed his absences, sometimes for several days. While their friendship had grown over the last year and a half, neither asked many personal questions about each other's lives. Tom knew Jake still harbored deep and conflicted feelings from the Vietnam war. He didn't bother wondering too much about it. If Jake wanted to reveal anything concerning this period of his life, he'd do it on his own time, or more probably, wouldn't mention it at all. Once after drinking a few Buds he'd said that he'd never married, but came close a couple times. He said the war took all the tenderness out of him and marrying him wouldn't be fair to any woman. Tom thought that a little harsh. Jake could be warm and gregarious, thoughtful even. But what went on in the head of Jake was for Jake to judge and Jake only. Maybe he was right.

Tom had grown fond of Jake in a way that went beyond a couple guys bonding over conversations in a den or attending a cage fight. Tom thought of Jake as more of an older brother, a mentor for time spent outside and away from academia and campus life. Jake was a sort of life coach for the real world, a world that could be anything but the neutral, non-threatening environment of Laurel College. Sometimes Tom felt more like an observer of life than the participant Jake certainly was. Where Tom had ink on his hands, Jake's were covered with grease and grime. While Tom read poetry about nature, Jake was getting dirt on his knees from being down in it. Tom's reading and teaching literature, along with the corresponding philosophy and humanity contained within, were anathema to Jake who was simply living it, not bothering to waste time analyzing its every aspect. Once he'd told Tom, "If you're constantly examining your life too closely, you might not find the time to live it."

Tom found Jake's common sense approach to life refreshing. It seemed in literature most conflicts were rarely black and white, but were instead an endless shallow sea of gray that had to be waded through for a satisfactory conclusion. Jake often proclaimed simply, "People generally do what they want," and that summed up a situation. He also said, "People end up getting who and what they think they deserve." How could Tom disagree with any of this? Jake was like the wise uncle you'd visit with a complicated problem expecting to spend hours in consultation only to leave five minutes later scratching your head thinking *now, why didn't I see it that way?* Jake said that deep down most people knew what needed to be done in most circumstances. When they got bogged down making a decision it was because they didn't like doing what they knew in their hearts was the right thing to do and in actuality were trying to talk themselves into doing something else. He was a man who despised inaction, who on more than one occasion would stop a discussion about a pending problem by simply saying, "So, what are you going to *do* about it?"

Logic too, was one of Jake's strong attributes. For example, how could Tom really dispute when Jake dismissed the notion he heard so often in the media and elsewhere that the chances of needing a gun for personal protection were so small as to negate the argument for keeping a weapon. Jake responded angrily to this by stating, "The people who say this are the same ones who wouldn't think of driving their cars across a K-Mart parking lot without buckling their damn seatbelts even though they haven't had so much as a dented fender in twenty-five years!" Then he'd mumble under his breath, "Bunch of jackasses."

For all his talk of self protection and refusing to be anyone's victim, Jake was a peaceful sort who avoided conflict when ever possible. Even at a small restaurant when Jake ordered a steak and received a chicken dish instead, he wouldn't send it back. He said, "This waitress is busy enough dealing with all these assholes in here. She doesn't need another asshole giving her grief. Chicken's just as good as steak in my book. Let's just eat and enjoy." At the end of the meal he tipped thirty percent.

Tom figured it was Vietnam that made him gravitate toward subjects like personal protection and security. Once he'd made the comment that during the war the only thing keeping him alive were the guys watching his back and his weapons. To his mind, they were both equal and indispensable.

The day after buying the Porsche, Tom heard Jake return from one of his absences. Tom grabbed a six pack of Budweiser – he'd learned to keep plenty on hand, much to the dismay of Sue – and walked out of his house.

"So you finally bought a *real* car, huh Doc?"

"Yes, what do you think of it?"

"That's one hell of an automobile," Jake said walking around the Boxster. "Got the S model too. Good decision. Gives it a little more power. Yes sir, you did good, real good!"

"Didn't go over too well with Sue, as you can imagine."

"You didn't trade in her car did you?"

"No, of course not. But it still caused quite a ruckus."

"So what? Tell her she can still be happy putting around in her rice-burner and you can be happy driving this. That way you're both getting what you want. What's the big problem?"

"I think her problem is more with me than the car, actually."

Jake looked at Tom for a moment and said, "Unless you're planning to drink that six pack all by yourself, why don't you come on inside and tell old Jake what's bothering you. Can't be that bad."

Tom and Jake sat in their usual positions – Jake on the sofa, Tom in the chair. Tom pulled a Bud from the six pack and handed it to Jake who surprised him by saying, "Thanks Tom. I really shouldn't be having this, but one shouldn't do any damage."

"Why is that?"

"I'm on some medication. Not supposed to drink alcohol."

"Are you ill, Jake?" Tom asked with obvious concern in his voice.

"Nothing for you to worry about. Now, tell me what's going on with you."

Tom hesitated a moment and took a drink from his can. He reached into the drawer by his chair for one of his cigars, but there were none left. He closed the drawer, took another sip of Bud and as offhandedly as he could muster said, "Sue wants me to leave."

"Is that so?" Jake deliberately said no more and waited for Tom to continue.

"Yes. She wants me to leave Kingston, leave her for a while. I'm supposed to *find myself* and not return until I'm the Tom she married."

"And when did all this happen?"

"It's been happening for a long time now. I think it's been building over the last year or so, slowly, but irrevocably gravitating toward this inevitable conclusion."

"That sounds like a college professor's way of saying things are going to shit."

Tom laughed and said, "You have a splendid way of cutting to the chase, Jake. That's something I always admire in you."

"Go on."

"Perhaps unconsciously, or maybe even cognizantly, I believe I've propelled the situation toward this end... "

"Doc, you really need to cut the professor crap," Jake interrupted Tom's train of thought and continued by asking, "Are you trying to say that you wanted things to go this way, that you want to leave?"

For a long moment Tom – lost in thought – looked back at Jake. Then he gazed down at the floor and said softly, "I'd say so. Yes."

"Alright then. You're getting what you want. Where's the problem?"

"Maybe now I'm not so sure it's what I really want." Tom knew he sounded sheepish and weak, but it was how he felt.

"Let me ask you this," Jake said, sitting straighter on the sofa and looking directly at Tom who was once again staring at the floor, "Are you happy with your life? Are you happy with your marriage to Sue?"

"I suppose not," Tom said, again aware of the same feelings of weakness and sheepishness, but now combined with self loathing.

"You suppose? C'mon Doc, face this thing one way or another. Either you like the way things are and you want to go along as you have been or you don't like the way things are and you need to split. Which is it?"

"To be honest with you, Jake, I absolutely *do not* like the way things are going, but I'm afraid to, as you put it, split."

"And why is that?"

"Well," he hesitated a moment, "I don't know if I could handle the loss."

Incredulously, Jake repeated what he'd just heard, "You don't know if you could handle *the loss*? What loss? If something is not good you should *want* to lose it. You got a headache; you want to lose the pain! You owe money; you want to lose the debt! What loss are you talking about?"

"I suppose I'm talking about the loss of companionship, support, the loss of my routine. I just don't know if I can handle that loss."

Jake stood and glared down at Tom. Trying to control his temper he said, "You talk about loss. You don't know shit about loss!" With mounting anger Jake nearly shouted, "You wanna know about loss? Goddamnit, I'll show you loss!" Jake walked to the door, turned and demanded, "Get in the truck! Don't say another word; just get in the Goddamn truck!"

With Jake behind the wheel of the F-150 pickup, they left the neighborhoods of Kingston. Jake turned onto back roads and soon they were in the rolling countryside typical of upstate New York. The trees were in full leaf; winter's hold on the land had loosened. Tom said nothing, waiting for Jake to speak first, which he didn't.

Passing through the small village of Maple Hill, Jake made a left hand turn down a narrow lane and passed through the open iron gates of Crestview Cemetery. Still without a word, he shut down the engine and got out of the Ford. Tom followed.

Walking by some graves, Tom began casually reading a few of the first headstones they encountered.

Jake finally spoke, "Don't bother with these. This is the newer section; just a bunch of old codgers who croaked in the last ten years. Let's go to the old part toward the back."

They walked to where the headstones were weathered and obviously old. Some had fallen. Some were leaning and about to fall. Many were ravaged by so many years of wind and rain and snow that they were now difficult to read.

Studying a tilting headstone, Jake said, "You want to know about loss? Here's a boatload of loss." He paused a moment before continuing.

"Look at this guy," and Jake read from the headstone, "Samuel Lewis – born 1860 and died 1909. Forty-nine years old. And here's his bride Ann – born 1861 and died probably in child birth at age nineteen on June 4th, 1880… Right next to their baby daughter – unnamed – who died June 5th, 1880 – one day later." Looking over to Tom he said, "That, my friend, is real loss. And look over here. Old Samuel gets married again. This time he marries Margaret – born 1863 – who dies at age twenty-one in September 1884 – don't know what of. Might have been an accident or some illness they couldn't diagnose or treat back then. Their son Harold dies in January 1887 at the age of five. He's lying right next to her. You can often tell the graves of kids because they liked to put carvings of lambs on top of the headstones. Look around. You'll see a bunch of folks who died in January of 1887. Probably influenza got them. So Samuel is alone again – no wife, no kids. Talk to *him* about loss. He knew. He surely knew. Take your time. Wander around in this section. You'll see more loss than you can imagine."

For a short while both Tom and Jake walked slowly in different directions, reading headstones as they went. When they wandered back together again, Jake spoke in an agitated and annoyed voice.

"Last week I read in the newspaper about a kid got killed in a car crash. He was a freshman in high school. Tragic accident. The school closed down for a few days and offered counseling to the kids, the teachers and their parents. Nobody could cope with it." Jake opened both arms wide as if addressing all the dead in Crestview Cemetery and said, "Hell, the kids in Samuel's time went to their first day of school in September wondering how many of their classmates would survive the winter and still be alive in June!"

Turning once more to Tom who stood expressionlessly staring for a second time at little Harold's headstone, Jake quietly, almost peacefully concluded, "These people knew loss. They understood loss. They accepted loss. They didn't need any counselors. Loss was just a part of life for them."

Back in Jake's driveway, Tom got out of the pickup saying, "Thank you, Jake. You have a way of guiding my vision – my awareness – like nobody else I've ever known."

"I don't know about all that, Doc. I've just found that sometimes you have to look to the past to get a grip on the present."

"That's a very astute philosophical way of viewing life."

"I don't know if I'd put it that way, but it's just a good way to help understand things. I found that cemetery last summer while I was just out for a ride. After wandering around there for a while, it kinda put a lot of things in perspective, if you know what I mean?"

"I think I do now," Tom answered thoughtfully.

"And you wanna know something, Doc? The country's full of cemeteries just like that one."

Tom simply nodded his head in agreement and understanding. Jake looked at his watch and said, "Hey, I gotta go. Doctor appointment. Why don't you come over after dinner Sunday, say about seven. There's something we gotta do."

"Sounds good. I'll be there. And Jake…?"

"Hmm?"

"Thanks again," Tom said and grinning at his friend finished with, "I've got some plans to make."

Thinking it best not to bring beer, Tom walked next door to Jake's, knocked lightly and let himself in.

"In the den," Jake called out when he heard the knock.

Tom settled himself in his usual chair facing Jake on the sofa. Jake said, "This may not look like much of a celebration, but it's your send off party."

Jake left the den and returned from the kitchen with a bottle of champagne. "You know me. I'm mostly a beer guy, but tonight's special. As I said, I shouldn't be drinking anything, but what the hell."

Popping the cork he poured the champagne into two tumblers saying, "Sorry I don't have the right glasses for this, but it'll taste the same anyway." He lifted his glass to Tom, "Here's to our journeys."

Tom drank and asked, "Our journeys? Are you going on an excursion?"

"We'll talk about that later. This is mainly a celebration of your journey, your *sabbatical,* if I got the word right?"

Smiling, Tom said, "Yes, you got the word right, although I don't know where I'm going exactly. I think I still have quite a bit of planning and research ahead of me."

"Bullshit! You're going and that's the important part. Where doesn't matter half as much. You'll have an adventure wherever you end up, trust me on that one."

Tom's mood was lighthearted. A carefree attitude seemed to have settled over him since the announcement of his sabbatical. The term was ending and the timing couldn't have been better. Sue, in her usual measured and intelligent manner, agreed this was the best course of action for both of them. All that remained was choosing a place to go and the actual leaving. Money, within reason, wasn't a problem. With both him and Sue working full time, living modestly without children, and keeping their savings and investments separate, Tom felt truly free and independent. It had been many years since he'd felt this way and the freedom was like the welcoming home of an old friend.

"I still need to decide on a destination."

"Old Jake has that one covered," Jake responded, closing the den door and exposing a map of the United States thumbtacked to the back. Jake opened a cabinet and produced three matching darts. "Let the darts decide for you!"

Laughing, they both downed their glasses of champagne which Jake quickly refilled.

Handing a dart to Tom, Jake said, "Now then, let's find you a new home."

Knowing what was about to come and playing along anyway, Tom asked, "What exactly do you expect me to do with this dart?"

They were facing the map on the back of the door. Jake bowed ceremoniously to Tom, pointed to the map and said, "Take your best shot."

Tom shut his eyes and threw the first dart. It landed off the coast of Biloxi, Mississippi about eighty miles into the Gulf of Mexico. Jake asked, "You wouldn't happen to have a yacht, would you?"

"Afraid not."

Handing over the second dart Jake said, "Try again."

Closing his eyes, Tom threw again. Walking to the map Jake peered at the tip of the dart, "Trenton, New Jersey. Nope, too close to here. Give me the last dart. I'll find you a home."

Jake took two steps back, looked intently at the map for a few seconds then closed his eyes and threw the dart with surprising force.

It landed with a sharp thump. "There, that sounded better. Third time lucky. Let's see where I hit."

They both walked to the den door. The dart stuck firmly in the center of Arizona. "Ever been to Arizona, Doc?"

"No. Aside from a paper I gave in Dallas and one in Los Angeles, I've never been west of the Mississippi River."

Looking closely at the last dart Jake said, "Well, my friend, you're going to live in Lunden, Arizona!"

Tom broke into a loud laugh. "This is rich! I'll tell everyone I'm on sabbatical in Lunden and of course they'll all think I mean London, England. Let them try to find me there!"

"Then it's settled? Jake asked, "Lunden, Arizona?"

"Yes, it's settled. Lunden, Arizona it is."

Jake raised his glass to Tom, "To Lunden, Arizona, your new home on the range."

They both drank to Lunden. Putting his glass down, Tom asked, "Now tell me about your journey. Where are you off to… wait, don't tell me… it's got to be a motorcycle trip?"

Jake suddenly looked serious. He put his glass down also and said, "Listen carefully to me Tom. I don't want to get into a big discussion here, so just let me do the talking."

"Whatever you say, Jake."

They took their usual seats and Jake began. "As you've noticed, lately I've been away a bit. Well, I've been having tests done – medical tests – and I've been examined by a bunch of doctors – at the V.A. hospital and by others too. When all is said and done, I escaped Vietnam in the 1970s, but it got me in the end anyway. Might have been the Agent Orange or some other shit. Doesn't matter now. What does matter is that I've got cancer – the kind they can't do too much about. The doctors say they can try some things, but all they can do is prolong the inevitable. I'm going to die pretty soon. Might be months, but not much more and maybe a lot less. I already feel it inside me."

Tom didn't want to believe what he was hearing as Jake went on, "Remember the things we talked about? About loss? Well, you're going to know another loss now. I've known about this for some time. I didn't want to tell you. Didn't want anything to spoil the good times we had and the good friendship we have now and will always have.

I've taken care of my affairs and starting tomorrow I'm going to be staying with family."

Tom interrupted Jake saying, "Jake, I can't leave now! Not with your illness. I can help you through this."

"You're not listening, Doc. No one can help me through this. I'm not going to get through this. I got one adventure left and it's to the great unknown. I won't have you see me fall apart little by little. I don't want you to remember me that way. After tonight we won't ever see each other again. Please Tom, don't try to contact me. Remember me the way I am now. What's to come won't be pretty. Last memories are the ones that stay with you and I don't want anything beyond tonight to be in your head."

Jake got off the sofa and walked to the wall where the poster of the blonde on the chopper hung. He took down the knife and walked back to Tom who was suddenly looking colorless and frail. "You seemed to like my Randall knife. I have no further use for it. I want you to have it. It's been a good friend to me, just like you. It's also saved my hide more than once. Keep it oiled and sharp and it'll serve you too."

Tom stood in front of Jake and couldn't help the tears that left his eyes to streak down his cheeks. Jake handed the Randall to Tom who started to speak, but Jake cut him off. "Don't say anything, Doc. Just take the knife." Jake smiled weakly and concluded, "Now, get out of here and go on your sabbatical. And think of me when you have a beer."

In the weeks that followed, Tom could not bring himself to drink beer.

SIX

Dust plumed from the back of the open yellow Jeep as Joseph drove the rutted dirt road back from the reservation to his house. Overhead from horizon to horizon stretched a clear blue sky. Wind streamed through his hair. Bouncing on the passenger seat were large zip lock bags of deer jerky and loaves of fresh baked bread – offerings from grateful parents. His mood was good. The two kids he'd tutored – one he worked with on math, the other he helped with writing an English paper – were improving and kept good attitudes toward school. It was a refreshing difference from his teaching experiences in Montana. Still, he knew these were only two Indian kids he helped today – two out of the many who needed help, but didn't want it. So be it, he thought. Nobody said life was fair. If they want to do well, they will. If they want help, here I am. If they don't, then they don't. Simple really. Better to concentrate on the kids he can help rather than on those who are already probably lost.

Joseph looked at his watch. Almost 6:30. Plenty of time to grab a bite, take a shower, put on some fresh clothes and head to the Oasis. Being Friday, Mae would be singing and Tom said he'd stop in around 9:00. It was good to have another friend.

Joseph still cringed when he thought how he'd first met Tom. Not the best first impression. Smiling to himself as he drove, Joseph thought how Mae's first impression of him had been good, but her second one was bad. Now, with Tom, his first impression had been bad, but his second one was good. Who said you have to be consistent, especially among friends?

Tom's story last Sunday had been a surprise to both him and Mae. Shows how hard it can be to accurately read people. Tom appeared to be just another out-of-town tourist from the East, but without their usual annoying attributes like gawking at the giant cacti, taking photos of local people without asking, speaking too loudly, and generally being critical. Tom merely *looked* out of place. Sure, he was pompous, but that's a carryover from his life on a college campus in New York of all places. He'd lose that soon enough, but Joseph recognized more in Tom. He seemed like a zoo animal that'd been captured in the wild and caged for a long time – and then suddenly released. For all his obvious smarts and education, there was something almost childlike in Tom. Joseph had to conclude the years married to Sue and being a professor were only part of a more complex story. Maybe just the second half of a larger tale. Joseph felt pretty sure that in time, if there was a first half, Tom would tell that story too. Joseph considered Tom's neighbor Jake. He wondered if he were still alive. Too bad, he seemed like someone worth knowing.

When he reached his home, Joseph was still thinking about Tom. He decided he absolutely liked him. He had good qualities and his also good sense of humor was a definite plus. For his first long year in Arizona he'd had no friends at all, which was probably a good thing. But too much solitude isn't a good thing and maybe without even being fully aware of it, Joseph had reached his limit. Then Mae appeared. She became a welcome addition to his solitary life and had since developed into a good friend. Now, in Tom he looked forward to some male companionship. Joseph was keenly aware that friends were about the only thing he had truly lacked. He thought about Mae and his new friend Tom. And he felt gratified.

Usually at Chuck's Desert Oasis, Friday nights were slower than Saturday nights, but tonight the parking lot was nearly full. Good for you Mae, Joseph thought as he parked the Jeep. Chuck certainly lucked out when her car broke down over two years ago.

Joseph walked in and spotted Tom sitting alone at a table in the front. This time Tom sported a new pair of Wrangler jeans and a white dress shirt. He wore scuffed cross-trainers instead of the loafers he had on last time. Not exactly cowboy attire, but at least not the eastern preppy look that instantly marked him as an outsider.

"Hey Tom, mind if I join you?"

"I was hoping you'd show up. Have a seat. Mae just went on break – said she was going to 'freshen up' and be back soon." Tom waved to a waitress and ordered another wine for himself and asked Joseph, "What's your pleasure?"

Coors Light," he said to Julie who took their drink orders, smiled warmly at Joseph and left for the bar.

"Do you know her – the waitress, I mean?"

"Yeah, I met her once or twice before. It's a small town, Tom. Hard not to know people."

Tom nodded his head slightly as he pondered what Joseph had said. It certainly seemed the women found him appealing. Remembering the last time he was at the Oasis, Tom said, "It's good to see you actually inside this establishment. I was quite convinced you only frequented the parking lot."

Joseph laughed loudly. "Actually you're exactly right. This *is* my first time in here," and looking around he said, "Nicer than I thought…"

Now it was Tom's turn to laugh. It felt good to laugh again. Aside from some amusing times with Jake, he realized his life had become nearly devoid of merriment. Putting his hand on Joseph's shoulder he said, "Seriously, I'm glad you are here."

Joseph looked deeply into Tom's face in return. "Yes, me too," was all he needed to say. They both knew that after Tom's revealing narrative about his life in New York, a bond had formed – a three way bond that would probably only strengthen over time.

Their drinks arrived. Tom couldn't help notice Julie lean over Joseph and make contact as she put his beer on the table. "Anything else, Gentlemen?" she said flirtatiously, mainly to Joseph.

Joseph replied, "Thanks Julie, that ought to do it," and as she was turning he added, "at least for now." Julie smiled back at him.

"Seems like a nice girl."

"They all seem like nice girls until you really get to know them. Sometimes the trick is to stop before you really get to know them. That way you only get to see the nice side."

Tom smiled awkwardly. He still wasn't comfortable with what Jake referred to as *guy talk*. Since meeting Jake and leaving Kingston Tom was frequently reminded of the sheltered nature of his life with Sue.

How could he have been so blind to the world outside of academia and Sue and Laurel College? But he had been and that was purely the fact of it. No point in thinking too much about it. Anyway, all that's in the past now and this is a new life. He'd adapt.

Following up on Joseph's comments about Julie, Tom said, "That certainly seems a logical approach to relationships with the fairer sex." Joseph laughed aloud again.

"Tom, I gotta say it. You have a wonderful way of putting things. I'm an impulsive guy and tend to say the first things that come into my head. That's not always a good thing, you know. I've gotten into some pretty sticky situations for exactly that reason on a number of occasions. But you on the other hand seem to instinctively know what's on your mind and can just say it as if it were lines from a play. It's great! I hope you don't lose that by hanging around with the likes of Mae and me."

Before he could answer Mae returned from break and took her chair at the front of the room. She picked up her guitar and adjusted the tuning slightly. Looking up she said, "Did you miss me?" The room applauded. "Thanks, I missed y'all too."

Mae looked to Tom's table and saw Joseph had joined him. She gave them a private wink and said, "Anybody like Patsy Cline?" A few whistles and applause followed. "I thought so. Let's try this one…"

She played and sang and kept up a light banter with the patrons. Occasionally she'd say something to a specific person in the room. Other times she spoke to them collectively. Mae had developed an easygoing rapport with the folks of Lunden. By this time nearly all of the single men had given up their efforts to go out with her. The majority of them were too young anyway. She knew she was in a sort of in-between age. Most men around her age were married. Those that weren't probably had reasons why they couldn't find a wife. The rest were divorced with baggage. She realized her cynicism, especially as she was not without her own baggage, but it remained simpler this way. No complications in that regard.

Joseph – thank God for Joseph – was there as a great friend and supporter. Now Tom seemed to be joining their small team. He took a little getting used to, but after last Sunday's dinner and reveal, she felt she understood him better. She both liked him very much, but also felt sorry for him in a way that was hard to define. Best not to look too deeply into these things right now. Better to just go with the flow, as they say, and enjoy them both. She felt lucky to know Joseph and probably lucky to know Tom too.

Sometimes, but not often and less as time had gone on, she'd felt a little male-to-female tension with Joseph. It was nothing serious, but she did find him handsome and she wasn't exactly unattractive in her own right. Only once a long time ago had things started to progress beyond friendship. As she had to, Mae didn't allow anything to transpire. A long discussion had followed and Joseph was completely understanding after that singular episode. In some ways it brought them closer. After that, they both knew that if anything intimate were to happen, their friendship would be forever changed and probably end. That's just the way these things went. She desperately did not want to lose Joseph being in her life. Having Tom around might act as a good buffer for them all.

At a little past 10:00 Mae saw Roger enter the Oasis. He'd towed her car that first day in Lunden over two years ago. Mae had since felt fortunate she broke down where she had. It altered her life and she was glad of it. In hindsight, it was too bad Roger had been in the garage when she needed a tow and not an employee. Seeing Roger, Mae could only hope this didn't mean trouble tonight.

Sitting at a front table Joseph didn't see Roger until he was almost past them on his way to the bar. Tom had no reason to take notice of him until Roger turned and said, "So Little Joey is back with the grown-ups. Your momma know you're out this late?"

Joseph stood with such quickness his chair went over backwards. In an instant the ever-watchful Chuck wedged between them at the table. "I won't have trouble in here tonight, Joseph. You got a problem with Roger, you can take it outside."

"He's already done that once, Chuck. I don't think Little Joey here would want to try it again," Roger laughed and sauntered to the bar and took a seat, his back to Joseph and Tom.

Mae had just finished a song. She saw what had occurred and during the light applause silently said, "Please, God, don't let anything bad happen tonight." She put her guitar down and announced she needed a drink. More applause to that. Lunden after all was a drinking town.

Full of rage, Joseph righted his chair, sat back down and took a deep swallow of beer.

"What was that all about?" Tom asked with genuine concern.

"Tom, that guy is an ignorant piece of shit and sooner or later… "

Mae's arrival at the table cut him off mid-sentence.

"Joseph, by God you better put your masculinity back in your pants or wherever you keep it and let this thing slide. I swear I won't go through what I did last time you tangled with that dumb-ass redneck son-of-a-bitch!"

Tom chimed in with, "I'm quite afraid I'm abandoned to the dark on all of this. Obviously there exists bad blood between Joseph and that fellow at the bar, but let's not forget I'm here also. You two are my only friends and if there is anything I can do to assist or to rectify this situation, well, you can count on me."

Mae looked at Joseph and Joseph returned the look. In an instant the near violence was diffused and replaced with uproarious laughter from them both. Tom stared at his two companions and finally said, "I don't understand. Have I said something…?"

May leaned over and put both arms around Tom's neck and gave him a long and tight hug. "Tom, you are a darling. No, you didn't say anything funny, but how you said it was priceless."

"I don't understand any of this…"

Joseph spoke this time, "I know you don't. That guy Roger from the garage is a total and complete asshole." He looked briefly at each of them and said, "I'm going home before I get myself in trouble. Mae, as always, you sang beautifully. Tom, thanks for the beer and offering to back me up. Adios you two."

Mae drank the Diet Coke that appeared as it always did. "I better get back to work. I've only got one more set and I'm done for the night. I'll join you then and tell you about Joseph and Roger, Okay?"

"I'll be right here."

"Good. Is there something in particular you'd like me to sing?"

Tom thought a moment and grinned, "Sure, Billy Joel's *New York State of Mind* would suite me just fine."

SEVEN

MAE'S JOURNAL, 2ND ENTRY: TWO YEARS PREVIOUS

I was planning on writing every day and here it is five days without an entry. Life is full of surprises and not all of them are good. As I of all people know, the world can be a hard and violent place. There seems to be nowhere, no matter how remote (Lunden, Arizona included) that is immune to this fact.

To catch up on the days since my first entry: I last wrote on Thursday after Chuck, the guy who owns the restaurant/bar and this room I'm staying in, gave me a job singing. Who could have guessed that my first night would end the way it did. The singing went okay, but I have some practicing to do. The Carly Simon classics and old folk tunes I happen to like apparently don't turn on the locals here. After all, I'm being paid to sing for them, not me. I did find some material they liked, so I think I know what songs I need to work on. It shouldn't be a problem. The first night tips were surprisingly good!

Anyway, the main part of all this is that Joseph, the Indian – or maybe part-Indian – came in to hear me sing. I was flattered actually. God he's cute! (but so young!) He took a table and I saw him drink a beer. Then another and another... He sat through a couple of sets. When I was done with my next to last set for the night, he motioned for me to join him – which I did. I needed a twenty minute break by then. He'd had a lot to drink, but wasn't drunk or obnoxious in any way. We mostly made the usual small talk. He asked how the room was and actually apologized for not helping me move my stuff in. This is one nice guy! After I finished my Diet Coke (I am being a good girl) and was about to sing again, in walks Roger – the tow truck man who was fixing my car. Something about him just gives me the creeps. He's in his 30s I'd guess. Kind of greasy blondish hair. Tall – maybe six-two or six-three – thin with a beer belly just starting. Few years and he'll be gross. Some people you just don't like instantly and this guy was one. Maybe that's unfair of me, but that's how I felt about him. And I think I'm right about that!

So, I'm still at the table with Joseph, all very pleasant and innocent. Then this Roger guy sits down at our table uninvited. At first I thought he must be a friend of Joseph's, but that wasn't the case. In fact, I noticed he totally ignored Joseph. He started asking me questions about where I'd been, where I was going – the usual stuff guys say while trying to pick you up. Joseph finished his last beer, ordered another and just sat there watching Roger give it his best shot. I'm sure he could tell it wasn't working and that I had no interest. Finally, just out of the blue, Joseph said, "Roger, why don't you go somewhere else to find some new friends. You're obviously not succeeding here and Mae's not really your type."

They looked at each other and I could see the dislike in Joseph's face and the humiliation in Roger's red face. I hate it when guys get this way! It was time for me to get away from them both! I said something like, "If you'll excuse me boys, I've got a job to get back to."

So I went back to my chair to sing the last set. I could see, Joseph and Roger talking. From the look of them, this was far from a friendly conversation. By the end of my first song I saw Joseph leave. The beer had affected him as he was a little unsteady walking out of the place. A short while later Roger left. I don't think he ever ordered anything to drink. I didn't think much more about either of them as I was concentrating on singing some songs the people in Chuck's might like. I took a few requests – fortunately I knew some of them enough to sing. By the end of the evening I was getting a feel for the place and the people who came here on weekends. Actually, a pretty friendly bunch of folks. They seemed glad to have me in their town for a while. I don't think much goes on here in the way of live music or entertainment. I screwed up one song some guy requested and when I apologized for messing up everyone just laughed and someone yelled out that if that was messing up, I could mess up all night long! Kind of restored my faith in humanity – for a few short minutes anyway, judging by what was to come.

I finished up my last set earlier than I'm used to. Couldn't have been much past 10:00. But considering this was a restaurant and bar combination, and I started earlier in the dining side, I'd been there a while. I put the Gibson away feeling pretty good. I was surprised at the tips. This job might not be so bad for a while.

As it was kind of warm and stale in the bar, I decided to go outside for a walk and some fresh air. I walked around the side of the building and that's when I saw Joseph.

Oh my God, he looked awful. My first thought was that he was dead! He was lying in the dirt next to his old yellow Jeep. His face was so bloody and swollen I hardly recognized him – at least he was breathing. I ran inside and told Chuck. He called 911 and in a few minutes an ambulance came. A few people gathered around to watch, but nobody seemed to care too much and soon the ambulance left. I was the only one remaining in the parking lot. I looked in Joseph's Jeep and saw nothing of value, but the keys were in the ignition so I took them for safe keeping.

Well, there I am, standing alone in a dirt parking lot after seeing the only person I know – a person, I might add, who showed me a lot of kindness – a bloody mess and taken to the hospital. He'd been so nice to me the day before that I had to do something. Since earlier in the day I'd taken a drive around to familiarize myself with Lunden, I knew where the little hospital was. I drove there and sat in the waiting room until a nurse came out and asked if I was related to the patient. I told her I was just a friend. I can't say I liked the way she looked at me, but maybe I imagined something more.

A short while later a doctor came out of the room where they'd taken Joseph. I asked how he was and the doctor said he'd be okay. He told me he was mostly just banged up pretty badly and that he was lucky no facial bones had been broken. He had bruised ribs and his lip was split, but didn't need stitches. His teeth were fine (thank God his smile will stay the same!). And he'd have black eyes for a while, but no permanent damage. Joseph was to stay in the hospital overnight for observation and to sober up. In the morning he could probably go home. Before the doctor left he said, "Drinking and fighting don't mix. He's a lucky man this time, next time he might not be." Isn't that the truth!

The next morning I called the hospital to check on Joseph's condition. They said he was sore and swollen, but getting ready to leave. I told the woman on the phone to keep him there for a few minutes longer and that I'd come by to help get him back to his Jeep. I remembered I still had his keys.

He was waiting outside the hospital when I drove up. He slowly got in the car and said something like now it was my turn to give a lift to a wayward soul. I drove him to his Jeep still parked at the Oasis. It was all he could do to get out of my car and into his. Even though his eyes were swollen almost shut, he swore he could see well enough to drive home. I told him that wasn't good enough and that I'd follow him to wherever home was and make sure he got in okay. He didn't argue. Even if he had it wouldn't have done any good. I'd never have left him to drive home alone. He told me Lunden was a small town and people liked to talk. He said I should let him leave first, wait a few minutes, and then circle around a back street and he'd be waiting on the main road out of town where I could follow him. I thought it really considerate that he didn't want people seeing me follow him. Obviously he understands gossip.

We followed his plan. I had to let him get way ahead of me as the roads were dirt and the dust from the back of his jeep was blinding. I'd never driven on roads like these before. The desert has a beauty all its own – a kind of starkness that at first seems empty, but when you really look, is full of color and life. Even though I'd been in Tucson for a while, Tucson is a big city and now I'm sorry I didn't explore the surrounding area more. Apparently Joseph's house is a rented one on the edge of an Indian reservation. The house is small and comfortable, but situated in the middle of nowhere. He told me there were no other homes for miles around. Joseph also said that's just what he was looking for when he moved here a year or so ago.

Anyway, I'm getting ahead of myself. I got to Joseph's house and helped him inside. He tried not to show it, but I think he'd stiffened up on the drive and was in a lot of pain. Before leaving the hospital they gave him a small bag containing some pain pills, but later he refused to take them saying last night he acted like an idiot and the pain was his punishment. Being a typical guy, he also said if he hadn't drunk so much beer he'd have "kicked that hick's ass all over Arizona." Typical guy! I only hope he lets go of his anger. I remember what the doctor said about fighting.

I got him into his house. He wanted to stay on the sofa instead of the bed so he could listen to music or read. There wasn't a TV, which I thought odd. I noticed a dish mounted on the outside of the house, so the previous occupant must have had one.

Anyway, I got him as comfortable as I could and went into the kitchen to fix some food. I was surprised to open the refrigerator and find it full of fresh veggies – all in bags or containers with labels on some. He said he kept more in the bigger freezer in the garage. Again, I was surprised by the number of containers. Each was labeled – some stews, some casseroles, some just had meat or fish in them. He yelled in to me that those with a big "C" on the labels meant they were already cooked and only needed to be thawed and heated. I picked one labeled with a "C" that said "casserole – grouse" and brought it into the kitchen to thaw.

returned to the living room and sat in a chair across from Joseph. He said there was nothing else I could do for him and that he was really grateful for my help. He asked me to put some music on, which I did. He has a big collection of CDs and I found an ancient Beatles album – an Indian who likes the Beatles? I guess so. I think a lot of my preconceived notions need adjusting! I put it on and turned the volume low so we could talk.

Again he thanked me for my help and apologized for me having to see him in this condition. He does have a good sense of humor as he also said he'd pretty well convinced himself I was impressed with him yesterday. However, today I must think him trashy, and he has his work cut out for himself if he was to regain his prior standing in my estimation! Who is this guy? He lives alone in the desert, cooks amazingly well, is a music aficionado, is obviously well educated... and looks like a Greek God! (Well, maybe a shorter, smaller Greek God).

So, we talked for a long while and he asked me to put the casserole in the microwave. The meal was ready in no time. I'd never eaten grouse before. It has an unusual flavor that I can't really describe, but whatever else he put into that dish made the whole thing heavenly! He said he had to go up into the mountains for grouse, but that often people on the reservation give him some for tutoring their kids. I gather he was a teacher in Montana, but he didn't seem to want to talk about that too much. We did talk about our lives and what we'd done and where we'd been, but I knew we both kept it mostly surface without delving too deeply. That was fine with me, and probably fine with Joseph too.

Time went by quickly and before I knew it a good portion of the day was shot – but aside from singing in the evening as it was Saturday, I didn't have anything else to do. Actually, the day was far from "shot" (poor choice of words). I couldn't remember a more interesting and relaxed day in a very long time. There was still some grouse left and Joseph said he'd finish it later. I told him I'd better get going and again he went on and on thanking me and apologizing. I told him I'd check in on him the next day. He said I didn't need to do that and I responded that I know I didn't "need" to do anything, but that I wanted to. I think he was pleased.

Singing at the Oasis last Saturday went well. I think I'm getting a better feel for what the locals want to hear, so I'll work on songs they'll like. Thankfully, Roger didn't make an appearance. I don't know what I'd have said to him if I had seen him. I better just act as if nothing out of the ordinary has happened. I don't want to get into something that really doesn't involve me – although, I guess in some way it's because of me that this whole nasty business got started in the first place.

It's late and I've been writing a long time. I'm getting tired, so I'll just finish by saying I stopped by Joseph's place each day since following him home Saturday morning, and each day he got stronger and seemed in a little less pain – although I sense the pain was still pretty bad. Once when he went into the bathroom I did peek into his bag of pain killers and, just as I thought, he hadn't taken any of the pills. In a strange way, I'm sort of impressed by that. It's nice to see a man who is tough, but also likes music and can cook etc. Each day we shared one of his frozen meals. Apparently when he cooks he prepares enough for several meals, eats what he wants and then freezes the rest. Smart way of doing things and they all tasted great!

When I saw him today, aside from the bruises that are starting to fade, he said he was feeling pretty good again. Of course, he thanked me over and over and said we'd have to get together again – maybe in *a week or two. I took this to mean he didn't want me stopping in again tomorrow. Thinking about it on the drive back, that was a nice way to let me know that enough nursing was enough. I certainly don't want to smother him. I hope we stay friends. I also hope he stays out of fights!*

EIGHT

The Arizona morning air always felt cool and invigorating to Tom. He had made it a ritual to start each day with a run and was surprised at how quickly he'd been improving. The first runs were more run-walks. Tom would run for a minute or two before slowing to a walk to regain his wind and then, when rested sufficiently, continue running again. He set a course of two miles. He'd been running for a while in Kingston, but the preparation for his move to Lunden, dealing with Sue and cleaning up his calendar at Laurel College left little free time. He'd mostly given up running there. No matter, he was running again now and liking it. Tom wasn't discouraged by his first run-walks. He wasn't competing with anyone – especially not with himself. Running was *for* Tom, not *against* Tom. That was his new attitude. The air felt dry and good. The sky was often clear. And so was his thinking process.

The move to Lunden had been uneventful. That was always good. He'd made friends almost instantly. And that too was good. In the short time he'd been in Arizona he felt certain Mae and Joseph were genuine and real, not like so many of the friends – acquaintances actually – that Tom knew back in New York. Jake would approve of these two. Tom wondered if Jake was alive. He willed himself to leave Jake in the physical past, but in his spiritual and intellectual present. Tom wasn't exactly sure what he meant by spiritual present, but wasn't going to get too deeply into that. He knew he was indebted to Jake on many different levels. That would suffice.

Tom realized he'd run for nearly a mile before his first walk. The streets he ran were mostly flat, so running was easy. Each morning he noted where he ended his last run and began his first walk and took satisfaction in seeing that point passed by a little more distance each day. Not going to push it – just run for the pure enjoyment of it. Life needs to be lived in the same way – for the good in it, not the pain in it – at least for now, for this point in his life. The future will sort itself out.

The two miles ended with more running than walking. Soon he'd increase it to two and a half miles. Then three. His eventual goal was to run hilly streets, and maybe later, even trails in the desert, but not yet. When he did that, he'd be in better shape. He'd wait until he could run without needing to walk as much. Right now Tom knew he very much needed something to look forward to. He had no real plans. Maybe he'd write, he'd read the books he'd brought – and hopefully some he saw on Joseph's shelves – he'd run and get into good physical condition. Beyond that, who knew? The *who knew* part would have been unthinkable a month ago. That was in his regulated, old life. Now, the unknown was welcome, something he actually yearned for. He'd come to cherish the idea of an uncertain future.

The few Sunday runs he'd taken were his favorites. Lunden slept until the first church services beckoned at which point local traffic increased. And then all was quiet again for a while. What was it Mae called this church time? Yes, *lull time.* Lull time runs were quiet and a fine time for thinking – or not thinking. Just running for the sake of running was often good enough.

Today's Sunday run was early, dark and cold early, before the sun early. Apparently Mae went to Joseph's most Sunday mornings. She often arrived before sunup and stayed for lunch. Tom felt accepted, even honored to be invited this Sunday. He didn't know what to expect, but the food was apt to be unusual and probably excellent. Don't think about it too much, just run, feel alive, feel good, shower and wait for Mae to pick you up. What came next would develop on its own. He stepped up his pace, as if running faster would make time quicken too. Silly thought, but he did look forward to both the drive to Joseph's and whatever might follow.

Mae's Taurus pulled in front of Tom's house. She didn't turn in to the driveway, just stayed along the curb. Tom knew she wanted a fast getaway before any neighbors might recognize her and start some unwanted gossip. He got in the car and they were off.

"Well, good morning to you, Tom. I hope you didn't mind getting up so early."

"Not in the least. I've already gone for a quick run. You know, early to bed, early to rise and all that."

"More than I can say for myself. I hate getting up before light, especially after singing the night before. You know, late to bed, late to rise and all that."

Tom smiled to himself. He was used to her chiding and mocking and he knew he deserved it. Tom said nothing for a while, just enjoying the ride and company.

After a few miles Tom asked, "What am I to expect on this predawn sojourn of ours?"

"Hard to say exactly. We'll take a sunrise walk to the kiva and see what we feel like when we get there. It's not a long hike. Sometimes we sit and watch the sun rise. Sometimes we just talk. And sometimes we get spooky – my term, not Joseph's – and use the kiva. We'll see."

Tom thought about what Mae had said. All very laid back and unplanned. Spontaneous. How wonderful! "Whatever takes place, I'm sure it will be enlightening," he said.

"It just might be that. You never know. I can at least promise you some good food though if it's not *enlightening*."

"That in itself will be a pleasure." A moment later he added, "But what do you mean by *spooky* exactly."

"I'm not sure, *exactly*. Joseph is into some spiritual stuff. Nothing wacky or really off the wall. And nothing overly Native American. More transcendental, I'd say."

"Ah, our old friend Henry Thoreau revisited once again."

"Maybe not revisited. Maybe he never left."

"Now who sounds spooky?"

"C'mon Professor Tom, you must have taught Thoreau at some point in some English 101 class back East. If he's not relevant today, then you were just teaching a history class."

"Excellent point. Yes, I believe he's relevant, but not particularly practical in contemporary American society."

"Well, according to Joseph, that's because we've become too technologically dependent, too civilized, too far removed from nature. I think that's exactly what Joseph is trying to reverse in his life. At least for a while."

"Sounds like he and Thoreau have something in common that allows them that privilege."

Mae looked over at Tom briefly, "And what is that?"

"They both are men of some independent means. Thoreau came from a family of at least some modest wealth and our young Mr. Curley has unearned income. Makes all the difference when pursuing idealism."

"To use your own words Professor, *excellent point.*"

Joseph's house was a mere gray outline in the dark. Mae turned the car lights off and shut down the Ford. "I do love the quiet out here this time of day or morning or night or whatever the hell time this is."

"And I love your succinct eloquence, Mae."

Joseph approached the car, steaming coffee mug in hand. "And a fine good morning to you both."

Tom was already rounding the front of the car with his right hand extended, "And a fine morning to you too, Joseph."

Mae slowly emerged from the driver's side and said, "Enough with all the salutations and loud talk. Joseph, if you don't get me a cup of coffee right now I'm going to climb in the back seat and go to sleep for a couple hours… or maybe a couple days."

Joseph chuckled, "Great sense of adventure, Mae. Plenty of coffee inside. C'mon in and warm up."

May stretched out on the sofa while Tom took a chair. Joseph filled two mismatched mugs with hot coffee.

"How do you like yours Tom?"

"Just some cream or milk would be fine."

"Mae, the usual?"

"Yup, bring it on."

Joseph handed out the mugs and retrieved something by the front door. He then sat on the end of the sofa, putting Mae's feet in his lap. He untied and removed her sneakers and replaced them with ankle high moccasins.

"Tell me if I'm tying these too tight."

"No, that feels just fine. Thank you."

Tom watched without saying a word. When Joseph completed his task he turned to Tom, "Good you've got runners on. They'll be fine for where we're going."

"I gave up hard shoes a couple weeks ago. Marvelous improvement these."

Joseph and Mae smiled to each other and Mae pointing to her mocs said, "And a more marvelous improvement these."

Joseph said, "Ignore her rudeness, Tom. She's always cantankerous until she's had coffee."

"I'm not cantankerous in the least. Just… feisty."

"More like a pain in the ass," Joseph responded. "Anyway Tom, you might want to try some mocs for desert trekking. Amazingly comfortable."

Mae added, "You can really feel the earth in these, but still have enough protection against sharp rocks and cactus. You'd love 'em."

Tom asked, "Are they made locally? On the reservation?"

"Nope, the good white folks at Carl Dyer Moccasins in Indiana make these. Best mocs in the world. You should order a pair. I've got an extra catalogue around here somewhere you can have."

Before leaving the house, Joseph went into the bedroom and closed the door. A moment later he returned wearing only his mocs and a pair of cut off jeans. His upper body was bare except for a small leather pouch on a thong around his neck. On his belt hung a four inch bladed sheath knife. He wore a rolled blue bandana as a headband to hold his center-parted hair.

Mae turned to Tom, "Don't worry, Tom. He's a friendly Indian, not the scalping kind.'

"Then why the scalping knife?"

"In case I need to gut… or maybe scalp something along the way."

Joseph walked to the wood gun rack by the wall and selected a light rifle. From the drawer beneath he removed a small rectangular green box of cartridges and put a few in the pocket of his cut-offs.

Tom asked, "Are we on a hunt?"

"Always on a hunt when I take a rifle. Just in case we spot lunch or dinner, it'll pay the check."

Mae said, "What Joseph means is should he see some poor defenseless creature that he wants to eat, he'll have the means to dispatch him and place his carcass in an iron cook pot."

Ignoring Mae he asked Joseph, "What kind of rifle is that?"

"It's a single shot Winchester .22, made before World War II. It's a little beat up on the outside, but has a perfect bore and a pretty decent peep sight."

"I thought most hunters use telescopes on their rifles?"

"Yup, most do. I had a gorgeous little scoped Cooper .22, but it got stolen from the U-haul on the way down. I found this gem in a pawn shop for seventy bucks – nobody wants these anymore. Out to forty or fifty yards it's just as deadly on small game as the Cooper. Past that range a scope is a real advantage, but knowing I have to get closer makes me a better hunter."

Tom gestured to the bow and quiver of arrows over the fireplace, "Do you hunt with that too?"

"I have, but I admit to being a pretty poor shot with a bow. I need to practice more." Pointing to the bow, "That was another pawn shop buy. It's a recurve bow, you know, without all the pulleys and gizmos of a modern compound bow. I've got a target on a hay bail in the back. You can give it a try sometime if you like."

Before Tom could respond, Mae got to her feet and said, "Enough talk about guns and bows. Let's get going."

Tom was glad for the fleece jacket he wore. Zipping it fully he noticed Mae wearing a long sleeved heavy wool outer shirt buttoned to the neck. Why Joseph wore next to nothing was a mystery and how he managed to not be cold was another. He wasn't going to ask, at least not just yet.

Joseph took the lead with Mae following and Tom behind. There was no conversation. The sun was just beginning to turn the horizon to rose when Joseph stopped and looked intently to his right. After a few seconds he continued on. Within a short time this occurred twice more. On the last stop Tom whispered to Joseph, "Do you see something?"

Joseph whispered back, "Not sure, more like sensing something or maybe hearing something faint."

He didn't elaborate and Tom asked no more questions. This was all new to him. Hiking in the cold desert before sun up with two friends –

one, an Indian mostly naked! Going to a kiva for some kind of ritual… or something! Bringing along a rifle! Sensing game! How unexpectedly remarkable! Tom was glad the darkness hid the smile on his face that he was unable to vanquish.

They arrived at the kiva while the first edge of sun broke in the distance. Long shadows instantly formed where only darkness had been moments before. The world was coming to life. Birds fluttered and an out-of-range jack rabbit ran for cover. Joseph stood the .22 against a nearby towering saguaro cactus.

"Well," Joseph said, "What do you think, Mae?"

She looked to Tom and winked, "I think you should put Tom in the kiva like you did my first time here and give him a little *enlightenment*."

The kiva was stone lined and dark. The sun hadn't risen high enough in the east to illuminate its circular inside. A short pole ladder rested against one side.

Joseph pulled a rolled straw mat from under a tarp and handed it to Tom saying, "Unroll this on the bottom. The ground may be a little cold and damp so the mat will help. Just go down, lie on the mat and make yourself comfortable. Mae and I will be up here. Mae's not going to say anything. I'll do all the talking. It's important you listen and do exactly as I say. And don't let yourself fall asleep. If you feel anything that makes you uncomfortable, that's okay. Just tell me enough and come back up. Any questions, Tom?"

"Sure lots of them, but I think whatever you have planned will answer them in due time."

"I'm glad you take such a good and open attitude. Some people would reject this whole kiva thing before even giving it a try. Alright then, in you go."

There were only about four rungs on the ladder. Standing inside, the rim was only a few inches above Tom's head. Inside felt cooler as the cold air sank to low spots until warmed by the sun. There was also a dankness to the interior of the kiva from the earthen bottom and stone sides. Tom spread the mat which was just long enough for his entire body and slightly wider than his shoulders. The floor of the kiva was smooth and without jutting rocks or debris to poke through the mat. He thought a pillow or rolled up shirt would be nice, but didn't ask for anything. He trusted Joseph and Mae. For all their joking and fooling around, Tom knew this was not one of those times.

While Tom was situating himself in the kiva, Joseph and Mae retrieved their folding chairs from under the tarp and set them up a few feet from the rim. They waited until Tom seemed settled and quiet.

Joseph asked, "Are you relaxed and comfortable, Tom?"

"Yes, quite."

"Good. Now we're going to start with some basic yoga relaxation to get you in the right physical and mental state of readiness. Unless you want to quit, just do as I ask, listen to what I suggest, be sure you don't fall asleep, and don't speak."

He waited for a few seconds. When he heard no reply he began, "Tom, I want you to raise your left leg a few inches from the ground, hold it a couple seconds and let it drop. However it lands, just let it lie. If it's not comfortable, do it again. Now do the same with the right leg. Good. Rock your left foot back and forth a few times and now just let it stop on its own. Very good. Now the same with the right. Lift your right arm from the shoulder and let it fall, now the left. Very good. Now wiggle your left hand at the wrist and let it stop on its own. Now the right hand. That's fine. Lift your head an inch and let it fall back to the mat. Now rock it slowly side to side a few times and let it stop on its own. Good, almost there. Arch your back and let it relax back to the mat. Now your butt and hips. Take a very deep breath and hold it for a count of three... one... two... three. Let it out slowly. Once again... one... two... three. Let it out slowly. If any part of you is not relaxed and comfortable, do that part again as before."

Joseph heard Tom raise a leg, let it fall and then rock a foot back and forth. Then silence.

"Very good, very good. I'm going to wait a minute or two. Keep your eyes closed, enjoy the silence, feel the earth under you and think of being so heavy you can't move. Sink into the earth. Listen for me to continue in just a short while. And stay awake."

Joseph whispered to Mae, "I think this will be good for him."

"I think so too."

"Tom, I want you to try to clear your mind of everything except what little you are feeling in the kiva. Allow me to guide your thoughts. Think only about what I am suggesting. It's very important to realize you are going to open your mind and soul to the forces of the world. As you know, there are forces for good and forces for evil, the ever present yin-yang of the universe. We're going to concentrate only on the good forces, the positive energy. Expel any negativity you encounter. You are ultimately in control here. No force or power can come to you without you willing it. Stay focused and stay positive and stay awake."

Joseph stood and faced the east. He closed his eyes and with his left hand grasped the leather pouch suspended on his chest. He placed his right thumb and pinky on each of the scars on his pectoral muscles. Mae had never seen him do this, but how could she if she'd been in the kiva? Still, watching him like this was unsettling in a way she couldn't define. She knew there was a side of Joseph she didn't share. She wasn't sure she wanted to know this side. It seemed foreign, too different to bridge with her sensibilities.

Joseph released the pouch, dropped both arms to his sides, and briefly opened his eyes to the sun before returning to the chair next to Mae.

"Let's begin, Tom. I want you to know this kiva was built around a thousand years ago. It was used by people for many years before being abandoned. You are now connected to these ancient ones who are long gone. You are also connected to the earth which is made up of tiny particles of once great rocks and mountains, bits of bone and teeth, shards of pottery, microscopic particles of all life. You are connected. You are one with all life and non-life. See black in front of your eyes. Feel the immensity around you, not just in this kiva, but this entire planet earth, this whole unimaginably vast universe. Think of yourself at its center. Everything radiates from you. Everything gravitates toward you. Time does not exist for you. You are content where you are. Enjoy this. Be a magnet for the positive, the good, the all powerful forces that strengthen and illuminate."

Tom went into the kiva with an open mind. The yoga relaxation exercises were remarkably soothing. He did indeed feel heavy, too heavy to move, and relaxed. At one point he caught himself drifting toward sleep, but brought himself back to alertness.

From Joseph's suggestions Tom did feel connected to the ancients, to the earth and the universe. He found himself starting to think about the pre-Civil War Transcendental Movement, but forced cognizant thoughts from his mind. He blanked his mind and listened to Joseph. He saw black and held it.

When Joseph ceased his suggestions, Tom was able to enjoy this suspended state between the physical and the metaphysical. Time really didn't exist in the kiva. He began to think about the passage of time, but again forced it from his mind. Blackness again.

At some point Tom realized his heaviness had transitioned to lightness. He felt himself begin to lift. Don't think, just feel… blackness, lightness and blackness. More passage of time, but how much? Doesn't matter. An outline appeared in the darkness of his consciousness and slowly grew closer. Tom felt himself rise to the now vague silhouette before him. Closer and closer. They were on a course to merge when Tom recognized the form of Jake. He was holding out his hand to Tom. Tom felt his own arm reach toward Jake's. I'm here Jake! No, he was not beckoning; he was pushing me back…

"Tom! Tom! Tom!" The voice was faint and mixed – male and female. There it was again, "Tom! Tom! Jesus Christ, Tom can you hear me?"

Tom felt a slow spinning sensation that gained in velocity until he felt caught in a tornado. He tingled and let out an uncontrolled gasp followed by a deep breath. Then another. A twirling, pulling sensation and then back to stillness and coldness. He was aware of someone leaning over him. Hands on his shoulders. He heard, "Tom? Tom? Are you okay? Tom?"

"Yes. Yes, I'm okay."

Now the female voice, Mae, "Let's get you out of here. Can you sit up?"

"Yes, I think so."

The male voice, Joseph, "Good, now can you stand?"

Tom stood.

"Take the ladder slowly. Hold the sides tight. That's good. Now, sit in this chair and get your bearings." Joseph watched Tom's face intently. "Do you know where you are, Tom?"

"Yes, of course. I was down in the kiva and now I'm back."

"Are you sure you feel alright?"

"Yes, I'm fine now. What was that all about?"

"Just tell me, Tom. Did you fall asleep or were you fully conscious."

"I thought I was falling asleep once, near the beginning when you were still talking, but I made myself remain awake. I was not asleep, but something like a dream happened and then a spinning tornado feeling."

Joseph turned to Mae who was staring at Tom. "That was no dream, my friend; that was a vision. Dreams occur from our imaginations during sleep. Visions are revealed only when you are awake."

Tom did not speak. He appeared drained and exhausted. Joseph continued from before, "You were in the kiva a long time. Mae and I thought you might be asleep, but we weren't sure. After about forty-five minutes we thought we heard movement, so we looked in. Your right arm was raised and you'd gone completely pale, lost all color. I couldn't see you breathing. That's when I jumped into the kiva. Mae came down too. I've only read about things like this, but never witnessed it. We were frightened for you, Tom. I assume we stopped whatever vision you were having and I'm sorry for that, but I was truly concerned you might not return – you might not survive it."

"Thank you both," Tom looked from Mae to Joseph, "That was the most incredible experience! I don't know where it was leading, but Jake told me to go back."

"Jake?" Joseph said looking again at Mae.

"Yes, Jake. I thought he was holding out his hand to me, but he was trying to stop me, motioning for me to return, to go back."

"Jesus Christ, Tom! You're sure it was Jake?"

"Certain."

Joseph said nothing and seemed to stare at Tom in awe for a long moment. Finally, almost absently he said, "So, Tom, how'd you like visiting the *other side*?"

The hike back to Joseph's house was a quiet one. Tom seemed lost in thought. Mae simply seemed concerned and confused. Joseph was unreadable. He led the three person procession back along the same ridge they'd taken earlier. At one point Joseph stopped and stared out over the rocky landscape.

Mae came alongside him and quietly said, "There's a rabbit just by that rock to the left."

"I know. I've been watching him."

"Aren't you going to take him?"

"Not now. It doesn't feel right. I don't want to kill anything today."

Mae didn't understand. He brought the .22 rifle for just such an easy opportunity and now he won't use it. Joseph could be hard to figure out. Since helping Tom out of the kiva, he's been acting strange… no, not really strange, more like he's in a partial daze. He'll explain it if he wants to. If not, well, that's okay too. Everything doesn't need an explanation. And now Tom is quiet and not communicating. Crazy day!

Joseph began walking again. This time there were no stops. They reached his house in short order. Once inside, Joseph seemed more himself again.

Joseph put the rifle back in the rack and replaced the .22 shells in their box. Turning to his friends he said, "That's better. It was getting pretty warm out there. What can I get you guys?"

May spoke up first, "Anything cold and wet."

Tom asked for some water. Joseph went into the kitchen and returned with both. He also popped the top of a Coors can for himself. "Well, so how was your day, Tom."

This was the ice breaker they all needed. The three broke up in laughter. They took the same seats they'd had before they left that morning and Tom said, "My day? Oh, you know, the usual I guess."

This caused more laughter still. Joseph got out of his chair and, passing behind Tom on his way to the stereo, grabbed both his shoulders and gave him a friendly shake saying, "You gave us quite a scare back there, Pardner."

"I'm really sorry for all that. It seemed a little out of my control."

"Mae, what would you like to hear?"

"Anything but the soundtrack to *The Exorcist*!"

"Okay, I'll go with my second choice then."

Once more they all chuckled together. And again Mae felt relieved. She thought this was more like it. A little lightheartedness was what they all needed.

Joseph pulled a CD from the shelf. "Mae won't let me have my first choice and she thought you were showing off with the classical you chose last time, Tom. So, today we'll try a little country."

Tom wasn't exactly a country music aficionado, but he had listened to some in a couple of the bars Jake had taken him to. He thought that seemed a lifetime ago, no pun intended – especially on this bizarre day! He did recognize the first sounds of a *Rascal Flatts* song. He tried not to think about Jake, but that was impossible. When Joseph returned to his chair Tom asked, "Joseph, what do you think that meant today?"

"I haven't a clue as to what you might be referring to, Professor Sloan."

Mae laughed uneasily. She was hoping they wouldn't get into a heavy discussion of Tom's experience in the kiva. But that was hoping for too much.

"You know what I'm talking about. Seriously, you said you'd read about what you thought was happening to me, but had never witnessed it. What did you mean?"

"If you really want to know, I can tell you that first of all, I'm not an expert in this stuff, but I've done some reading. There's New Age religion, Native American spiritualism of all sorts, Inuit or Eskimo beliefs – you name it. Every culture manages to dabble in the metaphysical. Here in the western world, Christianity has angels and fallen angels plus the Holy Spirit. It's basically found footing in every time period and in every corner of the globe. How we go about it is a reflection of our culture and time in history. I read a definition a long time ago that summed things up so well that I memorized it. It goes like this, 'religion is a cultural manifestation of a universal spirituality.'"

"Okay," Tom said, "but what did you read that pertained to my experience?"

"I was just getting to that. I've read where people who go into a deep trance or meditation can leave their physical bodies. Meaning their consciousness or souls depart for destinations unknown, literally. Some call it astral projection. I don't know this for a fact, but some say it can be dangerous. I do know that it's not easy to do and those that practice it, or at least claim to practice it, have to train themselves. It's a goal that is supposedly very difficult to reach."

Joseph saw he had Tom's and Mae's full attention. He took a drink of his Coors and continued, "I believe it is the Inuit who have shaman or medicine men that do this. I've read where it's possible for the soul – for lack of a better word – to go so far away from the body that it gets lost or decides not to return. When this happens the person can die. I don't know if there are actually recorded cases of this or not, but I've read it in more than one source. I think it's the kind of thing scientists and the medical profession shy away from. Kind of like UFOs – if you show an interest, you can be branded as a whacko. And once viewed in this way, your reputation is always suspect. Grant money goes away too. Cultural anthropologists can get away with studying it, but they have to be totally objective and keep it at arms length."

In a surprisingly matter of fact way Tom asked, "Why do you think I encountered Jake in this supposed *vision*?"

"Remember I suggested in the beginning when you were getting relaxed that you were in control? I meant that completely. Well, perhaps you sought out Jake – maybe subconsciously or consciously. From what you said, he wasn't trying to lure you any place. If anything, he was pushing you back or sending you away."

Tom thought about this, took a swallow of water and slightly nodding his head said, "Jake was more than a friend to me. He was like a teacher or mentor. I think of him often and at times wonder what he would think of this situation or that. I've wondered how he would view my new life here in Lunden. I find myself wishing I could talk to him."

"Perhaps you just answered your own question of why you encountered Jake. I think you were looking for him… and found him."

"That makes sense, but I don't even know if Jake's dead. I don't know if all this was just my imagination. Saying *I don't know* sums it up actually."

Joseph hesitated a little and quickly added, "Look, I know something of visions. And unless you tell me you were asleep and dreamed this whole thing up, which is doubtful given the physical condition I saw you in when I jumped in the kiva, you were anything but simply sleeping and dreaming. Tom, trust me when I say you were treading on thin ice."

Tom seemed to consider this. He asked, "Why were you so insistent I not fall asleep?"

"That's a personal thing with me. I alone uncovered a holy place, the kiva, that hadn't been used in centuries. The people who built it need to be respected. It's a place for connecting with a world we can't see or measure or fully understand. It's not a place for sleep. I consider myself a caretaker of the kiva, and sleeping in it, well, that would be disrespectful."

"I see, yes," Tom reflected. "You are to be commended for your convictions. It's a rare quality in people today. Did you learn this growing up on a reservation?"

Mae quickly looked to Joseph and was yet again relieved to see him smile.

"No, actually I didn't grow up on a reservation. Luck has a way of singling out people, and I was one."

Joseph walked into the kitchen and tossed out his empty beer can. He opened the refrigerator and grabbed a second Coors. "I'm going to have another beer. Tom, you were open enough to share your story about Jake and how you ended up in Lunden, so unless you're in a hurry to get back to town, I can repay your story with one of my own."

May stretched on the sofa and said, "Joseph, I think it's time to break out another bottle of your finest wine."

NINE

TWENTY-NINE YEARS PREVIOUS

Helen Curley was a nineteen-year-old Crow Indian. And she was giving birth. She was in her one bedroom home on the reservation. Her neighbor, a midwife, assisted her. Like most things in her life, the pregnancy had been easy and uneventful. She was single and kept the father's identity to herself. He was gone anyway, so what did it matter? Helen knew his first name and thought she knew his last, but wasn't sure. That didn't matter either.

Helen worked part time at a convenience store along the highway. That gave her some spending money – *fun m*oney she called it. Usually she spent it on cigarettes, liquor and weed. Occasionally, if she worked extra hours, she might score a little coke. Food and housing came mostly from the agency as well as a little cash which she used for basic necessities.

She'd been pretty clean during her pregnancy though – a bit of partying was surely okay – just a little to drink and smoke, nothing more. And she did cut down on the cigarettes. Helen instinctively knew her baby would be just fine. And he was.

The delivery was uncomplicated, a snap really. A couple hours in labor – that wasn't as bad as everyone said it would be – and then motherhood. Her son weighed seven pounds two ounces and she named him Joseph. It was a Bible name she knew, but it was also an Indian Name. Chief Joseph! She wasn't exactly sure who he was or when he lived, but that wasn't a concern. It was just a name after all.

Joseph was light skinned and had striking blue eyes. That wasn't too much of a surprise considering his dad was mostly white. Helen knew of at least one grand parent on her side who was white also. Besides, she thought, mixed babies were usually the best looking.

The problem with being a mom was the boredom. The baby seemed to need feeding and changing all the time. Helen couldn't even watch a TV show without being interrupted. She kept her job at the store – she could always stick Joseph with neighbor kids in another house somewhere. There were lots of other women willing to look after one more kid.

For the next year her routine consisted of taking care of the baby, working and being bored out of her mind. Helen missed hanging out with her friends. She couldn't expect them to tolerate a screaming, smelly baby for very long. She wondered how she managed it herself. Well, if she couldn't hang with her friends, she could at least get high.

At first it was beer and a little weed thrown in for good measure, but having a baby to care for took most of her extra money. She needed more if she was going to keep from going crazy staying at home so much.

Helen knew a guy who always liked her, always made gross comments to her when nobody else could hear. He dealt a little pot and coke and always seemed to have some money. Trouble was he was fat and pimply. His breath smelled bad too. None of the girls would go out with him. Helen weighed what he could offer her against what she could offer him and came to an easy conclusion. If she could get high enough, often enough, he could do what he liked with her. She'd get what she wanted and he'd get what he wanted. This was a no-brainer really.

At the time of the phone call, Jennifer Curley who was nine and a half years older than her sister, Helen, was baking bread in her kitchen. She'd married a white man named Paul Jameison who owned a ranch about eighty miles from the reservation. The ranch had been in his family since the Montana homestead days and now it was his. At thirty-three, he was four years older than she. Paul was an honest man and a good provider. They'd met when he was working on his master's and doing an independent study on various native grasses that grew on the reservation. She was finishing up a degree in social work and serving as a tribal administrator. That was seven years ago. They'd been married for six.

Since then, Jennifer and Paul ran a successful ranch. The work was hard and lasted from morning to dusk, but it was good and satisfying work. Neither complained. They'd planned for children, a big ranching family, but plans and reality don't always coexist. Children did not happen. It was Paul, not Jennifer. They'd discussed adoption, but the paperwork never seemed to get filled out and filed. Jennifer didn't push; it was a sore and unspoken topic for the present.

The phone call came from tribal social services. Agnes Pale Horse was on the line. Jennifer knew her from high school and later from working on the reservation. After a few pleasantries Agnes said, "Jennifer, I didn't know who else to call. I think you are Helen's only known relative at this time."

Jennifer braced herself. It wasn't the first call she'd received about Helen, "Yes, that's right, Agnes. What's wrong this time?"

It's been brought to our attention that Helen's using again. Pretty heavily, I'm afraid. Her son isn't getting the care he needs. If he's not taken in by a family member, he'll end up in foster care."

"Agnes, I haven't heard from Helen in over a year. I didn't even know she was pregnant."

"It must have been more than a year since you heard from her, 'cause the baby's already a year old, Jennifer."

Jennifer didn't know what to say. Could it really be that long since she'd spoken to her sister? Finally she said, "How much time do I have to make a decision, Agnes? I have to discuss this with my husband."

"We've got the baby, a boy by the way, in the infirmary, but he can't stay there much longer. We're trying to get Helen into rehab, but she's... resistant."

"Agnes, thanks for calling. Just give me twenty-four hours. I promise I'll get back to you in that time."

There was no discussion in the Jameison house. Paul was in one of the barns when Jennifer found him and explained the phone call. "Of Course, without question," was all he said.

Jennifer impulsively leaped into his arms and nearly strangled him. It was only then that Paul realized how much Jennifer wanted a child. He held her tight and said, "Me too, me too."

While Jennifer drove to the reservation to pick up Joseph, Paul had driven to Billings to buy a crib, high chair, Huggies, and a seeming thousand other things Jennifer had written out for him on two lined sheets of notebook paper.

Agnes met Jennifer at the infirmary. They hugged briefly and Jennifer was taken into a makeshift nursery. Joseph was sleeping soundly when she gazed down at him for the first time. So perfect, so peaceful, she thought.

"I'd like to see Helen. I need her to know I'll be taking care of her baby."

Agnes hesitated a moment. "I'm afraid that's impossible."

"Go on."

"When you called back to say you'd take the baby, I phoned Helen with the news. She was pleased and said I should come by the next morning to get Joseph's things. First thing this morning I drove to her house." Again Agnes hesitated. Then she continued, "The place had been cleaned out. Helen was gone. There was a letter with your name on it taped to the baby's car seat." Agnes produced the letter with *Jennifer Jameison* scribbled on the envelope.

Jennifer opened the letter – a note really – and read: "Thank you Jennifer. Joseph will find a better home with you and Paul than anything I can provide. Don't try to find me. I am gone. Love, Helen"

By age seven, Joseph was already riding horses and hunting with his dad. He was a ranchman's son through and through – a Montana ranchman's son. He kept his hair short and aside from appearing perpetually suntanned, he looked like most of the white kids at the small rural elementary school he attended. His teacher was pleased with his progress and on parent-teacher night told the Jameisons he was in the top five of his class.

Jennifer often said Paul was more Indian than she was. From an old movie, Paul took the line *Being an Indian is not a matter of blood, it's a state of mind.* Since marrying into the Crow tribe, Paul had read extensively about Indian history and cultures. He also took several Native American Studies correspondence courses offered through Montana State University.

Having grown up on the reservation, and while appreciating Paul's interest in all things Indian, Jennifer was glad to be away, leading a different life. She rarely returned to the reservation and over time lost track of most of her old friends. To Jennifer, the reservation held little promise for its population. She'd recognized this early on when she'd lost several school mates in alcohol induced fatal car crashes and drug related incarcerations. She was determined to go to college and find a life elsewhere. Falling in love with Paul came at a perfect time in her life.

Paul on the other hand, felt it important to instill a sense of Indian Pride – as he called it – in his son. From day one Joseph was never anything but *his son.* He told him of the famous chiefs, of his great and powerful name sake Chief Joseph of the Nez Perce tribe who famously said, "I will fight no more forever." He took Joseph to the Little Bighorn Battlefield and walked him through the stone monuments that indicated where soldiers of Custer's Seventh Cavalry fell to the Sioux and Cheyenne warriors on June 25th, 1876. He told Joseph he was descended from Custer's favorite Crow scout, Curley, who died with Custer on that historic day. He said to his son, "You have warrior's blood in your veins. Always be proud of who you are."

On Joseph's twelfth birthday he went with his father to the Big Sky Sportsman's Store in Billings. His father bought him his first big game hunting license – twelve was the minimum age in Montana. On the drive home, Paul said offhandedly to his son, "Oh, I almost forgot. I've got something for you when we get home."

"What is it, Dad?"

"You'll see," was all he said.

To Joseph the ride home from Billings seemed twice as long as usual. Once in the ranch house Paul took his usual easy chair in the living room and picked up the Billings Gazette pretending to read. In truth he was at least as excited to give Joseph the gifts he'd been planning for the last year as Joseph was to receive them.

"Umm, excuse me, Dad? Did you say you have something for me?"

"Did I?" Paul was not really very good at this sort of thing, but Joseph played along. "Oh yes, I almost forgot. I think I do have something around here for you. Let me see now, where did I leave it?"

Joseph smiled patiently through his dad's nonchalance act. "Let me call your mom in, maybe she knows where I left it."

Paul called to Jennifer who was in the kitchen preparing Joseph's birthday dinner, "Hon, would you come in here and bring that box for Joseph, please."

It was a long, rectangular box. Joseph knew instantly what it must contain. "Happy birthday, Joseph," his mother said handing him the wrapped package.

"Thanks Mom. Thanks Dad," Joseph said while already beginning to tear at the birthday paper.

With the wrapping torn off, printed on the box was the name Sturm, Ruger and Co. Joseph broke the tape holding the lid down and removed his first big game rifle. It was a Ruger No.1 single shot rifle. The stock and forend were beautifully figured walnut. On the side of the barrel was stamped the caliber designation – *.270 Winchester*. It was a classic and expensive rifle.

Paul could barely conceal his enthusiasm. "The stock may be a little long for you, but you can put up with that. You'll grow into it in no time. The .270 is a great caliber. It'll kick you a little, but you'll learn to handle it. You can take any game in Montana with this rifle, but remember, it's a single shot. You have to make sure your first shot counts. If you miss, you probably won't have time to reload to get a second shot. This rifle will make you a better hunter. I've got a scope we can mount on it."

Joseph wrapped his arms around his mother wordlessly expressing his gratitude and then once more he thanked his father. Paul couldn't hide that his eyes had filled. He'd waited a long time for this moment.

"I've got one more present for you," Paul said walking to a cabinet and pulling a drawer. "You'll need this too."

He handed another box to Joseph. This one was small and wrapped like the rifle box. Joseph tore the wrapping off and opened it. Paul said, "That's a Ruana knife, son. Hand made here in Montana. It's not a fancy knife, but for a pure working knife, there's none finer. Anyone sees you with a Ruger No.1 single shot and a Ruana knife, well, that'll tell them you know what you're about."

Joseph's high school years were successful and pleasant. He found his classes interesting and not particularly difficult. He'd always known he was college bound and high school was just a stepping stone. Unfortunately, at least to Joseph's thinking, he'd stopped growing at just over five foot six and his weight leveled off at about 140. Joseph lifted weights almost religiously, but the physical bulk never accumulated. Hard ranch work had strengthened him, but the additional weight training only sculpted and refined the muscle mass that refused to increase. He was too light for football, too short for basketball and had little interest in track. Instead he wrestled.

The weights and ranch work made him strong beyond his weight class and what he lacked in wrestling technique and know how, he more than made up for in agility and sheer strength. In middle school he was usually one of the smaller boys and this caused him to be picked on by the bigger kids from time to time – nothing serious, not really bullying – just an annoying understanding that others could dominate him physically. Wrestling put an end to that.

Joseph also saved his money and when he had enough, bought a heavy bag and pair of training gloves. Paul could hear him in the barn relentlessly pounding the bag. His father didn't say much about it, but inside he was proud of his son's masculinity and toughness.

Joseph got his varsity letter for wrestling in his junior year and then seemed to lose interest in the sport over the summer. Even with the wrestling coach pleading with both him and Paul, Joseph declined to go out for the team his senior year. Paul stayed out of the decision. It was Joseph's to make. To himself, he thought it a mistake, but was wise enough to realize wrestling was just a high school sport that wouldn't affect Joseph's college career or future life in the least. He should do what he liked.

Two things took the place of wrestling in Joseph's life. The first was a new found love of reading. Even Joseph didn't know how it took root except that he'd been assigned a short summer reading list between his junior and senior year. Most of the kids ignored it and couldn't be bothered to read during summer vacation, but Joseph picked up the first book, *Kon Tiki* by Thor Heyerdahl, read it in two days and was hooked. He realized there was a huge world beyond

Montana and if Joseph hadn't been there yet, he could sure as hell go there through books!

The other replacement for wrestling was the opposite sex. Joseph had discovered girls, or perhaps more accurately, they had discovered him. His easygoing manner combined with his flash smile and blue eyes were only part of the attraction. Joseph was also exciting intellectually. While other boys talked endlessly of sports or cars, Joseph talked of distant times and places, people who achieved greatness, and he even tried writing a little poetry. This made him stand away from the general senior male population in school. Joseph was viewed by the girls as a mixture of handsome athlete and brain. There was also something almost exotic in his deep tan and overall visage. If anyone thought of him as Native American, it was never spoken. He certainly wasn't like any Indian anyone in school had ever known. The girls thought Joseph was just… well, different in a refreshingly, and to their closest friends admitted, sexual way.

Once, toward the end of his senior year, three of the most promiscuous girls in school conspired to ambush Joseph at a school dance. By drawing straws it was decided the first girl would seduce him at the beginning of the dance, the second would make her move during the middle of the dance, and the third would find him at the dance's conclusion. Each would find a place to take him away from the other students and faculty chaperones. Later they'd compare notes.

Their plan worked perfectly and Joseph went home having danced little, but feeling exhausted nonetheless. The following Monday at school, Joseph passed the three girls walking together down the hall between classes. In unison they giggled and waved to him. One blew him a kiss. Joseph figured if this was what was meant by being had, well, he'd be glad to be had on a regular basis. By graduation, any girls who put-out had willingly been conquered by Joseph Curley.

The Jameisons and two other families thought long and hard before giving their sons the same high school graduation gift. Jennifer was less enthusiastic about it than Paul, but the decision had been made and, like his two friends, Joseph was given a plane ticket to Paris, a two month Eurail train pass, a new backpack and enough cash to lodge in hostels and eat modestly for the eight weeks he was expected to be away. The only stipulation was that the three had to promise to use the pre-paid cell phone plans their parents provided to check in with home at least once a week.

The threesome lasted five days before Joseph split off on his own. It seemed his two buddies were more interested in beer gardens and bars than seeing the sights of Europe. A night or two of this was Joseph's limit. There were museums and historical sites to visit. The drinking and partying he could do when he got to college.

Hostels were full of student travelers and Joseph trained Europe with a number of new acquaintances. He traveled alone when he wanted to and rarely had to look far for companions when the mood struck for company.

The eight weeks passed rapidly. As much as Joseph enjoyed the adventure, near the end of two months he longed for the wide open spaces and mountains of Montana. He was also excited to start college. He hadn't decided on a major yet, but there was plenty of time for that.

With his excellent grades and high SAT scores, Joseph had many options for choosing a college. Throw in his Native American status and even more doors and scholarships would open to him. Still, Joseph felt a loyalty to Montana. He planned to work on the family ranch in the summer, hunt in the fall, ski in the winter… and wish he were any place *but* Montana in the spring! He knew he'd invariably travel throughout the states in the years to come, but in his heart he always assumed he'd make his home in Montana.

Joseph entered Montana State University in Bozeman that fall. The university was situated close to some of the best skiing, fly fishing, hiking and hunting in the West. This fact was not unknown among professors from around the country with outdoor interests. Because of this, MSU attracted some of the highest regarded faculty of any state university in the country.

In his second year Joseph took a basic course in Native American Studies called *NAS 268: Contemporary Reservation Problems and Solutions.* He also picked up a history course titled *HIS 211: The Winning & Losing of the West.* To Joseph, the two classes seemed to bounce off each other. The main problems on reservations today seemed to revolve around substandard education and substance abuse.

The historical perspective of subjugating the Indians and removing them to reservations while the rest of the country exploited the opportunities west of the Mississippi River seemed to coalesce in Joseph's mind. He suddenly knew his majors. He would double major in history and education.

With these degrees he could teach on a reservation. He would begin a change, a metamorphosis. He could and would start to reverse the course of reservation life starting in the present. He'd open the eyes of reservation kids to the truths he'd learned from the books he'd read, from the places he'd traveled, from the knowledge he'd gained in college and from having Crow blood coursing through his veins, by God!

Joseph imagined his future and saw a clear path. It was from this epiphany that Joseph decided to be an Indian and to look like an Indian. He grew his hair to his shoulders and parted it in the middle. He wore a rolled bandana headband and went in search of a good pair of moccasins.

Much to the consternation and disapproval of his mother, but tolerance of his father, Joseph was the only student to walk at his college graduation ceremony with robes and mortar board in a pair of Carl Dyer, made in Indiana, double-soled mocs.

TEN

The moment Mae drove off with Tom, Joseph began working his phone. As soon as Mae dropped Tom off at the curb in front of his house and pulled away, Tom was thinking of his laptop. When at last Mae pulled into her driveway, she jumped from the car and trotted to her front door. Before she could unlock it and get to her computer, her cell phone vibrated. It was Joseph.

"You been on your computer yet?"

"Not yet. Just got home. I'm at my front door."

"I'll save you the effort. I know we were all thinking the same thing, but nobody wanted to say it. *Is Jake dead yet?* Well, he is. I did an obituary search for Kingston, New York and a Jackson "Jake" Taylor died six days ago. Had to be him. The obituary talked about his service in Vietnam and his love of motorcycles. I don't know about you, but I'm almost shaking."

"Tingles for me. And they won't stop."

"Mae, I've got another call. It's Tom. I'll get back to you."

"Hello."

"Joseph, I have some news."

"What kind of news, Tom?"

"This is unnerving, to say the least."

"Oh?"

"I went online and searched Jake Taylor – Jackson Taylor actually. It seems Jake passed away six days ago."

"I'm sorry, Tom." He waited for Tom to continue.

"Joseph, do you recall I told you the last thing Jake said to me was to think of him when I have a beer?"

"Yes. You also said you hadn't had one since that day. Before you go any further, let me just say if the day comes when you'd like to have another beer, I'd be honored if you'd drink it with me."

"How 'bout tonight? I know its Sunday, but we're apparently both gentlemen of leisure at this point in our respective lives and the days of the week, especially the working days of the week, don't typically hold significance to the likes of us. We can certainly afford to sleep in tomorrow morning."

"Agreed. I know a place Jake would approve of too. It's down the highway a ways, but so what? I'll pick you up at nine."

"Sounds grand – but Joseph?"

"Yeah?"

"I'll pick *you* up at nine."

Joseph was waiting when Tom pulled up in his black Porsche Boxster S. He wore a white dress shirt with the sleeves rolled to his forearms, jeans and a pair of well worn cowboy boots. His hair was pulled into a pony tail. Joseph walked around the passenger side and got in.

Tom noticed his boots and said, "No moccasins tonight?"

"Nah, not tonight. No point inflaming any hostilities with the locals. Same with the hair. I can get away with this, but the headband thing might be pushing the envelope. I'd be seen as either a hippy – bad news around here – or an Injun – maybe worse news. Last thing I need is trouble.

"I can't say I understand why one's appearance matters so much in this vicinity."

"Do you really want a historically based socio-economic and demographic explanation of the social mores and customs of this part of the West?" Before Tom could reply Joseph added, "Good, didn't think so. Besides I am sick of thinking about it. I've seen it and dealt with this crap my whole life. Tonight you and I will toast Jake with a beer or two, listen to some rock 'n' roll and kick back."

They headed south on the highway. After twenty-something miles Joseph had him turn left. The sign read *Reedville 8 miles*.

"Reedville isn't much of a town, but they have a bar where Lunden people don't usually show up. There's some kind of music every night and often some stray women hanging around. Being a Sunday things will be quieter, but for gentlemen like us, gentlemen of independent means, what difference does the day of the week make?" He laughed and Tom looked over at him smiling.

The Cactus Saloon was typical of any number of road houses in Arizona. Tom found the parking lot reminiscent of the one he and Jake used at the cage fights. It was littered with an assortment of mostly pickup trucks and SUVs. Tom parked the Porsche off to one side of the lot where there was little chance of getting a door ding from someone parked too close.

Walking to the front door, Joseph noticed Tom was wearing jeans, runners and a chambray shirt. He'd gone shopping. Inside the Cactus, nobody paid any attention to them. Tom noticed Joseph wasn't the only one with a pony tail. Clearly, he knew what he was doing.

They took a couple seats at a small table and Tom ordered a pitcher of Budweiser, King of Beers. He turned to Joseph and said, "For Jake." Joseph simply nodded and a minute later the waitress brought the pitcher and two frosted mugs. Tom poured and impulsively stood, raised his mug and said, "To you Jackson Taylor. Thank you for everything. And thanks for sending me back today!"

Joseph stood. They clicked glasses and drank deeply. Still standing, they lowered their mugs and Tom grinned. "God, that tastes good."

"King of Beers, indeed!" Tom pronounced while they took their seats.

Around 10:00 the band assembled, plugged in, tuned, wasted time, bantered with the Cactus patrons and finally started their first set with the Lynyrd Skynyrd country-rock classic "Free Bird." A few couples made an attempt at dancing, but this wasn't exactly a dance song. With the band starting to play, more tables and bar stools filled. Joseph viewed the tables and bar. He recognized a few faces from other nights at the Cactus, but knew nobody. He looked toward Tom. He was listening to the band, drinking Bud, seemed relaxed and oblivious to the other people in the place.

During the fourth song two women entered the room and took a table. They looked to be in their thirties. Probably late thirties, Joseph thought. One, a blonde, wore a tight, short blue skirt and blouse. Her friend, a brunette, had on equally tight fitting black leather jeans and a red tank top. Both wore boots with heels. Joseph watched them order beers and then scan the room for familiar faces.

"See those two?" Joseph said to Tom and indicated the table.

"Yes."

"I've seen them in here before. Usually they aren't alone, but tonight they seem to be."

"So…"

"So, I think we should wait a few minutes and if nobody shows up for them, we'll give 'em a shot."

"What do you mean exactly when you say, *give 'em a shot?*"

"We'll ask them to dance and then take it from there. Gotta start someplace."

"Joseph, I'm a married man. Well, sort of."

"Not really, you're not. But suite yourself. If in doubt, try to imagine what Jake would tell you to do. This night's for him after all."

"Point well taken."

Just as Joseph was going to walk over to their table and ask for a dance, another two guys beat him to it. The music blared. It was a fast dance and these girls were more than just a little suggestive in their moves. Joseph smiled, nudged Tom and motioned with his head in the direction of them.

Tom drained the last of his beer, poured another from the pitcher and said, "not exactly wilting wall flowers these."

Joseph found this particularly funny and he laughed loudly and said, "Nicely and very poetically put, Professor."

"Thank you."

The song ended. The couples split up and returned to their tables. The next song was slow. Joseph wasted no time. In seconds he was dancing with the blond, holding her close. She closed her eyes. They barely moved to the music.

Toward the end of the song Joseph saw their table was empty. Maybe Tom's in the restroom, he thought. He glanced around as best he could under the circumstances. No, not the restroom. Tom was dancing with Leather Pants. This time Joseph thought, *Thank you, Jake.*

After the dance the four returned to Tom and Joseph's table. Stephanie, the blonde, said she worked the desk at a local motel. Gloria – Leather Pants – was between jobs. This worked out well as Tom said he was between jobs too. Gloria scooted her chair closer to Tom and said, "I'll bet we have lots in common."

Tom waved to the waitress for another pitcher, winked at Joseph and said, "I'm most certain we do too."

They made small talk around the table and drank most of the second pitcher of beer. When the next slow song came around they were back on the dance floor. Tom hadn't held an *enthusiastic* woman in years. Not since... well, not in years. That was the only word that came to his mind – *enthusiastic* – and the sensation was thrilling. Gloria had both arms around Tom's neck and shoulders. He had his around her waist. It was a long, lingering song. They swayed to the beat barely moving their feet. Tom allowed one hand to drift down to her lower back and then further to the beginning swell of her butt. She pulled him even closer.

Sue hadn't responded to him in this way since their first year of marriage... or maybe not even then. Tom couldn't remember Sue ever reacting to him like this. Holding this Gloria woman was like a distant memory coming back out of the deepest, most forgotten recess of his brain. An area he'd blocked years ago. A place he tried to forget existed. But why? My God, this was exciting and arousing and... oh Jeez, Tom thought, am I showing? Gloria knows. She senses, no actually feels, his arousal. She wants his arousal. Now she's giving a little pelvic push of her own.

Tom pulled her tighter still. He felt her lips on his neck. Her hair brushed his cheek and ear. Was that a moan he heard? No, not a moan; she's humming to the music. Then the lips again. Tom dropped his hand to the full curve of her ass and squeezed. Gloria reached behind and raised his hand higher to her lower back and cooed in his ear, "Not here, baby." Did this mean he could do that somewhere else? It had to. All these years, and he'd forgotten this. The books, the teaching, the papers, academia, Sue... they all took the place of these raw, almost bestial desires. Jake must have known... no don't think of Jake now... but this is his night... Jake would want me to... no, it doesn't matter what Jake would or wouldn't want. This life belongs to Tom. Tom decides. Tom is in the here and now. And Tom likes being right where he is, holding whoever-the-hell he's holding. It could be anyone he finds attractive, anyone he desires. Gloria – right, that's her name – and she's attractive. She's more than attractive – she's – what did the students call it now... yes, *hot!* This Gloria in the smooth, tight black leather pants, that need to come off, is outrageously *hot!* Tom felt his mind swimming in lust and wanting. He had to have this woman. Who was she anyway? It didn't matter. Who was he anyway? This was not him. This was not Professor Sloan from Laurel College in Kingston, New York. Yet it was Tom. Maybe a new Tom. Maybe the old Tom. Maybe the Tom that always was – just hidden, sleeping somewhere waiting to awaken. Whichever Tom this was, he liked being the one dancing with Gloria Leather Pants in the Cactus Saloon in Reedville, Arizona.

The band played. Joseph and Stephanie, Tom and Gloria danced only the slow songs and drank beer through the fast ones. Tom nursed his beer now. He was driving. He was also determined to see those black leather pants empty of their present occupant at some point in the night. Hopefully soon. Too much beer might ruin his abilities, but he couldn't imagine anything impeding what he wanted to happen – needed to happen. Still, why take any chances?

The table conversation was both distracting Tom from his ultimate goal and boring. Gloria had worked in various shops and a Walmart in the past couple years. She asked Tom what he did, or used to do, now that he was also "between jobs. " He said he was a teacher.

"Wow, a teacher. I've never been out with a teacher before. What did you teach?"

"School." Tom wasn't trying to be condescending or rude, he just wanted one thing from Gloria and conversation wasn't it.

"Oh, stupid me! Of course, school. I think I've had too much beer. My mind is going. So Tom, do you live around here?"

"No, I'm from New York."

"You came all the way from New York to be at the Cactus Saloon?"

"I must have, because I'm in this establishment."

"You talk funny."

That was the third time she'd said that. The other two were in earlier conversation. Tom addressed it, "Yes, it's the bane of all New Yorkers to speak the way I do. Our speech patterns and euphemisms are ingrained in us as small children. Speaking clearly and succinctly is a weighty burden all New Yorkers must carry."

"Well, I for one like the sound of that!" Gloria slurred.

"Me too," said Stephanie.

Joseph was alternately smiling and laughing at the whole situation. He enjoyed Tom's banter and wit with Gloria Leather Pants. His Stephanie Short Skirt was entertaining too. She'd pushed her chair so it touched Joseph's and took his hand. That hand eventually found itself under the table resting high on her thigh. She held it there while drinking beer with her other hand.

Joseph knew the time had come to move this party out of the Cactus and into more intimate surroundings. "It's loud and stuffy in here. Ladies," Joseph said standing up, "would you be interested in some fresh air?"

Stephanie drained her glass and stood. "Sounds good to me, I'm ready."

Tom was on his feet too. "Let's go.'

Gloria stood unsteadily and said, "Tom, what's your last name anyway?"

"Edison. Thomas Edison."

"Okay, Thomas Edison, lead the way."

With arms around each other, the two couples walked out to the dark, star-filled night. They staggered to Tom's Boxster. Gloria said, "Oh wow, is this your car?"

"Does it have New York license plates?"

Gloria untangled herself from Tom and walked around to the front of the Porsche nearly stumbling, "Yes, New York, The Empire State."

"Good, then we're at the right car. They all look the same these days. It's easy to approach the wrong vehicle in a dark parking lot. And I know, Gloria, I speak funny."

"Take me for a ride, Thomas Edison," then she giggled to her friend, "Steph, you can take Joseph for a ride in my car, but I need the blanket from the trunk in case Thomas wants to stop somewhere."

Stephanie Short Skirt said to all three, "Sounds like a plan. Let's meet back here in an hour from now. I gotta go to work in the morning."

Gloria retrieved the blanket and handed the keys to her Chevy to Stephanie. She walked past Tom and got in the passenger seat of the Boxster.

"I love this car, Thomas. Is it fast?"

"It is indeed. You know this area, so you can be the navigator. I'll pilot this New Yorker-mobile anywhere you say."

They sped out of the Cactus Saloon's parking lot, slinging gravel with the acceleration. Tom worked through the gears until they were doing nearly a hundred miles per hour.

Gloria screamed her delight in the night air, "I love this car!"

"So you've informed me before. Which way would you like to go, navigator?"

"In a little bit turn down the dirt road on the left."

The road she'd indicated dead ended with just the desert surrounding them. It was a dark night with only a sliver of moon for illumination. The stars shone brilliantly overhead. A lone coyote yipped and howled in the distance. Gloria got out of the car and spread the blanket on a level spot near the Porsche.

She reclined on the blanket and said, "Come over here, Thomas."

As if he had to be asked! Tom slid next to her and took her in his arms. They kissed deeply. Now Gloria moaned. There was no music to hum to.

"Tom, how 'bout putting the radio on for a little romantic music? 100.4 FM is a good station."

Well, maybe there would be music to hum to…

In a minute they were back at it with a country music serenade. Their clothes were shed piece by piece and were thrown to the blanket's edges. Gloria panted, "These leathers are tight. I need some help getting them off."

At last! A couple strong tugs at the ankle and they too were on the edge of the blanket. She wore no panties and they embraced in nakedness. Tom caressed her small but firm breasts. He slid his hand down over her stomach. Further down. He was almost startled when he realized Gloria had shaved almost her entire pubic region except for a short stripe of hair in the middle.

"I hope you like my Mohawk," she gasped as Tom slipped a finger inside. She was obviously ready.

Tom rolled her on her back and with an urgency that surprised him, entered her. He hadn't felt like this in years. "Of course I like your Mohawk, Liz."

"Liz? Who the hell is Liz? Call me some other bitch's name again and I'm outa here."

Oh Christ, Tom thought. Where did that come from? But he knew exactly. Thinking fast without losing his rhythm he said, "Don't be silly, Gloria. Of course I know your name. Liz is a character in a Shakespeare play who allegedly also sported a Mohawk. She was the most beautiful and desired woman in all of Venice. And I'm so besought with your charms and Mohawk I feel I'm an actor caught up in Shakespeare's erotic plot." *Charms and Mohawk*, Jeez, is she really buying all this?

"Oh Thomas... Oh don't stop... oh... faster... oh... oh, Tom you're making me cum."

Two more times they acted in *Shakespeare's* plays. Gloria seemed to get off on Tom's "funny way of speaking" and urged him to keep talking while they made *the beast with two backs* – she had another orgasm when Tom used that term.

"Oh my God, that was great, but what time is it?" Gloria found her watch inside her bunched shirt. "Shit, we gotta get back. We're gonna be late and Steph will be pissed."

In minutes they were dressed and driving back to the Cactus Saloon. "C'mon Thomas, can't you make this car go any faster?"

In a few seconds the speedometer read one twenty-two. "Fast enough?"

Gloria screamed again, "Did I say I love this car?"

"I think so."

They pulled in to the Cactus parking lot exactly sixty-seven minutes after leaving. Suddenly the exuberance left Gloria's face. "Oh, Shit. Oh, Mother-of-God!"

"What's wrong?"

"See my car over there? Under the light? That's Stephanie's boyfriend and my boyfriend talking to them. Oh shit. Listen, I can handle this. You just keep your mouth shut and I'll do the talking." Tom noticed Gloria tuck the blanket as far as she could under her seat.

Tom parked the Boxster near Gloria's Chevy. A tall guy with a short, dark beard and wearing a ball cap opened the passenger door and pulled Gloria out by her arm. Tom saw the name *Jimmy* embroidered on his shirt over his pocket.

"What the hell do you think you're doing, Gloria. Who the fuck is this guy? Tell me quick or I'll kick both your asses."

"Oh for Pete's sake, Jimmy," she laughed easily, "This is Thomas Edison. He's a school teacher from New York. He's new in town and I was just going for a ride with him to show him a few things... 'cause he's not from around here... he's just a school teacher, Jimmy. He was telling me about Shakespeare."

To Tom, "Is that right?"

"Shakespeare was a most marvelous poet and playwright. He was quite accomplished. I was just exposing Gloria to his gifts."

Jimmy looked confused. "Well you sure talk funny – like a teacher, I guess."

Gloria took Jimmy's arm and hugged it to her. "See, I told you he was just a school teacher."

At Gloria's Chevy voices were getting louder. Tom heard Stephanie yell, "For Christ sakes, Alvin, you never showed. You were supposed to be here two hours ago. Look asshole, you're the one who stood me up. What was I supposed to do? Sit on my hands waiting?"

"Don't call me asshole you bitch. And where do you come off going for a drive with this little ponytail pussy?"

Joseph, who'd been leaning against the car with his arms folded on his chest trying to look invisible, suddenly dropped his arms and took a step closer to Alvin. "Watch who you're calling a pussy you fucking desert redneck…"

Tom yelled to them all, "That will be enough of that –" but was cut off from saying more when Jimmy stepped in front of him and put his hand on Tom's chest saying, "Stay out of this, Teacher-man. This ain't none of your business. Alvin can take care of what needs taking care of."

When Jimmy walked behind Alvin to back him up, unseen, Tom reached through the open window of the Boxster and from under the seat pulled a dark object. Holding the handle in his right hand and the stained leather sheath in his left, he spoke loudly and firmly, but without yelling, "I said before and I'll say only one more time, that will be quite enough."

Everyone looked at him. It was at this point Tom punctuated his statement by unsnapping the protective sheath and drawing the long, fighting knife with his right hand. He pointed the blade at Alvin. Tom watched as Jimmy stared at the blade. He seemed to shrink a little when he turned to his friend and hissed, "Alvin, don't mess with this guy – that's a Randall."

"What the fuck are you talking about? What's a Randall?"

"The knife. It's a Randall knife. I saw a few of them in Iraq. Only Special Ops guys had them – you know, Navy SEALS, Army Rangers. Those guys were all badasses. That knife's seen a lot of use. This guy will fuck you up in a heartbeat."

Tom saw his advantage and pushed on, "That man you just called *a pussy* is my brother. He saved my ass more than once. Insult him – you insult me."

Joseph looked to Tom with fire in his eyes, "I don't need you to bail me out, General. I can make quick work of this candy-ass."

"Stand down, Corporal Upham!" There was no response, "Now!"

"Yes sir!" Joseph yelled back as if to a drill sergeant and took his previous relaxed pose against the car.

Alvin looked over to his Dodge pickup parked only a few feet away. More specifically he glanced at the rifle hanging in the back window gun rack.

Slowly and quietly, but with force, Tom urged, "Go for it Alvin. I'm just itching for an excuse to use my old friend here again," he waved the blade in a short back and forth movement. "There's not a jury in the world that would convict me for killing a man who's threatening me with a rifle when I merely have this knife. Besides, everyone likes servicemen."

It was Jimmy now who said, "C'mon Alvin. These two aren't worth it. Nothin' happened here anyway. Let's let 'em go."

Alvin turned to Stephanie and growled, "Get in the truck." She did. "Jimmy, why don't you and Gloria follow us. We can have a party somewhere else."

Back in the Porsche, Joseph turned to Tom, "Corporal Upham? Wasn't he the coward in the movie *Saving Private Ryan*?"

"Sorry about that. It was the first military name that came into my mind. Be glad I didn't say *Corporal Klinger.*"

"Corporal Klinger… Corporal Klinger… who was that?"

"I forgot, you're too young to have watched *MASH*. He was the soldier who dressed like a woman all the time in hopes of being booted out of the army."

They both chuckled. Now Tom said, "What about calling me *General*? That was a stretch. Generals aren't usually in combat with corporals. How could you have saved my ass? And more than once?"

"Don't you remember? I saved your ass when you were a captain. It was after that you became a General."

"Oh, I see. I feel much better now. Thank you for explaining that."

They snickered over this for a few minutes. Changing moods, Joseph said, "I was wondering if you'd kept Jake's Randall. May I see it?"

Tom reached under the seat and handed the knife to Joseph. He pulled the blade from its sheath. "This is one hell of a knife, Tom."

"Do you know anything about Randalls?"

"Sure. One of the most recognizable knives in the world – for people who know this kind of stuff, that is... Yeah, this is one hell of a knife." He sheathed it and handed it back to Tom.

They sat in silence while Tom drove back to Lunden. After a few miles Joseph let out a short guffaw. Tom followed with a laugh of his own and in a few seconds both were hysterical. Tom pulled the Boxster to the side of the deserted road and stopped.

Joseph said, "Thomas Edison!" and the hysteria got even louder. Oh God, that was funny!"

Between fits of laughter Tom managed to stammer, "My word, what a day!" A moment later he said, "And what a night!"

Joseph thought a minute, laughed, turned serious and said, "One of the most amazing days, wild nights and funniest times I've ever had in one twenty-four hour period."

"Really?" Tom said incredulously looking at Joseph. Then putting the Porsche in gear and continuing to drive added, "Fairly typical day for me actually."

The laughter started again and halted, then started all over. Back at the house Joseph said, "Can you come in for a minute?"

"Sure." Tom cut the engine and walked with Joseph through the front door.

"Have a seat. I'll be right back."

Tom slumped in the same chair he'd sat in early that morning – a seeming lifetime ago. A moment later Joseph appeared with two tumblers and a bottle of Jack Daniels.

"You okay for one more?"

"I think it's only fitting."

"Good." He poured them each a drink and toasted, "We drink in Jake's memory. And we drink to Jake's Randall knife that clearly was the only thing that saved our collective asses tonight."

Tom raised his glass, "Amen to that, Brother."

ELEVEN

    Tom's usual early morning run wasn't so early this day. He didn't even know what time he'd gotten back from Joseph's house, taken a shower to wash Gloria's scent off and actually turned out the lights. Tom didn't know and Tom didn't care. It had been a night designed to awaken, rather than sleep. Lying in bed in total darkness, Tom relived swaying with Leather Pants and grabbing her ass on the dance floor, driving over a hundred miles an hour – sometimes a lot over a hundred miles an hour – through the desert in a Porsche with a joyous woman screaming from the passenger seat, "I love this car!" He thought of each of the three times he'd had Gloria on the blanket under the stars with country music playing from the car radio in the background. He shuddered just a little remembering Jimmy and Alvin in the parking lot. Jake warned him about threatening a man with a girl, much less two men with two girls! Things could have gotten messy. But Tom and Joseph were able to diffuse the situation, thanks to quick thinking and Jake's knife. It was also good to drink beer again. First one since leaving Jake's house that last time. Tom forced himself not to dwell on his experience and supposed *vision* in the kiva. It was beyond explanation. Perhaps he'd borrow some books he'd seen on Joseph's shelves relating to Indian spiritualism, but probably not very soon. He fell asleep realizing he missed Sue not at all, but feeling a deep, unfilled void with Jake's passing.
    Running the usual course through Lunden, Tom realized he'd run the entire two miles without walking. His body was free from last night's alcohol and his mind was still cruising along at full speed. He hadn't felt so alive and invigorated and full of fun in years – maybe not since getting married. He had to remind himself he was forty-one,

not twenty-four, even though that's exactly how he felt. Three times in one hour last night, well, he hadn't done that since he was twenty-four!

Tom decided two miles wasn't enough. He'd run two more. What a great feeling! Life was good – crazy, but good. Here in Lunden Tom could be anyone he liked. He could be a Native American spiritualist vision-seeker. He could be a desert hiker, maybe even a hunter. He pictured himself a sports car driver of back roads at ridiculously high speeds. He'd shown himself to be a honky-tonk dancer and carouser, a pick-up artist who got himself laid – three times – on a blanket under the stars in the middle of nowhere. What would Sue think of him and his new life now? Sue? Sue who? Tom was passing the three mile mark when he thought this and actually laughed out loud. He was getting back in shape. He was enjoying his very existence and the carefree attitude he'd acquired.

He was suddenly startled by a car pulling alongside as he ran. The window opened and Mae said, "Looking good, Tom. Very impressive! I can put some coffee on if you want to run to my place, or I can give you a lift?"

"Put the coffee on. I'll run a little more and end up at your house."

A hand waved as the car pulled away and the window closed.

Ten minutes later Tom knocked once on Mae's front door and let himself in.

"I'm in the kitchen," Mae yelled to Tom, "Make yourself at home. Be right with you."

Tom took a straight-back wood chair. He didn't want to sweat on her upholstered furniture. Tom could see Mae getting coffee mugs from a cabinet.

"How 'bout some cold water before the coffee? I need to cool off. If I'd run only a half marathon I wouldn't be so hot, but twenty-six miles always heats me up a little too much for coffee."

"That's why I never run more than thirteen miles myself," Mae laughed from the kitchen.

She brought a glass of ice water for Tom. "You really don't need to sit in that uncomfortable chair, Tom."

"I'm fine here. Thanks for the water." He drank half the glass with one breath. "Ah, that's just what I needed. It's really good to be running again."

Ignoring this, Mae said offhandedly, "I tried to call you last night."

"Oh?"

"I was just concerned about you. That was quite an experience you had at the kiva. I just wanted to make sure you were okay."

"Well, thanks for the concern, Mae. Means a lot to me. Don't worry though, I'm just fine."

"Actually, I called several times. When I didn't get you I became a little worried. I'm not trying to get into your private life, I was just, well, like I said, concerned. I called Joseph too. You know, just to see if he'd heard from you, but there was no answer from him either."

Tom took another drink of water. "I don't like to keep my phone turned on. Nobody in New York really knows where I am and that's just fine with me. I check my calls every so often. I'm enjoying my anonymity."

"I figured maybe you and Joseph went out last night. He usually answers his phone."

Tom looked at Mae. Was she checking up on him? Was she keeping tabs on Joseph?

Or was she, like she said, just concerned? It had been an unusual and particularly intense day. "Actually, we had a much deserved and overdue boy's night out together."

"Really? I think that's great. Joseph needs some male companionship. Probably good for you both. Have a good time?"

"Sure, we just went out for a beer."

"The *Oasis?*"

"No, a place Joseph knew. Kind of off the beaten path, called the Cactus Saloon."

"Oh, God. What a dive! He took you there?"

"Yes, seemed like a decent enough place to me. Cold beer, band playing some music, people dancing – everyone seemed to be having a fine time."

"I hope you two behaved yourselves."

"Most certainly," and Tom couldn't help but smirk just a little sheepishly.

"I've seen that look before. What did you two get up to?"

"Seriously?" Tom wasn't sure how to respond. "Mae, are you and Joseph… I mean, do you and Joseph… what I'm trying to ascertain here is, well, what is your concern with Joseph… oh hell, Mae. I'll just come out with it. Are you and Joseph more than friends?"

Mae blushed and said, "I think the coffee is ready." She quickly got up and went back to the kitchen. Walking from the living room she said, "You like just cream, right?"

"Yes, right."

A minute later she returned to the living room with the two mugs.

"I'm sorry, Tom. I had no right to question you. What you do is your business, but I was concerned about you."

"Thank you, Mae – for both the coffee and the concern. It's nice to be cared about."

They both sipped the hot coffee without saying anything. Finally Mae said, "Tom, you look cooled off now. Why don't you sit here on the sofa and I'll answer your question."

Tom moved from the chair to the sofa next to Mae.

"Okay, sometimes I'm a little confused about my feelings toward Joseph. I admit to being very fond of him, maybe even more than fond. I also know nothing can come of our relationship. For one thing, I'm just too old for him. He's still in his twenties for goodness sake! He's smarter and wiser than most people twice his age, but the fact is he's a young, single man and I'm almost forty. I have to remind myself of this from time to time. When I first got to know him, I admit to thinking we might be more than friends. But reality got the better of me and now I think of him as a younger brother – someone I love, but not romantically. I know he cares for me in much the same way. If circumstances were different, maybe our relationship would be different, but facts are facts and nothing can change them. So I consider myself incredibly lucky to know him and have him in my life. If he were to leave Lunden, I don't think I'd stay here. He keeps me sane and balanced. He's my sounding board and advisory board all rolled into one. He's also funny as hell and keeps me on my toes. But I do worry about him. He drinks too much sometimes. He'd also rather fight than consider the source and walk away from trouble. Joseph is smarter than just about everyone around here and being an Indian – he *chooses* to look like an Indian, you know – doesn't help much. I'm frightened he'll be out someplace – someplace like the Cactus Saloon – say the wrong thing to the wrong person and go missing… like forever.

There's a lot of empty space out here to get lost in, or more to the point, be buried in."

Mae looked into Tom's eyes. "Look, Tom, you saw the way that creep Roger – you know, the tow truck guy – tried to provoke Joseph. How long do you think that will continue until something happens? And if not with Roger, then probably someone else. Joseph is quite the ladies man. Girls around here can't seem to resist him. Some of them have boyfriends too. Sooner or later all this animosity will catch up with him. I don't know what happens then. I'm actually relieved to know you were with him last night. He goes out alone; he's apt to get into trouble."

Tom picked a coaster from a small stack on the coffee table. He put his mug down and sat back in the sofa. "I know what you mean. I've seen it myself. Now that you mention it, I'm concerned for him too. This isn't the most progressive and tolerant community. Having a non-traditional appearance, speaking with erudition and being truculent might be a bad combination around here."

Mae laughed, "You do have a way with words, Tom."

"I know, I've recently been told *I talk funny.*"

"I'll bet you have," and she laughed out loud again. "Tom, I have no right to ask anything of you, but I believe you have developed a fondness for Joseph too."

"Unquestionably, I have."

"Good, well, let's try to keep an eye on him when we can. I know we can't follow him around – that's not what I'm saying. In fact, I don't really know what I'm saying, except we need to be watchful. If you two have another *boys night out* try to keep an eye out for trouble." Mae smiled again, "And I'm not interested in what you two got up to last night. Well, actually I am, but it's best I don't know."

They both laughed. Tom looked at his watch out of habit. He was aware he had nowhere to be, but said, "Thanks for the coffee, Mae. I better be on my way."

They both stood and Mae walked him to the door. As he left to walk home Mae called, "Thank you, Tom."

For what? he briefly wondered, but didn't turn around.

TWELVE

MAE'S JOURNAL, 3rd ENTRY: 23 MONTHS PREVIOUS

I seem to start each entry with the same apology about not writing regularly, but who am I apologizing to anyway? Regardless, here I go.

Since I haven't written much lately I'll do a quick catch-up. I've been singing at Chuck's Desert Oasis for a month now – just Friday and Saturday nights. The local crowd is definitely into more country than folk. No big deal, I like both. If it's country they want, it's country they get. I found out soon enough that if I sing them the songs they want, my tip jar fills quicker. The other night some guy who was already half under the table offered me a twenty if I could sing Willy Nelson's song Whiskey River. I knew it, played it and am twenty bucks richer for a drinking song I've never been overly fond of anyway. Thanks, Willy. I do wonder if this makes me a song request whore. Nah, but if he hadn't offered the twenty I might have said I didn't know it well enough to sing it...

Roger the tow truck jerk came in recently. He tried to buy me a drink while I was on break. I told him I didn't drink when I was working. He asked if he could buy me a drink when I wasn't working. Fat chance of that. I told him I needed my own space and didn't want to drink with anyone. I think that let him down easy, letting him think I didn't want any company, not just his. Men can be so damn bothersome.

Well, not all men. I'd hoped Joseph might stop in those first days after I helped him heal. But that was not the case. A couple weeks passed and still no sign of him. Then just last Friday he came in during my last set – I think he planned it that way. The place was full and I asked for any requests – my last shot at increasing my tips! Joseph asked for a song I'd never heard of by someone I'd never heard of. I said I didn't know it, so he asked for another song I never heard of by another person I didn't know. Everyone in the place laughed. Well, this went on four or five times. He had the place in stitches – at my expense, I might add, but I knew it was all in fun and he was just giving me a hard time. Finally he asked if I knew anything by Jimmy Buffett. Everyone applauded – I think as much to finally get me off the hook as to hear a Jimmy Buffet song. I sang them Margaritaville, which by that time half the people in the Oasis could relate to!

After the last set I sat with Joseph. Thank God Roger didn't come in! Joseph had completely healed and acted as if nothing had ever happened. He's smart and funny and one of the more interesting people I've known – I should say I'm still getting to know.

Well, that was Friday night and now it's Sunday night. This is important because Friday at the Oasis Joseph invited me out to his house Sunday (today) for a sunrise hike in the desert and lunch.

I'm not much of an early riser, but I do make exceptions! I drove in the dark and arrived at his house well before sunrise. It was pretty cold out and I was glad to have my old Woolrich Alaskan shirt. To my surprise, Joseph wore nothing but a pair of shorts, moccasins and a headband! He never seemed cold. He looked so good without a shirt on that I wasn't going to question him! There was one thing puzzling about his appearance. He has two fairly fresh looking scars above each nipple. The scars are almost identical. Each has two parallel lines a few inches long going vertical about two inches apart. In the middle of each, between the lines is a ragged bit of scar tissue connecting the two lines. He caught me staring and just said he'd explain the scars some other time. At least I take this to mean he wants to see me again.

I just reread that last part and I sound like some silly school girl with a crush on an older boy when actually I'm the older woman thinking I might have a crush on a younger guy. Not good!

After a wonderful cup of strong coffee, (thank goodness!) we hiked into the desert along a ridge behind his house. The sun was just beginning to rise and warm up the day. It was a glorious morning. The stars gave way to a pink dawn without even a hint of a breeze. We walked a short way to a hole in the ground lined with rocks along the sides. It was about six or seven feet deep and maybe eight feet across. Joseph said it was called a "kiva" which is some kind of ancient Indian place for worship or rituals or something – I'm still not completely sure. He said he goes into the kiva and meditates. Sometimes he says he stays in it for a few minutes – sometimes for an hour or more. He said its quiet and peaceful inside. "Close to the earth," as he put it. He asked if I'd like to try It and I agreed.

I climbed down a short ladder and Joseph unrolled a matt for the bottom which was packed dirt. I lay there and he went back up. He told me to close my eyes and relax, which I did. He then said he'd describe in words a peaceful place he would lead me to. I should listen to his "suggestions" as he called them – and try to imagine being in the place he suggested. He said I should blank my mind as much as possible and only concentrate on what he was saying. He also said I shouldn't go to sleep, that if I felt myself slipping into sleep I should quit and come back up. I did this as best I could, but my mind wandered a few times and I almost did fall asleep. I can't say it did much for me, but I did feel peaceful and content while in the kiva. I was there for about ten minutes. I admit to being a little afraid of falling asleep and disappointing Joseph, so I climbed up and out. Joseph said I did well for my first time. He said it took discipline to blank one's mind and get the full benefit of the kiva. I didn't question this too much, but I don't think I'll be a very good candidate for kiva-girl of the year. Still, I'm open to the concept, not that I really understand it.

Joseph set up a couple of folding chairs he keeps under a tarp there and we sat facing the rising sun. We're very comfortable together. We talked about things in our lives, but mostly kept to the present. I was glad of this, but a while later I felt compelled to bring up the past.

After a couple of hours we decided to put the chairs away and head back to Joseph's place. I felt so good to be walking with him that at one point climbing over some loose rocks I reached for his hand. After getting through this rough area and back on the trail, I kept holding his hand. It's been years since I've wanted the touch of any man. I didn't have this planned. It just happened. Innocent really.

I held his hand the rest of the way back to his house. In the kitchen Joseph had some kind of deer pot roast that had been cooking slowly since the middle of the night! I guess he must have gotten up and started it simmering while the rest of the world slept! He offered me beer or wine, but I had a soft drink. Joseph had a Coors. We were both in the kitchen, which is pretty small. He reached for a glass that was in a cabinet over my shoulder... Okay, it's obvious where this is leading. We kissed in the kitchen. I really wanted him and I could tell he wanted me too. Then the flashbacks kicked in, the darkness returned, I was in the basement again...

    I pulled away and, I hate to say it, burst into tears. Not just tears – sobs. It was an awful scene. Joseph was confused, but also concerned. I didn't know if he would be angry or frustrated or what. He seemed just... concerned. And he stayed that way!

    He is intuitive and knew enough not to prod or pry into my obvious distress – what else can I call it? I told him I was sorry and it had nothing to do with him. He walked me into his living room, sat me on the sofa and poured me a glass of wine. I didn't argue. He sat across from me in a chair and said nothing. He waited for me to speak first. Any other guy would be asking insensitive questions and acting offended, but not Joseph. He sat patiently. I think if I didn't say anything we might have sat in silence for an hour. I started to apologize again, but without saying anything he waved the apology away. I owed him an explanation. After all it was I who took his hand. It was I who got in his way (intentionally?) in his kitchen. He sure didn't have much of a chase to catch me!

    So I told him what I was going to say hadn't been said to anyone in years. The last time was at the inquest! I can't believe how long ago that was. Makes me wonder what I've been doing all these long years! In short, I told him. Everything. It took me over an hour.

    In the end he hugged me, kissed the top of my head and said, "Good thing its pot roast or we'd be eating burned lunch." It was so unexpected and off the cuff I broke into tears of relief and, somehow, sobs of laughter. If you can laugh and cry at the same time, that's what I did.

    We ate his tender and flavorful pot roast without a mention of what I'd just told him. At one point, just as we were about finished, he said, "Just as well, Mae. If anything had happened between us, it'd never be the same again. Much better this way."

    I knew he was right, yet the disappointment I felt was crushing. Deep inside I wanted him to fight for his desire to have me. I didn't want him to give up so easily! Any way I logically think about this *situation, I know this is for the best. Perhaps if we were closer in age, I'd try to work through things. But we're not. Maybe that's good. Maybe I just need more time... But how much time is required to recover from this? Twenty years? Thirty? Am I so damaged I can never be complete again? Maybe Joseph can put me in his kiva, make some suggestions and bring me up a normal woman – yeah sure, and maybe at the same time I can grow wings and fly...*

A wonderful, beautiful, delightful, yet oh so troubling day!

THIRTEEN

Aside from the power, phone and credit card bills, Tom's mailbox was usually empty. There was the occasional junk mail or other miscellaneous bill, but rarely anything else. Because of this, after several months he only checked his mail a couple times a week. When a hand addressed letter arrived at his box Tom was more than a little surprised – especially when he recognized the handwriting and saw the return address was Kingston, New York. It was from Sue.

Tom took the envelope inside and opened it at his kitchen table. It was a to-the-point two page letter:

Tom,
When you said you were going on Sabbatical to "London" I, and everyone else, assumed you meant the United Kingdom. Foolish us, we should have naturally assumed "Lunden," Arizona. Perhaps you thought this little joke amusing. I, for one, found it childish and annoying. That you don't answer or return phone calls is also childish and annoying.
Did you truly believe you could lose yourself in some Godforsaken town in Arizona and nobody would be the wiser? There is such a thing as technology, Tom. Did you neglect to realize the credit cards you use are in my name too? A few minutes on the internet disclosed where you'd used your card, where your bills were being sent etc. etc. etc. You don't play this game of hide and seek very well, Tom.
To the point of this letter: I have been offered a position at Fairleigh Dickenson University in New Jersey. I've accepted it. You left Laurel College in somewhat of a scandalous manner, leaving me to make the excuses. I did not and do not appreciate your lack of consideration then or now.

When you departed, I asked you to find yourself, straighten yourself out and come back the Tom I married. I now wish to rescind that sentiment. I find I am more complete without you, more content without you. I still hope you are able to find yourself and straighten out, but I no longer want you in my life as either the Tom I married or the vexing, contemporary Tom you seem to have become.

I wish to be granted a divorce. Since most of our assets are in our separate and respective names, that part will be easy. Only the house is in both our names. I propose to sell it and split the proceeds equally with you. I believe my realtor may already have lined up a buyer. Upon sale, I will put your possessions in storage and pay for the first year rent out of your half of the house equity.

If this is agreeable to you, please affirm with either a call or a written letter and I can get the divorce papers drawn up and sent to you.

Sue

P.S. I read in the newspaper that our next door neighbor died recently. As you seemed to be attracted to him in some unfathomable male way, I thought you would like to know. His house is being sold to a professor in the psychology department. I'm sure the neighborhood will be pleased.

Tom stared at the letter after reading it twice. Not even *Dear Tom*, he thought. Not even *Love, Sue* or *Fondly, Sue* or *Sincerely, Sue*. He sat for a full minute holding the letter and then let out a loud laugh. Without hesitating he went to a kitchen drawer, pulled out an envelope and a sheet of lined yellow paper from a legal pad. He quickly addressed the envelope, addressed it to Sue Sloan, Ph.D. at his old address. He then wrote his response:

My dear Sue,
I wish to thank you for your recent letter. Regarding your requests: I can only respond with a most emphatic Yes! Agreed!

Your soon to be x-husband,
Tom

P.S. The only disturbing part in your entire letter was the sad news of Jake's passing.

Tom folded the letter, put it in the envelope and stamped it. He next put on his running shoes, shorts and a T-shirt. He'd literally run this letter to the mail box by the Safeway store and deposit it directly into the box himself.

He felt lighter on his feet and faster than he'd felt running any time in the past. Searching in his mind for a way to describe his thoughts as he ran to the Safeway holding the letter, Tom summed up his new situation with two words, *extraordinarily marvelous!*

After opening the mailbox and nearly flinging in the letter, Tom ran another four miles.

Relaxing with a Budweiser after a cool shower, Tom called Joseph and Mae – dinner at Chuck's Desert Oasis – on him – 6:00 pm. No questions.

The night was cool and clear. Tom enjoyed the short, invigorating drive in the Boxster. He felt rejuvenated, alive and vivacious. He felt young, or at least, youthful.

They all arrived on time at the Oasis and were shown to a table by Chuck.

"It seems strange to be eating here on a Saturday night," Mae said.

Joseph asked, "So, what's your new schedule now?"

"Well, it seems I'll only be singing here on Friday nights now. Chuck was really nice about it and I've seen this coming for some time. I've been singing here about two years and folks need something new to hold their interest. I hate to admit this, but I seem to appeal to the older crowd and Chuck's been losing revenue lately because the younger bunch is not showing up like they used to."

Tom asked, "Who will be singing on Saturdays?"

"A young guy named Horace Johnson. He's just back from Arizona State University. Good kid from a nice family. I do their taxes. He plays guitar and sings with two others – a guy and a girl. I've heard them. A good sound – very talented. Actually, this works out great for me. I still get to sing and now I have more time to do accounting and tax prep. Don't worry, I'm a happy camper."

Joseph said, "As long as you are okay with the new arrangement, that's all I care about."

"Me too," Tom threw in while motioning for Chuck to return.

"Chuck, how 'bout a bottle of champagne tonight to start us off?" Mae looked at Joseph and said, "Okay, what's this all about, Tom."

"Yeah, something's up. What is it?" Joseph said.

Tom smiled broadly and began, "Well, I received a missive from my estranged wife, Sue, today. Apparently she wishes to divorce yours truly in a most timely fashion."

Joseph responded first, "I take it this is a good thing?"

"Indeed it is!"

Mae asked, "Were you expecting anything like this?"

"No, I hadn't given it too much thought, really. I assumed I'd be the one asking for the divorce at some point in the not so distant future. Now I don't have to feel guilt or betrayal." Then looking at Mae he added, "I too am a happy camper!"

"If you two are happy campers with your new arrangements, then I too am to be considered a happy camper!" Joseph looked from Tom to Mae and smiled, "I absolutely will join you in your camping contentment!"

The champagne arrived while they were all still laughing. Chuck poured each a glass, placed the bottle in an ice bucket and returned to the bar. A waitress arrived at the table to take their orders.

The dinner lasted well over an hour and a second bottle of champagne. Tom was finishing his dessert, New York cheesecake of course, when he noticed Joseph and Mae who were facing the door stop eating and put their silverware down. The gaiety in their faces vanished. Tom turned toward the door in time to see Roger the tow truck guy enter the Oasis and take a stool at the bar. He ordered a shot, threw it back and ordered another. He then turned in his seat and surveyed the room. When he saw Mae, Tom and Joseph, he finished his second shot and ordered a third. Taking it in hand he approached their table.

"So, I see a little celebration going on here." He stared down at Mae and continued, "You know Mae, a long time ago you said you didn't want to drink with anyone. I think you said you just wanted to be left alone. I guess that's all changed now, huh?"

Joseph was slowly beginning to stand when Mae said, "Why don't you move along, Roger. This is a private party."

Roger laughed and turned as if to walk back to the bar, but stopped himself. He turned back to Mae and said, "You stuck-up bitch!" and threw the remainder of his shot glass in her face.

Joseph's right hook came so fast that Roger was on his back on the plank floor before his empty glass landed next to him. Chuck was there in a flash, "Joseph, I told you I won't have fighting in – "

Tom stood and stopped him mid-sentence, "Hold on there Chuck. Roger started this whole ruckus by throwing is drink in Mae's face. Joseph did what every other man in this establishment wishes he'd done first. You're placing misdirected blame and I strongly suggest you have this objectionable piece of refuse escorted out before I have a go at him myself!"

Chuck looked shocked. He didn't know Tom well, but this display was surprising and unexpected to say the least. Chuck motioned for the other bartender to help him and the two lifted the semi-conscious Roger to his shaky feet. Halfway to the door, Roger regained enough of his senses to slur over his shoulder, "I know where you live, Joey-boy. Same with you, New York. Better watch out, both of you."

Now Mae stood. "Quite a spectacle we've made here tonight. I feel this was all my fault. I'm so sorry to ruin your dinner, Tom. Joseph, you need to control your temper, but thank you."

Tom replied sincerely, "Mae, don't be ridiculous. That Roger cretin is out of control. He deserved everything he got, thanks to *Sugar Ray Joseph* here. I hope he didn't completely spoil your evening."

"Not completely," she laughed. I think I need a shower. I smell like a distillery."

Mae hugged Joseph and said, "Thank you, my knight in shining armor."

"And, Tom, thank you for being quite the generous and charming host." She hugged him tightly and whispered in his ear, "Thanks for standing up for Joseph too."

Mae left Tom and Joseph standing at their chairs. Joseph turned to Tom and said, "Damn, that felt good. Son-of-a-bitch had it coming. I'm just sorry it happened here, tonight, at your special dinner."

"No worries, Joseph, just another interesting episodic adventure between friends. Besides, the conversation was becoming tiresome anyway."

"Nicely put, as always, Professor." Joseph waved to a waitress. "Two brandies are in order – make them doubles."

The plates were cleared and replaced with amber colored snifters. Joseph held his toward Tom, "To your impending divorce and future independence. May you survive the first and enjoy the latter."

They both laughed and drank. Tom put his glass down and said, "Survive the divorce? Nay, my good Native American Friend, I'll relish it!"

"Tom, if you don't mind me getting personal... can I ask you a question?"

"Naturally."

"From what you've told me, us really – Mae included – Sue wasn't exactly, how shall I put this…"

Tom finished his sentence for him, "...wasn't exactly adventurous? Humorous? Exciting? Easy going? Fun? And let's not forget erotic or sexual?"

"Yeah, something like that, in so many words…"

"Right on all accounts, Joseph. She could be an intolerant bitch too. Oh, and we neglected to add controlling."

"Okay Tom, I get the picture, but my question is why did you marry her in the first place? Or did she change over time?" Joseph took another sip, "If I'm overstepping my bounds, forgive me. You certainly don't need to answer it. But the question has crossed my mind."

"It's still early and I don't think Chuck will mind us monopolizing his table a little longer. It would be cathartic to elaborate on your question."

FOURTEEN

EIGHTEEN YEARS PREVIOUS

I

Jeff Ingerson was a near perfect roommate. He was reasonably neat and clean for a twenty-four-year-old guy. He was also friendly and outgoing, yet knew enough when to stay out of the way and give Tom the quiet space he needed for his academic work.

Jeff and Tom met when Tom enrolled for his master's program at the University of Vermont six months ago. Jeff had been living with his girlfriend until their recent break up. Now he needed an apartment of his own, but couldn't afford to rent one by himself. He posted the *roommate needed* card at the student union building bulletin board which led to his introduction to Tom. They had a beer together, talked about their respective lifestyles and living requirements at the present, then shook hands, walked two blocks to the Briarwood Apartments and signed a lease for a two bedroom flat.

Jeff had graduated from the University of Vermont and was currently working at the Textbook Center on campus until he "found his real direction in life." Athletically built, Jeff spent a good portion of his spare time working out at the university gym – a perk for being employed by UVM. Years of weight training had sculpted his body into a tight mass of muscle. He was six foot two and two hundred-five pounds. Blessed with intelligence, a good sense of humor and boyish good looks – blue eyes and longish sandy hair – Jeff kept a busy social life.

Tom was a serious grad student. His love of books and reading led him to the English department. Since his parents both taught at the high school level, Tom decided to carry on the family tradition. However, he wanted to go one better and teach at the university level.

That's were the intellectual challenge would be, not to mention better pay. With a master's degree he could teach at a community college while he worked on a Ph.D. Eventually he'd make professor; he had no doubt of this. It seemed like a solid plan.

Tom had been a cross country runner in high school, although not a particularly gifted one. He ran to clear his mind, to gather his thoughts. He ran because he simply liked to run. He wasn't overly competitive because he wasn't truly good enough to be a challenge to the more serious runners. That was okay. A varsity letter was always a positive addition to any college application. Later, at Colby College, Tom continued to run. He ran alone, sometimes for six or eight miles at a time. He was light on his feet, if not particularly fast. Running kept him in shape and seemed to keep his mind sharp.

Jeff was a lifter and Tom was a runner. Each looked the part. Tom was lean and wiry while Jeff was powerful and bulked. In the very beginning of their friendship Jeff invited Tom to lift with him at the gym. Tom agreed. The first workouts left Tom exhausted and sore, but as time went on his body adapted and he felt his strength increase. However, the muscle mass never did. He looked at himself in the mirror and saw fine definition, but not much bulk. Likewise, Tom invited Jeff to run with him and the results were similar, but in reverse. Jeff was slow and heavy on his feet. In the beginning he often stopped to walk while Tom ran ahead and then looped back for his friend. Over time Jeff ran longer distances, but could never equal Tom, just as Tom could never come close to packing on the iron plates to the bench press and curl bars that Jeff added. Jeff good-naturedly kidded Tom about his lack of weight improvement and Tom gave it back to Jeff about his slow running. Good friends, especially guy good friends, could get away with this with no bad feelings.

Toward the end of the spring term, Tom and Jeff went to the gym as usual. They nodded recognition to the regulars in the gym who tended to work out at the same time as Tom and Jeff. But today there was a new face. She wore an athletic tank top with tight black stretch shorts. Tom noticed a white UVM name badge pinned to her shirt indicating she was probably a trainer. This made sense as she was helping a slightly overweight student with the easier side of the climbing wall.

Tom watched as she demonstrated to the girl how to use her feet and legs to propel her body upwards, relying less on arm strength. In an instant, like a spider she was eight feet off the ground. Her long, straight, almost-black hair hung half way to her waist. She kept it under control with one elastic hair band close to her neck and another near the end. It billowed slightly in the middle as she moved. She was tall; Tom guessed five foot nine or ten. He noticed the olive tinge to her skin and that her arms were defined, but not muscular. He also noticed her firm bottom, held tight in those shorts. When she turned sideways to show the student something about the wall, Tom saw a profile of full, high breasts that balanced her round ass perfectly. Tom was instantly smitten. Jeff saw this in his friend and gave him a smile and a nudge.

"You better get over there and take an interest in climbing; you're sure as hell built for it. Looks like she's built for it too, in more ways than one."

"I don't know. She might be out of my league."

"What the hell is that supposed to mean? Out of your league? Are you crazy? You, my friend, need to take a long look in the mirror and see the stud you are. Now get your ass over to that wall and make some kind of contact. Tell her you want to learn to climb or something."

Her name was Elizabeth, but she went by Liz. She'd recently graduated with a degree in Athletic Training and this was her first job. She had an easy smile with straight white teeth and deep pools of brown for eyes. Tom noticed her skin seemed flawlessly smooth. His attraction was immediate.

Their first date was a quick beer at a popular local bar and then a movie. Their conversation in the quiet bar was typical of couples getting acquainted. She asked about his master's program and what he intended to do with his degree. He asked about her interest in athletics and work as a trainer. Tom had to concentrate on not staring at her. He looked into her face and wanted to kiss her. He dropped his gaze and wanted to fondle her. This girl was a magnet to all of his senses. He liked what he saw; he liked the sound of her voice and laugh. Tom caught a whiff of her scent – a little soap and a little... well, something else he couldn't recognize – and he liked that also. What remained was his sense of touch and taste. Without question he knew he'd like those too. Tonight he yearned for them.

The movie seemed deliciously long to Tom. They sat toward the middle of the theater with Liz to his left. There were empty seats on all sides of them. Tom chose a movie recommended by one of his professors. It was an offbeat melodrama that drew a small audience. By choosing this film, Tom hoped to impress Liz, make her know he was intelligent, thoughtful, not some average jerk who went to the movies to see mad car chase scenes and a variety of things eventually blow up. He wanted to get off on the right foot with her.

However, Tom wasn't prepared for such a dull and slow-moving film. He was distracted by Liz in the seat next to him, of course, but after fifteen minutes of monotony, Tom lost focus. He could only think of the girl beside him. He let his hand slide from the armrest. She grasped it in both of her warm and moist hands. At this point the movie ended for Tom. Seconds and minutes didn't exist. His world consisted of only Liz squeezing his hand, and then gently running her other hand up and down his forearm. At some point – was it seconds later, minutes – she snuggled closer to Tom and exchanged his arm for his thigh. Just fingertips at first, knee to crotch and back again. Slowly, teasingly, down to the knee, up, up, barely touching, then a little pressure and a squeeze, pause, and back for the long slide to the knee again. On and on, up and down, back and forth, light then forceful, fingertips, then full hand contact. She must be aware of his response, his arousal… She was. Once more, nails lightly dragging downward to his knee, then up and up. This time she didn't stop. Tom felt her hand pause just before the obvious bulge in his jeans. He felt warm, almost ready to sweat. Then, in an instant her hand traveled upward still and surrounded him, fingers kneading. Seconds, minutes, again it was impossible to judge. Tom slumped lower in his seat, Liz pulled yet closer, continuing her massaging. She whispered, "As much as I want to, we better save this for later."

Tom whispered back, "Later is a relative term. Every second is later than the one before. I think it's *later* right now."

Liz gave a hushed laugh and a final caress, "This movie sucks. Let's get out of here."

Liz lived alone in a tiny efficiency apartment. Upon opening the door she said, "Like the old saying goes, 'it ain't much, but it's home.'"

The kitchen, eating area – too small to be called even a breakfast nook – and living area were comprised of one square room. An alcove to one side barely contained a king size bed made up with red satin sheets, matching pillow cases and a black blanket. There was no bed spread. The headboard rose up two feet and contained a shelf and several small drawers. Candles in different degrees of melted height stood along the shelf like random notes on a line of sheet music. The few walls of Liz's apartment contained posters. One showed a whitewater kayaker going through a class four chute, another was of a climber planting a flag on a windswept and barren mountain peak and a third showed a scene in the Dallas Cowboys locker room with incredibly muscular football players wearing only game pants and holding jerseys in their hands. They had black under their eyes, were sweaty and obviously pumped from the game. Small smears of blood could be seen scattered on their pants and skin. Awesome is an overused word Tom had come to despise, but that was the only word that described these stadium warriors. Momentarily he felt inadequate in the presence of such masculinity, but he checked himself thinking that's as ridiculous as women allowing themselves to feel ugly when passing a newsstand full of girly magazines.

"No, it's fine. Cozy actually."

"Either you're too kind or just full of bullshit."

Tom didn't know how to respond. Liz followed with, "I'm only kidding. Relax."

Tom took a seat on the room's single option, a sofa. The only other place to sit was on one of two oak stools at the cramped kitchen counter. Liz went into the kitchen and returned with a bottle of inexpensive rose and two glasses. She poured them full, handed one to Tom and said, "To us."

Tom repeated, "To us," but before he could drink, Liz put her index finger in his wine glass and rubbed it on and around his lips. She leaned over and kissed him, finishing by running the tip of her tongue around his mouth.

Tom regained his composure, took the first sip of his wine – from the glass anyway, and said, "You have an interesting way of punctuating a toast."

"If you think that was interesting, you've come to the right place."

"Oh, I know I've come to the right place." The double meaning was intended and not lost on Liz, who merely smiled, downed her glass and refilled it.

The flickering candles created a surreal mood around the cave-like apartment. In her bed Liz dribbled wine on Tom's neck and now bare chest. Her tongue followed the drops and runs. She had left her hair loose and it tickled Tom's skin as she bent over him.

"You'll get wine in your hair and on the sheets," he said.

"Both can be washed." She said dismissively, dribbling more wine and undoing his jeans. "There is still a lot of wine left in this bottle. You might have to follow my lead."

Well, Tom thought, that would take care of the final two senses he'd longed for at the bar earlier in the evening. "It would be my pleasure."

"Good. 'Cause I think it's my turn."

Liz stood to full height straddling Tom lying naked on his back. She removed her blouse and bra, tossing them to the floor. Showing remarkable balance she next undid her Capris and standing on first one leg and then the other removed them. She moved forward standing over Tom's face, wearing only a black thong. Ever so slowly she bent her knees and lowered herself into a squat, stopping inches from his head. "You Like?"

Tom was too overwhelmed to say anything.

With the same deliberate slowness Liz stood back up. "Maybe you'll like this better." She executed the same balancing act as before and removed this last wispy piece of clothing.

The same achingly slow descent followed as before. Tom was stunned when he saw in the wavering candlelight that Liz was completely devoid of hair. Every detail of her femininity was exposed to him… and getting closer and closer. Again she stopped a few inches from Tom's face. "Ask me to go lower. Beg me, or I'll get dressed."

"Go lower."

"Not good enough, Tommy. You're running out of time."

"Please Liz, go lower."

"Getting better, but I'm about ready to throw you out…"

"Oh, God Liz, put your pussy in my face… NOW!" Tom almost yelled. He was nearly out of his mind with lust for this woman, this crazy, sexual creature. Tom grabbed the swell of her hips and forced her down.

At 1:30 in the morning, after three additional rounds of sex in positions Tom had only imagined, Liz said, "You have to get out of here, Tommy. I have a training session at 8:00 and if you stay any longer I won't get any sleep at all."

He didn't answer. As exhausted as Tom was, he knew he had one more session left in him.

"I know what you're thinking, you bad boy, but I mean it, I have to get up in the morning."

"Okay. But I need to see you again. How about dinner tomorrow night?"

Liz laughed, "Slow down, Tommy. That might be too soon to handle the likes of you. I might be a little sore tomorrow. Give me a few days to recover."

II

A dinner date was set for a Saturday night the following week. Tom's academic work load was heavy. The spring term was coming to an end. Aside from reading, he had a number of short papers to write as well as one longer creative work – a short story. As he always did, Tom kept current. He'd learned early in his college career to never fall behind with either required reading or written assignments. If he attended all his classes and did the work on time he could usually breeze through.

Liz was a distraction. Tom would be reading and suddenly realize he was reliving his evening with Liz instead of concentrating on what he had just read. Several times after their first date this had occurred. Tom almost embarrassed himself by having to retreat to either his bedroom or the bathroom to relieve his own sexual tension so he could focus on his work. He hadn't done much of that since leaving high school. At least not until this one date with Liz.

Saturday finally arrived. Tom picked Liz up and they drove to a small Italian restaurant. Liz looked radiant in a white skirt and blouse. Over dinner she talked of rock climbing and camping – two topics to which Tom could not relate. He'd grown up in a household of books and ideas, but not much activity. Sitting over his baked ziti and listening to Liz's enthusiastic talk of exhilarating climbs and warm lakeside campfires seemed new and refreshing. Everything about this girl seemed new and refreshing. Tom found her enthusiasm for adventure and challenge – and no doubt, sex – stimulating and even inspiring. Liz promised to take him rock climbing the following weekend.

They managed to polish off a bottle of Chianti between finishing their meals and talking. Actually, Tom mainly listened. He was enthralled. Time flew by. Twice after clearing empty plates, their impatient waiter asked if he could bring them anything else. Twenty minutes after the check arrived Tom paid it and they left.

Walking to his car Tom asked, "Where to?"

"It's such a gorgeous evening, let's go for a walk."

"Fine. Any place in mind?"

"How about the campus? It's usually deserted on a Saturday night."

Tom parked in the empty library parking lot. They walked side by side along one of the many paved pathways through the UVM campus. The night was dark and moonless, but unseasonably warm for this time of year. Liz took Tom's hand and spoke more of rock climbs and a canoe trip she hoped to plan in the summer. Their random wandering led them to a small, secluded duck pond. A group of mallards were huddled together under a nearby spruce tree for the night.

They sat on a backless concrete bench. Liz put her arm around Tom's waist and rested her head on his shoulder. "You're a good listener, Tommy."

There was that *Tommy* thing again, he thought. Only his parents had called him that – until he reached middle school. After which it was Tom or perhaps Thomas. But if she wanted to call him Tommy, that was okay. "You're interesting and refreshing to listen to, *Lizzy*."

She playfully began poking him in the ribs and he instantly turned to grab her offending wrists. She lifted her head and they kissed.

With Tom still holding her wrists, Liz rested her head on his chest and said, "Seriously, you do listen well. Most guys are more interested in talking about themselves. You're different."

Tom took this as a compliment. Liz gently pulled her wrists from Tom's light grasp and pulled his head down for another lingering kiss.

"I want you," she said.

"I want you too. Let's go."

"No. I want you here."

"Here?"

"Now."

She slid from the bench to her knees in front of Tom and began undoing his pants. Tom weakly said, "I don't know if this is such a good idea, Liz. There could be people around."

"I don't care," she said, unzipping him.

With a tug she released him. In an instant he was in her mouth. "Of course, if you'd rather I didn't, Tommy, you could always just drop me back at my place." She smirked teasingly before continuing.

Tom could say nothing. He looked down and saw his lap enshrouded in straight raven hair that gently swayed with her movements. Liz could feel him building and stopped. In a single fluid motion she stood, turned, hoisted her skirt and mounted him.

Slowly she moved and somehow knew just when to stop motionless and keep him from climaxing. Then the slow undulations would begin again. Once she stopped and said, "shhhh," as two people walked past several yards away. They didn't seem to take notice of the girl sitting on the guy's lap by the duck pond. Liz giggled when they were out of hearing and continued. Finally she demanded, "Fuck me hard, Tommy!" and she rapidly bounced and ground herself into him. They climaxed together and sat stacked in silence.

Liz finally disengaged and sat next to Tom on the bench. She reached in her small purse, found a packet of tissues and removed a couple. With uninhibited indifference, Liz spread her legs wide and the tissues disappeared. "That'll plug the dam," she laughed. "I could feel you cum a lot. Gravity can be annoying."

Tom was still breathing hard and found himself yet again speechless. This girl was so open and unabashedly candid that he was lost for words. But, she said she liked him as a listener and that was fine. He could listen to her forever.

III

The week passed as agonizingly slow as the one before. Tom borrowed a book on beginning rock climbing from Jeff who considered himself no more than a casual or *social climber*, as he jokingly put it. At least, Tom thought, when Liz was explaining basic climbing to him on Saturday he'd not be totally clueless. The book was a great help and Tom memorized the names for the different kinds of equipment and the climbing terms they were apt to use. The last thing he wanted to seem in her eyes was *feeble*!

Tom worked long hours on the required reading and papers he was writing. The time spent was doubly long because of his inability to fully focus on his work. Mental images of Liz haunted him. He'd be writing a critical paper and find himself in the middle of a sentence envisioning Liz standing over him, then squatting inches from his face, taunting and teasing him. He'd see her hair cascading over his lap at the duck pond… Running helped, but instead of clearing his mind for productive work, as he ran he thought of Liz, adventurous Liz, enthusiastic Liz, crazy Liz, *sexual Liz*. Thinking these thoughts while running, Tom burned up the miles. If his usual run was three or four miles, he now ran six before he was even aware of the distance. He enjoyed these running fantasies, figuring in time they'd diminish or retreat beyond recall into an insignificant sector of his brain. But for now, he relished the thrill of this new experience, this new woman in his life, this wildly uninhibited woman. Sometimes he smiled as he ran.

During the week when Tom and Jeff worked out at the gym they'd see Liz. She took her work seriously and was usually intently working with students, some of whom were recovering from injuries or illnesses. She might hear her name, turn, smile and wave, but she rarely left her charge for more than a minute. A few times when Liz was between appointments the three would talk, but Jeff was usually more eager to lift than socialize. Once when Tom had a few minutes to talk to Liz, Jeff came up to them and asked Tom to spot him on the bench press. When they both started to walk to the bench Jeff said in a surprisingly serious tone, "Just one of you to spot me, I don't care which. I'm going for a max and need a spotter who's not distracted."

Liz said, "Sorry, Jeff. You're right." She then turned and said, "Tom, I'll see you later."

After she left Tom said to Jeff, "Thanks a lot. That made me look like a jerk."

"Don't be so sensitive. Relax. You're not being judged all the time." Jeff positioned himself on the bench. "We're here to lift, not gab."

Tom was relieved to see Liz walk to another part of the gym and not take notice of the huge amount of weight Jeff was attempting. Compared to what Tom lifted, spotting for Jeff made him feel thin and weak.

After a quick warmup set, Jeff worked a hand hold on the bar over his face. Tom stood behind the slightly bent bar stacked on each end with iron plates. Speaking aloud to himself Jeff said, "Okay Jeff, let's get this. Do it!" and he lifted the bar from the rack.

Tom called Liz on Thursday night with the excuse of wanting to know what time to pick her up for climbing on Saturday. Actually he just wanted to hear her voice. They spoke only briefly. He thought Liz seemed a little preoccupied and Tom didn't want to come across as a pest. She said he could pick her up around noon. No need to get up early. They could spend the afternoon together.

The climbing area Liz chose was not a long drive away. There was a wide cliff face tapering to one end. She said this was a good place to practice. The low end toward the left was rocky and full of hand and foot holds. A great area to learn the basics, she said. Further to the right, she explained, the cliff grew higher and more sheer. The degree of difficulty grew the further along one ventured.

"Follow me," Liz said, hoisting a coiled rope and equipment bag from the backseat of Tom's car.

They walked a well trodden path around the low, left side of the cliff to its top. Liz chose a spot where a stout tree had grown. Around the tree was a nylon strap with a solid oval ring already attached. "We'll use this as our belay anchor. She pulled her own nylon web strap and metal ring from her bag and fastened it to the tree above the other. Tom used this to show his new climbing vocabulary.

"Why are you using your own webbing and carabiner when there's already one here?"

"I only trust my own equipment. Who knows how long that webbing has been there? It's probably perfectly safe, but I trust my own stuff."

Liz ran half the length of her rope through the carabiner and then threw the entire coil over the edge. "C'mon, let's walk back down and get you started."

Back at the bottom, Liz showed Tom how to affix the end of her climbing rope to the carabiner on his nylon harness. She pulled the other end of the rope connected through the anchor ring until there was no slack and ran it through a devise on her own harness and explained how Tom could climb while she controlled the rope along his progress. If he fell, she'd simply pull the rope sideways and brake his fall. Tom was glad for Jeff's climbing book. He had a general understanding of how things worked and he was anxious to try his first climb.

"Go slowly and try to use your feet and legs. Think of it as sort of stepping up the cliff. Don't use your hands and arms for more than hand holds for balance unless you have to position yourself for a foot hold. If you try to pull yourself up with your arm strength you'll be exhausted in no time. That's the biggest mistake beginners make. If you can avoid that, you'll be way ahead of the game."

Tom listened to her instructions and was determined to follow them. He didn't want to seem inept or clumsy. She said this was an easy, beginner's climb. He hoped so.

"All you have to do is put a foot on anything sticking out that seems like it will hold you, try some pressure to make sure it's solid, and then step up like climbing a stair.

"Okay."

"All set?" Liz asked.

"I am."

"One more thing, your shoes. Runners won't help much here. What size shoe do you take?"

"Usually about an eleven."

Liz dug deep in her equipment duffle. "These are a ten and a half. They're friction boots – shoes really – bit worn, but they're better than what you've got on. Might be a little tight, but you want them that way. They'll grip pretty well even on tiny stuff that you wouldn't think would hold you."

Tom pulled off his runners and replaced them with the friction shoes. "They feel fine."

"Good. Oh, and another thing. We're wearing shorts which are okay for what we're doing today, but watch out for your knees. You can really shred them on these rocks if you're not careful."

Tom approached the rock wall, saw a jutting ledge a foot above his head and put a hand on it. Just before trying to pull himself up, Tom remembered what Liz had said about using his legs instead of his arms. Replaying Liz's instructions, he still held the ledge for balance but found a protruding bulge slightly above his right knee. He put his foot on it, seemed solid, and stood. Another to his left, this one a small outcropping. The second friction shoe grabbed, a little pressure... a bit more... it held. An additional hand hold above and to the right – good. Hold tight, no pulling, use feet only. That's it, step... pressure – extend the leg... grab the depression... now hold. Step again, up... and hold for balance. Feel for a foothold... good... now the next.

With each step of his ascent, Tom could feel the tension on his rope lessen just enough to slip through the carabiner on the anchor webbing above. He felt confident in Liz's ability to keep him safe. His own confidence grew with each foothold and step up. Tom glanced over his shoulder and down at Liz. Surprised at the thirty feet that now separated them, Tom gave her a smile. He couldn't tell if she noticed. Back to the climb.

As he became more comfortable with finding footholds and handholds, Tom started to notice more of his surroundings. The rocks in the sun felt warm to his hands. Those in recessed shadows were cool, almost damp. There were sharp edges and others that were smooth, rain worn depressions. Looking closely, some of the stone held miniscule chips of mica that reflected the sunlight like miniature flash bulbs as he changed angle and position. Sometimes the breeze came at his back and sometimes it seemed to slide along the side of the cliff as if seeking a way around. Tom spotted a tiny dried leaf in a crack in the rock wall too narrow for his fingers to grasp as a hold. He wondered what the chances were of a wind blown leaf finding such a purchase.

He looked up and judged he was just about half way. Tom realized that what at a distance seemed sheer was actually full of seemingly friendly and helpful places to support feet and hands. Resting after a particularly awkward foothold and step, Tom put his cheek to the cliff. It felt rough and cool. It felt hard and unyielding, but it also felt good.

A dozen feet from the top, Tom was feeling confident. Anxious to finish his ascent and using his feet to feel for holds, Tom's right foot caught and held. He quickly extended his leg and reached for a handhold at the same time. He sensed his actions go wrong as soon as he began the extension. It was too late to correct. The move was set in irretrievable motion. Tom had forgotten to test his foothold with pressure while maintaining his handhold before trusting it. The gray pebble wedged in a crack wasn't a solid hold – just a temporary part of the cliff's eternal erosion process. The fragment of rock gave way with Tom's weight, saving it a thousand years of weathering, to fall in a clinking, rattling descent along the cliff face to the bottom.

Liz felt the reversal of rope and instantly broke Tom's fall. He fell, slid really, only a foot, but it was an unnerving, totally insecure sensation. Dangling by a rope on the side of a cliff seventy feet above the ground was a uniquely terrifying experience. Tom began to flail for anything to grab. He kicked his feet feeling for a hold. Then he heard Liz yelling.

"Tom! Tom, listen to me!"

He relaxed. The rope was secure. He was safe. He turned his head as best he could and looked down to Liz who appeared inhumanly small from this height.

"Tom, are you okay?"

He waved.

"Good," she called. "Now just calm yourself. Everyone falls. It's part of climbing."

Tom waved again and was still.

"There's a hand hold to your right and lots of footholds. Take your time. You're doing great."

Tom looked up and to the right as Liz said. Why hadn't he seen that? Easy as before, he reached and held. Slowly raising and lowering his left foot, he found purchase again. This time he tested it with half his weight. No problem. In a few steady movements Tom reached the cliff edge. He was up and over in one final push. He unclipped the rope from his harness, stood and called down "Off belay!" as he'd read in Jeff's book. He thought he heard Liz laugh before calling back, "Belay off!"

Liz took the trail around the side of the cliff to the top. She gave Tom a big hug and said, "You did great! I think you're a natural at this." Then looking down at Tom's legs she said, "Did you know your knees are bleeding?"

Now Tom looked down, "Never felt it. Must have happened when I fell."

Tom looked very serious when he added, "By the way Liz, thanks for saving my life."

He looked quizzically at her as her smile turned into a full laugh. "What?" he almost stammered.

"Tom, listen, I suppose technically I saved your life, but like I yelled to you before, everyone falls. That's why we use ropes. It's all part of the sport. If you don't fall, you don't learn. Think of it like skiing. If you don't fall down once in a while, you're not pushing yourself. You did wonderfully."

"Well, I guess that does make me feel better."

"Sure. It should."

Liz pulled up the rope, coiled it and unfastened her anchor from the tree. "There's a climb I've wanted to do for a while. Would you feel comfortable belaying me from above? I'll show you how to do it. It's simple."

"If you're sure you're okay with it?"

"I'm sure. Follow me."

Liz led Tom along the top of the cliff. He could see where other climbers had found anchor spots. He also noticed several crosses chiseled into the rock. He asked Liz about this, almost certain he knew the answer. "Accidents. Deaths." Was all she replied.

Liz stopped, looked over the edge and said, "This is the place. We'll anchor around this boulder and then I'll tie you in."

She ran a section of rope around the rock, making sure to inspect every inch of the rope for wear or fraying. She then tied both ends to a solid ring and pulled hard on it. "Good," she said to herself. Next she made sure Tom's harness was secure.

"Step back and sit down." Tom did. "Good," she said again. "I'm going to clip the back of your harness to the anchor. Then I want you to scoot forward as far as you can to take up any slack." Tom did this too. "Great, there's no way you can be pulled forward now, understand?"

"Yes."

"Okay. Now I'll attach a belay device to the front of your harness. The rope goes through this," she said, threading the line first in and then out. "All you have to do is pull the rope in with your left hand as I climb to take up slack and pull the rope out with your other hand at the same time. It's like a rhythm. You'll feel it right away."

Liz quickly attached one end of the rope to her harness. "Let's practice. I'll step back as if I'm beginning a climb." She walked a few yards along the cliff's edge away from Tom. "Now, as I start walking to you just pull the rope in one side of the belay device and straight out the other side. Good. Keep taking up the slack. If you feel pressure on the rope like I'm falling, all you do is take your right hand – the one pulling the rope out, that's your brake hand – and pull the rope to the side. That's the brake. Try it when I start walking backward."

As soon as Tom felt the line go taught he pulled the rope to the side and immediately it stopped feeding. "Ingenious little contraption," he said smiling.

"Very simple and effective. Another thing," she continued, "if the brake is on full and say I'm hanging in midair, you can lower me by bringing in your brake line a little at a time to the forward or free position. You can control the rate of descent by just this method. It's simple. You'll do it naturally without thinking. Let's try. You put on the brake." Tom did. "Good, now I'll try to walk backward. Keep the brake on and don't let me. Good. Now I'm going to really lean back. Let me go a few inches at a time."

Tom brought his right hand in from the side and just as Liz said, the rope very slowly played out. He put his hand to the side again, and the rope stopped.

"I can do this."

"I know you can. Like I said, you're a natural." And she walked up to him and kissed him full on the mouth. "That's your reward for being such a good climbing student."

"Makes me want to climb some more."

"My turn now."

Liz unclipped herself and re-coiled the rope. Looking over the side she yelled, "ROPE!" and tossed the coil far out and over the headwall. She turned to Tom sitting at the edge, "Oh, and don't let the rope run over the rocks or edge. That'll wear it out and weaken it."

"Okay, I won't."

"I'm going to walk back down the trail and tie in. When I yell 'on belay!' you yell back 'belay on!' like you did before. Then take up the slack. I'll yell 'climbing!' and you call back 'climb.' You probably won't be able to see me much, so just keep the rope taught. Just pull enough to keep the slack out and keep me from dropping more than a foot or so if I fall. If I need some rope I'll yell to you and you can release a little out as I pull. That probably won't happen, though. Okay?"

Tom said very seriously, "Okay."

"Relax, it's easy. You're doing fine. If I had any doubts, I wouldn't let you belay me." She kissed him again and left.

Tom heard the commands and responded in kind. He couldn't see Liz but could judge her progress by the amount of rope he was pulling through the belay device. He was surprised at how fast and constant he was able to pull the rope through. She was right; he got into a rhythm of pulling in the rope with his left hand while simultaneously pulling the rope out of the belay device with his right.

After a few minutes and probably forty feet of rope had been pulled through, Tom heard Liz call, "I'm going to rest here for a minute."

"Okay," he yelled back.

A few moments later he heard Liz yell "climbing."

"Climb!" he called back and the rope piled once more at Tom's side.

Tom was able to peek over the edge enough to see the top of Liz's head about fifteen feet below him. She looked up and smiled at him. Suddenly she bent her head, did something to her harness and without looking back at Tom yelled, "Off belay."

"What? Liz, what the hell are you doing?"

There was no response. "Liz? Liz?" Tom called in near panic. "Are you okay? What are you doing?"

He could hear her climbing, even hear her heavy breathing, but she said nothing. Tom quickly pulled in the loose rope, somehow hoping it would go taught again. But it didn't. The end of the rope came up. Tom reached behind himself, found the carabiner and released himself from the anchor and stood just in time to see Liz come over the headwall and stand in front of him with a beaming smile on her still sweat-dripping face.

"Liz, for God's sake, what were you doing…"

"What a rush! Wow!"

"Are you insane? Why did you take the rope off?"

"Calm down, Tommy. I knew I could make it. Climbing without a rope is indescribable. It's like a blast of adrenaline and getting high all at the same time. It's like being close to death and being born again all at once. Oh Wow! Oh God!"

Tom just stared at Liz in incomprehension. This was crazy.

Liz stepped out of her harness and walked to Tom. She undid his and it fell to the granite underfoot. She stepped back and looked into Tom's face. Tom thought she had a faraway, unfocused look in her eyes and an odd half-smile on her face he'd not seen before.

"You have to fuck me right now, Tommy!"

"Liz, there could be people around. It's broad daylight.I'm all sweaty…"

"I know you're sweaty. You smell great. There's no one around. Fuck me now, right here."

Liz pulled off her top and athletic bra. Next her shorts and panties landed by her feet. "I'll leave my friction shoes on, if that's okay," she joked.

As she turned from Tom and walked back to the cliff edge she said, "Take your clothes off, Tommy."

Liz put the toes of her shoes over the edge, spread her arms wide and let out an almost animalistic, triumphant howl. Tom stared at her back, the curve of her hips, her perfectly round ass. In a moment he struggled out of his shirt and shorts.

"Come here behind me." Liz said without turning.

Tom walked the few steps to her and put his arms around her clutching a breast in each hand. After a few seconds she removed his hands. Then slowly, without bending her knees, Liz spread her legs slightly and bent at the waist until her finger tips touched her shoes.

Tom traced a line with his middle finger from her lower back, down her crack and into the shallow, slick crease between her labia. He was fully aroused and Liz knew it.

"Now, Tommy. Fuck me now! I want your blood on the back of my legs!"

He grabbed her hips and plunged deeply. Liz let out a long moan and then a series of short sighs as he pounded her from behind. She stayed in the same position and gasped, "Oh, yes, Tommy. Oh, yes, fuck me more… hard Tommy… bleed on me Tommy… Oh, don't stop, don't stop."

Liz came first and panted, "Oh God I needed that. Now you have to cum, Tommy. That's it… faster… umm, oh, that's so good, fill me up."

And he did.

Arriving back at the parking lot, they passed four young men getting their climbing gear out of a car. One had binoculars suspended around his neck. They all looked at Tom and Liz chuckling. Had they noticed his skinned knees and the bloody smudges on the back of Liz's legs? Finally the one with the binoculars said, "Nice ascent, man. Way to go."

Tom said nothing, aware of his face turning bright red. Liz let out a high-pitched laugh. Turning to the four, she put an arm around Tom and replied, "I can always rely on him to be the first on top and to finish the job."

Everybody laughed now, even Tom.

IV

In the following weeks Tom was forced to spend the majority of his time on his work. The term was ending and for the first time in his entire college career he'd allowed himself to fall behind. He wasn't behind much, but for Tom who'd always prided himself on keeping totally current, this was as new an experience as was his seeming whirlwind affair with Liz.

The short papers and literary critiques based on his classroom discussions and readings were never a problem. If needed there was always plenty of outside support reading and critical essays to review, but Tom rarely needed these aids. Early in his first semesters at Colby College he'd learned to make it his own course requirement to get acquainted with his professors, to understand their points of view, their likes and dislikes, their prejudices. He also made sure his professors got to know him as a student and as a person. Professors, he'd quickly learned, were human after all and enjoyed personal contact – and often personal compliments – like anyone else. Tom also learned to slant his essays and papers to the ideology of his respective professors. This strategy seldom failed to keep his grades high and their opinions of him favorable.

But it was the required creative writing paper, the short story that gave him the most angst. Tom had worked out a storyline, but beginning consisted of a multitude of deleted material and false starts. For someone more imaginative and free spirited, Tom thought, this assignment would be a breeze. Perhaps Liz was right or at least partially correct when she told Tom he was too uptight, that he needed to relax – *float a little* as she put it. Tom overheard others comment on how they'd written the short story early in the term. They said this part of the course was easy and once out of the way allowed them more time for the critical work. The first time he heard this, Tom started wondering if there was some essential part of his nature that was incomplete or missing altogether. No, he concluded, he merely targeted a different set of priorities.

Tom continued to struggle with his beginning, but finally felt satisfied with one attempt and built on it. Once he overcame this primary hurtle, the body of the story and conclusion followed more easily. He read and re-read his work, making small corrections until he felt there were no more to make.

Liz was on an afternoon-to-evening schedule the week Tom finished his story. She'd made it a habit to stop by for coffee and a visit with Tom and Jeff before work if they were around. Sometimes the three would plan a run together. Secretly, and Tom could admit this only to himself, he encouraged the runs because it was the only area in which he knew for certain he could outshine them both. After the first mile or two, Tom would announce he needed to "stretch out a bit" and he'd pace a fast quarter-mile distance between himself and his two companions. Then he'd slow to a jog, loop back and rejoin them. He often found them laughing and throwing good natured barbs at him for being such a show off. Pretending to shrug off their comments, deep inside Tom glowed with the veiled praise.

After one such run, the three returned to the Briarwood Apartment. Jeff took a quick shower and headed for his job at the Textbook Center. This left Tom and Liz relaxing in the small living room. Assuming Liz wasn't particularly interested in his course work, Tom rarely discussed it with her in any depth. But the short story he'd written might be different. He wanted to share more of his life with Liz, to reveal more of his mind, his thinking. This might be a good opportunity.

"You know the short story I've been working on? Well, I finally finished it."

"That's great, Tom. I know you said you were having trouble getting it started. When did you finish?"

"A few days ago. I've been doing a little revising and polishing, but I've finally got it to its final form."

"That must be a relief. I'm glad for you."

Tom hesitated before speaking. Liz had never asked him about the story – what it was about, when it took place, if it was tragic or comedic or ironic. Perhaps she was just not interested, or perhaps she merely didn't wish to pry into something she might consider too personal.

"Would you like to hear it?" he nearly blurted.

Liz smiled at him, "Okay."

Tom went into his bedroom and brought back a thin yellow binder. He sat in a chair across from Liz, opened the cover and began reading.

The story was nineteen pages long. It took place in a small English village during the early Victorian era. A moderately affluent sheep farming family consisting of a husband, wife and three children were in conflict with an adjacent farm over property boundaries and water rights. Tensions built between all members of the two families until the court ultimately settled the matter. Tom's goal was to contrast the more civil English system of dealing with land and water issues with the frontier American system where violence and lawlessness often determined the outcome of such disputes.

Tom read for slightly over an hour. He tried to read with some appropriate emotion in his voice, a little drama here and there. When he finished, he put the folder on a table and looked to Liz.

"Well?"

"I think it's very good. Not the most thrilling story I've ever heard, but I know that wasn't you're intent."

Tom explained the allegorical nature of the work, trying to put it into perspective from the viewpoint of civilized versus uncivilized societies. Liz listened to him and finally said, "Tom, I liked your story. It's very good, but I was an Athletic Training major. My teachers were jocks and M.D.s. You're in the English department. Most of this stuff is lost on me."

Tom sat thoughtfully for a short while. "You're right, of course. This must seem pedantic and irrelevant to you. I'm sorry to have made you suffer through my poor attempt at being creative."

Liz stood up from the sofa and stretched. She smiled down at Tom and said, "Don't be silly. Your story was good. I'm just the wrong person to hear it. It's over my head, Tommy."

He looked up into Liz's face. She bent down and kissed him. "I've got some clean clothes in my car. How 'bout I get them and we can take a shower together?"

In Tom's mind the story was put aside. This was real. This was here and now. Nineteenth Century English villages and frontier Americana be damned. An exotically beautiful and sensual woman wants to shower with me. This is life – a life of intensity – a life perhaps avoided or detoured around for too long – way too long. Tom realized how desperately he wanted – no, needed – to enter such a life. The door had always been locked, but Tom saw Liz as his key.

V

A few days before the term ended, Tom received a message requesting he make an appointment to see Dr. Edmonton, English department head, University of Vermont. Not knowing what this might be about, Tom nervously made the call and set up an appointment for that afternoon.

Dr. Edmonton's door was open when Tom arrived. "Come on in, Tom," he said getting up and extending his hand as he walked around his desk to greet him.

"How are you?"

Tom shook his hand saying, "I'm just fine, thank you, sir."

Dr. Edmonton was in his early seventies. A well liked English professor, he had been at UVM over twenty-five years. His easy laugh and portly physique combined with an unruly shock of white hair and matching beard gave him a jovial Santa Claus-like appearance.

"Sit. Sit. Make yourself comfortable. Can I get you anything? Something to drink, maybe?"

"No, I'm just fine, sir, but thank you."

"So Tom, how did this semester go for you? Were you pleased with your classes?"

Tom barely had time to consider where this might be going, "Everything went well. I'm quite pleased."

"Good. Good. Glad to hear it."

They looked at each other for a moment before Tom spoke, "Is there something wrong, Dr. Edmonton? I am unsure why you requested an audience with me."

Dr. Edmonton laughed his Santa laugh, "*An audience?* Come now, Tom, I'm not the Pope." He laughed again and continued, "It's about your short work of fiction."

"Oh?"

"Yes, Dr. Walther who assigned it, of course, read it and gave it to me suggesting I read it too."

What's this all about, Tom thought, but said nothing. He waited to hear more.

"Tom, I'll get to the point. Your writing is excellent. The story you wrote is both provocative and historically fascinating. Dr. Walther wishes to have your permission to use it as required reading in his class and also keep a couple of copies on permanent reserve in the library to serve as a model for the benefit of other, future students."

Tom was more than surprised. He was overwhelmed. "Yes, of course. That would be an honor, sir."

Dr. Edmonton said, "Good. Good indeed. I'll inform him of your generosity. I know he'll be pleased. I'm sure you're aware there's not a large market for short stories, but with the department's connections I feel safe in saying with confidence that we can find a venue for publication. It probably won't pay much, if at all, but would look good on your resume nonetheless." He leaned back in his creaking desk chair, put his hands behind his head and said, "Tell me Tom, do you have any plans for the summer?"

"Nothing definite, sir. I thought I'd probably look for a job. With course work," and with Liz he thought to himself, "I haven't had too much free time to seek employment."

"Well, good. Good. I have a proposition for you then." He sat upright in his chair and put his forearms on his desk looking directly at Tom. "Would you be interested in TA-ing a couple of freshman English classes this summer? You know I can't give you a full teaching position, but the classes would be basically yours. You'd be under Dr. Walther, but from his glowing report of your academic abilities, he's intimated he feels confident to give you free rein in the classroom. He'd show you the syllabus and as long as you cover the required material, all should be copacetic. The pay wouldn't be great, but probably more than any summer job you could land around Burlington. What do you say?"

"Again, I'm honored, sir. I'm staggered, really."

"*Staggered?*" Dr Edmonton paused a moment, "You have an interesting, if a bit archaic, way with words." He grinned at Tom and said, "I'll take that to mean an answer in the affirmative. Make an appointment to see Dr. Walther in the next day or two. He can go over the details with you. And congratulations," he added, "I look forward to following your progress here at UVM."

Tom left the building feeling euphoric, his mind reeling. His work used as a model, a copy kept permanently on reserve in the library! Publication! A teaching job for the summer! His head was spinning. He needed to call Dr. Walther. He couldn't wait to call his parents. He was dying to call Liz.

"I told you I thought your story was good, Tom. I'm really happy for you. See, just like I said, it was just over my head. The right people needed to read it. And I know you'll do great teaching this summer. I'm so proud of you!"

"Thanks," Tom said a little demurely into the phone, "I just had to call you with the good news."

"I'm really glad you did. Are you busy?"

"When?"

"Right now."

"No, why?" Tom asked a bit perplexed.

"Because I've got the afternoon off and I think you deserve a little reward for being such a great author. Why don't you come over, unless of course, you have something important to write about that can't wait…" she teased.

"Give me ten minutes."

Aside from the night of their first date, Tom had only been to Liz's tiny apartment a few times, usually just to pick her up when they went out. Their lovemaking had taken place largely outside or at the Briarwood Apartment when Jeff was away. On the way to Liz's, Tom couldn't help thinking of the smooth red satin sheets, the candles, Liz standing over him. Instead of ten, he was knocking on her door in seven minutes.

"Come in. It's open."

Tom closed the door behind him. It took a minute for his eyes to adjust to the darkness. Then he saw the shimmering candles, the blanket pulled back from the bed, those red sheets. Naked, Liz lay on the bed, propping herself up on one elbow.

"Hey Mr. Author, how 'bout coming over here and making some poetry."

Tom walked to the bed and sat on the edge.

Liz shook her finger at him, "Not with your clothes on. I want some skin poetry."

Tom stood, kicked off his shoes and removed his shirt and jeans.

"Everything's got to come off if you want to *bare* your literary sole to me, Tommy."

Tom complied. "So what's my reward?" he asked slyly. He was already beginning to breathe faster.

"Lie here," Liz said. She reached to the shelf with the burning candles and brought down an octagon shaped bottle containing a brown liquid. "Massage oil. Cinnamon," she said, opening the cap. "First you, then me. After, we can play slip-and-slide."

Liz dribbled a small amount of the oil on Tom. He gave a start from the surprisingly cold temperature of it. "I should have heated it first," Liz said, massaging the oil into first his neck and back, then legs and finally his buttocks. "How's that feel?"

"Wonderful."

"Good, now turn over. And don't worry about the sheets – this will wash out."

Liz worked the slick oil on Tom's arms and chest, then his legs and stomach. "Any place else you'd like to be massaged?"

"Surprise me," Tom said

"How's this for a surprise?" and Liz took him deeply into her mouth and throat.

"Mmm-oh, *surprisingly* much better than the oil."

Liz knew when Tom was near orgasm – knew when to stop. At the last possible moment she pulled back and lay down next to Tom. "Now me," was all she said.

Tom was glad she'd stopped when she did. He wanted this to last. With this interruption, he'd be able to hold out longer next time. Liz rolled over and Tom applied the sweet oil, following the example she'd set with him. After about ten minutes she rolled over on her back and said, "Take your time with this side, Tommy."

He applied oil to his hands, rubbed them together and massaged Liz's cheeks and around her ears. "Mmm, that feels so good," she whispered, her eyes closed.

Next he let a drop land in the hollow at the base of her neck. With a light finger tip motion he traced her throat with an up and down motion. "I think you've done this before," she said just above a whisper.

"Nope, never. You're my first massage-ee," Tom said feeling a little silly afterward.

"Well, don't stop. You're doing a great job."

"I have no intention of stopping."

He streaked oil down her arms, working the oil with long strokes, wrapping his hands around her upper arms and bringing them to her forearms, wrists and hands where he used his thumbs to massage her palms. Then he put a series of drops in a line between her breasts to her navel. Massaging her stomach and breasts, he made sure to stop short of touching her dark, erect nipples.

"You're missing the best parts," Liz said in a whiney voice.

"Surprise." Tom replied and took first one and then the other nipple between his lips.

"Nicely done, Mr. Author," Liz sighed.

Next the oil was worked in to the legs and feet, then up her thighs in a single wide oily path. Tom lightly kneaded her thighs with open hands, feeling their silky smoothness. He allowed his hands to wander to her upper inner thighs and to the velvety mound surrounding her vaginal lips.

"You're so smooth," he said. "You must shave every day."

"I never shave. You can only get this smooth from waxing – neck to toes, twice a month. But enough talk," she purred, "surprise me again, Tommy."

He bent over her and tasted her warmth and wetness. Liz arched her back slightly and let out a long, barely audible moan. She moved her hips with his oral stroking.

"You surprise well," she said, sitting up to pull his head back to her breasts. "I feel sorry for you men," she began while he sucked her nipples, "You only have one part to please. We women have it much better. I love what you're doing now. Ooh, that's so good," she said breathlessly. "But women have other places too. I get really turned on when you're in my mouth, I can almost orgasm just thinking of you spurting down my throat." Tom listened with increased arousal and reached down to rub her clit. "Oh yes. That's it Tommy, suck me too. Ooh, that's so good. And when you eat my pussy I could go crazy. But I also have another place you haven't explored yet."

Liz pushed Tom gently back and got on all fours. "There's a tube of K-Y jelly in that drawer. Use some of that and explore."

Tom reached in the drawer she'd indicated and withdrew the tube of lubricant. "It's almost empty," he said.

"There should be another one in there. Quick, I can't wait much longer."

Almost frantically Tom felt in the drawer and found the full tube. He squirted a large amount in his hand and slapped it on her ass cheeks. The impact splattered some of the lube on himself and the sheets.

"Ooh, I like it when you're forceful, Tommy. You don't have to be gentle. I won't break." Tom rubbed the lube on her ass and down her crack.

"That's good – Oh yes, explore me there." Tom ran his fingers over and in both exposed openings. Liz rocked back and forth slightly with his probing and fondling. She moaned and pushed back forcing his fingers in deep.

"Oh Tommy, I want you inside. Lube yourself and go slow until I get used to you. Let me do the pushing at first."

This was a new experience for Tom. He positioned himself behind Liz and let her take over. She felt warm and tight. As she'd wanted, Tom restrained himself from moving as much as possible.

"Oh yes, mmm that's so good Tommy… You're so good… Oh, I love you so much… Oh God, Tommy, you can fuck me now… Oh yes, keep moving, I love you… I love you fucking me like this…"

Liz moved in the opposite direction to Tom's thrusts, making a slapping sound when the front of his thighs met with the back of her thighs and ass. She reached back and Tom could sense the furious rubbing she gave herself while Tom penetrated. Tom peaked only seconds before Liz let out a hoarse cry and shuddered for a few moments before stretching to her full length on her stomach with Tom sliding onto her sweaty, oily back.

Catching his breath, Tom rolled off and lay facing the ceiling. Most of the candles had burned down to swelling puddles of different colored wax or burned out completely. Liz rolled over too and took Tom's hand in hers.

"So, how did the future Professor Sloan like his reward?"

"Delightful. Unexpectedly so."

"I liked it too," she said giving his hand a squeeze. "Let's take a shower and get all the oil and K-Y off us. Then you can take me to dinner."

"I thought that was dinner," Tom said, squeezing Liz's hand as she had done to his.

"Nah, that was just an appetizer. Now I want dinner."

VI

Summer in Burlington, Vermont: the trees were green; the temperature warm, the VMT campus was more relaxed than at any other time of the year, and everyone seemed content. Tom ran most mornings. It had become a habit he looked forward to, even longed for each day. At least during his short running time, it freed him from thoughts of teaching responsibilities, obligatory office hours for students and grading papers and tests.

On this August 12th run, Tom recalled something referred to in one of his English 101 classes. A student made reference to the writings of Robert Louis Stevenson. Tom forgot what it pertained to, but it got him thinking about his famous work, *The Strange Case of Dr. Jekyll and Mr. Hyde.* Tom smiled to himself as he ran. He, Tom Sloan, grad student and TA for the summer was leading a version – a mild version, but a version just the same – of Jekyll and Hyde. The major part of each week was spent preparing for his classes, classroom teaching, speaking with students and grading; while another part of each week, albeit a smaller part, was spent with Liz in a totally different world. His association with Liz was adventurous, completely unpredictable and, for lack of a better word, decadent. Books were left behind, ideas and hypothetical thought didn't exist, the future would take care of itself, the present – aah, the present – was alive with possibility.

Rock climbing, hiking, drinking cheap wine, drinking expensive wine, eating inexpensive take-out food, fine dining, quick sex on the fly out of doors, long, lingering experimental sex lasting half a night… everything about Liz was sensual and unlimited in scope – *Mr. Hyde's turf.* Yet it could also be unfulfilling intellectually. So he prepared for his classes and taught. He threw ideas out and discussions raged. He conferred with Dr. Walther and Dr. Edmonton and was scintillatingly challenged – *Dr. Jekyll's world.* When he needed, was desperate for, the physical, the emotional, the erotic, he became Mr. Hyde with Liz. In the heady academic circle of VMT he was the staid, erudite Dr. Jekyll.

Running past a towering blue spruce, his five mile marker, Tom laughed out loud for the world to hear – for nobody to hear. He wasn't the least bit fatigued. He could run forever. Tom Sloan would become the brilliant Dr. Sloan. He would also remain Tommy Sloan – the adventurer, the free-living, free-loving cohort of Liz, the fire starter, the arsonist of love. He could turn to VMT for the cerebral. He could rotate to Liz for his bestial desires. No man could ask for more. Few men, in fact none that he knew or was even remotely aware of, had achieved this delicious duality somehow bestowed on Tom Sloan, recently of Burlington, Vermont. The Gods had chosen him. He had been gifted the life most other men couldn't even begin to imagine, yet it was his. When he turned left he was satisfied, when he turned right he was equally fulfilled. There were no such things as a win-lose or a lose-lose situation for Tom. His life was win-win all the way. How he deserved this he hadn't a clue, but he wasn't going to question his gilded fate. He'd savor it instead.

By late August Tom viewed his life as enchanted. Liz never ceased to surprise him. On a recent overnight camping trip to a lake, she'd insisted they take their rented canoe out at midnight. It was a moonless, inky sky she wanted to experience lying in the bottom of the canoe. Staring at the brilliant Milky Way, like a child Liz would shout with excitement at each shooting star. Seated in the stern, paddle in his hand, Tom was more transfixed by the sight of this dark-haired beauty lying at his feet than with any other heavenly body. Without warning, Liz shifted her head back to look at Tom.

"Put that paddle down. I want you."

"Where? Here?"

"Yes, here. And now."

Tom slid the paddle next to Liz in the bottom of the canoe. "How are we going to manage this?"

"We'll change places. You lie down. I'll sit on top."

Removing his clothes and putting them on the bottom of the canoe for padding, Tom took Liz's previous position. Liz pulled her shorts and tanktop off, tossing them to the bow.

"Looks like you need some encouragement, Dr. Sloan."

"Actually, that's Mr. Hyde to you madam."

Bending over a thwart to reach him with her mouth she managed to say, "I don't know what the hell you're talking about Tommy."

Liz sucked him deeply until he grew to a size that was too much for her to take all the way down. "That's better. Now we have to find a place for my big friend here."

She straddled him with her knees on each side of his hips. Holding the gunwales she tilted her head back to view the stars and began her rhythmic movements. Looking skyward in the near blackness, Tom could barely make out her breasts between swaying, straight hair. He was plunged into a gently shifting colorless cocoon, aware only of the rounded sides of the canoe, the desperate rising and grinding of Liz above him with a vast array of stars as a backdrop. As her excitement grew her movements gained momentum. She again tilted her head back and let out a low, gasping moan. Then she started to chant in an almost inaudible voice, "Oh, ooh yes, let me fuck you… I want you deep… mmm, like that… oh yes… yes… I love you so much Tommy… I love the way you fuck me… make me cum Tommy…"

She began to get louder as she approached orgasm, "Oh Tommy, oh Tommy, fuck me like you want to hurt me… Do it hard… You know I love you so do me better… faster… Yes, yes… Ooh I'm almost there…"

Tom wondered how much easier sound would travel over water than land. He thought he heard laughs and whistles from shore, but that was at least a couple hundred yards away. It didn't matter. He'd long past the point of caring if some unknown, unseen people heard Liz cry out her passion. He just accepted that as *de rigueur* for these outdoor scenes. What did he care? Would Mr. Hyde care? Of course not! Go with it. Enjoy it. This was his time…

But his time was cut short – startlingly, abruptly cut short. Liz had worked herself up into a vocal and physical frenzy. At the conclusion of her voluminous pronouncement to the heavens that she'd indeed cum, Liz threw her weight to one side and flipped the canoe. Trapped under the thwarts, Tom took in a mouthful of water and went into near panic until he realized, like some ancient brass diving-bell-contraption of yore, the canoe had flipped and was now floating at the surface with trapped air running its entire length. Tom untangled himself from the thwart and bobbed breathing the air under the canoe. A moment later a laughing Liz popped her head out of the water next to him. Before he could say an angry word her tongue was filling his mouth.

Their clothes sank to the bottom. Tom was glad his pockets were empty. Naked and with Liz laughing they swam the swamped canoe to shore. If there were people on the shore before, they'd left by this time. Unseen In the almost total darkness they made their way to the tent.

"I'm cold, Tommy. Warm me up."

A week later Liz packed a lunch and took Tom on a short hike through deep woods to a narrow, cascading waterfall. It was a warm day with a cloudless sky. Liz carried a blue daypack containing their lunch and a bottle of Lambrusco. There was a small clearing in front of the waterfall with a rocky pool of clear, cool water.

She said, "I'll just put this wine in the water to cool."

"This is a picturesque spot you've found. You must have been here before."

"Once or twice. I thought you'd like it."

"I do."

Liz fumbled with the contents of her pack and said, "I thought you'd like this too."

She stood by the pool and removed her hiking boots and socks. Sitting on a flat overhanging rock she let her feet into the water. "Come join me. This feels wonderful."

Tom did as she asked and sat next to her with his feet playfully splashing water on her smooth legs. She turned her head and kissed him. When they pulled apart Tom surprised himself by putting his arm around her, pulling her close and saying, "You know I love you, Liz."

For a short time she said nothing. Then abruptly standing she whispered, "Then you better show me."

Her shorts and top were off before Tom could even get his feet out of the water and stand next to her.

"I've got you beat again. Now, get those clothes off, Mister!"

They both laughed as Tom complied. Liz knelt over her daypack and rummaged around, pulling out a water bottle, taking a drink and putting it on the ground. By the time Tom was naked and beside her Liz was on knees and elbows.

"Tommy, I want you to do me doggy style. You're certainly ready," she said glancing at him, "and so am I. I don't need any warm up, just fuck me now."

Tom knelt behind her and removed a sharp twig from under a knee. He felt Liz reach between her legs and grab him.

"Mmm, I like this," she purred and guided him into her wetness.

Tom leaned forward and held her shoulders. He let her start a slow rhythm and then pulled her to him, forcing himself fully inside.

Liz gasped, "Oh, I love it when you do that, Tommy. Do it harder… Yeah, that's it… Pull me back hard… Ooh, like that, yeah… Oh, I love you… Oh, I love you forcing yourself in me…"

Tom was used to Liz talking during lovemaking. He had to admit it heightened his own arousal. When she, for lack of better terminology, got down and dirty Tom could have trouble holding back.

Liz stopped momentarily and seemed to place something on the water bottle next to her right hand. From Tom's position he couldn't see what it was. The thought was fleeting as Liz resumed her back and forth motion and coaxing, "Ahh, that's so good, Tommy. Think of me sucking you, taking you deep into my mouth and throat… Think how soft and warm I am for you… how I love you and love getting you hard… Think how you can fuck me any way you want… how I love it all… how I love you… and how I want you in all my openings…all of them…"

Tom could feel Liz start to tense for her own orgasm as he was ready to explode in his own. Before closing his eyes for a final deep plunge, Tom looked down at Liz. She'd moved the flat-sided water bottle under her face and he heard her breath in deeply through her nose. She relaxed her arms, letting her cheek rest on the ground while her entire body tensed and shuddered, tensed and shuddered. She let out a guttural moan and a series of shallow sighs with her breaths. Then she lay still. Tom was spent and motionless behind her. Seconds turned to a minute. No movement.

Still inside her, Tom spoke softly, "Liz, are you okay?"

He heard a muffled sound. Then Liz suddenly brought her head off the ground and let out a raucous, seemingly primordial laugh. "Oh my god, that was the most unbelievable, mind fucking orgasm I've ever had. Oh, Jesus Christ, what a rush!"

"Liz, what's going on? Are you sure you're okay."

"Of course I'm okay. I'm better than okay. God, I've wanted to do that for a long time. Oh God, was that worth the wait!"

Tom stood putting his shorts and shirt on, "What are you talking about? Worth what wait?"

"I thought you saw…"

"Saw what?"

"Just as I was about to cum, I snorted a line of coke off my water bottle."

"No, I didn't see…"

"Don't be upset, Tommy. I just had to try it once. If you'd like, next time you could do a line off my back."

Tom was stunned. This girl was incredible. He'd learned a while back not to be judgmental, to trust her when she said he needed to relax, to go with the flow. If it got her off, so what did it matter? Maybe, like she suggested, he'd try it himself. It would all be in the spirit of Edgar Allen Poe. He liked that idea.

Tom walked back to her, hugged her tight and said, "Maybe I will. Just maybe I will."

As wild and satisfying as the sex was, Tom liked to hear Liz say she loved him. The first time she said it he was more than a little surprised, but now lovemaking wasn't complete without those words. Several times Tom answered her back saying, "Oh Liz, I love you too." But she never spoke of it afterwards. This was fine with Tom. He had not used the words before and felt a little uncomfortable, a little awkward saying them now. How his life had changed from only a few months before! He was a highly regarded teacher at VMT, or so he assumed, and he was enraptured with a beautiful woman who proclaimed her love for him in the heat of passion, the apex of his satisfying her deepest needs. Life was good. No, life was great.

Toward the end of August Tom received a phone call: "Hello, is this Tom Sloan?"

"Yes, speaking."

"Tom, this is Susan Ellsworth. I'm not sure if you are aware of me or not, I've had a couple classes with you before…"

"Okay, I think so. Your name is familiar…" Tom lied.

"Well, I just read the story you wrote for Dr. Walther's class and to say I'm deeply impressed would be an understatement."

"Thank you, that's very kind."

"The reason I'm calling is that I'm starting a study group for the fall semester. Nothing formal, just a bunch of grad students in the English department getting together maybe once a week – or more if needed – to discuss our work and maybe help each other out from time to time."

"Sounds interesting."

"I wanted to know if I could count on you to be in our little group," Susan said. When she heard no immediate response she went on, "Of course, I realize you'd be helping us out probably a lot more than we could help you, but I was hoping you'd still join us."

"I'd be delighted provided your meetings don't conflict with my schedule or work," Tom realized what a snob he sounded, but let it slide without an apology.

"Great. I'll call you when the semester begins and we get organized."

"Fine, just call me then. And thank you for thinking of me."

Tom hung up the phone. He hoped nothing would come of this study group. He had enough on his own plate without trying to help out a bunch of other people. Still, it was a nice compliment, he thought.

The summer term ended. Dr. Walther was well pleased with the test scores and papers of Tom's freshman students.

"You've obviously succeeded, Tom," he told him in his office. "These kids did well under you."

"Thank you. They were a good bunch. A couple show particular promise."

Tom thought Dr. Walther seemed to view him as an equal when he said, "You certainly did a fine job. It was nice working with you this summer."

"It was nice working with you too, John."

Tom had entered the building a teacher, but realized he was now leaving once more as a student – a grad student, but a student nonetheless. That was okay. He was looking forward to the challenge of his fall courses which would begin in a couple weeks. Until then, he could concentrate on a little vacation with no responsibilities or obligations to anyone but himself. He could devote more time to his relationship with Liz – more than the one or two days a week he'd allowed himself this summer. He'd try to make up for that. But first, there was something he needed to purchase.

VII

Tom wasn't sure of when they'd actually have a ceremony and be married, but he knew this was the right step to secure his future with Liz. They could decide on a date anytime – probably in a year or so after he got his master's. That wasn't a concern. Tom wanted his ring on her finger, his love for Liz displayed for all to see. He'd spent an hour in a local jewelry store pricing diamond engagement rings. What he wanted and what he could afford were two concepts that would not coalesce. He would prefer a simple solitaire diamond in a classic setting, but anything of a reasonable size was completely out of his present financial realm. He settled on a ring with a quarter karat diamond in the center with several smaller ones clustered around it. This gave the impression of a larger diamond without the cost. Tom made the purchase and felt pleased with himself.

Upon arriving home at the Briarwood Apartment, Tom could hardly wait to call Liz.

"Hi Liz…"

"Oh, hi Tom."

"Liz, there's something I'd like to ask you... Something we need to discuss."

"Sure, is something wrong?"

"On the contrary, just something I'd like to go over in person with you."

"Umm, sounds mysterious, Tommy. What have you got in mind?" she said with a teasing tone to her voice.

"No, nothing like that, at least not at the moment. This is serious. Can you come over around 5:00? I'll take you out for dinner after."

"Sure, see you in an hour."

Tom took a quick shower and put on fresh clothes. He wanted to look respectable yet relaxed in khakis, a button-down shirt and loafers instead of his usual jeans and running shoes. This was to be one of the most important evenings of his life and he'd appear mature and confident.

Coming out of his bedroom after dressing, Tom saw Jeff in the kitchen making a sandwich. Seeing him, Jeff said, "What are you all dressed up for?"

"Liz is coming over. I anticipate this to be quite an evening."

"Oh? Big plans?"

"You could say that, yes. I'll show you something I bought today."

Tom reached in the small white bag he'd placed on a table by their sofa and pulled out a square leatherette box. He opened it and held it for Jeff to see.

Jeff's initial smile vanished in an instant. He stared at the ring for a long moment then said, "Shit. Oh no, shit… Shit… SHIT!"

Tom was utterly lost for words. This was not the reaction he'd expected. "What is wrong with you, Jeff? I'm going to ask Liz to be my wife and all you can do is say 'shit.'"

"Listen Tom, we need to talk."

"What's your problem? I don't have time to talk. Liz is coming over in a little while and I want you out of here."

"Don't worry about me being out of here – but we need to talk – and I mean right now."

"Fine, but make it fast. I've got other things on my mind."

"No, you don't, Tom."

Tom sat on the edge of the sofa. Jeff slid a kitchen chair to face him.

"This isn't going to be easy, Tom. Not for either of us, but you better listen carefully."

"Go on, but make it quick. I really don't have time for all this."

Jeff began, "Tom, we've been friends for a year now. I respect you and wouldn't do anything to intentionally hurt you, but… well, I'm not sure how to say this…"

"Just say it. Come on, we don't have a lot of time here."

"Tom, I had no idea you and Liz were serious. I mean, you know, thinking about marriage. If I'd known…" Jeff paused as if trying to find the right words to say.

"Out with it, man!"

"Okay, there's no other way, Tom. Listen, Liz and I have been screwing each other for weeks. She told me you two were just friends."

Tom stared at his buddy. He couldn't believe what he had just heard. Lamely he said, "You're lying."

"For God's sake, Tom. Do you really think I'd say this after you show me an engagement ring if it weren't true? Jesus Christ, Tom. You think I want to tell you this? I'm telling you this as a guy who cares about his friend. Would you rather I kept my mouth shut and let you get engaged to… to someone like her?"

Controlling his temper, Tom said, "What exactly do you mean *someone like her*?"

"Tom, you're the smartest person I know. But you need to think with your head instead of your crotch. I'm telling you man to man, this girl isn't the kind you want to spend the rest of your life with. Maybe if she settles down in five or eight years, but not now. She's a hellcat, Tom. She's dangerous. You're so blinded by her looks and the sex games you can't see straight."

Jeff looked at the stunned and silent Tom still holding the ring box in his hand. "It's best you hear this from me now, than make a huge mistake or maybe hear this from someone else when it's too late."

All Tom could do was weakly respond with, "Continue."

"While you were teaching this summer, Liz would stop in before going to work at the gym. She called us fuck-buddies. Sometimes she'd call and I'd go to her place. Sometimes outdoors. It was casual, harmless sex. That's all."

Tom was looking down at the floor saying nothing. Jeff went on, "You must have seen the candles, the red satin sheets, the tubes of K-Y. C'mon Tom, think! Did you really believe you were the only one? Didn't you know about the threesomes? And the drugs? The ecstasy and coke?"

Jeff saw the destroyed look on Tom's down turned face. The ring box had slipped from his fingers and now lay on its side by his feet on the carpet. Jeff softened his tone and continued, "Tom, Liz is the kind of girl you enjoy for the moment. Maybe when you're married to someone else for ten years and drinking and bullshitting with your married buddies, she's the one you remember from your past and laugh about. You build memories with girls like Liz, but you don't build a life with them."

Tom sat motionless, numb. "Thank you, Jeff," was all he could mumble.

"You need to know I'm not the only one either. She works at the gym. She knows and hangs out with jocks. I know of at least four or five – "

"Enough!" Tom shouted at his friend and roommate – his ex-friend and ex-roommate. "Get out!"

Jeff opened the door to leave at the exact moment Liz was about to knock.

"Oh, hi Jeffrey, where are you off to in such a hurry?"

He pushed passed her and vanished.

Tom sat motionless in the same position he'd maintained while listening to Jeff. Liz took the same seat Jeff vacated. Staring at Tom hunched on the sofa, she said, "Tom honey, what's wrong?"

There was no reply. They sat without speaking for a few moments until Liz spotted the ring box between them on the floor. Picking it up she said, "What's this?"

Except for briefly looking up, Tom remained motionless, "That was for you."

"Liz opened the box. She viewed the contents and whispered, "Oh Tom, it's beautiful."

She removed the ring and was about to slip it on her finger when Tom barked, "Don't you dare put that on!"

Liz immediately placed the ring back in the box and closed the lid which made a snapping sound that seemed almost deafening in the silent room.

"Tom, I'm so sorry…"

"You lied to me."

"I never lied to you, Tommy."

"You told me you loved me."

"When did I say that?"

"On numerous occasions, Liz. When we were, well, intimate."

"Tom, I said that because I thought it got you excited, got you hot. I never said that any other time."

"Well, I took you literally. I told you I loved you, and I meant it, at least at that point in time I did."

"We can work this out, Tom. No damage has been done."

"No damage? NO DAMAGE! You were screwing my best friend behind my back!"

Liz sat expressionless for a short time. Then a bit of annoyance, even anger, crept across her face, "Look, I never told you what you could or could not do. We never discussed our relationship in those terms. We got together and enjoyed each other… in a lot of ways... but if you felt you needed more you should have said something. You seemed very happy to see me when it was convenient for you, when you weren't teaching or meeting with your students or writing. I have a life to lead too, you know. I put no expectations beyond what we did with each other and, goddamnit, you have no right, no right at all, to have expected some kind of unspoken restrictions on me."

Tom looked at Liz with a mixture of confusion and loathing as she continued, "I'd like to keep this ring, Tom. I won't wear it until you want me to. We can work this thing out. I believe we can have a future together, but Tom – Tommy – I've only just turned twenty-two! You have to cut me a little slack here. I wanted to try everything, explore life, grab some adventure. I wasn't ready to settle down with one person, get married and have children. But if you're serious about wanting to share your life with me, I can be with just you. We can start new. We can start right now, Tommy."

Tom gently took the ring box from Liz's hand. He looked her in the eyes, the same eyes in which he'd seen so much passion. Softly he spoke to her, "Liz, I've never said *I love you* to anyone but you and I've also never said to any woman what I'm going to express now." Tom stood facing Liz who gazed at him expectantly. He waited a few seconds gathering his thoughts and words carefully, then concluded, "You can go to hell for all I care. I want you out of my life." Tom forced a bitter smile and cryptically added, "And when you go, take Mr. Hyde with you."

Tom sat on the sofa. He didn't know for how long. He simply sat. That interminable August day gave way to dusk and then night. The apartment was silent. At some point Tom went to his bedroom to lie down. Time had no meaning as he lay on top of his covers. Later, he glanced at the clock on his bedside table – 3:14 AM. Sometime after, he dozed fitfully. By 6:00 he had taken a seat at the kitchen table. He thought about going for a run, but he was too emotionally drained and too physically exhausted from lack of sleep. Tom had no appetite, but knowing he hadn't eaten since lunch the previous day, he poured a half glass of orange juice and forced a small bowl of cereal.

He was eating slowly, mechanically, when the door opened. It was Jeff. Seeing Tom in the same Khakis and shirt as the night before, he said, "Jesus Tom, have you been up all night?"

"More or less," Tom said, barely looking up from his bowl.

"Are you okay?"

Again, Tom glanced up briefly, but said nothing. Jeff took a seat on the sofa.

"Where were you last night?"

"I didn't think you wanted me around, so I stayed out."

"Where?"

"What difference does it make? I'm just concerned about you."

Tom put his spoon down and looked directly at Jeff. "Did you stay with Liz?"

Jeff thought a minute. "I'm not going to lie to you. She was very upset last night. She needed to talk."

"You didn't answer my question."

"Yeah, I stayed at her place. I had nowhere else to go."

"Did you... I don't even want to know."

Jeff remained silent. Resting his elbows on the table, Tom put his head in his hands. A while later when he looked up, Jeff was not in the room. He could faintly hear the shower in the bathroom. Whether five minutes went by or fifty, Tom didn't know or care.

He felt as if he were in a suspended reality where time didn't exist – or if it did, moved almost imperceptibly slow.

Tom looked up when he heard the bathroom door open. He caught a glimpse of Jeff's muscular and athletic nude body walking the few feet to his bedroom. Tom's reaction was immediate and visceral. He just made the kitchen sink as he vomited the meager contents of his stomach. Trying to be as quiet as possible, Tom heaved until nothing but acidic bile drooled from his lips.

VIII

The note Tom left for Jeff read:

Jeff,
After carefully screening a number of applicants, I believe Glenn Jacobson will be an acceptable roommate to take my place. He appears seriously studious, reserved and responsible. I have sublet my lease to him and requested he pay to you his half of the rent ahead of time. I have also paid this month's power bill in full. Do not concern yourself with reimbursing me for your portion. You can also have my half of the security deposit.
I regret the circumstances of my leaving. Please do not attempt to contact me.

Thomas Sloan

Tom found a one bedroom furnished apartment on the other side of the UVM campus. From there he could walk to the College of Arts and Letters building without passing the athletic department and gym. Perhaps sometime in the future, somewhere else, he'd continue his weight training workouts. For now, he grew sick to his stomach at the thoughts of entering that part of the campus. From lack of sleep and lack of food he felt too weak to run. He could try that again too, some time in the future.

The two weeks before classes resumed went by as if encased in fog. During this interlude Tom had little recollection of what he did to occupy this time. All he knew was that he longed to begin again his academic career, his academic life. If Mr. Hyde had been abandoned, Dr. Jekyll was certainly alive and well. Hyde had been an experiment – an experiment that failed. Only a fool would not learn from such a failure, and Tom considered himself anything but a fool.

A week into the fall semester, Tom was already slightly behind in his work. Every time he attempted to read, his mind would uncontrollably drift to vivid images of Liz. They were usually sexual in nature –

disturbingly dark – especially when the memories mixed with imagination and he envisioned Liz with Jeff or in one of the *threesomes* he'd mentioned on that dreadful evening. Was Liz with another guy and girl? Was she with two guys at the same time? Then the nausea would begin to take over. If Tom believed in the occult, he'd swear Liz had a spell on him.

Tom handed in his first short paper which was returned to him the next day. Hand written across the top was: *After reviewing some of your previous work, this is unacceptable. Summer is over, Mr. Sloan. It's time to refocus and clarify your academic intentions.*

Summing all his powers of concentration, Tom immediately rewrote the paper. It took him nearly twice as long as it normally would have to complete, but at least this one was deemed *acceptable* and slowly over time Tom began to catch up with his reading and course work.

A second week passed before Tom received a call from Susan.

"Hello Tom, it's Susan – you know, Susan Ellsworth… I spoke with you during the summer about joining our study group…"

"Yes, I recall the conversation."

"Good. Well, we're having a little get-together tomorrow night to get acquainted and go over some basics of the group. Can I count you in?"

From the moment Tom heard her voice, he realized he'd barely spoken to a soul in the past several weeks. He was instantly aware of a feeling of revitalization, of refreshment in the simple act of conversing. "Yes, I'd be happy to," he said without hesitation. When the call ended Tom was surprised that he was actually smiling.

The group met sporadically throughout the semester. Usually the meetings began with talk of courses, professors, papers and exams, but quickly gravitated to the more personal. Someone would relate a humorous anecdotal incident from a class or outside job and the direction of the meeting would shift. It became clear to Tom most of the seven members were looking for camaraderie with people in similar circumstances with whom they could relate. They drank coffee, or beer or wine, ate snack food and generally relaxed around the few people who could identify with their lives as liberal arts grad students at UVM.

After the second meeting broke up early, Susan suggested to Tom they go to a nearby coffee house. The main room was dimly lit with a small raised stage in one end. Looking around, Tom told Sue he thought the place was reminiscent of the old Beat Generation coffee houses where aspiring poets recited incomprehensible lines and were accompanied by goateed partners who punctuating their recitations with bongo drums. Susan thought this hilarious. She said she could envision Jack Kerouac and Allen Ginsberg sauntering in with a group of adoring and innocently twittering female fans.

They drank espresso and talked casually, familiarly, for nearly two hours. It was obvious to Tom that Sue – he called her Sue now instead of Susan – admired his mind and was impressed with the fact that he was invited by the department head to TA for the summer. It was the exact elixir Tom needed. He could feel his confidence returning. If his affair with Liz had robbed him of any past feelings of masculine prowess, Sue returned to him her intellectual admiration. His perception of Liz needing more than what Tom could apparently offer physically caused him to feel inadequate, weak, less than what a man should feel about himself physically. But, he reminded himself, Mr. Hyde was dead and buried. That part of him didn't exist anymore. He was a scholar – not some kind of unbridled playboy. He found solace in the idea that his affair with Liz added to his overall life's experience. But that was past now, and good riddance too.

When they were about to leave, Sue turned to Tom and unknowingly began a lasting tradition that would follow them for years whenever they left a restaurant, coffee house, bar or movie theater. Looking directly at him, she took his arm and in her best 1950s Beat Generation voice drawled, "Let's split this crazy scene, Daddy-O," to which Tom replied, "I can dig it, man."

Sue was about five foot three and of average weight. She considered her pale blue eyes and small nose to be her finest features. Sue's brown hair was cut in a sensible page-boy style. She told Tom she used to wear it longer, but that she got tired of going to early morning classes, especially in winter, with cold and wet hair. She was a practical girl who carried herself with confidence, but without bravado or haughtiness. Tom found her intellect attractive, her wit unexpected.

As the weeks passed, the study group shrank from seven members to six, then four and then it seemed to dissolve altogether. Tom and Sue continued their coffee house discussions, often after they'd been to the movies. Sue was a fan of foreign films and art flicks. Popular movies they saw for fun, but both usually came away feeling that because the films were mainly active; there was little reactive thought for later discussions. This was okay though. A little fun could be a pleasant break from study and course work.

Sue and Tom's affection for one another grew slowly over the fall semester. Everything had been platonic for months until Sue invited Tom to her apartment to watch a movie she'd rented. When Tom arrived at her place, he sensed something was about to change. Sue had cleaned her usually cluttered apartment, extinguished the lights and lit an antique kerosene lamp she'd purchased at a flea market. The lamp usually sat dust-filmed on a shelf for use in the event of the occasional power outages that occurred, especially in the winter when snow-covered dead tree limbs were apt to fall onto electrical lines. The lamp gave a soft, warm glow to half the room, leaving the other half in semi-darkness. The TV was located in that half and Sue had placed a few huge blue pillows on the floor in front for them to lounge on while viewing the movie. There was also a folded patchwork quilt on the floor. A chilled bottle of German Riesling sat in an ice bucket with two stemmed wine glasses nearby.

Even though it was January, Sue was barefoot and wore a pair of baggy elastic-waisted gray warmup shorts with UVM on the left leg. She covered her top half with an equally baggy green football jersey with the number 24 in faded white numerals on the front and back. Sue was small breasted, but Tom still thought he detected she was bra-less under her jersey.

Sue poured them each a full glass of wine, and then another. They settled in to watch the movie. After about fifteen minutes Sue snuggled next to Tom. He turned his head and they kissed lightly. Sue said, "I've wanted to do that for a long time now."

"I hope you're not disappointed."

"No, of course not." And she wrapped her arms loosely around his neck and kissed him more deeply this time.

Sue reached across Tom for the remote and clicked off the movie. "I hope you don't mind me turning that off," she said softly, kissing him again.

"If you hadn't, I would have," Tom said while holding her.

Sue lay back on one of the giant cushions while Tom kissed her lips and neck. She made no effort to stop Tom's hands from exploring her body, starting with the outside of her jersey and shorts, then continuing underneath. Tom couldn't help draw a comparison between Sue and Liz. Where Liz had been long-limbed and firmly toned from constant exercise, Sue was shorter and soft – not flabby, just, well, *soft*. Her breasts were peach-sized with tiny pink nipples. She gave no indication whether they were sensitive when he rubbed one between his thumb and forefinger. Working his right hand lower over her winter pale stomach and into her shorts, Tom was momentarily startled by Sue's hand size patch of coarse pubic hair. Kissing and fondling Sue, Tom felt almost guilty comparing this aspect of her to Liz. Where Liz was artificially waxed *from neck to toes*, as she'd once remarked, Sue was natural, real. She was comfortable with the way she was, with who she was. Sue was also comfortable with Tom. Liz needed excitement and teasing in her lust. She required massage oil or the danger of being caught having sex out-of-doors in public. Sue didn't appear to desire anything but Tom's gentle fondling and closeness. As exciting as Liz always was, Tom told himself often that her ways would grow tiresome, become mundane. Sometimes he actually believed this. Sue's physicality was relaxed, unthreatening, unchallenging. That, Tom convinced himself, was timeless.

Sue pulled out of her jersey and shorts. Tom lost his shirt and jeans. Before he entered her, lying on her back, Sue asked Tom to go slow, to be gentle, saying it had been a very long time since she'd been intimate with anyone. Tom understood and complied. They moved languidly together, and except for their quickened breathing, silently together.

As a matter of practicality, Tom moved in with Sue, sharing her apartment. Splitting bills and rent cost them both less than living separately. It was an agreeable arrangement. Months later they made the decision to get married once they'd earned their master's degrees. There would be no engagement ring, no big wedding to arrange, just two thin gold bands and the local courthouse. Later they could probably teach at a community college while working on their Ph.D.s. They made a plan and followed it through to the letter.

FIFTEEN

They called their weekly outings *Desert Sundays.* None of them gave the term much thought. It evolved naturally from "Are we going to the desert Sunday?" or, "Tomorrow is Sunday; I'll see you in the desert.*"* or, "I'm really looking forward to Sunday's hike in the desert." While Lunden either attended church or slept in, Mae had already swung by Tom's place and together they were on their way in the darkness to Joseph's house. Weeks of this routine had turned these times into a tradition. Mae and Tom looked forward to the relaxed morning and lunch with Joseph. And Joseph found himself counting down the days until he could plan a meal and share his home and kiva with his two friends.

Joseph had come to think of the several years he'd lived outside Lunden in his secluded desert home as possibly nearing an end. In the beginning, over three years ago, he yearned for solitude, the time to read, hike and hunt, to forget his last years in Montana. But now he yearned for the company of his friends Mae and Tom. It distracted him from his earlier contentment with living a solitary existence away from society – even the limited society of Lunden. He began to find his thoughts shifting to other places – maybe Santa Fe, New Mexico or The Big Bend area of Western Texas – maybe even back to Montana. But the realization of leaving Mae and Tom quashed any real motivation to relocate, at least for now. Perhaps in time the dynamics of their friendships would change or one or both of them would move on. That might be the time to seriously consider leaving. There were no constraints on him, no obligations to meet, no pressing matters with which to be concerned. He'd deal with his life day by day, trying to make each one count for something, if but a casual observation of some aspect of the desert he'd not noticed before, tutoring some kids, trying a new recipe or simply researching an idea online or in a book. He knew he had to be active and productive in his life, otherwise he might slowly turn into some kind of deranged desert hermit. That he'd never allow to happen. Sometimes he thought that if Mae and later Tom hadn't entered his life, becoming an eccentric desert recluse was exactly the direction his life would have taken.

The Taurus pulled up and parked a half hour before sunrise. Mae and Tom were both met with long hugs and back pats from Joseph.

Mae said, "God it's cold out here. Is that coffee I smell?"

Joseph replied, "No, Mae. Sorry to say I'm fresh out. You're smelling the hiking boots that I'm airing out."

Mae punched him lightly on the arm. "You know better than to run out of coffee on these god-awful early Sunday mornings. Couldn't we make these visits begin around ten or eleven o'clock?"

Now it was Tom who chimed in, "Gee Mae, never heard you offer up that suggestion before."

They were all laughing going into the warmth of Joseph's house. "Coffee's ready to pour. Make yourselves at home. I'll be right in with it."

Mae took her usual sprawl on the sofa. Tom sat in the upholstered chair. Joseph emerged from the kitchen with the steaming mugs, handing one to Mae and the other to Tom.

"I think I'll just stay here. You two can go off and play with the spirits all you want while I sleep here where it's cozy and warm."

Tom said, "One of these times we might just take you up on that."

"Actually, you'd be desolate without me. In fact the only reason I come out here is to offer solace and kindness to you two lost souls."

Joseph chimed in, "It's getting pretty thick in here. Let's get ready to go."

Tom and Joseph walked to the bedroom and emerged a few minutes later dressed only in shorts and moccasins. While they were dressing, or undressing, Mae had laced her own mocs. Mae had long since run out of jokes and sarcastic remarks about their insistence on hiking half-naked in the cold desert morning. Instead she merely looked at them and shook her head in mock disgust.

"If you weren't such a sissy Mae, you'd have given this a try long ago. The freedom it affords is quite remarkable really. There's a decided merit to it."

"And what, pray tell Professor Sloan, would you have me wear exactly?"

Joseph answered for him, "A bikini would be nice – or better yet, a thong."

"Fat chance of that. Maybe fifteen years ago I could have gotten away with wearing a bikini. I don't think it would be a pretty sight today."

"Bullshit Mae," Joseph said. "You'd look great in a bikini and you know it, but if you hesitate at that suggestion, what about the thong? I fantasize about that image all the time."

"Now who's slinging the bullshit?"

"Enough of this nonsense," Tom broke in. "Sun's about to break the horizon and the morning's getting away from us."

Joseph and Mae looked at each other and laughed. Mae spoke first, "I think either our bawdy talk has offended the good professor, or he's gone native on us."

Joseph walked to Tom and put his hand on his shoulder, "I can assure you Mae, Tom doesn't offend easily by a little *bawdy talk*." He gave his friend a conspiratorial wink and said, "He's definitely gone native."

As was their custom, nobody spoke on the walk to the kiva. The sun was half over the horizon when they arrived. Tom had come to enjoy this time of long shadows and rapid warming. Once, weeks before, in a particularly romantic frame of mind, he thought the sunrise in the desert was a symbolic reflection of his present life in Arizona. From cold darkness he'd arrived in a new land where he found warmth and enlightenment from both the natural surroundings and his two good friends. He tended to reflect on this for a moment or two each time they walked to the kiva.

Joseph removed the three folding chairs from under the tarp and set them up facing east to the sunrise. Tom asked Joseph if he was going to use the kiva and he responded he'd spent a little time there during the week. He was content to sit in the sun now.

"How about you, Mae?"

"Yup, just what I need. Maybe ten minutes. Just a little relaxing meditation. Some mind and soul cleansing this morning would be nice."

Tom pulled the rolled mat from the tarp and climbed down the short ladder. "I'll spread this out for you, Mae."

"Thank you, sir. Such a gentleman!"

Mae handed her watch to Tom, who like Joseph didn't wear one anymore on Desert Sundays. "Call to me in ten minutes. I don't want to fall asleep or get too heavy into anything."

Tom and Joseph sat in the warming sunlight. Every so often Tom looked at Mae's watch. He still felt a little uncomfortable about the whole kiva thing. His first experience shook him up and although he didn't speak much about it afterwards, he'd researched and read significantly on the topic of out of body experiences with regard to astral projection and Native American rituals. Tom was still unable to intellectually get his mind around the subject, yet he knew what he'd experienced. That was no dream. Finally he decided to simply accept what had happened and be comfortable with the notion that he could not fully explain it. For now, at least, that would have to suffice. There really was no alternative.

Tom looked at the watch again. "Time's up, Mae. You doing okay?"

here was no response. Joseph called, "Mae, everything alright?"

"Yep, just give me a moment to come back to the real world."

Tom looked to Joseph with concern. "Don't worry Tom, you've seen her like this a bunch of times." he said, "Mae's fine. She just gets relaxed down there." Then he smiled and whispered, "I also know sometimes she falls asleep, although she won't admit it. Don't equate anything Mae might experience down there with your first time. You – not Mae – are the one who needs to be careful."

A moment later Mae climbed the ladder from the kiva. "That was just what I needed. Well, aside from a longer night's sleep anyway."

Joseph turned to Tom, "You're up."

"Just ten minutes for me too."

Joseph took Mae's watch. "Okay, ten it is. And listen, Tom, if you start to feel yourself –"

"Don't worry," Tom stopped him mid-sentence, "If I feel myself start to leave, I'll turn back. I can control this thing. A ten minute mind clearing would be good for me too."

The mood was always different, somehow less somber, on the walk back to the house. Perhaps, Tom thought, it was the light of day that changed things. The desert at night seemed full of mystery and presence, where as in the daylight the landscape was revealed. It was what it was.

Nearing the house Tom asked, "So what's lunch going to be this time?"

"I, for one, hope it's nothing overly exotic," Mae said with a grin to Tom.

In his best southern accent, Joseph answered, "Well, since I'm plum outa porcupine liver and skunk spleen, you'll have to be satisfied with trout almandine."

Mae said, "Now that sounds like a good second or third choice. When did you go fishing?"

"Actually, I didn't. Grandparents of a kid I tutored the other day caught them. I teach a little math, help write a short paper and presto! It's trout almandine for all."

As seemed another tradition that evolved on its own, once back at the house, Joseph and Mae went to the kitchen to prepare for lunch while Tom put on his usual jeans and shirt. He then removed the old Bear Archery target bow and quiver of arrows from its hook over the fireplace and headed for the back of the house where Joseph had a target attached to two stacked bales of hay. This was expected now and Tom didn't bother to ask permission to use the bow. He'd purchased his own finger tab and arm guard which he kept in the zipper pouch on the quiver. Joseph had showed him how to string the old recurve Tamerlane Model HC 300. He explained to Tom that the bow was another pawn shop find. Not many people are interested in traditional target archery anymore and the equipment that was once expensive is now considered out of date, used stuff that's hard to sell. Times and styles change, but the laminated wood and fiberglass bow was magnificent in its symmetry and form. Being a target bow as opposed to a hunting bow, the draw weight was an easy and comfortable thirty-four pounds.

Tom had little experience with such things, but believed Joseph when he said that the let off on this particular model bow was wonderfully smooth.

With a small wood stake in the ground, Tom had marked off a distance of twenty yards from the target. Months before, Tom was barely able to keep his arrows anywhere on the target, but now he was hitting the center bullseye with regularity and, as Joseph had instructed, was considering his total arrow group size rather than the number of center hits. With time, Tom noted with satisfaction, the groups were shrinking.

A short time later, unseen and waiting for Tom to release the arrow that he held at full draw, Mae announced, "Professor Sloan, it is with much pleasure and satisfaction that I have the honor to inform you that luncheon is served."

Tom turned slowly to Mae, bowed slightly and said, "Indeed!"

The trout had a delicate flavor complemented by the bottle of Mosel Joseph had supplied. The conversation too was light, but lively. Mae spoke of some of the amusing and surprisingly personal things people tell her while gathering tax information. Joseph told of happenings on the reservation and tutoring. As usual, Tom did more listening than talking.

At the end of the meal when the apple strudel desert was finished along with the last of the Mosel, Tom innocently asked Joseph why he didn't teach full time.

Mae said, "This might be the wrong time for that discussion, Tom."

"No, that's okay, Mae," Joseph said. He turned to Tom, "I had a rough couple years teaching high school in Montana. I don't know if I could ever get back in the classroom again, or if I'd even want to."

"Can I ask what happened?"

"Sure. You've opened up a lot about your past. I don't mind telling you some more about mine."

"I've heard this story before," Mae said.

"Why don't you two go out and play Indians with your bow while I clean up the dishes and kitchen? You can talk there."

"I won't argue with that," Joseph said.

They carried their plates to the sink and Mae said, "Don't worry about clearing the table. I've got it. Go. Have some guy time."

They each took a few turns shooting arrows. Joseph complimented Tom on his form and his improvement.

Tom said, "Are you certain you don't mind revealing this obviously troubling part of your past?"

"No. It was a long time ago. If you look at the chain reaction effect of things, if it hadn't happened, I might still be in Montana instead of being here with two good friends eating Trout Almandine and drinking expensive wine."

"That's a fine way of viewing things that, as you know, I've been contemplating myself."

"My mother used to tell me that we are all born pulling a cart. As life progresses we fill the cart with our experiences – some good, some bad. This becomes our baggage cart. Certain people use it to build fortunes and empires, while others are crushed under the weight of their own baggage and never create anything."

"She sounds like a wise and insightful woman."

"She is." Joseph handed the bow to Tom and said, "You can shoot while I talk if you'd like."

"No. I've shot enough. Besides, I need to fully concentrate when I shoot and I'd not want to split my concentration. I'd rather hear about this experience in Montana."

Tom carefully unstrung the bow and laid it and the quiver of arrows on top of the hay bales. Joseph said, "I've got another bottle of that Mosel. Would you like some more?"

"Do you really believe you have to ask that question?"

"Just being polite. I know how you New York socialites require protocol. I'll be right back."

Tom found two folding aluminum chairs leaning against the house and opened them on a shady spot. Joseph returned with the second chilled bottle and two glasses. The cork had already been pulled.

"Mae's going to finish cleaning up and then take a nap, so we've got time."

"This is a great wine," Tom remarked.

"And this is a great day to go along with it."

They sat in the chairs. Joseph pushed the bottle into the sandy ground. "There, that should keep it from spilling."

Tom held his glass up to Joseph, "To another fine Desert Sunday. Thanks for being such an accommodating host and chef."

"My pleasure."

They downed their wine and Joseph refilled the glasses. Joseph said, "Okay, are you ready?"

"I'm teetering on the brink of exquisite expectation."

"Very nicely put, Professor."

"Thank you."

Joseph took a sip of his wine and began.

"I got out of college with History and Education degrees and a minor in Native American Studies. I was twenty-three years old and determined to hit the ground running. My future students were gong to go to college. They would be the first to break the cycle of poverty and ignorance and alcohol and drugs and government assistance. These kids would shine. They'd get good jobs and be prosperous. Mr. Curley's students would raise the bar and set an example for all the younger kids to follow. They'd grow up proud and have only me to thank."

Joseph took another swallow. "I was pretty cocky, huh?"

"If you're a first year teacher and you're not, as you say, *cocky*, you'll probably be a poor educator. Good teachers all start their careers in an idealized state of over-confidence. Never mind all that, I'm not here to sit in judgment of you. Please continue. This is fascinating."

Joseph looked at Tom a moment and continued, "Okay. So, I landed a job teaching high school Social Studies on a big reservation in Montana. They provided me housing and paid pretty well. The first year went badly. These kids just weren't motivated. I thought I could reach them, but I was wrong. Because I wasn't brought up on a res they were skeptical. Thought I was an outsider. The school administrators said I'd find my way and that first years were always a bit shaky. They said not to worry, that in time I'd be accepted and find my place. So I made myself believe that my second year would be different, but it wasn't.

"I'm teaching U.S. History to juniors and by the last few weeks of the school year I was getting pretty burned out. The kids weren't interested and I was losing heart. My patience was about gone too. Then one day I'm still reviewing half a year's worth of American History before the final exam. I've had it by this time and simply want the year over. I ask the kids to open their texts to a map page. I look around the class and one kid is sitting with his arms folded on his chest and no book on his desk.

"I barely remember his real name now, but he was called 'Cottonwood' by everyone. This kid was huge. Had to be six-feet-four and weigh two-forty. He was our football and basketball star. Dumb as shit, but the kid was a bull. I assume he was called Cottonwood because of his size, but probably also because he had chronic dandruff. This guy's not exactly teacher's pet material. He probably showed up to school about half the time. I was more or less told I had to pass him so he could continue in sports. A year before I'd have fought this sort of bullshit, but by this time my idealism was shot. I just didn't care. If they wanted me to pass him, I'd pass him. It didn't mean anything to me anymore.

"Anyway, I ask Cottonwood why he doesn't have his book open and he says he doesn't have one. 'No big deal,' I say and walk to the back of the room where the spare texts are kept. I grab a copy and drop it on his desk. 'Problem solved,' I say with a big stupid grin on my face. I notice the classroom goes motionless – not a sound. I think the other kids knew something was about to happen, but I didn't give a damn. I walk back to my desk and sit down. Before I can continue, Cottonwood stands up and with a swipe of his hand, sweeps the book off his desk so hard it actually hits the wall about ten feet away. I'm not in the mood for this crap and now I stand up. Cottonwood says, 'Why do we need to waste our time learning this shit? This is white man's stuff anyway.' I answer him with something like, 'You need to learn this so you don't remain just another dumb reservation Indian on welfare.' There's silence in the classroom – again, not a sound. Cottonwood just stands there. Then he says, 'You think you're better than us, don't you? You think we're all a bunch of dumb Indians. You're saying my mother's just a dumb Indian. Someone ought to kick your ass.' And he walks up in front of my desk.

"I knew I was handling this badly, but like I said, I really didn't give a damn. I should have known the hammer was going to fall when he mentioned his mother. It just didn't register and it should have. I was supposed to be the example. I was supposed to correct their wrong ideas and explain things so they could understand. But I didn't and that was my fault.

"What happened next shouldn't have happened at all. The kid was stupid and I wasn't doing anything to change that. All I was doing was feeding his frustration and ignorance. In his own way he was trying to protect what little he had, maybe what little dignity he had. I should have recognized that, but I didn't. What occurred in the next minute probably did as much to fuck up his life as it did to change mine. At least I had something to fall back on. He had nothing. All I saw was a threat to my classroom – my territory. I also saw it as a threat to me and my misplaced masculinity. I was the alpha male in that class and I'd be damned if some jerky kid was going to unseat me."

Joseph stopped speaking. He drained his glass, refilled it and wiped his eyes. "Sorry, Tom. I don't mean to get emotional. I can't help it though. Even after all this time, it still gets to me."

Tom said, "You don't have to continue with this, Joseph."

"Yeah, I know, but I want to." He dabbed at his eyes again and took a deep breath to compose himself.

"Look, I'm twenty-five years old and think I'm smarter than anyone else in a ten mile radius. This stupid kid may outweigh me by ninety pounds and be nearly a foot taller, but I work out and hit the heavy bag and speed bag. I'm the toughest little bastard around and no idiot seventeen-year-old junior in high school is going to threaten me. I walk around the desk and face him. We're maybe a foot apart. A few calming, intelligent words on my part would have diffused the whole situation, but I didn't say them. Maybe subconsciously I'm thinking words haven't worked so far, so it's time for action or some other such shit. Instead I say, 'Touch me and we'll see who gets his ass kicked.'

"I see confusion in his face. But all I did was offer him a lose-lose situation. If he backs down from little Mr. Curley he'll never live it down. If he hits a teacher he'll be in deep shit. A year before another boy tried to get in my face. He backed down, of course, but I found out if a student is aggressively physical and makes contact the teacher is allowed to fight back. I stored that information in the back of my mind. Sometimes I think I was sort of just waiting for a time to act on it – like a trained sniper in peace time itching for a little war. These kids were more physical than cerebral and I'd match them on their own level. I was smarter than them and I'd show them I was tougher too. Now that I've had a lot of time to rehash this situation, I think Cottonwood and I had something elemental in common. We both shared a kind of frustration. He was frustrated because he either didn't want to or couldn't change anything about his life. I was frustrated because I wasn't able to make a difference in his or anyone's life. I think Cottonwood, for all his dullness, at least aspired to being a great athlete if only for a couple of glory years in high school. That's more than a lot of people will ever achieve. But he had to know – even if he succeeded – any greatness was small, fleeting really, and would fade away in time. I mean, who really cares about last season's star player? Beyond another year of high school sports, he would be lost. I was angry at him for being shortsighted, for not seeing a better way out, but how could he see these things? I saw them because I was taken from the reservation before it got its claws into me. If I hadn't, maybe I'd be just another Cottonwood. I was doomed to failure just as Cottonwood was doomed to the reservation. This was a bad mixture at the worst possible time. It rose up out of nowhere and had nowhere to go."

Joseph took another deep breath, sipped at his glass and, Tom thought, seemed to be trying to steady himself.

"I can still see Cottonwood standing in front of me. He doesn't understand how this has escalated to such a level and neither do I, but things were said and an impasse was reached. I know Cottonwood doesn't want to hit me, so he goes half way. Remember, this guy is huge and probably doesn't realize his own strength. Adrenaline is pumping through each of us. With both hands he gives me a chest push. I don't think he meant it, but it was one hell of a shove and sent me back against the black board. If I hadn't stumbled against it I'd have fallen. I remember hearing someone in the classroom laugh and that did it. I regained my footing and walked up to Cottonwood. Before he had a chance to react I hit him with two quick left jabs and a hard right hook. The first jab broke his nose and the second split his lip. The right should have ended it, but somehow it had no effect. Cottonwood just stood there dumfounded for a second. I remember looking into his eyes which went from emptiness to rage in an instant. Next thing I know he's got me in a bear hug with my arms pinned to my sides. We're face to face and he's lifted me a foot off the ground.

This kid's strength was amazing. I couldn't breath. I couldn't even struggle much. He walks to the side of the classroom and starts pounding my head against the wall. Thank God it was the cork bulletin board instead of cinder block!" Joseph laughed and shook his head.

"Anyway, he's breathing hard and choking on his own blood. I remember feeling the splattering of warm blood and mucus in my face as he smashed my head to the wall. I could actually taste his snotty blood as I tried to breathe out of my mouth. At some point I lost consciousness. I later found out a girl in the class ran next door and got the basketball coach to break things up. I'm pretty well convinced he'd have killed me if she hadn't. I woke up in the school's infirmary a short time later. The police took Cottonwood and got statements from the kids confirming he had touched me first.

"After a couple days I returned to the classroom. Cottonwood was gone, of course, but I could see the hatred in every kid's eyes. Cottonwood was expelled – the end of his sports career. The kids all knew Cottonwood didn't have a chance. I was just the *system* crushing the *individual*. They knew it and I knew it. I finished out the last week of school, gave out the final exams and passed each kid whether he deserved it or not.

"Word spread of Cottonwood's expulsion. I was shunned by everyone on the reservation. I fucked up big time and had no one to blame but myself. So I handed in my resignation and went back to my parent's ranch.

"I helped run the ranch for a couple years until some California land developers offered more for the place than it was worth. My folks were tired of the hard life and sold out. They did section off the ranch house and a nice piece of land which they gave to me. Then they bought a house outside of Billings and retired. I lived alone in the house and ran some cattle for a while, but Montana winters are long and cold – especially for a single guy. So I leased the place and figured if I was going to play *wild Injun* I'd be wise to do it some place warmer than Montana."

Joseph blotted his eyes with his fists and smiled at Tom.

Tom remained expressionless, but Joseph could tell he was still digesting the story. After a moment Tom said, "I have a nagging feeling that there is more to this story."

"You're very perceptive, Tom. There is more. Soon after I'd moved here to Arizona, I went online to check the local newspapers from Montana. You know, just to see what was going on back home. Well, I came on a short announcement that Cottonwood had committed suicide."

"How did you take that?"

"I blamed myself. If I hadn't gotten him expelled, maybe he'd have had a different life. I fucked up the only thing he had going for himself – sports. Once he couldn't play sports he was an instant nobody."

"Like I said, I believe there's still more to this story."

"What makes you think that?" Joseph asked suspiciously.

Tom thought a moment before speaking. "After my first experience in the kiva – you recall my short sojourn to the *other side*? – I started my own condensed version of researching Plains Indian rituals and practices. In so doing, I came upon the Sun Dance Ceremony…"

"Very astute of you. Maybe I should reword that to very *observant* of you."

"After hearing the emotion in your voice as you told me about Cottonwood, I put two and two together and the mystery surrounding your pectoral scars began to unravel."

Joseph let out a short, gruff laugh. "I'm sure Mae is still napping and this bottle is only half empty. Wanna hear the rest?"

SIXTEEN

THREE YEARS PREVIOUS

Joseph sat in the cramped second bedroom of his house staring into a computer screen. He'd settled in to his new home and after six weeks was still in the exploring stage. He'd bought a simple GPS devise as the desert was still a vast unknown to him. The last thing he wanted was to find himself lost and alone in a new and strange and potentially hostile environment. Hot days, cold nights, little water, not a place to take lightly. Hiking in each direction for a few miles had made him familiar with the immediate vicinity of his house. It was part of the settling in process. He was sleeping soundly now after fitful nights during the first several weeks. Still, this was all new and as much as he enjoyed his surroundings, he couldn't help but feel a little homesick for his familiar ranch back in Montana. It was comforting to know he'd only leased it by the year. If Arizona didn't work out, he could always return or try somewhere else.

For as little or as much as he liked, the internet kept him connected to Montana. Every so often he'd peruse the Billings Gazette, The Bozeman Daily Chronicle, or The Great Falls Tribune. During his first few weeks in Arizona he'd checked the Montana newspapers every couple of days, but now he viewed them once a week or less. Probably over time he'd lose interest all together and concentrate on his current locale.

Scanning the Billings Gazette, he came on a small notice and photograph of a young man. Joseph read the brief write-up and to no one at all shouted out loud, "Oh, shit! Oh, fuck! No! No! No…"

He walked out of his house with clenched fists at his side and his eyes squinted into slits of rage and tears. To the ground he yelled, "Goddamnit, NO! Why the fuck…" His words trailed off to silence with only the desert breeze to carry them away. He picked up a rock and threw it as far as he could. Then he threw another. With buttons popping, Joseph ripped his shirt off and flung it backhanded to the ground. He put his hands on his hips and looked to the cloudless, blue sky. He closed his eyes and tilted his head back down to the ground. A moment later he fell to his knees in the sand and cried out, "You stupid, stupid fuck. You son-of-a-bitchin' idiot. Goddamn you..." Then Joseph sobbed into his hands.

Five minutes later, maybe ten, he didn't know how long, Joseph wiped his eyes with his hands and his running nose on the top of his forearm. Still on his knees with his head down he spoke aloud again, "This is my fault, isn't it? You fucking did this to me, not to you, to me. Didn't you? You fucking asshole!"

Remaining on his knees, Joseph thought about his life since leaving his teaching position on the reservation. Everything had gone wrong. The ranch ran okay, but he was alone, in some kind of self imposed exile. Ranch hands were unreliable. They came and they went. Women were the same. They'd come into his life and after any cerebral attraction ran out of steam and they sensed he had little real interest in them aside from sex, they'd move out of his life. He found some comfort in nature, but being alone in nature during long Montana winters offers little but cold. Day after day, week after week, from late November through April – cold with wind, cold with snow, cold with clear skies, cold with cloud cover – always alone with the cold. A family working together might find it tolerable. Growing up, his family had. That was a lifetime ago. Now, as a single young man, it could only be considered little more than an obvious mistake.

Driving to Arizona was energizing. Joseph was fixing the mistake. He was alone, but he was leaving. Something new would come his way. It had to. And it did in southern Utah. A shower in a motel bathroom, fresh clothes from his overnight travel duffel, then one final day of driving would bring him to his new home in Arizona. A fresh start waited. Joseph was eager to get behind the wheel. He left the room carrying his duffle and car keys – except there was nothing to drive. The new Chevy Suburban was gone; his rented trailer un-hitched with the back doors hanging open, a cut padlock lay beneath on the pavement. Joseph's world had just contracted even further. Inside the trailer were a few torn-open boxes of books and CDs, some scattered clothes. Everything else was gone.

Collecting himself, Joseph sat on the back of the trailer floor. He could deal with this. What he lost were just things. Insurance would pay for the Chevy and he'd get compensated for the contents in the trailer. To hell with it. He didn't need all that crap anyway. It was a hindrance. Or at least, he convinced himself it was.

Now, in his desert house in Arizona six weeks later, he was still being punished. It's because of Cottonwood. Cottonwood cost him his teaching career, his life on the reservation. Maybe he'd have done better if he'd stayed and taught a third year. No use thinking about that. He couldn't have stayed. He was shunned. He was hated by students and staff. He was not welcome on the res. He had to leave.

Eleven hundred miles away and more than two years later the torture and disaster would continue. Cottonwood's suicide hung over Joseph like an angry, gray-clouded electrical storm. What would be next? When would the next bolt of lightning strike him? He felt inextricably tied to Cottonwood. In life, he could run from him, separate himself by miles, but now that he was dead, he'd never be able to escape him. His memory, his spirit would be a part of Joseph forever. He wouldn't allow this. He had to do something. Joseph knew what he could do.

Joseph's mother was a vaguely defined non-practicing Christian. Similarly, his father was a vaguely defined, semi-practicing spiritualist. After marrying into the Crow tribe, he became fascinated with the subject of Plains Indian religions and practices. From a comparative standpoint he found parallels between Indian beliefs and many other religions. He felt there was a clear link between them all separated mainly by culture and custom. For a man who lived a life on a ranch surrounded by nature, a transcendent spiritual realm made sense. He passed this along to his son Joseph, who accepted it without trying to empirically examine or put it to a test. Joseph and his father intuitively believed in a universal spirituality, an omnipresent force manifested in all things – living and inanimate. Its presence wasn't relegated to churches or holy sites or certain days of the week or holidays. It was merely an unseen part of each day – like the limitless sky above, the earth below, or a softly spoken word.

Joseph found the interaction with spiritual forces something that happened naturally. If he opened his mind and soul he could allow entrance to beneficial insights and wisdom that came from outside his sphere of existence. Joseph didn't know from where they came or perhaps even from whom they came, but he knew absolutely that they did come. That is what he acknowledged. Explanations were beyond his scope of understanding, beyond the scope of anyone's understanding. From a young age Joseph made the decision to accept this aspect of life, rather than challenge it. If he wanted to interact with the spiritual world, it was available to him. If he chose not to, he could simply absent it from his life. Joseph also knew from personal experience that desired or not, at rare times the spiritual universe could intrude on his life. He learned to be aware of the subtleties of this intrusion, to know when something of this nature was occurring and, more importantly, to pay attention to it.

The Sun Dance Ceremony was widely practiced by the Plains Indian tribes until missionaries reported to the government on the barbarity of the spectacle. By the late 1800s it was officially outlawed, but the practice was never fully obliterated. Small Sun Dances were held in secret locations and the tradition lived on. Today the outright ban on this sacred ceremony does not exist and to at least a limited degree, the Sun Dance continues.

The general theme of the Sun Dance is one of prayer, thanksgiving, healing, renewal and rebirth. The sacrifices made by the dancers demonstrate their devotion and gratitude to their tribe and to the spiritual world. Joseph had never witnessed a Sun Dance, but through reading was familiar with the subject. There were variations of the dance with differing emphasis. Some of these seemed little more than friendly gatherings where participants danced to drums around an erected Sun Pole in thanksgiving and recognition of past Sun Dances and Sun Dancers. Others, replicating the more ancient and extreme, involved the self torture of the *pledgers* or dancers in the form of fasting, thirsting and bodily piercing.

The Sun Dance was held over several days in summer. Being July, the time seemed particularly appropriate to Joseph. The ceremony involved a number of people. Aside from the pledgers were family members, onlookers and holy men and women. But Joseph was alone. He would be the single pledger in his own unwatched ceremony.

Joseph drove his Jeep to a pine forest on higher ground where the mountains loomed over the reservation. Selecting a straight and stout tree of about eighteen feet in height, Joseph knelt down and thanked the essence, the singular spirit, which connected all things – including trees and men. He then cut the trunk a few inches from the ground, neatly trimmed away the branches and removed the last few feet of the tapering top. Joseph also cut two four inch long pieces from a three quarter inch thick bottom branch and placed them in his pocket. He was left with a sturdy, and now sacred, Sun Pole around which he would dance and seek rebirth and renewal.

A few days after arriving at his home, on one of his first exploration hikes, Joseph had found the remnants of a kiva. It was little more than a depression in the sand surrounded by carefully fitted stones. This would be a good and proper site for his Sun Dance.

An hour before sunrise on next-to-the-last-day of July, Joseph hoisted a small backpack containing water, his Ruana knife, strong parachute cord, a lightweight camp trowel and some pemmican he'd made the day before from dried meat and berries pounded into bite-sized squares. Suspended by a thong around his neck, Joseph wore a leather pouch the size of a child's fist. Inside was a piece of fur from the first rabbit Joseph had killed in the desert, a fragment of an ancient pottery shard he'd found near the kiva, pine needles wrapped tightly in thread from his recently cut Sun Pole, and other personal items that symbolized to Joseph his connection with the natural and spiritual world of today, ancient times, and people from the past and of the unknowable future.

The Sun Pole was heavy, but once Joseph found the balance point he was able to lift it to his right shoulder and settle the weight on top of the padded backpack shoulder strap. Wearing only gray cotton sweatpants he'd cut off above the knee, his ever present moccasins and a rolled bandana to keep the sweat and hair out of his eyes, in darkness

Joseph hiked the mile to the kiva site. He put down the pole and placed his backpack on the ground. Choosing a spot about fifteen feet from the ring of exposed kiva stones, Joseph retrieved the trowel from his pack. He took a scoop of red sand and, facing first to the east, let some drop in a tiny dust cloud back to the ground. He did the same facing west, north and south. He gazed to the sky overhead for a few seconds and then took a kneeling position, placing both hands on the ground. In this, his own personal way, Joseph paid homage and respect to his universe.

Joseph placed a stone to mark the spot he decided to plant the Sun Pole. Next, for a distance of a dozen or more feet from this stone, he cleared all stones and debris from the area. He worked slowly, methodically removing the largest rocks and sticks first. Then gradually he picked smaller and finally the smallest particles. By the time the sun was three hours above the horizon, Joseph's Sun Dance area was carpeted with only the finest sand.

Finding the circle to his satisfaction, Joseph discarded the center marking stone. Taking his trowel, he began to dig on the spot where the stone had been. He could have brought along a shovel, but that would make the job too easy. Too short. Joseph needed to feel the earth he dug, to be a part of it, to make the work last. When a mound of dirt and sand built to a height of only ten inches or so, Joseph would very carefully, so as not to spill any in his cleaned area, take a scoop from the pile and walk it out of the sacred circle where he'd scatter it. Then he'd return and repeat the disposal until the mound was gone. Again and again he followed this pattern. The higher the sun rose in the sky, the hotter it became. Joseph allowed himself no food or water. He had to find a balance between fasting and thirsting and keeping strong enough to complete what he knew would be a long process. He finally rested for a short while and drank a tiny amount from a canteen. For now, food he could do without.

Joseph paced himself. Using the little trowel, he dug with a monotonous rhythm. Dig and scrape, make a mound, remove the mound, dig and scrape some more, make a mound, remove the mound, careful not to spill any, walk slowly, now return and dig. He left the circle only briefly to relieve his bodily functions. By nightfall the hole was four feet deep. Enough for day one.

Joseph allowed himself another few short swallows of water. He'd spent many days in the outdoors wearing little but shorts and mocs, so his skin was already deeply tanned and didn't burn in the relentless sun. The night cooled quickly, then turned to cold. Joseph sat by his newly dug hole and stared to the horizon. He was hungry, chilled and exhausted. This was good. He had no idea when he fell asleep, but he woke from his dreamless slumber to a clear pink dawn. He stood with a handful of sand facing the east. He let some escape back to the earth. Again, he made this gesture to the west, south and north. He tilted his head to the last fading stars, then crouched putting both palms on the ground. Joseph was ready for day two.

Taking his Ruana knife, he cut a notch near the top of the pole. Removing the olive drab parachute cord from his pack, Joseph cut four equal lengths of about fifteen feet each. He then tied all four ends to the notched top of the Sun Pole. He pulled the knots as tight as he could. The cord would not come undone or slip from its anchor point. Carefully he pulled the four lengths and trimmed them, making sure all were exactly equal in length. Finally he tied a tiny half inch diameter loop in each cord end. They had to be just the right diameter and all the cords had to be precisely the same length. This process took many tries and was accomplished through trial and error. Loops were tied and untied, tied and untied, until finally they were identical.

The Sun Pole seemed heavier than the previous day as Joseph lifted it, placed the base end in the hole and, stepping along the shaft with his hands over his head, pushed the pole ever higher until it slid into the ground. Joseph was surprised that the effort took so much out of him. He felt famished, but tried as best he could to put the idea of food far from his thoughts. A sip of water he needed.

Next, trowel by trowel, Joseph walked from the circle to collect sand and small rocks to refill his hole around the Sun Pole. With each few inches of replaced material, Joseph would tamp the dirt and stones with a stick he'd found the day before until it felt like a solid, compacted mass. Find a few rocks, drop them in the hole, one at a time, evenly around the pole – now earth, more earth, a few more trowels full, don't spill, walk slowly – carefully as lack of food makes for clumsiness – that's good, now tamp… tamp some more… look at the pole… make it straighter… a little to the left… wedge a rock to hold it there… a little more… that's good… more dirt… tamp it down. By the second sunset the hole was filled and tamped. Joseph could not hold thoughts in his head. His mind felt blank. Listening to a pair of howling coyotes, he sat with his back against the Sun Pole and wept. He cried in his thirst and hunger. He cried in his sweat cooled exhaustion. He cried in his aloneness. He sobbed in desperation until rescued by sleep.

Day three began with the sun already hot on Joseph's face. Weakly he sat up, leaning against the Sun Pole for support. He allowed himself a short drink from the sun-warmed canteen. His head was light and he nearly stumbled when he stood to dribble sand from his hand to the four directions, the sky and earth.

Before leaving the circle to relieve himself, Joseph pushed hard against the pole with his shoulder. As if it had grown in this spot for decades, the Sun Pole yielded nothing from his effort. Joseph was satisfied the job had been completed correctly. Returning a few moments later, he picked up the trowel and noticed the pain from the bloody blisters on his palms and fingers. He looked at his hands and smiled wearily. This was good.

Stepping into the center of the kiva ring, Joseph began day three digging again. He piled the dirt from the deepening pit on the opposite side of the Sun Dance circle. By noon he'd removed a foot of dirt from the kiva, exposing several rows of the stone lined circular wall. A little water in the early afternoon and then it was back to digging – slowly, mechanically digging and piling dirt into an ever expanding and heightening mound. A foot and a half deeper and the sun sank below the distant horizon. Joseph realized he no longer felt hungry. A few sips of water were all he required. He wasn't even aware of the heat. He'd stopped sweating. He'd stopped thinking. A weary comfort fell upon him like a soft veil. This was not good. He needed to act fast. Any hesitation and he might fall asleep and not wake up.

Joseph was alone. There was no one to aid him in his Sun Dance preparation. He was attempting a Sun Dance in Arizona, not South Dakota or Montana. This was a far harsher environment than either of those. He could perish alone in the desert if he allowed himself to ignore the danger signs his body was trying to communicate to his numbing mind. Under these circumstances, feelings of contentment and comfort meant death was not far from visiting.

Joseph stepped out of the kiva and sat by his backpack. He drank slowly from another canteen and fished out a Ziploc plastic bag containing the pemmican he'd made. A wave of nausea passed through his guts with the first swallow. He ate no more until the sick feelings subsided. He had to keep food inside. He needed strength to continue. He'd pushed himself too far for too long in this blazing mid-summer sun and heat. He must care for himself. There was simply no one else.

He ate more pemmican and drank more water. When the nausea returned he knew he'd had enough. He sipped water and sat as still as possible against the Sun Pole. The nausea returned in waves each time he tried to lie down or move in any way. The little food in his stomach meant life. He was not going to give it up.

He woke on the fourth morning curled around the pole. How he ended in this position he didn't know. He slept dreamlessly through the cold night. Joseph stood unsteadily and for the final time let the sand drop from his hand to the four directions, the sky and earth.

Before returning to the kiva, Joseph ate a few squares of pemmican and drank from a canteen. The water was cool from the night and Joseph thought nothing in his memory had ever tasted so refreshing and good. He rested in a sitting position, forcing himself to focus on who he was and where he was. He needed his wits about him on this day. Still Feeling lightheaded, he ate another two squares of pemmican and drank a few swallows of water. A pressure in his lower abdomen took him from the Sun Dance circle where he defecated for the first time in three days. His mind began to clear. He saw the trowel and knew what he would do. He saw the cords hanging from the pole and understood what waited. This was the day. And he smiled to nobody at all.

By the time the sun had reached its zenith, Joseph had the kiva dug to four feet deep. The ground he dug was cool and damp. It had not seen the light of day in centuries, nor had the uncovered circular rock wall. It was time.

Joseph climbed from the kiva and took a cloth from his backpack. Wetting it with water, he removed his shorts and moccasins and washed four days of dried sweat-stuck dust and grime from his body and face. He needed to be naked, to be clean, to be pure.

Next he unsheathed his Ruana knife and carefully peeled the bark from the pair of three quarter inch thick sticks he'd saved from the branch removed from the Sun Pole days before – a lifetime before. When the four inch long pegs were barkless and smooth, Joseph whittled one end of each to a sharp point. These too he smoothed with light strokes of his blade, making the tip needle sharp. Reverently he placed the two sharpened pieces of wood in the hot sand by the Sun Pole. He stood and stared at them for long minutes, concentrating, knowing what was required, wanting with all his heart to complete his rebirth and renewal, wanting his freedom, wanting the dance to begin. He was beyond fear. Pain had no meaning for him. Heat was unimportant. Joseph knew he must proceed now. To wait would distress his body to the danger level he'd experienced the day before. He was not at the brink of slipping into unconsciousness, but he was not far from it either. He was right where he wanted to be – needed to be.

The honing stone was pulled from the bottom of the pack. Joseph barely had enough spit in his mouth to correctly moisten the abrasive surface. He took a couple of swallows from the canteen – warm again, mid-day. He spit on the stone and slowly, evenly ran the Ruana's blade across the surface. One stroke on the right side of the blade, turn it over, and one stroke on the left. Right, then left, right, left again, on and on… one side… the next… more spit… right… left… ten minutes, twenty minutes… more? Maybe less. It made no difference. The sun would remain high for hours. Joseph tested the edge of the blade against his thumb as he'd done since receiving the knife on his twelfth birthday. He knew the blade, understood the characteristics of the steel. He could feel when it cut with a sharp edge and when it was dulling. He understood the angle to hold the knife when sharpening for the keenest edge. He used all his skill today. The blade was as sharp as it had ever been. As a final test, Joseph shaved a swath of fine hair from his arm in one smooth stroke. He walked to the Sun Pole, placed the Ruana on top of the two pegs and took two steps back. Closing his eyes, he prayed to the earth and sky. Silently he asked for forgiveness, for a fresh beginning, for a new life. He began to feel dizzy and opened his eyes. Balance returned. He mustn't wait any longer.

Barefoot and naked, Joseph walked to the Sun Pole, stooped and picked up the Ruana. Looking down at his chest he realized that in a few minutes it would forever be changed. He placed the tip of the blade four inches above and to the right of his left nipple. He pressed the blade inward. For the briefest of time the skin buckled, then relaxed as the blade separated it. He drew downward with the knife until he had made a three inch incision. It took a few seconds for the blood to well and run. Joseph felt no pain – only the beginnings of an indescribable if unclear relief. He made the second identical cut above and to the left of his nipple, two inches from the first. Joseph looked down at the twin rivulets of blood running from his chest over his stomach and now down the inside of his thigh. He felt as if he were watching someone else from afar, peering like a voyeur at the nude figure of a stranger. Don't drift away, he thought, reminding himself to hang tight to reality. Stay focused a little longer. Concentrate! Joseph closed his eyes momentarily and then opened them wide. He could go on, but barely. Normally, the pledger doesn't make his own cuts, but this was anything but normal. The Sun Dance, especially in the Arizona desert, was anything but normal. Joseph was glad to be alone, content in his suffering. This was what he needed. This was what he wanted. He didn't want or need an audience. His Sun Dance was a private affair between himself and… well, he wasn't sure what, but he knew at least in this respect he was not alone. He might not be surrounded by people, but he still felt surrounded, surrounded by the land and sky, the breeze that blew warm, sometimes hot, the cactus and the mostly hiding desert dwellers – the coyotes, bobcats, the little wild pigs known locally as javalinas, jack rabbits, owls, and more. Joseph was alone by his Sun Pole, but crowded by an unseen universe of spirit that threaded through everything like arteries and capillaries extending out from one central beating heart.

Joseph looked down and made two more matching parallel cuts on his right breast. Gently he laid the knife by the pole and brought up the two wooden pegs. Pinching the skin between the twin cuts on his left breast, Joseph pulled outward and simultaneously positioned the tip of one sharpened peg in the middle of the incision closest to his breast bone. With a quick shove it drove through the skin and flesh to emerge from the center of the outer incision. The pain was sharp and intense, but not unbearable, not unwelcome. His knees felt ready to buckle, but he held straight. Birthing was a painful affair. Rebirth should be no different. The second peg was inserted like the first. His mind cleared with the pain and he was ready to proceed, to dance into a new world, to dance into a new life, a purified life devoid of his past crippling misdeeds.

Stepping closer to the Sun Pole, Joseph took the first of the four dangling cords. He forced the tiny looped end over one tip of a skewer. The cord stretched just enough to encircle the wood end and hold it tight by the first vertical cut. The second cord went over the other end of the skewer. He secured the remaining two in the same fashion and surveyed his work. Drooping from his cut and skewered chest were four thin, but extremely strong cords. He was now standing in a sacred circle, naked except for his medicine pouch dangling between the blood and cuts and skewers and cords. Joseph stood on consecrated ground connected to the life giving Sun Pole – the conduit to the spirit world, the birth-giving mother of forgiveness and repentance. The cords were his umbilical to The Great Mystery, to The Earth Mother, to The Grandfather, to The Great Spirit, to God. The power rushing through to Joseph was his for the taking, his for the suffering, his for the hunger and thirst and bleeding… and his if he were worthy. He could retain the power, but he had to first sever the cords, to move back from the spiritual, the metaphysical, and return to the reality of his life. The time for dancing had come.

Feeling the flesh pull and resist under the skewers, Joseph raised his arms wide and faced the sun. "I give up myself!" he screamed as loud as he was able. The words vanished in the thin desert air. Only a single bird flew startled from a dry bush at the disturbance.

The bottoms of Joseph's bare feet were calloused and hard from wearing moccasins, but he could still feel the warm, even sand underfoot. Nothing separated him from the earth as he took the first steps of his Sun Dance.

Joseph had not considered this aspect of the ceremony before. He'd contemplated the four days of fasting and thirst, the monotonous digging. He wondered if he'd be able to cut himself and skewer the flesh after. The actual dance steps never really occurred to him. Others on the reservations with which he was familiar, embraced traditional dancing as an ongoing activity, a sport even. There were categories of dance for men and women, elaborate beaded and feathered dance costumes, competitions at pow-wows across the country. Tourists and spectators watched in fascination, choosing and rooting for their favorite participants. But Joseph wasn't a dancer. He was a hiker, an explorer of nature, a wanderer in unadorned moccasins. He would do the dance steps of a seeker, a lone and naked repentant soul wishing a new start to life in a new land.

One step in the orange sand in front of the other, slack in the cords connecting him bodily to the Sun Pole and beyond, around the sacred circle he walked. It felt wrong. This was a celebration, not a jaunt through the mountains. He must do the dance of renewal, take the steps of a child learning to walk. Yes, he was a child learning to walk! A toddler taking his first cautious steps. Little more than an infant who must fall and get back up to fall again. Joseph gave a clumsy hop and two steps to the side to regain the balance children find so difficult to maintain. He lost himself in childhood, to childhood. He stumbled around the pole, fell to his knees, rose and like a dizzy toddler swayed first to the left and then to the right. He laughed out loud like a child. He could walk! At long last he'd crawl no more. He was on his feet like his parents! Watch me! Come to you? I can do that! Catch me when I make it… Wait! I'm not a child! I'm Joseph Curley! I'm a man! Joseph had trouble focusing his thoughts. Had he just been stumbling around like a giddy child? This is delirium. No, he thought, this is the Sun Dance. He gazed down at his chest. The bleeding had mostly stopped. Streaks of blood turned brown as they dried and cracked on his sun-darkened skin. It was time to do what must be done, to pull.

Joseph did a little hop-step around the pole. He wasn't a trained dancer, but this felt okay. It would have to do. For him, the steps meant little. This was not a show. Let's get on with the birthing process.

He faced the Sun Pole and sidestepped to circle it. The cords wound around the pole as he moved, taking up the slack until there was no slack. Joseph stopped when the cords began to tighten on the attached skewers, pulling the skin outward just slightly. He took a deep breath and leaned back away from the Sun Pole. Heat flashed behind his eyes. Blinded he fell forward on his knees. The bleeding started anew, the lines went slack, he'd begun the birthing.

Joseph stepped and hopped. He shuffled when he tired. When he rounded the pole enough times to tighten the cords he'd lean back. Burning pain exploded through his chest and down his arms with each pull. Hop... quick step... step again... now hop and face the pole... back... back... lean with more weight... take it... you can take this and more... pull back harder... ease up... forward now... shuffle... don't fall... stay with it, stay alert and focused... do what needs to be done... step, step, hop... NOW! PULL HARD! LEAN BACK! MORE! AGAIN! ONCE AGAIN! Maybe next time around... this can't go on forever... how many pulls so far? A dozen? Twenty? Shuffle... shuffle... hop, step, hop, the line's getting shorter... it's taught... now pull... GOD ALMIGHTY PULL! IT WON'T RELEASE ME! I'M PULLING, I'M PULLING! I CAN'T PULL MORE! I CAN'T LEAN BACK FURTHER! It's getting dark. What time is it? Don't pass out! Dance, move, keep it going, you're not done... step, hop, step, hop, step and shuffle to the side, no slack, it's time again, PULL! HARDER! OH GOD, I CAN'T STAND IT, I CAN'T TAKE IT! YES, YES YOU CAN! I PUT THE SKEWERS IN TOO DEEP! THEY WON'T LET GO! IT'S NOT GOING TO WORK! I WON'T BE ABLE... YOU WILL! YOU CAN! EASE NOW... NOT YET... NOT YET.

Joseph stopped. His arms lay at his sides. His head drooped He saw the circular bloody trail through the sand he'd trodden. He didn't feel defeated, he felt ready. He knew what would release the binds. Pain was the new norm of his existence. The shock of more pain as he pulled and pulled over and over again and again dulled and diminished with repetition. Several times he caught himself blacking out and eased up until he regained his senses. There was not much daylight left. Joseph would not let the dance continue all night.

Joseph danced counterclockwise until the cords tightened. He did not pull back. Instead, he danced clockwise unwinding the cords and then rewinding them in the opposite direction until they were taught once more. It would all be over in less than a minute. He danced now to remember the moment, to honor the Sun Pole one last time, to burst free ultimately.

Reversing the dance, Joseph watched as the four cords unwound yet again. When they were at their longest, when none were wrapped around the pole, Joseph calmly walked across the circle as far from the kiva side as the cords would allow. He bent down and then stood with a handful of sand. He faced the east and let some slide from his fist. Then to the west, south and north, each time allowing a little more sand to cascade over his fingers and drop to the ground. He looked to the sky, closed his eyes and slowly collapsed to his knees, placing both palms on the earth. "Now Joseph," he spoke calmly to himself as he stood facing the partially dug-out kiva.

Joseph ran across the sacred Sun Dance Circle. He passed the Sun Pole gaining speed. For this brief moment his strength had returned, his mind had sharpened. The cords slackened as he approached the pole to which they were attached and quickly began to tighten as Joseph neared the outer edge of the circle on the opposite side. At the last possible moment and at full run, Joseph let out a roar as he leaped into the air and turned his body to face the center Sun Pole. White light blinded his vision. The tearing, searing pain from the skewers ripping free shot from his head to his toes. He heard the snapping sound they produced when the flesh gave way. He landed on his back, then rolled and felt himself fall, bouncing hard as he thumped to the kiva floor. Struggling to his side, Joseph could not regain his breath. He tried to breath, but his lungs would not expand. He watched as the even stones lining the wall of the kiva melted into blurred darkness and then miraculously took shape again as his breathing resumed in longer and longer rasping gasps.

Joseph rolled to his back staring up at the deep blue afternoon sky. He watched a single raven float high above on the thermals. A moment later, a second raven joined him. They circled and dodged each other playfully. Together they'd fly until one would veer off, fold its wings and spiral like a thrown football for a distance before spreading wings to regain control. They bobbed and weaved like airborne shadow-boxers in a no-contact bout. Joseph was no longer aware of his pain and exhaustion, his hunger and thirst. He lay staring up, then floating up. The ravens got closer. Joseph could see their ruffed necks and watch their beaks open slightly as they breathed. He looked directly into the eye of one raven until the second approached from behind. He looked into this one's eye too. The two birds flew off to the west and Joseph spread his own black wings and followed. They were losing him, leaving him behind. He opened his beak and coughed a loud, raucous caaw! The two ravens answered with croaking sounds of their own and returned. They flew in a three raven circle until Joseph felt tired, his wings refusing to flap until finally they folded against his body and he spiraled in a long slow arch. He gained speed and saw the earth rising fast. Don't crash! He thought. Stop the fall! With all his strength he opened his wings and soft landed on his feet.

Joseph lay in the bottom of the kiva. It was dark, cold dark. He drew his knees to his chest and wrapped his arms around his legs for warmth. Sleep arrived to take away his pain and thirst, his hunger, his exhaustion, his cold and discomfort. He remained in a black void until the sun rose over the desert as it has since the beginning of time. Joseph tried to sit up, but could not. His thirst was too great, his muscles too stiff to respond. He slept again.

Before he opened his eyes a second time, Joseph heard a rushing, roaring sound. Confused, he raised his lids to see an orange brown sky of billowing dust. The roar was the wind. Four feet below ground level, he was shielded from the power of the dust storm, but he could hear its ferocity. His tongue was swollen and dry. The first spattering rain drops felt cool, even cold on his dirt-crusted naked body. The rain kept pace with the increasing wind which was now deafening. Joseph opened his mouth, letting the rain quench his thirst. A trickle of water found its way over the stone lip of the kiva by Joseph's head. He squirmed the few inches toward it until he could tilt his head and sip from the thin stream. Starting to revive, Joseph lifted his head and saw how the rain was beginning to wash the orange dust from his skin, the dried blood from his wounds. He felt chilled again. He had to get out of the kiva. He had to get to his backpack.

Joseph forced himself to sit up. The bottom of the kiva was turning to mud. Grabbing a rock at the top of the kiva, he managed to stand. He put both hands on the wet stones and jumped. His chest felt on fire with the effort and he again lay on his side with his arms tightly folded across his bleeding chest. The pain subsided. Joseph crawled weakly across the Sun Dance circle. He passed the Sun Pole and saw the two wooden pegs attached to the cords hanging limply. The rain had washed the blood from them and they were once again bone white. At some point Joseph had lost his headband and now his hair hung wet over his face as he rummaged through the sodden pack for the bag of pemmican.

Lying on his side again, he placed a pemmican square in his mouth and chewed slowly. He ate another and felt strength return, felt warmth radiate out from his stomach to his arms and legs, then his hands and feet. He drank from a canteen and sat upright. The dust storm and rain had moved to the west being replaced by a pure, cloudless sky. He watched as the brown torrents moved over the desert and grew smaller and smaller until it was completely gone. The air fell still and silent. It warmed rapidly, soothingly.

Joseph was able to stand now. He found his moccasins in the backpack where he'd left them before beginning his Sun Dance. He sat and laced them. He ate a few more pemmican squares before stumbling home naked.

SEVENTEEN

This Desert Sunday was to be different. During the week Joseph had called Mae and Tom. His meat freezer was getting near empty. It was time for a refill. Joseph intended to hunt deer and asked if Tom and Mae wanted to come along. Both did.

They arrived at Joseph's house at two in the afternoon.

"This is a more civilized time of day for a get together," Mae said to Joseph when they took their usual places in Joseph's living room – Tom in a chair and Mae stretched out on the sofa.

Joseph laughed. "Civilized or not, there's a reason for you guys coming in the afternoon."

Tom said, "Yes, I was a little surprised when you wanted us here late instead of early. I was under the impression that hunters set out before sun up."

"That would have been my first choice, but when you see the road – trail really – that we have to drive, you'll see why I didn't want to be traveling before sun up."

Mae asked, "Where exactly are you taking us, Chief Joe?"

"It's an area I know on the reservation. We'll take an old supply road that hasn't been used in years to get there. It's a place I found a long time ago that nobody ever goes. Probably because it's just too hard to get to. It's near where the foothills to the mountains start. There are always deer there. Shouldn't be hard to bag one and be on our way home in no time."

Tom said, "The way you speak of it, the hunt sounds easy. I thought these things took planning and often days to accomplish."

Joseph chuckled, "You're not in New York anymore. This is the west. Mule deer aren't all that quick-witted. If you know where they hang out, you can usually spot them and get a shot. That's it. All over quick and easy. I suppose if you were out trophy hunting, you know, looking for a record buck with huge antlers to hang on the wall, that can be a different ball of wax altogether. Me, I'm a meat hunter. I kill to eat, not to brag."

"So you're not looking for a male to shoot?"

"Actually, I *am* looking for a buck. This time of year most of the does are pregnant. I don't want to kill two birds with one stone. A young buck would be ideal for eating."

"When does the deer season end?" Mae asked.

Again Joseph chuckled, "Well, technically it ended last weekend, but we'll be on the reservation and I'm an Injun, in case you hadn't noticed."

"Which means what exactly?" inquired Tom.

"It means, hunting seasons aren't really enforced on reservations when it comes to Indian residents who are hunting for food. If some guy from New Jersey shows up and gets caught, he'll be in trouble for sure, but nobody cares if a local is out in nature's supermarket checking out the meat department. Besides, nobody will see us."

"You're sure this is okay?" Mae asked again.

"Look, I'm not going to go hungry or be forced to buy beef pumped full of antibiotics and growth hormones just because of some arbitrary hunting dates set by a bunch of old white men for a bunch of white sportsmen."

Now it was Mae's turn to chuckle and shake her head, "Looks like we're in the company of a rebellious, angry savage. What do you think, Tom?"

"I think we should get our stuff ready and put some meat in Joseph's freezer."

Joseph smiled, "Good to know I'm in the company of at least one other *rebellious, angry savage.*"

Tom watched as Joseph selected a rifle from the standup rack. From the drawer underneath, he took out a box of shells.

"What kind of rifle is that?" Tom asked.

"It's not real pretty, but it gets the job done. This is a cut down U.S. Military 1903 Springfield, .30-06. The barrel's dated 1921. Somewhere along the line someone cut down the stock and put a recoil pad on it. They also changed the sights. Probably a depression era chop-job. Ruined a pretty valuable collector's item, actually. Now it's just a cheap shooter modern hunters wouldn't want."

"Another pawn shop purchase?"

"Yup, same place I got the .22 Winchester and the Bear bow. Paid ninety bucks for it."

"I don't know, but I suppose that's inexpensive for a deer rifle?"

"You can spend a couple grand easy for a nice big game rifle and scope. I had some beauties, but, as you know, they got stolen."

Joseph put the rifle in a zippered case and Tom followed him to the garage where he placed it next to a daypack in the small space behind the backseat of the Jeep. He then placed a heavy gauge aluminum hauling platform into the trailer hitch. "This thing is called a *hitch-haul*. It's handy 'cause there's not a lot of spare room in this rig. Plus, I can put game on it and not have to sponge blood out of the back or worry about it getting on the seats."

With a couple bungee cords Joseph secured a rolled tarp to the hitch-haul. "I put this around the deer for the drive home. Keeps the dust off."

Tom asked if there was anything he could do and Joseph said, "Not until we get a deer. Then you can help drag it to the Jeep. Aside from that, just enjoy yourself."

"I am already."

Joseph drove a few miles down the road from his house and turned onto little more than a twin-rutted trail through the desert. They could see the mountains twenty miles in the distance.

"We're on Jasper Road, even though there aren't any signs to say so. Some of this is going to be slow going, but we should get there in about an hour. Relax and enjoy the scenery."

From the back seat Mae said, "Relax? Are you kidding? I gotta hold on tight just to keep from being bounced out of this thing!"

Tom turned to her and uncharacteristically taunted, "Don't be such a sissy, Mae."

"Maybe we should switch seats Mr. Tough Guy!"

"Impossible, Mae. A simple matter of logistics, really. I wouldn't fit as well as you in that petite seat. Otherwise, you may be sure; I'd change seats with you as a matter of gentlemanly obligation."

All Mae could do was laugh and say, "In all my life, I never heard such a bunch of crap! And in case you're wondering, I am quite familiar with the concept of *noblesse oblige* and I don't think you have an ounce of it in your quasi-highfalutin pretentiousness!"

Joseph tossed in, "Well put, Mae. I'm impressed!"

Tom looked over the seat again and said, "Forgive me My Dear. I stand chastised and diminished."

"I should hope so too," she mumbled feigning annoyance just as the Jeep hit a rut and Mae left the seat by nearly a foot.

"Sorry, I didn't see that one till it was too late." All three couldn't help but laugh as barely ahead of their own dust they rumbled and bounced closer to the mountains.

With the gradual gain in elevation, the desert gave way to pine forest. Joseph stopped the Jeep. "Every time I've been here before I've seen deer around that bend up ahead. There's a small pond just beyond where they like to hang out."

Tom asked, "What do you want us to do?"

"Just wait here. The more people moving around, the more chances of spooking any game. I'm going to walk to that rocky outcropping," he pointed ahead. Mae and Tom nodded. "Then I'll take a little peek around and see if Mr. Buck is at home today. If I see anything, I'll wave and you'll know I'm going to try to get a shot."

Joseph went around the Jeep and lifted his daypack. He removed a compact holstered snub nose revolver and put it on his belt. "This is a finisher," he explained to Tom.

"If I shoot a deer and he's still alive when I get to him, I can shoot him in the head to finish him off. I hate to see an animal suffer."

Tom asked, "Why not just shoot him with the rifle?"

"Too powerful. It'd make a mess of things at such close range. The .38 Special does a neat, quick job of putting them out."

He put the pack on and cinched the shoulder straps. Next he unzipped the rifle case and opening the Springfield's bolt, inserted five cartridges into the magazine and one in the chamber. He closed the bolt over the five reserve rounds and flipped the safety on. He turned to Mae and Tom and said, "Hopefully this will be over in a few minutes and we can be on our way."

Joseph walked the few hundred yards ahead of the Jeep to the rocky outcropping he'd indicated before. When he was out of hearing Mae said to Tom, "This is the part I have mixed feelings about."

"I confess to being a little conflicted myself. I gather you've done this before."

"Twice."

"And how did you do the last times?"

"I did fine. There wasn't much for me to do. It was like this only in different places. I stayed back and Joseph went ahead."

"And?"

"And when it gets to this point, part of me wants there to be no game to shoot and part of me wants to join him in the kill."

"Interesting. That is exactly how I feel right now. I hate the thought of a beautiful, healthy animal being gunned down, but on the other hand, I understand everything Joseph has spoken about concerning hunting for food." He looked to Mae for approval but she was stone faced. "I also know how good those venison steaks taste!"

"Okay, I'm with you," she grinned, "Let's hope he can get a shot."

Tom quietly laughed with Mae and without thinking put his arm around her shoulders and pulled her gently to him. Mae responded by encircling his waist with both of her arms and giving him a hug before pulling away.

Joseph reached his place of concealment. His moccasins allowed him to move over the ground and rocks almost silently. He then flattened himself to the ground and with as little movement as possible carefully peeked around the base of the rocks. A moment later he waved to Mae and Tom before removing his pack and inching almost imperceptibly forward on his belly. A short time later he was out of sight around the rocks.

Mae took a step closer to Tom and again put her arms around his waist. She closed her eyes and rested the side of her head against his chest. Tom could feel her tension as he replaced his arm across her shoulders. Without opening her eyes she said, "This is the part I hate."

They stood motionless for what seemed like an eternity, but in reality was only a couple of minutes. As the shot rang out, Mae jumped and let out a soft "oh." She released her hold on Tom and said, "C'mon, let's see how he did." Before joining Joseph, Tom reached into the Jeep and removed the Randall knife from a small duffle he'd brought containing some snacks, water and a jacket. He hung it from his belt and the two of them walked to where they'd last seen Joseph, picking up the daypack he'd left behind.

Suddenly another, but less loud, shot broke the silence. Tom looked at Mae, "That must be the finishing shot Joseph mentioned."

"He didn't need one on the last two hunts," she said.

They rounded the bend and about two hundred yards further toward the boggy pond they saw Joseph bent over a tawny mound in the grass.

Mae said, "Give him a few minutes. Wait until he waves us down."

"What's he doing?"

"Apologizing."

"Can you explain?"

"It's what his father taught him. He apologizes to the deer for taking his life. He thanks it for the meat it will provide. I don't know whether it's an Indian thing or just something his father instilled in him, but I like it. Kinda makes everything alright."

"I agree."

In a minute they saw Joseph wave and they walked over to him. The deer was a three point buck. Joseph stood up and said, "He'll be good eating. I was tempted to shoot his buddy, though. Huge four point. Really massive rack. But this one is younger and will be more tender and less gamey. Still, he's big bodied for a three point."

"Well done, congratulations." Tom said.

"Thank you, sir," Joseph said taking the pack from Tom. He unzipped the main compartment and removed his Ruana knife, a folding saw and a couple of plastic bags.

"What can I do?" Tom asked.

For the first time Joseph noticed the Randall hanging from Tom's belt. "If you want to help, you'll need this," he said tossing the sheathed Ruana to him. "That knife you've got is a great military or survival knife, but for this kind of work, anything over a four to five inch blade will just get in the way. Self consciously Tom undid his belt and slid the Randall off, placing it in the daypack.

Looking at the Ruana he'd been tossed, Tom said, "I thought all of your stuff was stolen on your move from Montana."

"Most of it was, but the Ruana I always keep with me. It was in my travel duffle that night, so the sons-a-bitches who ripped me off never got it."

On a slight incline Joseph rolled the deer on his back, placing his head uphill. "We heard the finishing shot," Mae said. "Was your shot not good?"

"No, hit right where I wanted. See?" and Joseph pointed to a small hole just behind a front leg. "Perfect lung shot. About eighty to ninety yards. He ran another fifty before piling up. He was twitching when I got to him, basically dead, but I put a finisher in him to make sure."

"Tom, are you sure you want to do this? I can do it and you can watch, if you'd rather."

"No, just tell me what to do." He unsheathed the four inch blade Ruana.

"Okay, better roll up your sleeves. There are different ways to do this and all work about the same. What we want to do is remove all the guts from the body, just sort of hollow him out. Most people start at the bottom – I like to start at the top – but it doesn't matter really."

Joseph instructed Tom to hold the knife with the edge side up and how to cut along the breast bone and then down and around to the base of the tail. Once this was completed Joseph unfolded his saw and while Tom held the buck from rolling to the side, sawed easily through the rib cage and then the pelvis. "Now, reach in and grab the wind pipe." Tom did this. "Good. Now slice through the wind pipe and pull out and down on it."

Taking the knife from Tom he said, "Great, keep pulling and I'll cut away the connective tissue around the sides and back. Keep pulling; everything should come out into one gut pile. Just watch where you step and you'll stay pretty clean."

Just as Joseph said, the job was completed with little mess. With the deer gutted, Joseph rolled the deer on its stomach and splayed his four legs to keep it from shifting. "This will let any remaining blood drain out. One thing left to get," he said and moved his hand into the gut pile. Grabbing the heart he cut it away and held it in his hand. "Mae would you open a plastic bag, please."

She held the bag wide with her finger tips, not wanting to get blood on herself. Joseph dropped it in and Mae rolled the remaining bag around it before placing it in a second bag to avoid the possibility of blood leaking out. She placed the bagged deer heart in the bottom of the pack.

Joseph walked a little ways away and found a fallen tree limb. Using the folding saw he cut a four foot section and trimmed the branches off. Bringing it back to where the deer lay he said, "This will make hauling it back easy. Removing a short piece of rope from the pack, he tied the center of the limb to the antlers of the buck leaving about five feet of rope between. "There, that'll do," he said.

"I think we're about done. Mae, how 'bout some wipes?"

"Coming right up," she said rummaging in the pack for the yellow plastic container of moist baby wipes.

Joseph turned to Tom, "Best woods invention of all time – baby wipes!" He pulled a few for himself and in little time had clean hands. He held the container for Tom who did likewise. "Just because we're in the outdoors and hunting is no reason not to be clean," he said.

"In a thousand years, I'd have never thought to bring these. But couldn't we just wash off at the pond?" Tom asked.

"You'd be up to your ankles in mud before you got to the water."

"Right. I think I'll stick with the baby wipes."

"I never go without them. There's always a container or two of these in the jeep."

"It's refreshing to be in such civilized company," Mae threw in and they all laughed.

Joseph wiped down the saw and knife, placing them back in the pack. Next he slid the holstered revolver from his belt and placed that in the pack too. Picking up the Springfield, he removed the remaining cartridges and dumped them into a zippered side pouch. "I think we're ready," he said as he shouldered the pack and tightened the straps. "Mae, if you'd pull the Jeep up as far as you can, Tom and I can drag Mr. Buck there and meet you."

"Not a problem," she said taking the keys and unloaded rifle from Joseph. Without another word she began her short walk back the way they'd come.

"See you in a few minutes," he said to her back.

Joseph and Tom went to the deer and Joseph said, "It should be bled out by now," and he rolled the buck on his side. They picked up the tree limb that Joseph had tied to the antlers and stood between it and the buck. "This will make dragging easy," Joseph said as side by side they held the limb in the crux of their elbows and began to walk.

Tom said, "You're right, this is easy."

"It sure beats dragging alone. Feels ten times as heavy with just a rope over your shoulder."

"I really appreciate you allowing me to assist you in the field dressing," Tom said. "This is all quite a new experience for me."

Joseph laughed, "No, it's I who appreciates the help. You did fine. It was a nice end to a good hunt."

Tom said nothing for a minute as they dragged the deer together. Then he spoke, "It's hard for me to believe that last year at this time I was living with Sue in New York and teaching Brit. Lit. at Laurel College."

"Yeah, life has a way of changing on you quick. I think we all know that feeling."

"I prefer when the change is for the positive. Like this."

"Don't we all!"

Mae arrived with the Jeep just as Tom and Joseph brought the deer to the rutted trail. Joseph spread the tarp over the hitch-haul and they lifted the buck on top. The covering was spread over him and bungeed into place.

Getting into the driver's seat Joseph said, "It doesn't get much easier than that. Let's head home."

An hour later Tom helped Joseph hang the deer to cool in Joseph's garage. "I'll let him hang for a few days and then cut and wrap. Always a good feeling to know the freezer's full," Joseph said.

Back in the house Mae was busy in the kitchen. She'd unwrapped the deer heart, washed it out thoroughly and was cutting it into thin strips. Next to her on the counter was a glass mixing bowl full of seasoned flour.

Tom asked, "What culinary exotica have we in store, might I be so bold as to ask?"

Joseph said, "I'll interpret that for you Mae. I think he means to ask, 'so, watcha fixin?'"

"Actually I prefer Tom's rendition," she smiled to them both. "I'm preparing fried deer heart a la Chef Joe."

Tom said, "I've never eaten any kind of heart, much less deer heart."

"Well, you're in for a treat. Joseph showed me this recipe the first time I went deer hunting with him. It's kind of a tradition now. He hangs the deer while I cook the heart."

"Sounds like a good tradition," Tom said.

Joseph put on some classical guitar music and asked, "What can I get you two?"

Mae responded, "I've got a Diet Coke going here. I'm fine."

"Tom?"

"What are you having?"

"Coors."

"Sounds good to me. I'll have one too, if you have enough…"

"Always have enough." Then added, "It's good to have a beer with you again."

Tom smiled to his friend, "Joseph, I was just thinking the same thing."

EIGHTEEN

Mae pulled the Taurus in front of Tom's house. As usual, he was waiting and immediately walked to the passenger side and got in.

"God, it's cold out!" Mae said as Tom closed the door.

"I believe it is February twenty-sixth," Tom said looking at his watch, "And precisely five-O-two AM. Judging by that information Mae, I contend it is quite normal for the expectation of frigid temperatures."

"You're such a pompous ass!"

"I think that is particularly unkind of you, Mae. I'm only trying to be informative and helpful."

"You're trying, and succeeding I might add, to be a jerk."

"This treatment is painful, especially for someone as sensitive as me."

"As *I,* as sensitive as *I,* not *as sensitive as me.* Are you really a Ph.D. in English?"

"That was merely a test for you, and I'm happy to say, you passed. I laid that trap to gauge your level of alertness this morning. I'm delighted to see you actually are awake and functioning at a reasonably high level."

"Bullshit! You just slipped. The eloquent Dr. Thomas Sloan was actually caught in a grammatical faux pas. Admit it, you fucked up and got caught."

"Okay, you got me, but at least it woke you up and got your clever mind working."

Mae laughed, "My mind's always working."

"I never doubt that," Tom joined in her laughter. "Seriously, if you're tired and want me to drive, I will."

"No, thanks, I'm okay. Had a late one last night, though. Working on taxes. Didn't quit 'till midnight. I gotta get more sleep than this. It would be almost worth going on another deer hunt just to be able to show up at Joseph's later in the day."

"I don't know. I sort of look forward to these drives before sun up. It's so peaceful and quiet. No other cars. The stars still out. Alone with the best looking woman in Lunden…"

"Cut the crap, it's too early in the morning for this. I need coffee, not false compliments."

"I'm sure Joseph's brewing some as we speak."

"He better be or I'm turning around and going home."

"To work on taxes?"

"You got a point there. Okay, I'll stay with you two."

"And one more thing Mae – "

What's that?"

"I don't give false compliments."

"You're a sweetheart."

Tom smiled in the dark, reached forward and turned the heat up another notch. "We should be there in another minute and you can have your coffee."

"Yup, I can almost smell it now," Mae said as she drove around the last curve before Joseph's house. Then she said, "Oh, shit!"

"What's wrong?"

"I don't see any lights on in the house. The Jeep's parked in front. Don't tell me he slept in. I hope he didn't get drunk last night and pass out. I'm not in the mood for this."

Mae pulled in front of the dark house saying, "I'm about ready to turn around…"

"Hold it, Mae. Back up a little, I thought I saw something in the headlights."

Mae turned the wheel and backed up a few feet. "There! Stop the car."

Tom was out and running before Mae had the Taurus in park. He was bending over something by the side of the house. Mae's stomach did a quick turn. "Oh no, oh please God no," she whispered aloud as she got out of the car.

Joseph was lying on his side with his knees pulled up and his arms folded over his chest. Tom felt his forehead and was shocked by the cold, clammy feel. Mae arrived a moment later. "Get a blanket, quick!"

Mae ran to the house. The front door wouldn't budge. "It's locked!" she screamed.

"Check the Jeep. Keys might be in it."

Mae ran back to the Jeep. "Got 'em," she yelled and was in and out of the house in an instant. "Here put this around him," she said spreading the Pendleton Hudson's Bay wool blanket she'd snatched from Joseph's bed.

"He's hurt bad, Mae. I can't tell what's wrong. He's not conscious. Drive up closer so I can see."

As the headlights got closer, Tom saw the blood in the sand around Joseph. Then he saw the front of his white shirt also soaked in blood. Mae returned and they covered him in the blanket. Mae bent over him, cradling his head in her arms, and kissed his head.

Mae, we have to get him to the hospital right now."

She reached for her phone. I'll call 911 for an ambulance."

"No time for that. We can't wait for them to get here. We have to get him in the car."

"Is it safe to move him?"

"I don't know, but we don't have any choice. I'll get the tarp from the garage. We can roll him on that and lift him into the backseat. Keep him on his side."

Tom ran through the house to the garage and found the rolled tarp. He scrambled back, unfurled it and tucked the edge of the tarp under Joseph's side. "Okay now, we have to roll him on his back. Take his shoulders and I'll stretch out his legs. Real slow now…"

Joseph let out a low groan as he rolled onto the tarp. "Oh god, I'm so cold," Joseph sighed barely audibly.

"Tom! He's conscious."

"I heard him. Good. We have to keep him awake and talking. I'll grab the two ends of the tarp where you are – that's the heaviest part. You take the ends by his feet. I'll walk backwards and climb into the backseat with him. We can do this. Move slow and try not to bounce him around. On the count of three we lift, then follow me. One… two… three…"

Joseph moaned as his head and shoulders made it smoothly to the rear seat with Tom gently pulling on the tarp to slide him in all the way. "Mae, you're going to have to bend his legs a little to shut the door." She did. "Good. I'll get on the floor in front of him. Can you move the passenger seat up as far as it'll go?"

Mae did as Tom said, got in the drivers seat and hit the gas. "Better move it Mae – we need to get him there fast."

Tom could feel the Taurus fishtail on the dirt road. "Easy Mae. Stay in control."

"Tom, oh shit, it hurts so bad." Joseph managed to say.

"I know it does. Just stay with me, Joseph. Don't fall asleep. We're getting you to the hospital. Stay with me now. Talk to me, Joseph."

"Okay, I'm here. I'll try to stay awake. It hurts so bad though."

"Who did this to you?"

"Roger… that… son-of-a-bitch."

"Roger?"

Joseph grimaced with the pain, then seemed to relax a little. "I was at the Cactus Saloon. Stephanie was there. Remember Stephanie? Gloria's friend?"

"Yes, I remember her."

"She got rid of Alvin, so I moved in. We had a few drinks. I left to go take a leak. When I got back Roger was in my seat trying to take over. Stephanie wanted him to leave her alone, but he wouldn't. I came back to the table and told him to fuck off. He wanted to take it out to the parking lot… Oh Christ Tom, I hurt so bad. Oh shit, oh shit it hurts."

"Hang on Joseph. Just a little longer."

Joseph started to lose consciousness again. "Joseph – Joseph! Stay with me. C'mon buddy, wake up. Stay with me.

"I'm here. I'm just so tired Tom, I'm so tired…"

"Wake up now, Joseph. C'mon, talk to me. What happened with Roger? Keep talking."

"He wanted to… fight me, but I had… other things on my mind." Tom thought he saw the corners of Joseph's mouth upturn in a faint smile.

"Go on. Then what happened. Talk to me, Joseph."

"I told him I'd fight him another day and he left. A little while later Stephanie followed me... back to... my place... in her... car." Joseph began to fade again.

"Mae, step on it, we're losing him!"

"I can't go any faster. We'll crash!"

"Okay, hold steady Mae, just keep driving."

"Joseph! Joseph! Stay with me now!" Tom yelled at him, but he got no response. Tom slapped his face with his open hand and Joseph returned. "Joseph, you gotta stay with me. You gotta stay awake. C'mon now, keep talking."

"Okay... When we got... to my place... Roger was... there... waiting. I... got out of the Jeep. Stephanie saw him and... didn't want... any trouble... so she drove off. I was pissed... and went up to Roger. I was going... to... kick his ass good... but he pulled a pistol... and... shot me. Tom, he fuckin'... gut shot... me. He..."

"C'mon Joseph, we're almost there. Stay with me. Talk to me!"

"I'm so cold. Oh God, it hurts so bad..."

"Talk to me, Joseph."

"He... Roger... must have thought I... was dead 'cause he... drove off. That's... all. Then you and Mae... you and Mae... you..." Joseph's tense and pain-wracked expression slowly relaxed.

"Joseph! Joseph!"

Tom felt for a pulse. There was none.

"Joseph!" No response. He slapped his face. Nothing. He slapped again.

"Mae, he's gone."

"No!"

"We lost him, Mae."

"No. We have to get him to the hospital!"

Tom felt the car slide on the gravel as Mae accelerated. "Stop the car, Mae."

Mae did not answer or slow the car.

"Mae!" Tom yelled, "Stop the car, now!"

He could hear her sobs as the car slowed and finally came to a stop.

"Put it in park and get in the other seat."

Mechanically, Mae did what Tom asked. Tom changed places with her and adjusted the seat rearward so he could drive.

Weakly, Mae said, "We have to get him to the hospital or police station or somewhere…"

"No. Not yet anyway."

Tom put the Ford in gear and turned the car around. A couple of miles back the way they'd come he pulled off on a dirt side-trail that had no tire tracks on it and drove for a few minutes. Then he stopped the car, turned off the lights and engine. "I need to think," was all he said.

Mae tried to speak through her tears, but he held up his right hand and calmly said, "Just give me a few minutes."

She stared at him, not saying a word. The sun had just broken the horizon and in the first rays of the day, Mae watched Tom's expressionless face. He sat with both hands on the wheel, his eyes closed. As he thought, Mae could see his lips move slightly from time to time as if he were speaking to someone. Occasionally, almost imperceptibly, she'd see him nod his head as if he had made a decision only to shake it slightly in rebuttal. Minutes passed. Mae looked into the backseat. Joseph looked asleep. Maybe he's not dead… But she knew he was.

Tom released his hold on the wheel. He looked at Mae. "Do you trust me, Mae? Really trust me?"

Mae looked at Tom blankly. She seemed to be in thought herself now. Then she said, "Yes. Completely."

"Do you trust me enough to do exactly as I say and not question me or ask why?"

She looked into Tom's face and eyes. His expression was intense, but controlled.

"I'll do whatever you say."

"Okay. Listen to me carefully. If we take Joseph to town, we'll be mired in this for weeks. We'll tell the sheriff what Joseph said about Roger. Then Roger's *lawyer* will claim Roger acted in self defense. He'll say Joseph pulled a knife or gun on him first. Consider this; Roger owns a business in town and everyone knows him and relies on him to repair their cars. Joseph is just an Indian from Montana renting a house on the reservation. He drinks and fights and white girls love him. So, who are they going to believe?" Tom knew he was speaking about Joseph in the present tense, but couldn't bring himself to use the past. He was sure Mae picked up on it too, but wasn't going to correct him.

"What are you saying, Tom?"

"I didn't know Joseph as long as you did, but I loved him like a brother. I'm not going to let him die like this without any justice. I can take care of this in one day, if you'll help me. But we have to act deliberately and you have to do exactly as I say."

There was still no response from Mae. "Either trust me on this or not. It's up to you, Mae."

Again, she looked into his face. "I trust you, Tom. What do you want me to do?"

Tom drove the Taurus back to Joseph's house. On the way, Mae mainly listened. "First thing we're going to do is bury Joseph."

"Where?"

"In the kiva. Nobody knows about it. The kiva is a fitting resting place for Joseph. It's where he'd want to be buried." Tom thought a moment, "What we're going to do is what he'd want, but would never ask of us."

In what seemed like no time, the Ford pulled in front of the house. Tom and Mae picked up the corners of the tarp and gently pulled and lifted Joseph from the backseat.

They carried him a short ways from the car. Tom said, "We'll roll him in the blanket and I'll carry him down to the kiva."

"Not yet," Mae said and disappeared into the house. A few moments later she returned with Joseph's medicine pouch and moccasins. She slipped the leather thong around his neck and placed the pouch on his chest.

"Help me pull those boots off him," she said.

Tom carried them into the house while Mae laced Joseph's mocs. Then she knelt over his head, bent down and kissed his forehead.

"Oh Joseph," she whispered.

Tom returned. "Mae, we have to act fast. I don't want this to drag on any longer than necessary. This is the only time we'll have to say goodbye to Joseph. If you want a minute alone, I'll leave you."

"No. I've had my minute."

"Are you sure?"

"Yes. Let's just get on with it."

"Okay. I know you're still in shock, even though you may not be aware of it. There will be plenty of time to grieve, to come to grips with this whole thing, but now is *not* that time. Now is the time for clear thinking. Are you sure you can do this, Mae? Are you sure you are okay?"

"I wouldn't be if I were alone, Tom. I can do this with you."

Tom nodded his head. "Mae, when I was in the house I wrote a short list of things I want you to get from my house." He handed a house key and the scrap of paper to Mae. "You'll probably need some fresh clothes too."

Mae looked at the list, "Okay."

"I'm going to bury Joseph in the kiva while you're gone. After you pick up the things at my place and yours, drive to a store at least twenty or thirty miles from Lunden – some place where no one will recognize you. Wear sunglasses too. Buy a bunch of little things, snack food, cosmetics, anything you can think of. Also – and this is the important thing – buy two prepaid cell phones and a couple of those five-hour energy drinks. The other stuff will draw attention away from the phones. Pay with cash and throw the receipt out when you leave the store. I'm probably being over cautious, but better cautious than sloppy. If you see anyone who might recognize you, go somewhere else. Can you do that?"

"Yes. Of course."

"Good. Then before you come back here, fill up your tank with gas. Pay cash." Tom reached for his wallet, but Mae held up her hand, "I have money."

"Help me roll Joseph in the blanket, Mae. Then you better be off."

Tom lifted Joseph and settled him over his right shoulder. He squatted and with his left hand, picked up a shovel he'd found in the garage. Tom never noticed the weight he was carrying, nor was he aware of the distance he trudged to his destination. Lost in his own thoughts, Tom felt no fatigue, only purpose and determination.

He placed the rolled red blanket at the edge of the kiva. Then he removed Joseph's matt and the three folding camp chairs from under the nearby tarp and carried them down the ladder and placed them in the bottom. He spread the matt before climbing out. Again he lifted the rolled blanket to his shoulder and stepped down the ladder. He gently placed Joseph on the matt. "Goodbye, my friend," was all he said before returning up. Tom pulled the ladder from the kiva and dropped it back down sideways next to Joseph. Lastly, he folded the tarp and let it slide down the stone side to the bottom of the kiva. Tom looked around. There was nothing else but the pile of excavated orange dirt by the side of the kiva that Joseph had dug one trowel at a time during his Sun Dance. Tom took a handful of the sand and let it fall through his fingers to the blanket below. He stood for a moment looking into the kiva until the tiny dust cloud settled, but said nothing. Then he picked up the shovel.

Half way back to the house, Tom saw Mae sitting on a flat rock. Walking up to her Mae said, "Is it done?"

"Yes. The chairs and tarp are buried too. You'd never know there was anything there."

Mae wiped a tear from her cheek, "Sorry," she said.

"No need to be sorry. This isn't easy on me either. Why didn't you walk the rest of the way?"

"I didn't want to see…" Mae wiped her eyes again, "I want to remember the… that place, as it was in happy times – with the three of us sitting in the sun – you know?"

"I do know. It was smart of you to stay here."

"I thought so too."

They began walking to the house. Tom asked, "Did you get everything from my place?"

"Yes, everything."

"And the phones?"

"Not a problem. Store was almost empty. I bought the energy drinks with a bunch of little stuff and paid with cash. The cashier never even looked at me. I filled up with gas on the way here too."

"Good job. I'm proud of you."

"I didn't do much. And I'm not going to ask anything. Just tell me what you want me to do."

"First thing is to get back to the house. I need to look around a bit. There are a few things I need to get ready too."

While Mae lay down on the sofa for a moment, Tom searched the garage. He took note of another, smaller shovel, the hitch-haul leaning against the wall, gasoline cans and a kerosene lamp. Back outside in front of the house Tom looked down at the bloody tarp Joseph had lain upon in the Taurus. He pulled it over to the blood spot in the sand where they'd found Joseph. He flipped the tarp over and dragged it bloody side down to the concrete front steps. Along the way any rocks and sticks picked up Joseph's blood from the tarp. Tom made sure plenty got on the steps. He then carefully folded the tarp with the blood side in and walked around the garage where he hosed it off and played the hose over the ground until there were no traces of the washed-off blood. For good measure, from a hundred yards away he shoveled some sand into a bucket and scattered it over the hosed spot. By this time, the tarp which had been spread in the sun was nearly dry.

Next, Tom drove the Jeep to the garage where he secured the hitch-haul in the trailer hitch and bungeed the rolled tarp on it as Joseph had done before their deer hunt. He put the two shovels in the back of the Jeep along with the small duffel Mae had brought from Tom's place. It was time for stage two.

Tom found Mae stretched out on the sofa with her eyes closed. "Are you asleep?" he said tentatively.

"No. Just resting."

"Mae, let me explain what we need to do next. You're going to play a pivotal role in this, but I know you can handle it. You're going to need to put everything that's happened out of your mind while you do this. You have to be calm and act as if it's just another day."

"I'll try, Tom. Just tell me what to do. I want this over with – whatever it is."

Tom took his usual chair facing Mae. It seemed odd to be here talking to Mae without Joseph either with them or in the kitchen. Maybe Joseph was with them in some way, Tom thought, but now was not the time to start thinking along those lines. When he knew he had Mae's full attention, he explained what she must do and how she must do it.

Tom had her do a few short role plays until he was confident in her ability to get the job done. Mae could be charming and persuasive. She'd do well.

"Alright, let's get this show on the road," Tom said and made an attempt at a lighthearted smile. "I'll take the Jeep. You follow behind. We'll have to go slow in places, but I think you'll make it fine. Just in case, I put a tow chain in the back of the Jeep, but we shouldn't need it."

"Okay, I'm ready. Let's go."

"And one more thing, Mae… Don't forget the phone."

Now it was Mae who gave up a smile, "I'll try not to."

Tom drove the Jeep with Mae following just out of his dust trail. He turned on to Jasper Road, the same one they'd driven on the way to hunt deer. Mae heard the Taurus bottom out crossing a few deep ruts, but she kept moving and was sure no damage had been done to her car. At least there were no sharp rocks jutting up, just hard packed dirt and sand.

Three miles in, Tom shut down the Jeep and walked back to Mae. "Okay, this is it. I'm going to drive the Jeep off a ways and out of sight. When I come back we'll make the call."

Before leaving, he raised the hood on the Ford and, from the underside, loosened the small lightbulb from its socket until it went out. "We'll leave the hood up. I'll be right back." And Tom drove Joseph's Jeep down Jasper Road and then veered off until Mae lost sight of him.

"Are you ready, Mae? We can practice again if you'd like."

"No, I'm ready. I can do this."

From a pocket in his jacket, Tom removed a page he'd torn out of Joseph's phone directory. He skipped the regular number and read out the one listed below it under "emergencies and after hours towing." Mae punched in the number on the first prepaid cell phone and waited. She heard it pick up.

"Roger's…"

"Is this Roger?" Mae began pleasantly.

"Yes it is, how can I help you?"

"Roger, this is Mae… you know, from The Oasis…"

There was a pause on both ends. For a moment, Tom worried that Mae might not be able to pull this off – that Roger would hang up.

"What do *you* want?"

"I'm in a little trouble here, Roger and I need your help."

"What makes you think I'd want to help you – especially on a Sunday?"

"Oh come on, Roger. I realize I haven't treated you very nicely and I'm sorry for that. But you know this is a small town and people talk."

"Yeah, well you didn't mind hanging around with that little Indian friend of yours and that New York dude."

"Roger, you have that all wrong," Mae glanced to Tom who nodded his approval. She continued, "Joseph helped me out my first day in Lunden – you remember that, you towed me in."

"Yeah, I remember."

"Well, I felt sorry for him. He didn't seem to have any friends. I felt I owed him for helping me out."

"Well, maybe," Roger hesitated as if trying for something to add. "What about that guy from New York?"

"Roger, I hardly know him. Besides he's married. He didn't know anyone in town and I was just trying to be friendly."

The line went quiet. Again Tom thought he might hang up, but he didn't. "So what kind of trouble are you in?"

"I was out for a hike and left the lights on in my car. The battery's dead. I just need a jump."

"So why don't you call your little Indian friend or that New York fella?"

Because you killed him, asshole. "Roger, the New York guy Tom drives a Porsche. He'd never take it off the pavement. I don't even think he'd have jumper cables and I don't have any. As for Joseph, he's probably sleeping off a drunk somewhere. I wouldn't ask him anyway. Come on Roger, I'll pay you double."

"You'd pay me double anyway, it's Sunday."

"Okay, I'll give you whatever you want. I'm out here all alone, Roger. Please help me. I just need to be jumped." Mae looked over at Tom when she said this part; sure Tom got the double meaning and hoping that Roger did too.

"You'll give me anything?"

Mae purposely waited a few seconds and then in a soft, almost husky voice said, "That's what I said – anything."

"I'm going to hold you to that, Mae."

"And I'm counting on that, Roger."

Another pause, "Where's your car?"

"I'm about three miles out Jasper Road. Do you know where that is?"

"I run a towing service. I know where every road is. What are you doing out there?"

"Like I said, I went for an early morning hike to take some photos and get some exercise. The sun came up while I was driving and I forgot the lights. I just need to be jumped."

"I can jump you."

"I'm sure you can."

"I'll be there in forty minutes."

The line went dead. Mae looked at Tom who was nodding again. "You handled that perfectly, Mae. I'm really proud of you. That was no less than an Oscar winning performance."

"I was a little worried once or twice. I thought he might hang up on me, but it worked like we planned. Now what?"

"That was your part to play Mae, and you did a superb job. Now the rest is up to me. I only hope I can do as well."

"You're sure you know what you're doing?"

"As much as anyone can predict the future, yes, I think so. I've been going over this in my mind for a couple hours now and I'm as ready as I'll ever be."

"For what it's worth Tom, I've got complete confidence in you." Mae gave Tom a quick hug. "Whatever you're planning, I'm sure you'll do what you think needs doing."

"I'll do my best," he said almost offhandedly – then said, "Look Mae, when Roger shows up, just act like I'm not here. He needs to get out of his truck and walk over to your car. So stay by the car. Make him come to you. I'm pretty sure he won't bring the big tow truck…"

"Why do you say that," Mae interrupted him.

"Because he thinks he only needs to jump your dead battery. He can do that with his own pickup. He won't want to waste a lot of gas on a fuel guzzling tow truck. Plus, he wants to impress you. Everyone knows how he babies that pickup of his. I've never seen it unpolished. He'll want to show up looking cool, not like some grease monkey in a towing rig."

Mae looked at Tom in amazement. "You have all that figured out in advance?"

"Well, yes. I guess I do. I've got a lot figured out. We can't afford to make any mistakes."

"I'm feeling better about all this already."

"Just don't be too sure of yourself. Remember, this guy wants to jump more than your dead battery. Keep some distance from him," Tom said very seriously, "Even after I show up. No matter what, stay far away from us."

"Okay, what ever you say. Where will you be when he arrives?"

"See that clump of cactus by those boulders?" Tom said pointing to an area about fifty yards away.

"Yes."

"Roger will arrive in this direction and pull in here." Tom said sweeping his arm to show Mae how he envisioned the truck pulling in. "He knows he's going to jump the battery so he'll pull in very close to your car. While he's getting out of his pickup I want you to get to the other side of your car. I want you on the opposite side of the car from him. This is really important. Do you understand, Mae?"

"I do, yes."

"At this point, I show up at the dance and ruin all his plans."

Tom looked at his watch. "This guy's hot to trot. If he says he'll be here in forty minutes, I bet he makes it in thirty. We'll see his dust long before he arrives, but I'm not taking any chances. He might suspect something and check things out with binoculars. I'm going to wait behind those boulders." Tom turned and walked a few feet before turning back. "Don't worry. This will all be over soon. Things will be fine." He tried to smile, but the attempt was less than heartfelt.

At exactly twenty-seven minutes from the time the phone line went dead, Mae saw a dust trail coming up Jasper Road. She stood by the driver's side door and forced herself to wave and smile as the pickup neared. The *pickup* Mae thought, just as Tom predicted. Not the Tow truck.

Roger pulled in exactly as Tom said he would. He shut down the motor and at the exact time he turned his head and reached for the door handle, Mae walked around to the passenger side. Roger was out of the truck. "So you left the lights on and now you've got a dead battery, huh?"

"Yes, like I said on the phone."

"You also said you'd pay me double."

"That's right."

"You said you'd give me anything I wanted."

"What do you want?"

"I want to get what's owed me before I jump the battery."

"That, sir, is not very cavalier or gentlemanly of you!"

Roger spun around and faced Tom. His confused look turned to a grin and then into loud laughter. He unzipped his nylon jacket and put both hands on his knees laughing. "Well, well, well. If it isn't the little chicken-shit from New York!" He looked over his shoulder at Mae. "What kind of bullshit setup is this, huh?"

Tom answered, "It's the same kind of bullshit setup you planned for my friend last night. You do remember, don't you?"

"I don't know what you're talking about."

"You're not very smart, are you Roger? You should have shot him again. Any idiot knows you don't leave a live victim behind. Victims heal up and turn into witnesses. That's when attempted killers go to jail."

Clearly befuddled, Roger stopped laughing and stammered, "Who told you this?"

"My best friend, Joseph Curley, told me how you waited for him in the dark and ambushed him. Then like the coward you are, you shot him and ran away."

Roger stared blank faced at Tom. A moment later a smile formed on his face. Another moment later he was laughing again. "Well, I guess you got me then, don't you Tommy-boy. I took care of your little red-nigger friend last night and figured I'd take care of you too at some point. This makes everything all the more convenient."

Roger began a slow, measured walk to where Tom was standing. Still smirking, he said over his shoulder to Mae, "This won't take long.

After I'm done with him it'll be your turn, bitch. And don't worry, I'll take more time with you."

Roger stopped three feet in front of Tom. The second he stopped Tom took two quick steps closer. They were inches apart. Tom stared into Roger's eyes above his foul-breath smile. Out of the corner of his left eye he saw Roger slowly move his right hand under his jacket. Tom made the same move knowing Roger would never notice.

"One thing you need to know, Roger." Tom whispered, "*Tommy* left a long time ago. It's Professor Thomas Sloan now."

In an awkward, jerky motion, Roger's right hand came up and around at the same time Tom's left arm rose sharply. The nine millimeter pistol discharged with a deafening explosion a foot to the left after Tom's blocking maneuver knocked Roger's arm aside. While Tom's left arm had come up to block Rogers draw, his right hand flashed from behind his back in an upward thrust. The Randall's eight inch blade found its way under the center of Roger's rib cage, slicing through lung and piercing his heart.

Almost instantly Roger's knees buckled and the Glock pistol dropped from his grasp. Tom felt a warm flow wash over his fist, but he maintained his firm grasp on the Randall, holding Roger's full weight upright by the imbedded knife. Tom stared straight into Roger's half-opened lifeless eyes. Only then did he step back and pull the blade free. Roger fell limply, face down on the desert sand.

Mae walked around her car with both hands in front of her mouth, as if trying to muffle a silent scream. She stood next to Tom and stared down at Roger.

Holding the dripping Randall point down, Tom said, "Are you okay, Mae?"

Mae looked up at him and dropped her hands from her face, "Yes, I'm fine." She said. "But I thought you'd been shot when the gun went off. Did you know he had a gun?"

"Yes, I knew."

"How could you know that? Did you see it?"

"No, but stupid people are predictable and transparent. Roger's been in too many fights to be that confident with an adversary he knows nothing about. He told you, 'this wouldn't take long.' That telegraphed to me he was armed. Besides, he wouldn't come all the way out here without a gun. He would have used it to threaten you to get what he wanted if it came to that. That's why I stepped so close to him. If I was further away he'd draw his gun and point it straight at me. By getting that close I could easily block his shooting hand. I also had to be close to use the knife."

"So you planned it this way?"

"Yes."

"And you knew how to throw that block that knocked his gun aside?"

"I'd never done it before, of course, but I saw something like it at a cage fight once. It was a game changer. Thinking that move might come in handy some time, I memorized it."

"What if your block hadn't worked and he shot you?"

"Then, I'm afraid you'd be in a great deal of danger."

"No I wouldn't."

"Mae, I don't even want to think of what he had in store for you."

"I'd have had to go to *my* plan. Plan B."

"Your plan? What do you mean *Plan B*?"

Mae reached into the pocket of her jacket. Pulling out Joseph's snub nose .38 *finisher*, Mae said, "This was Plan B. If you didn't succeed in whatever you had planned, I'd have shot that motherfucker before he'd ever lay a hand on me."

"I see," Tom said, obviously impressed. "Do you have any more questions for me?"

"One more. What if he didn't have a gun?"

"That would have made killing him less risky."

"You'd have killed an unarmed man?"

"Yes. He gunned down Joseph who was unarmed. This is simple justice."

"Tom, you realize we just took the law into our own hands? If we get caught, that same law will crucify us."

"Being neutral between right and wrong only serves wrong."

"Did you just come up with that?"

"Unfortunately not. The credit for that simple truth belongs to Theodore Roosevelt."

"I think he makes sense."

Tom looked down at his blood-covered hand and knife. "Mae, do you know *why* there are serial killers?"

She looked at him strangely, not knowing where he was going with this and said simply, "No. Why?"

"Because they are smart. If serial killers weren't smart, they'd be one-time killers found guilty and they'd rot in prison." He waited for a response from Mae that did not come. He concluded by saying, "Serial killers do this all the time. We need to do it just once."

"That doesn't make it lawful."

"In Joseph's case, I'm going by his definition of *Indian law*. Roger murdered Joseph in cold blood – ambushed him in the dark after he'd been drinking and shot him. I believe with all my heart he deserved everything he got."

"I agree, he got what he deserved," she said, "and it was self defense, even if it was preplanned."

"Then I take it you are with me on this?"

"A little late for this discussion. Besides we've already had it. I knew something like this was going to happen. How could it not? I wanted it as much as you. I'm okay with it," she said adding, "I'm better than okay with it."

Taking her measure, Tom said nothing – just nodded slightly.

"So that's settled for now and forever," she said. What's the rest of your plan?"

"I can't do anything until I clean up. If you would be so good as to get the Jeep and drive it here, I believe it contains the baby wipes I require. Keys are in the ignition."

"Be right back, Professor Sloan."

From a canteen Mae poured water over Tom's hand and knife. He finished cleaning up with the baby wipes and told her to put them in her car. Drying his hands on his jeans, Tom said, "Now we have some work to do."

Walking a few feet away, he picked up the Glock, dropped the magazine into his hand and silently counted the rounds in it, remembering to add one for the cartridge in the chamber. He replaced the magazine and put the gun on the seat in the truck. He opened the glove box and was pleased to find a half full green box of Remington 9mm ammunition. Next he removed a thin screwdriver, put it in his jacket pocket and said to Mae, "Hold your ears, this is going to be a bit loud," and pointing the pistol at the ground, fired off all but two of the remaining rounds in the Glock. Tom then placed the gun under the seat in the truck and locked the doors. He turned to Mae who still had her hands over her ears. "Sorry about that, but it was necessary. Now, can you help me find the fired casings? Point them out to me, but don't touch any."

Tom pulled a plastic bag from the Jeep. Mae found the first ejected brass case. "Here's one," she said.

"Good." Tom walked over to where she was pointing and removing the screwdriver from his pocket, placed the tip in the hollow casing, picked it up and put it in the bag. The rest of the shells were close by and Tom treated each one the same. "We'll need these later," he said. Mae didn't ask any questions.

Unfastening the tarp Tom said, "Now for the work." He unfurled the tarp and spread it next to Roger's body. Grabbing Roger's belt and arm, Tom rolled him onto it. "I can help with that," Mae said.

"No. Thanks Mae, but you don't need to do this. I've got it. You can lock your car though."

Mae did not argue. Reaching under the tarp with a few quick lifts, Tom had the body rolled. He dragged the bundle to the back of the Jeep, scooped it up, and with one lift put it on the Jeep's hitch-haul. Mae couldn't help but be impressed with the quickness of Tom's work, not to mention his strength. He finished by wrapping a few bungee cords and said simply, "Let's go."

With surprising calm, Tom drove the Jeep carefully and slowly. He said, "We don't want any mechanical problems out here. This is rough going even for a Jeep. We'll just take it slow and easy. We don't have too far to go."

"Where are you taking him?" Mae asked and absently pointed over her shoulder.

"On the deer hunt Joseph pointed out where the reservation land started. We'll go there. It's just up ahead. That's the last place anyone would search for Roger's body." Tom let out a short grunt and said, "Not that anyone's going to be searching for a body."

A few minutes later Tom turned the Jeep off the trail and drove a short way over the rough desert before coming to a stop.

"This will do," he said.

Climbing out of the Jeep, Tom handed Mae the smaller of the two shovels he'd brought. "We still have a couple hours of daylight left. We'll bury him here."

The sandy orange dirt dug easily. In an hour's time they were down nearly three feet. Taking a breather, Mae panted, "How deep are we going to go?"

"Just another foot should do it. We don't want any animals digging him up and dragging him around."

"That's not such an unpleasant thought," Mae said.

"True, but this isn't a time for emotions. Right now, I don't want any trace of anything to be found, unless we want it found."

Mae wasn't sure what Tom meant by that last bit, but decided to continue digging instead of asking.

Fifteen minutes later Tom said, "Enough. This is good."

He unhooked the bungee cords, lifted the concealed body and carried it the short distance to the hole. Instead of dropping it in, he placed it next to Roger's final resting place, grabbed the edge of the tarp and walked backward, unrolling the body.

Surprised at this, Mae asked, "Why not just throw him in?"

"I don't want anything to protect the body or prolong decomposition."

Tom quickly emptied Roger's pockets, placing the contents in a pile – his wallet, cigarettes, lighter, a folding knife and some change. Unbuckling and pulling off his belt, Tom put the empty leather holster in the pile along with Roger's cell phone. Then, with one quick shove, Roger slid into the hole face down.

Looking in Tom said, "That seems fitting."

In a short time the hole was filled. "What about this?" Mae asked, pointing to Roger's stuff.

Tom pulled another plastic bag from the Jeep. "You'll see," he said, putting the items in. He folded the tarp, bloody side in, and secured it to the hitch-haul. "We're done here. Let's go."

Tom drove back to Jasper Road, which this far in was little more than a track, and stopped the Jeep. He pulled a broom from the Jeep and walked a short way back from where they'd pulled off. Mae saw him walking backwards, lightly sweeping the dirt with long back and forth strokes.

Tossing the broom in the rear of the Jeep and beginning the drive back, Mae asked, "What was that all about?"

"Just covering our tire tracks. Nobody needs to see where someone pulled off the trail. That's not going to happen anyway, but as I said before, I'm overly cautious."

Again, Mae could not help but be impressed with Tom's keen ability to think clearly – to protect them. "Now what?" she asked.

He brought the Jeep to a stop. "Now we dig one more little hole. This will only take a minute."

Once more Tom took a shovel and walked off a short way. He dug a shallow pit, returned and removed the folded tarp from the hitch-haul.

"I'm just going to get rid of this. Be back in a jiffy."

Another mile down the road, Tom repeated the previous hole digging. This time he emptied the contents of the plastic bag, smashing the cell phone with his heel before kicking it into the pit and covering it with dirt and rocks.

As the sun was setting with red and yellow streaks across the western horizon, Tom pulled the Jeep next to the pickup and Mae's Ford.

"Mae, I want you to drive the Jeep back to Joseph's. I'll follow in Roger's truck."

"What about my car?"

"We'll come back for that soon. We need to get going. I'll be right behind you."

Roger's bright yellow 4X4 pickup started with a low, guttural roar. Looking around the dash, Tom noticed an expensive after-market Bose stereo and about every option one could add to an already loaded and top-of-the-line GM truck. He was glad to see the fuel gauge showing three quarters full. An extra row of headlights across the cab roof gave the rig a no-nonsense appearance. This is perfect, Tom thought as he pulled out and followed Mae's dust trail in the rapidly darkening desert.

"Mae, we only need about fifteen minutes here and then we'll be on our way."

"Just tell me what I can do."

"Okay. You can drive the Jeep into the garage."

Mae did this as Tom walked to where Joseph had lain all night in the cold. His anger at Roger rose briefly, but he pushed it back down. Now was not the time for such thoughts. Besides, Tom realized with satisfaction, Roger had been dealt with.

Mae came around the house. Tom said, "Hold your ears one more time." He reached into his pocket and pulled the Glock. He fired two quick rounds directly into the blood spot on the ground. Turning to Mae he said, "We'll leave those fired cases for the Sheriff to find."

Walking into the house with Mae following, Tom turned on a light. "If there's anything of yours here, now is the time to retrieve it."

Mae picked up her moccasins and Tom's too. "Just these."

"If there's anything you want, take it now."

Patting her own jacket pocket she said, "I'll keep Joseph's finisher. He'd like that."

Tom walked to the fireplace and took down the Bear target bow and quiver. "I'll take this and," picking up Joseph's Ruana knife from the mantle, "this." Looking to Mae he said, "You're right. He'd want us to have these things. Would you put them in the pickup? I need a few minutes on the computer."

She didn't answer. Mae gathered their mementos and walked out in the dark. Tom booted up Joseph's computer. The old dialup internet was frustratingly slow, but Tom was none-the-less glad for it. It would pay off later.

While the computer warmed, Tom went outside, turned on the hose and pulled it to Roger's truck. "Mae, I'm going to wet the truck down. As soon as I'm done, I want you to drive it around fast. Hit the breaks and make it skid. Just do whatever you can to get it dusty and dirty. Be back in five minutes."

Mae sped off in Roger's soaked truck, spinning gravel as she left. He could see her break lights flash as she slammed on the breaks, skidding as he'd instructed. *She's an impressive girl,* he thought before going back in the house.

Mae returned and Tom said, "You haven't eaten all day. Grab a bite. I only need a few more minutes here."

"I'm not hungry."

Make yourself eat, Mae. We still have a long night ahead of us."

Looking past the computer screen, Tom saw Mae busy in the kitchen. She called in to him, "I don't have any idea what kind of meat this is, and I'm probably glad I don't, but I'm fixing us each a sandwich."

Tom wrote an address and directions on a scrap of paper and stuffed it in his pocket. "Good, I'm done here. Let's eat."

They stood at the kitchen counter and taking a bite, Tom said, "This is deer meat."

He knew it was a mistake the moment he said it, but it was too late now. Tom knew it caused her to remember their hunt and he was sorry he'd made the comment. Mae put her sandwich back on her plate and covered her face. She began sobbing quietly. Through her hands Tom heard her say, "I'm sorry, I can't help it."

Tom put his arm around her. "It's okay, Mae, it's okay."

She turned to him and Tom was momentarily surprised by the ferocity of her own arms pulling him close as she cried. They stood motionless clutching each other for a short while until Mae pulled back, wiped her eyes with her napkin and said, "I'm sorry for that." She looked up at Tom who was wiping his own eyes.

"Nothing to be sorry about," he said softly. "I feel the same way."

Without speaking further, they managed to finish their sandwiches. Tom broke the silence. "We need to clean up and put on fresh clothes – the good clothes I told you to bring. Use makeup. No time to question anything, just do it."

Mae freshened up in the bathroom first. She emerged looking tired but still radiant, Tom thought. "You look beautiful, Mae." She tried to smile in thanks.

Tom picked up his duffle and followed her lead. They now looked like completely different people from the ones who'd been eating in the kitchen a little while before.

Tom walked to the garage and returned with a kerosene lamp. Mae followed him into Joseph's bedroom where he removed the glass chimney and placed it on the nightstand by the bed. Next, he returned to the garage and brought out two fuel cans. He turned off the pilot light in the stove and made sure all the windows were closed tight. He then lit the kerosene lamp in the bedroom and closed the door, noting with satisfaction the half inch gap between the bottom of the door and the floor. Picking up the gas cans he said, "Mae, wait in the truck, I'll be there in a minute."

When she'd left, Tom poured gasoline around the edge of the living room, Joseph's cluttered office, garage and kitchen. He made sure to douse extra gasoline on the computer, carpet and sofa. Lastly, he turned one burner on the propane stove to its lowest setting before walking out the front door and shutting it behind.

Tom started the truck and headed back to get Mae's car. Mae asked, "Did you start a fire?"

"Not yet."

"What do you mean, *not yet*?"

I figure we've got about an hour or more before the house blows and burns."

"I don't understand. How's that going to happen."

"The whole place is doused in gasoline with the windows and doors shut. I turned on the propane so it's seeping very slowly into the house. The kerosene lamp is lit in the bedroom. After the house fills with propane, it'll seep under the bedroom door and eventually be ignited by the lamp. The place will explode and the gasoline will make sure everything burns."

"I'm tired Tom, and I know my mind is working slow. I think I'm still a little lost. Can you tie all this together for me."

"Okay, but it'll take a little time. In a few hours we'll be in one car and I'll explain it all then. Just hang in there with me a little longer. Next time you see the sun, this will all be over and we can work on forgetting about it."

"That's the best thing I've heard all day." Mae gave Tom a faint smile. "I just want you to know," she added, "I'm with you all the way."

"I never doubted you for a minute, but thanks."

They arrived back at Mae's Taurus. Tom put Joseph's bow, knife and the two pairs of moccasins in the trunk. "Follow me. We're going to be driving about half an hour."

Tom parked the dirt encrusted pickup on a nearly deserted side road. Mae pulled behind and he got in the passenger seat of the Taurus. "Okay, now where?" she asked.

"A block down and a couple more over to the left. We're going to the Cactus Saloon for a little celebration."

"Are you out of your fucking mind?" she nearly screamed.

"Calm yourself, Mae. It's still part of the plan. We need to be seen."

"I don't get it, but whatever you say…"

She parked her car in the lot and they walked in. Tom selected a table in the middle of the room. The band had just started their first set for the evening. Mae said, I'm surprised at the number of people in here – especially on a Sunday night."

"It's always busy here. That's why we came."

"And just how did you know that?" she chided with a grin.

"I just know."

The waitress came to the table and Tom said loudly, "Mae what would you like?"

"Just a Diet Coke," she said to Tom barely over the music.

"Mae will have a glass of your best champagne and I'll have…" He paused, put his hand to his chin as if pondering a difficult question and said to himself just loud enough for the waitress to hear, "What would Tom like… Let's see…" Then he yelled, "I think I'll have a glass of champagne too."

The waitress left and Mae said, "What's gotten into you? I said I wanted a Diet Coke."

"I wanted the waitress to hear our names. Nobody comes in here and orders *a glass of your best champagne,* Mae. I want her to remember us. Just take a little sip from time to time, then you can knock it over and I'll order you another. She'll remember us."

The band played a slow song and Tom said, "Come on. We need to be seen dancing. Try to smile and laugh. You can do it. This is important. I figure we should stay about a half hour. Make the best of it."

They sipped their champagne and danced three times.

"I need to use the restroom. I'll be right back."

Sitting alone at the table, Tom looked around the room. He spotted Gloria at a table with two other women. This was almost too much luck to be possible. As Mae was making her way back to the table,

Tom caught Gloria's eye and waved. She came over to Tom seconds before Mae could sit down. "Well, if it isn't Thomas Edison! I swear! I thought I'd never see you again!"

Before he could introduce her to Mae, Gloria threw her arms around him and said, "You have to dance with me!"

Tom disentangled himself from Gloria's embrace and said, "I'd love to Gloria, but I'd like to introduce you to my girlfriend, Mae."

"Nice to meet you," she said with disappointment in her voice. "Lucky girl," she added and walked back to her friends.

"How do you know her? And why did she call you Thomas Edison?" Mae asked incredulously.

"It's unimportant; you really don't want to know anyway."

Mae laughed. "You're full of surprises today." They looked at each other and then both broke into more laughter when the realization of what she'd just said struck them both at the same time.

In all the laughter, Mae managed to spill her champagne. Tom waved to the waitress and when she arrived at their table said, "Mae spilled her champagne. Could you bring her another glass?"

Before the waitress left, Mae quickly reached in her purse, pulled out a twenty dollar bill and handed it to her saying, "I'm so sorry to make such a mess. Would you mind wiping it up? Tom's so clumsy; he'll have his sleeves in it in no time." The waitress smiled warmly, pocketing the bill. "No problem, Mae. Be right back with a rag."

"Nicely done," Tom said looking at Mae with admiration. "I think one more dance and we can get out of here."

Tom paid the bar bill with his American Express card, being sure to leave a generous tip.

Back in the Ford, Tom said, "We passed a motel a mile back. Go there."

Mae drove to the Broken Wheel Inn, parked in front of the office as Tom wanted, and turned off the ignition while Tom went inside.

"I need a room," he said to the desk clerk who looked over Tom's shoulder to the parked Taurus and then back at Tom.

"No problem. Twin beds or a king," he said with a wink and a grin.

"What do you think?" Tom said returning a conspiratorial smile.

"A king it is."

Tom signed the register using his full title, Thomas Sloan, Ph.D. and paid with his credit card.

"How 'bout a room in the back?" he asked, pointing to the wedding band he'd slipped on his finger walking in from the car.

"I completely understand," the desk clerk said. "Take room 119. Nobody will see your car from there."

Tom laid a ten dollar bill on the counter and returned to the car. He could see the clerk looking through the glass door at Mae as she pulled out and drove to the back of the motel. "Pull over to room 119 and turn off the headlights."

Mae turned off the lights and sat in the dark car while Tom grabbed his duffel and went into the room. He messed up the bed sheets, tossed a couple of towels on the bathroom floor and exited wearing a tie and sport coat, leaving the key in the room.

"Good," Tom said, "Now slowly drive out the back of the lot and turn your lights back on when we're on the main road.

Once on their way, Tom instructed Mae to drive back to the parked pickup. "You're doing great, Mae. We're going to drive to Phoenix. There shouldn't be much traffic on a Sunday night. We can be there in less than two hours. Follow close. I know where I'm going. Hang in there, Mae. We're almost done. Have one of the energy drinks you bought. I'll have one too. We need to keep sharp. "

Tom set the cruise control at exactly the speed limit and pulled the scrap of paper from his pocket on which he'd scribbled the address and directions he'd downloaded from Joseph's computer.

Leaving the highway, Tom checked his rearview mirror. Mae was right behind. He drove through downtown Phoenix with little traffic to slow him and pulled into an all night gas station and car wash. *Time to make this rig look attractive*, he said aloud to himself while slipping a five dollar bill in the automated slot of the car wash.

Mae waited in the Taurus for him to leave the carwash bay and in a minute they were off again. Nearing his destination, Tom pulled over in an obviously poor Hispanic neighborhood. He got out of the truck and Mae opened her window. "I want you to stay here. Turn off your lights, but keep the motor running. Keep your door locked. This isn't exactly Rodeo Drive. I won't be long."

Tom drove down the street he'd left Mae on and turned right on another block. Some of the houses were boarded up with graffiti painted on the sides. Others were clearly occupied. Those that were inhabited had bars on the doors and windows. Tom drove slowly, looking. That's what I want, he thought as he drove by a group of hooded sweatshirt-wearing young men standing on a corner. Tom pulled over and parked the once again bright yellow pickup. He opened the glove box and put the Remington ammo box in his pocket along with the registration folder. To be safe, he took a handkerchief from his pocket and quickly wiped down the steering wheel, glovebox and turn signals. Before closing the glovebox, he grabbed a handful of small tools. Knowing he was being watched, Tom stepped from the truck, locked the doors and promptly dropped the handful of tools in the street. He let out a loud, "Shit," and, putting the truck keys on the cab roof, bent down to pick up all the tools and put them in his jacket pocket before walking away.

Striding briskly toward Mae's car, Tom couldn't help but smile. I bet they've already got Roger's truck heading for some chop-shop, he thought. Tom heard Mae pop the door locks. He got in the passenger seat and said, "Let's get out of here." A short distance from the highway they'd come down on, Tom had Mae pull into a Walmart parking lot.

"I can drive now, if you want."

"Yes, I'm beat. You take over." They both got out of the Ford and changed places.

Tom adjusted the seat back and said, "We're just about done. I think I've covered all the bases. One thing left to do."

"Oh no, not more. I can't do much more of this, Tom."

"This is easy. We can do it from right here. I want you to use the other prepaid cell phone and call Joseph's house number."

Mae hit the numbers on the second cheap phone. She heard it ring and then a recording came on: "You have reached a number that is either out of order or not in service at this time. Please check your number and try again." Mae tried again and got the same result.

"I think we can assume the house is no more," Tom said and pulled another scrap of paper from his pants pocket. Handing it to Mae he said, "This is the number for the phone company. Report Joseph's number as out of service. When you're sure they've taken the number, hang up."

Mae did this last thing Tom asked. "Now what?" she asked, hoping for the right answer this time. She got it.

"Now we go home."

Tom drove to the back of the Walmart and stopped by one of the big dumpsters. He reached in his pocket and pulled out Roger's truck registration folder. Tearing it into pieces, he tossed it into the bin. Next he took Mae's first prepaid cell phone and smashed it with his shoe before throwing it in also. They left the parking lot and within minutes were back on the highway.

"One detail, and that's it," Tom said while driving and looking out the window.

"Mae said nothing. At this point she didn't even want to know."

"Ah! That's what I'm looking for," Tom said taking an exit and a minute later pulling to a stop by a chain-link fence.

A short distance beyond the fence was a full flowing drainage canal. "This looks like a perfect spot for the Glock."

Tom took the gun from his duffle and got out of the car. He looked around, making sure the area was deserted. It was. To be extra safe, Tom swiped the gun down with a baby wipe. He then leaned back and with a mighty throw committed the Glock to its watery resting place. It landed with an almost inaudible splash. He got back in the car.

"Let me have the other cell phone." Mae handed it to Tom. It too landed in the canal.

"Now it really is over."

"All over except for the telling," Mae said.

As they cruised up the highway doing exactly the speed limit, Tom said, "First of all Mae, I can't tell you how proud I am of you – "

"Oh sure you can," she interrupted.

"Seriously, I couldn't have done this without you. You kept your head and kept your composure better than I could have hoped for."

"Thank you, Tom. But I did it for Joseph," she said. "I still can't believe he's gone. It's been less than twenty-four hours, but driving with him this morning seems ages ago."

"I know. We packed a lot into one day."

They drove in silence for a while, each lost in private thoughts and memories. Mae broke the quiet by asking, "Can you explain all this now?"

"Sure," Tom began. "If you can find any faults or flaws, speak up while we have time to alter things if we need to."

"Okay, I will. Explain all this to me."

"You know why I didn't want to take Joseph's body to the hospital and call the sheriff."

"Yes. I was okay with that. Tell me how this whole plan is supposed to play out."

"I buried Joseph in the kiva because that seemed a fitting place, even a holy place for him to rest. It was also ready-made and unknown to anyone. I wasn't going to let Roger fight this thing in the courts with his lies and lawyers, so I decided he needed to go. He also threatened me that time at the Oasis. I didn't want to live my life looking over my shoulder all the time or hearing a middle of the night house noise thinking it might be Roger coming for me. He had to go and I was convinced it was a just decision.

"You calling him on the prepaid cell phone meant that the call was untraceable. The number would show up on their records as coming from just what it was, a prepaid cell phone in nobody's name. You flirting with him and getting him out to Jasper Road was just a way to make sure he came alone to a place where we could dispose of his body where no one would look or have any reason to look."

Mae cut in, "Why would no one have a reason to look for his body?"

"I'm getting to that. Bear with me a little longer." Tom continued, "So we get rid of Roger out in the middle of nowhere and we go back to Joseph's. Somewhere by the house is the spent 9 mm shell casing from Roger's gun that killed Joseph. I assume the investigators will find that. Just to be sure, I fired two more rounds into the spot where Joseph bled all night. They should find the bullets in the ground and it'll look like Roger fired directly down into his body to be sure he was dead. It makes him more guilty of murdering Joseph. The two ejected shells will be close together to substantiate this.

"Remember I pulled the bloody tarp to the front steps? Well, that was to make it look like Roger pulled Joseph's body into the house before throwing gasoline on the place and burning it up. They won't find any remains, and this might be problematic, but it's possible Roger could have drenched Joseph in gasoline and he burned up to the point that when the house exploded from the propane tank, what little was left of him disintegrated. Remember, where not talking about a Kennedy or a Rockefeller here, just an unemployed Indian down from Montana who few people knew or cared about. He also had a documented history of drunkenness and fighting. The easiest conclusions about his death will be the best ones. They'll want this case off the books and forgotten as soon as possible.

"Since we were known to be friends with Joseph I expect we'll be questioned. We'll say we got together from time to time, but weren't particularly close. I'll say Joseph mentioned he was seeing a woman he met at the Cactus Saloon named Stephanie. I can add that I think she was friends with another woman named Gloria. Remember, Stephanie is the one who followed Joseph home that night and split when she saw Roger there. So, she'll be questioned and finger Roger.

"Well, Roger left unexpectedly the following morning and hasn't been seen since. It looks like he's on the run after killing Joseph. I did a quick crime search on the internet at Joseph's house and found the area in Phoenix where more cars are stolen than any other place in Arizona. So we dusted up his truck so nobody would recognize it until we got to Phoenix. I washed it and parked it in *Car Theft Central* with the keys left on the cab roof. I did good acting there for the benefit of some local gang-bangers in hoodies. Too bad you weren't there to watch. Anyway, Roger's truck is already in some garage being stripped for parts. It'll never be found and the search for Roger will continue indefinitely.

"We'll also be asked where we were at the time of the blast. They'll know the approximate time because you called in to the phone company on a different untraceable phone to report the number being out of service. Well, our waitress will surely remember the big spenders named Mae and Tom who ordered expensive champagne and left a nice tip about that time. I also paid with my American Express which can be scarched for the exact time of use. My friend Gloria can corroborate that. We also checked into a motel for a little romp because neither of us wanted to have a car left at the other's house all night in

Lunden. People talk, you know. Rock solid alibi, not that we would be suspected of anything anyway, but it's still better to cross all your Ts and dot all your Is."

"That all sounds good, but how will they know the shell casings were from Roger's gun. You got rid of it. That's kind of a loose end, isn't it?"

"That's very astute of you, Mae. I'm impressed. But I've got that covered too. Remember the fired shells you helped me collect in the plastic bag? Well, they will go into this ammo box I pulled from Roger's glovebox." Tom reached in his pocket and placed the green box on the seat. Tomorrow morning first thing, before word even gets out about Joseph being assumed killed or his house burning down or Roger being on the run, I'll stop in at the garage and ask that guy who works there to check the oil in the Boxster. While he's trying to figure out how to get to the engine, I'll stick this box of ammo on a shelf. When his place is searched – which it will be – they'll discover the fired shells that match the ones at Joseph's house. There's the definitive proof of Roger's guilt. End of story." Tom said as he pulled into Mae's driveway. "And timed perfectly."

"Can you come in?" Mae asked.

Tom looked at his watch. "It's after three in the morning. You sure?"

"Yes. There's something else I want to talk about. I know it can wait, but that energy drink still has its claws in me. There's no way I can sleep tonight or this morning or whatever it is."

Tom sat on Mae's sofa. "Can I get you anything?" she asked.

"How 'bout an energy drink," he laughed.

"Oh god, the thoughts of that could make me sick."

They sat quietly next to each other for a moment and Tom said, "What did you want to talk about?"

"Where we go from here."

"I've got that figured out too. I'm going to assume neither of us wants to hang around Lunden any longer."

"I have too many memories of Joseph here. I need to leave, put this behind me, start new."

"I feel the same. So, here's what I suggest. You and I are seen around town together. We'll go to dinner, take walks, you know, make the townspeople talk. We'll do this for a month. That'll give you time to give Chuck a thirty day notice and time to wrap up your tax work. By then nobody will be talking about Joseph's murder and Roger's disappearance. All you have to do is pretend for a month that we're a couple in love. Then we'll leave together, which won't surprise anyone. We'll leave the state and then you can go where ever you want."

Mae looked at Tom shaking her head. "I won't pretend, Tom."

Tom looked dumbfounded. "Come on, Mae. After all we've just done, what's the big deal? Just pretend for a few weeks and it's all over. You can put this completely behind you."

"That's not what I mean. I'm saying I can't pretend I love you because I *do* love you." Mae looked to Tom and didn't bother wiping the tears that ran down her cheeks.

Tom put his arms around her and held her until he could feel her tense and pull back. "What's wrong, Mae. What you just told me may be the best thing I've ever heard in my life."

Mae's soft crying turned to soft laughter. "I can't tell you how happy that makes me, Tom." She wiped her eyes and sat back from him. "But you need to know more about me. I'm damaged goods, Tom. I don't think you'll want me when you know how cold I am, how I can't love… I mean love in the intimate sense – the physical way."

Tom sat thoughtfully before he said, "Mae, I've always known something deeply disturbing haunts you from your past. I can't begin to fathom what that might be, but in my heart I know whatever it is, we can work through it. And let me add that if somehow I'm wrong and we can't, I promise to love you just as you are. The way I've felt about you for months now won't change. It's unconditional."

NINETEEN

TWENTY-TWO YEARS PREVIOUS

I

The day the Mill Valley, Tennessee High School yearbook arrived from the printer always caused excitement on campus. Voting for Senior Superlatives and the photos of the candidates was long in the past, but the results would be revealed in the yearbook, and just about everyone was anxious to see who had been chosen in the different categories. The yearbook staff had been particularly diligent this year in keeping the outcome secret all these weeks. There were rumors of the winners' names, but nothing concrete came to light. Some students even laid bets and it was thought even the faculty had a few wagers on the results.

Mae was as anxious as anyone to get her yearbook, but she was also feeling a combination of nervousness and embarrassment. She'd been nominated for several categories and winning one would have been fine – an honor even – but suppose she won more than her share? Suppose she was chosen in more categories than would seem modest and proper? Well, she'd just have to wait and see like everyone else. Whatever the outcome of the voting, it was out of her hands. Either way, she'd be graduating soon and then none of it would matter anyway. Maybe her children or grandkids would find the old Mill Valley yearbook some day and say, "Gee, Grandma, was this really you?"

The yearbooks were handed out in a near frenzy of grabbing hands. Mae received hers and walked off to be alone while she searched the Senior Superlatives section. The first page had a color photo of Marvin Bigsby for *Most Likely to Succeed.* No relief there as she wasn't a candidate for that honor. The next page was *Best Looking Male Student.* Mae looked at the full page photo of Adam Kessler, her boyfriend since the tenth grade. Good photo of him, she thought as she turned the page to *Best Looking Female Student* and saw her own photo with her name in script at the bottom – Mae June Holland. She thought it a good enough photo and with some hesitation went to the next page, *Most Likely to get Married.* The photo of her and Adam had been taken during a Halloween party they'd attended the previous fall. At least they weren't wearing any goofy costumes Mae thought, staring at Adam and her sitting atop a hay bail surrounded by pumpkins. Okay, at least nothing embarrassing about that one. She skimmed the categories of *Best Student, Most Popular Male and Female Students, Best Dressed Male and Female Students,* and stopped at *Most Talented Female Student.* This photo of Mae was taken during a talent night in the school's auditorium. It was a profile shot of Mae, her strawberry blond hair hanging loose over her shoulders, sitting in a chair playing her guitar. She was leaning into a microphone with her eyes closed and her mouth partly open, hanging on to a last note perhaps. Mae thought it a terrific photo. This was one category to be proud of. Anyone could be born attractive, but most talented was a true honor. To be honest, winning *Best Looking Female Student* was a little embarrassing. As for *Most Likely to get Married,* that was pretty much a given. She and Adam had talked about it and decided to marry after graduation. Both her and Adam's parents had done it and they seemed happy enough. Who else was she going to marry? The last Senior Superlative was the coveted *Best Male Athlete.* No surprise here. The photo was of Adam holding a football above his head with one hand. He held it triumphantly in the end zone after another touchdown run. He was the only member of the Mill Valley Falcon's football team to be offered a full football scholarship to the University of Tennessee. Everyone knew he would win *Best Athlete.* You'd have to be clueless to bet against him winning in this category.

Mae flipped through the remainder of the yearbook. She saw a full page devoted to the King and Queen of Homecoming. Again, she and Adam looked like the perfect, stereotypical high school sweethearts. Adam, the best looking Male Student; Mae, the best looking female student; Adam, the best male athlete; Mae the most talented student – they obviously had it all. The world awaited their post high school arrival with high expectations and an uncluttered road to success and happiness.

Eighteen years before yearbook day, on May 31st an hour before midnight, Mrs. Holland went into labor. Her daughter's head became visible just as clocks throughout Mill Valley were striking 12:00 am. By 12:01 on the morning of June 1st, her daughter took her first breath of air and bellowed out a cry. Mr. Holland, taking careful note of the time, declared her name would forever reflect her entry into the world. His daughter was born at the end of May and the beginning of June. With delight he declared her name, Mae June Holland.

Mr. Holland was a lover of popular music. His album collection spanned from Elvis to the present. Growing up, Mae could rarely remember the house being silent when her father was home. As a little girl she'd sit in the living room on her father's lap while he swung endlessly forward and backward in the huge – at least huge to Mae's little body – cushioned rocking chair, while music filled the house from two gigantic speakers in opposite corners of the room. As Mae learned the words to songs, to the delight of her father, she'd sing along. At eight she took piano lessons, but that fell away when at age ten she received her first guitar.

Mae sang in the local church choir and later in the Mill Valley High School Glee Club. Her voice developed strong and clear. She had good pitch and timing came naturally to her. She soon got over the fear of singing in front of people and learned to enjoy performing. Mae's confidence in her singing came across to her audience of listeners. For a number of years, Christmas Eve carol services at the Holland's Church were not complete until concluding with Mae's singing of "Silent Night" which always brought the congregation to their feet. Mae's parents were proud of her, as was the entire town of Mill Valley.

II

One month to the day after graduation, Mae and Adam became husband and wife. They spent a quick weekend honeymoon in Gatlinburg before moving to Knoxville.

For Adam, football practice would begin in the summer long before classes started. Mae had little trouble finding a waitressing job at The College Diner situated close to the campus and their one bedroom apartment. If she could save a little money, Mae hoped to begin her own college career after a semester or two.

For now, Adam was the focal point. He wanted to be in condition before football practice officially started. His days began at 6:00 am with a six mile run, then a high protein breakfast, an early afternoon lifting session in the UT weight room, followed by a nap and then an evening four mile run. At six feet three and two fifteen, Adam was in the best shape of his life. He felt strong and fast. Coming in as a freshman running back, Adam was determined to excel. If all went well, in four years he might have a shot at the pros – and if not, there were always plenty of business opportunities for University of Tennessee football stars. Football was his key to future success and Adam would give it one hundred percent and make the most of it.

Adam's potential and skill as a running back brought him more attention than he'd expected. The upperclassmen on the team accepted him as one of their own. He made friends quickly and it seemed every Friday and Saturday night was spent surrounded by UT "Volunteers" football players and their girlfriends. Mae and Adam were the only married couple in the circle of team players and their seemingly, at least to Mae, ever changing array of girlfriends.

On a Friday after the fourth week of practice, Adam burst through their flimsy apartment front door. "Amazing news, Mae!" he nearly screamed. "The backfield coach pulled me aside after practice today and told me he thought that even though I'm just a freshman, I should see plenty of game time this season!"

Mae threw her arms around her muscular husband, "Oh Adam, I'm so proud of you! You're going to do great, I just know it!"

"We got our jersey numbers. I'm going to be number twenty-six."

"Number twenty-six. That's got a nice ring to it," Mae said. "Soon everyone will know number twenty-six is Adam Kessler and I'll be Mrs. Number Twenty-six." They both laughed at this. Adam was ecstatic.

"Tomorrow a bunch of us guys on the team are going out and I'll have a surprise for you when I get home!"

"Tell me, Adam," Mae said. "You know I don't do well with surprises."

"Nope, this one you'll just have to wait to see."

"Will I like it?"

"You better, 'cause you can't take it back."

"Now you've really got my curiosity up. Come on Adam, you can tell me." Mae put her arms around Adam again, "Please…"

"No, I shouldn't have said anything. It really will be a surprise. Anyway, it'll be worth the wait."

The next afternoon Adam went out with *The Guys* just as he said he would. He referred to the teammates he'd begun hanging out with as "The Guys." They'd made no friends who weren't University of Tennessee Volunteers football players, but Mae knew that was to be expected. They were like brothers who worked together on the field, sweated together and often hurt together. Mae sometimes worried when she saw the bruises on Adam's back and arms. Adam appreciated Mae's concern saying, "running backs get tackled, Mae. You know that. It goes with the job. But I'm in great shape. It's no big deal."

Adam returned home for dinner wearing a light nylon UT Football jacket and a wide grin on his face. "I've got the surprise, Mae."

Mae had been through these surprise games before. On her last birthday using most of the money left over from his previous summer's job, Adam had given her a pair of pearl earrings. Another time it was concert tickets. The ritual was the same. Mae would close her eyes and hold out her right hand, or if it were a larger surprise, she'd hold out both cupped hands.

This time, to be on the safe side, Mae closed her eyes and held out both hands toward Adam. Instead of feeling her surprise, this time she heard Adam laugh. Cautiously opening her eyes, Mae said, "I don't understand…"

"This isn't that kind of surprise Mae," Adam said pulling off his jacket. Here's the surprise."

On the inside of Adam's left forearm was a large, fresh tattoo. In thick black old English letters it said **UNIV. TENN**. over **VOLUNTEERS** over **FOOTBALL** over **#26**.

Mae stared at his raw looking inked arm. She didn't know what to say, so she just stared in silence.

"Well? C'mon Mae, what do you think?"

Mae was still too shocked to respond.

"We all got 'em, Mae. It's who we are now."

"Well, I suppose – "

"I'm proud of it, even if you don't like it."

Mae could tell Adam was beginning to get defensive. The tattoo was there and nothing could be done to change that. Thinking fast she said, "No Adam, I think it's fine. If that's what The Guys all did, I suppose you had to go along too. I just need to get used to it, that's all."

The following Monday Mae received the call while working the afternoon shift at the diner.

"Mrs. Kessler?"

"Yes, this is Mae Kessler."

"Um, Mrs. Kessler, this is Danny Richardson from UT. I'm one of the trainers who's been working with your husband, Adam…"

"Yes, is something wrong?"

"Well, there is. Yes. You see Adam got tackled pretty hard today at practice. He's at the hospital right now. I just wanted to call you so you could go there to be with him."

Mae could feel herself shifting into panic mode. She forced herself to calmness. "Tell me what's wrong with Adam. How bad is he?"

"Don't worry Mrs. Kessler, Adam will be fine. I mean, he's not unconscious or anything like that. He just seems to have hurt his knee."

"How bad?"

"Well, I don't exactly know…" He seemed to stutter around a little. "You'll have to talk to the doctor about that."

"Could he walk by himself?" Jesus, Danny, she thought, give me some damn information here.

"Oh no, we had to carry him off the field. I mean, he might be okay now, but like I said, you'll need to talk to them at the hospital. He's probably having an MRI right now. I think one of the coaches stayed with him." Danny said nothing more and an awkward silence ensued.

"Can you tell me anything more?"

"No, Ma'am. They just wanted me to call you so you could get to the hospital."

Mae put the phone down without saying another word. She grabbed her jacket and told her boss an emergency had just come up and she had to get to the hospital.

Mae was not particularly religious, but she found herself silently moving her lips in prayer while she drove. *Please God, just let it be a sprain or twisted knee, please, nothing serious, please.*

She parked the Toyota in the emergency parking lot and ran inside. She explained to the receptionist who she was and was shown to a waiting room down a separate hall. She was told an MRI had been ordered and someone would be in shortly to explain the results. Mae was asked if she wanted to see Adam first, but she thought it best to wait and see him when she had all the facts.

Mae waited nearly an hour before two doctors in white coats approached her.

"Mae Kessler?" one of them asked.

"Yes," Mae said as she rose to stand.

"I'm Dr. Sanchez. I'm a radiologist – and this is Dr. Jenkins."

Dr. Jenkins held out his hand to Mae. "I'm an orthopedic surgeon, Mae." He smiled and said, "Let's all have a seat and we can talk."

Mae instinctively knew this was not going to be good. She sat and tried to prepare herself for whatever was coming. "How's Adam?"

Dr. Sanchez said, "Adam's resting now. He was in a great deal of pain when they first brought him in. He's been given a sedative."

"Let me get right to it, Mrs. Kessler," Dr. Jenkins began. "Adam tore his anterior cruciate ligament, usually referred to as the ACL."

"Yes, I'm familiar with the ACL," Mae said. "How bad was the tear, doctor?"

"It was a complete tear, as opposed to a partial tear, I'm afraid. However," he said, "there is some good news. This is a fairly common occurrence, especially with athletes in contact sports. With surgery we should be able to do a tendon graft in his knee. These procedures are almost always successful."

"When could you do this?"

"Really any time. I don't see any reason to believe after a reasonable recovery time and some physical therapy that Adam couldn't have pretty much full use of his knee again."

Mae felt relieved. "That all sounds great. How much of the football season will he have to miss?"

This time it was Dr. Sanchez who spoke. "I'm afraid he won't be playing football."

"You mean, he'll miss this whole season?"

"Mrs. Kessler," Dr. Jenkins began, "You're husband has suffered a very serious injury. Fifty years ago an injury like this could leave him partially crippled. Medicine has come a long way since then, especially sports medicine. But we can't work miracles. Adam will have to be content knowing after surgery and recovery he'll be able to lead a full and reasonably active lifestyle." He continued looking at Mae and said, "I know he was looking forward to playing football for UT. He's going to need you right now. I've seen this before. In his mind, his life may seem over. He'll need you to prop him up, show him there is a lot more to life than college sports."

"You don't understand, doctor," Mae said, "He was counting on this. Being on the team was his whole life –"

"No Mrs. Kessler, I do understand. Don't think this is the first talk like this one I've had to give. I see this all the time. It's not easy for me and I fully appreciate how difficult this is going to be for both you and your husband. It'll be up to you to urge him to stay at UT, to earn his degree and move on to a successful life. I also understand he's on an athletic scholarship. I would suggest you speak with whoever is in charge of scholarships and financial aid to see what can be done to keep him at UT."

Mae looked to Dr. Sanchez and then back to Dr. Jenkins. She realized all that could be said had been said. There was nothing left except to ask directions to Adam's room.

III

Adam's grandmother had recently moved into a nursing home. The small farmhouse she'd lived in for over fifty years sat four miles from town on nearly two hundred acres of prime grazing land. When she learned the new buyers of her property intended to bulldoze the house she'd spent most of her adult life living and toiling in, she reneged on the deal until they agreed to section off the house on two acres of surrounding land, supply an easement and purchase only the remaining acreage. Grandma Kessler had intended to rent the house, but since learning that Adam and Mae were returning to Mill Valley, she decided to deed it to them as a belated wedding gift.

Mae thought the house was furnished nicely, if a bit old fashioned. There were three bedrooms, a full bath with another half bath off the kitchen and a living room. A stairway leading down from the kitchen opened to a cool, windowless root cellar where Grandma Kessler stored her award winning preserves along with her canned fruits and vegetables. Mae was pleased to see that several shelves still contained rows of Grandma's paraffin sealed mason jars.

Moving their few possessions into the house, Mae tried to be cheerful and chatty. Adam took little interest in the place. He was at least off his crutches and needed only a cane to help him keep his balance and offer some support when he walked. Mae had been unsuccessful in convincing him to stay at UT. After visiting him once in the hospital after his surgery, not one of "The Guys" ever bothered to call on him. Mae decided Adam was a reminder of what could happen to any one of them at any time. That they didn't need. They lived for the day, for practice and for games. They felt invincible as a team, but each secretly dreaded the very concept of personal injury. They needed to be around each other, the warriors of the field. Injured non-players were discarded by necessity. They were a negative force no one could afford to carry.

Adam found a job at the Mill Valley Goodyear Tire Store and Service Center. He wore his Goodyear button-down shirts with the sleeves unrolled. He didn't talk about the tattoo with the untested #26, a constant reminder of a failed future. Secretly Mae searched websites advertising tattoo removal services, but there were none close to Mill Valley, and besides, the treatments were both expensive and long lasting. She spoke with Dr. Foster who'd been the Holland family doctor since as long as Mae could remember from her childhood. He gave no new information on the matter other than what she'd already found online. How, Mae thought, would Adam ever put this whole University of Tennessee Football thing behind him with that goddamn tattoo staring at him every day? If she let herself think about it too much, she build up an anger that could be hard to control. Better to think of something else. Perhaps some time in the future, there would be a technique developed for removing tattoos that would be quick and easy. He could take care of it then.

Mae took another waitressing job. This time it was at the local Waffle House. The pay was low, but because she knew so many of the patrons, tips were good. Between Adam's paycheck and hers, they made out okay. The house they owned outright and taxes and utilities were low. They'd do well enough until Adam got centered, got over the damn football thing and came up with some sort of long term plan. Mae mentioned going back to college which he'd never even begun in the first place, but Adam was resistant. She suggested Tennessee State University in Nashville, where nobody knew him, but he just pointed to his forearm and said, "This would go over big in Nashville." Mae made an attempt to say he could wear long sleeves, but he cut her off saying, "I don't want to talk about it, Mae. Just let it drop." And that's exactly what she did.

IV

The drinking began after work – only a beer or two with the other men who worked at the tire store. Adam would come home an hour later than usual, but he did seem happier after socializing with his new friends. If a couple beers helped him cheer up, that was fine with Mae. Along with the drinking, Adam's sexual urges intensified and became more frequent. Mae was glad of this too. Before they'd married, sex was on their minds all the time. Quickies during study hall with the help of bathroom passes, in the rear seat of the Toyota at the back of the deserted school parking lot after football practice, on the old army blanket Adam kept in the trunk of the car for use along any one of a dozen back roads outside of Mill Valley. Wherever they found themselves, with a little creative thinking, could be their temporary bedroom. Mae was attracted to Adam like she'd never been attracted to anyone else. Of course, she'd never had even preliminaries with anyone but Adam and that was fine with her. He could satisfy her lust and needs with his own sexual athleticism. At eighteen, the only thing stopping their activities was Mae getting too sore to continue. After Adam's injury his sex drive seemed to diminish along with his self esteem. This too worried Mae, but that might have run its course now, she thought. Some new friends, a little innocent socializing after a hard day at work, a beer or two, nothing in the world wrong with that. At least not until two or three Jack Daniels were chased by three or four beers..

The extra alcohol took more than a bite out of Adam's take-home pay. It took some of his past sexual prowess along with it. Sometimes Adam would initiate sex upon arriving home while Mae was in the kitchen fixing his dinner. She'd laugh and say something like, "Hold on there tiger. Let me just turn the stove off and put the oven down to one-fifty." Mae liked being wanted by her husband in such a strong and demanding way. After all, they were still newlyweds! It had usually been a long day for her too, so a little fooling around when they first got together was not only fun but a good stress reliever. A few beers didn't seem to make much difference, but Jacks on top could cause a problem. Half way into a session with Mae either bent over the kitchen table or perhaps sitting on the counter – at six foot three Adam was the perfect height for this – Adam might soften and not be able to continue. When this happened, Mae would just laugh and hug him tight. She'd say something like, "You've had a long day, Mister. You need some of Mae's good home cooking to perk you up!" And usually later that's just what he'd be and they'd continue where they left off before dinner.

One particular Friday night Adam came home later than usual. Mae had had a difficult day at the Waffle House dealing with an assortment of rude and annoying customers. She wasn't in the best frame of mind when Adam stumbled into the kitchen. She could easily tell that he'd had more to drink than usual. Thinking about the size of his bar bill didn't improve her mood either. When Adam came up behind her and grabbed her around the waist, she turned and faced him saying, "Not now. I'm busy and you're probably too far gone to be much good to either of us."

Mae regretted saying that the instant the words left her mouth, but it was too late. Adam roughly pushed her back and, taking a beer from the refrigerator, walked to the living room. He turned on the TV and fell into the overstuffed chair that was generally accepted as his. Mae brought his dinner to him there, but he told her she could throw it out for all he cared. And that's exactly what Mae did.

While Adam watched sports, Mae cleaned the kitchen and went to bed early, locking the bedroom door behind her. When she awoke at 6:00 after a fitful night, she found Adam still snoring in the same chair he'd occupied the night before. Next to him on the floor were six crushed beer cans. Mae showered and dressed as quietly as she could before driving to work.

When she arrived home, she noticed Adam's pickup in front of the house. With more than a little trepidation, she walked through the front door. The first thing she noticed was a water pitcher on the coffee table with a half-dozen red roses placed in it. The stems needed cutting down to set right, but they were roses nonetheless. Adam was in the kitchen. "I've got a couple rib-eyes ready for the grill. I'm not much good with anything else, but I put two potatoes in the oven and have some mushrooms and onions on the stove."

Mae walked into the kitchen saying nothing. Adam turned around and said, "Look, Mae honey, I'm really sorry about last night. I was a real asshole and you don't deserve that."

Mae's eyes filled. She walked up to Adam and put her arms around his neck. "Thanks Adam. It was the alcohol last night, not you."

"You're right. And speaking of that, as of today, I'm on the wagon. No more getting Jacked up, no more beer. I don't need that anyway. I've got you and you're more intoxicating than any booze."

"Well, aren't we becoming the poetic one?" Mae exclaimed.

"It's true, Mae. I haven't been treating you very nice and that's all over now," Adam said and added in the most matter-of-fact way he could muster, "I've been thinking it's time we started a family."

V

The first months of Mae's pregnancy were not easy ones. She knew she needed to eat for the sake of the baby, but the nausea and often violent vomiting made just the thoughts of eating a torture. She'd had no choice but to quit her job at the Waffle House – being around food and the smells from the grill made for an impossible work environment. Adam was supportive and as understanding as possible for a nineteen-year-old man with no experience with pregnancies or anyone who'd ever even been pregnant. As he'd promised though, Adam did stay away from alcohol and unless he had errands to run, came directly home from work each day. Without complaint he took over the cooking and anything to do with food.

Fortunately, after her thirteenth week, the nausea and vomiting suddenly ceased. One morning it was all Mae could do to get out of bed and face the sunshine of a new day, and the next she bounced from the bedroom into the kitchen to make a full cooked breakfast. Overnight, Mae's world seemed bright and full of promise again. She felt constantly energetic, optimistic, hopeful, enthusiastic and hungry. All this wonderment lasted a total of six days. It terminated with her pregnancy.

Adam came home to find Mae curled on the bathroom floor. The blood on the tiles led to an open toilet where an unflushable clot of fluids and fetus floated in a dead suspension of cold water.

The depression Mae experienced in the weeks that followed wouldn't leave like her morning sickness had. She felt even more lifeless with each passing day. Adam and Mae together consulted Dr. Foster who informed them both that postpartum depression was a normal occurrence for many women after a birth or miscarriage. He said in time it should pass. Then Dr. Foster wanted to speak with Adam in private. While Mae sat in the waiting room he told Adam it was imperative he be considerate and compassionate toward Mae. This was not an easy time for his wife, he explained. Some women could emotionally recover quickly and get back to their normal lives, while others found this difficult. The more Adam could be supportive and understanding, the shorter this time would probably be. He warned that Mae might be intimately unresponsive to Adam and that he needed to be especially patient in this regard. He assured him this difficult time would not last indefinitely and again urged him to be sympathetic and helpful to Mae.

Adam was the model of gentility. He treated Mae like a pampered princess, preparing her sandwiches wrapped in plastic in the refrigerator before leaving for the Goodyear store each morning and then doing the housework as soon as he arrived home in the evening. He watched only the shows on TV Mae liked and made sure she stayed warm and cozy on the sofa under one of Grandma Kessler's quilts. When Mae turned away from him in bed at night, Adam remembered Dr. Foster's advice and accepted this.

Over the next weeks, the depression lightened, but never fully floated away. Mae controlled the intimacy of their marriage and she unenthusiastically let it return on an infrequent basis. Adam stopped preparing lunches and doing the housework. Not only was he tired of pampering the princess, he thought it might be prolonging and facilitating her depression. He was also frustrated with his wife and felt taken for granted. It was time, Adam decided, to snap out of it and get back into the swing of things. And when Mae didn't shift into gear as Adam wanted, the drinking began again.

It started like it had the previous time. Adam justified breaking his promise to Mae by rationalizing that she had broken her marriage vows. Even though they might have been unspoken vows, the lack of intimacy, the sour moods, the undusted furniture – Adam felt betrayed. Here he was working his ass off at a goddamn tire store while she hung around the house all day doing nothing but watching TV or listening to music. It wasn't fair and if she was going to act that way, he could certainly find some of his own satisfaction and enjoyment in having a beer after work. Was that too much to ask? No, of course it wasn't. Being home was turning into a morbid and dull existence. Half the time, Adam realized, he'd rather be balancing tires at the store than watching some crappy show on TV with his sullen wife. When a girl he'd known from high school, Linda, came on to him while he was working, Adam rebuffed her of course, but later the thoughts of her haunted him. It's not so much that he wanted her as that he felt his wife didn't want him. He never tired of sex with Mae, but now she nearly always seemed too tired for sex with him. Adam could have Linda, who he didn't really desire, but he couldn't have his own wife, who he really did desire! Well, a few beers with the boys was the least he was owed.

The first time Adam came home with beer on his breath, Mae didn't explode on him as he'd expected. Instead, she quietly left the kitchen and the chicken dinner she had halfway prepared and went into their bedroom. For a brief moment Adam took this as an invitation and after hanging up his jacket quickly followed her. What he found was his wife on the bed, lying on her stomach and crying. Adam sat next to her and leaned down to brush the hair from her face so he could kiss her cheek. At his touch Mae rolled to her side. The crying stopped and the tears in her eyes turned to fire. "You lied to me, you son-of-a-bitch!" she screamed. "You're drinking again! Goddamn you, Adam!"

Adam's initial reaction to her sobbing was a compassionate one, but that was short-lived. In a controlled voice he said, "Who the hell are you to criticize me?"

Mae just glared at him. "I'm your wife, that's who."

"No you're not!" Now it was Adam's turn to yell. "A *wife*, especially a *new* wife, has at least *some* sex with her husband who, I might add, works the whole fucking day while his *supposed* wife hangs around the house sulking about a miscarriage! Goddamnit, Mae, get over it!"

Mae was taken back by what Adam had just said. Immersed in her own sorrow and self pity, had she really become a bad wife? Maybe so, but a little understanding would go a long way instead of a broken promise and now accusations. "Fuck you," was all she could mumble. Did she really just say that? Who had she become over these last weeks? Or was it months?

She didn't have time to answer her own questions. Adam said, "No, not fuck me, Mae. It's you who needs a good fuck. Maybe that'll pull you out of this god-awful state you're in."

Mae said nothing. She just rolled away from him and the tears began again. Through her quiet crying she felt Adam get off the bed. Good, she thought, let him get out of here.

But Adam had no intention of leaving. He merely stood and removed his clothes. The next thing Mae knew she'd been roughly turned over on her back. When Adam pulled her robe apart, She became aware that she'd never bothered to get dressed this day. She had a fleeting thought that hanging around all day in a robe was what old people sometimes did – sick, old women. Was that who she'd become?

There was no time for pondering. Adam was on top of her. Since leaving the University of Tennessee he'd also left running and working out. Adam had put on at least twenty pounds. His weight crushed the air from her lungs. Under better circumstances this was a position they avoided for exactly this reason, but that seemed ages ago. Mae struggled for each breath as Adam thrust into her with an urgency she'd never felt in him before. There was no preliminary kissing and soft caressing, no gentleness, no consideration for her desires or needs. This wasn't lovemaking, this was being fucked. Adam said this was what she needed, but no woman needed this.

Fortunately, this whole disgusting act lasted little more than a minute. When Adam went still, she grabbed his shoulders – was this the first time she'd lifted her arms from the bed? – and managed to roll him off of her. He lay there panting. Mae looked over at his heaving nakedness. The athletic, chiseled musculature was now covered with a thin layer of soft flab. For the briefest of moments, Mae didn't know who this man lying next to her was. Then her eyes focused on the *UNIV. TENN. VOLUNTEERS FOOTBALL #26* tattoo and all she could feel was disgust and desperation. Her life had been filled with such hope and promise. How could everything change in so short a time? And now she was reduced even further by being fucked. Was it rape? She put that repulsive idea out of her mind. Was she destined to work, childless, at a Waffle House and be fucked by some out of shape, beer swilling, tattooed loser? She started to cry again.

VI

The image of a bathrobed elderly woman shuffling around a dusty, unkempt farmhouse in frumpy slippers stayed in Mae's head. She was drifting without identity, without purpose. Her guitar sat propped in the corner of the spare bedroom, untouched and out of tune. On more than a few nights, Mae realized she'd not stepped foot out of the house the entire day. Had she gone two or three days shut in? She wasn't sure. What she was sure of was that this could not continue. She felt nineteen going on eighty and that was no way to live.

One bright morning after Adam had gone to work, without speaking a word, Mae glanced at the ancient, and until now unused, claw-footed bathtub. It had sat empty and pipeless since being gutted by some forgotten plumber who installed the small, boxy shower that Grandma Kessler had wanted. At least the drain was still attached. Finding a faded labeled bottle under the sink containing scented bubble bath powder, Mae poured some in the old tub. With a bucket from the garage she filled the bath with steaming water. Mae soaked until the bubbles had all dissolved and her hands had pruned. She didn't want to leave the now tepid bath, but the day was young.

Mae put on the first makeup she'd worn in weeks, combed out her thick red-blond hair, picked out a light and breezy sundress and, as an after thought, dabbed on a little of Grandma Kessler's abandoned Chanel No. 5. She found her car keys. How long had it been since she'd driven the Toyota? She left for town.

Opening the windows allowed the warm spring air to circulate in the stale Toyota. Mae breathed deeply and felt renewed. Some roadside flowers were already in bloom and seeing them, Mae decided to buy some flower seeds. She turned on the radio and found a light country station. Before she knew it, she was parked on Main Street in Mill Valley.

Mae walked the length of the street. People she knew greeted her as if they'd seen her just the day before. Where had she been these last months? She stopped in Suzy's Dresses and Evening Gowns. There weren't many evening gowns in the store, but it made the sign more impressive. That was okay. Mill Valley wasn't exactly Beverly Hills. Suzy's daughter Joanne graduated with Mae and worked in her mom's shop. Upon seeing her she exclaimed, "Mae Holland! God it's good to see you again!" Then catching herself she said, "Wait, you're Mae *Kessler* now. I'm such an idiot!"

"No, you're *not* an *idiot* Joanne!"

Mae and Joanne talked in the shop until Suzy came over. Smiling at them both she said, "Joanne, it's almost lunch time. Why don't you take Mae to Jerome's and you two can catch up on things over sandwiches." Suzy walked to the till, opened the drawer and took out some bills which she handed to Joanne. "This one's on me," she offered.

"Thanks, Mom," Joanne said taking the money. She grasped Mae's hand and said, "C'mon, I'm starved."

Mae was humming in the kitchen when Adam arrived home.

"What are you all dressed up for?" he slurred.

"You've been drinking again," Mae said, her mood changing.

"What do you care? And you didn't answer my question. Why the fancy clothes?"

"First, I care because I'm your wife and second, I just felt like getting out of the house. Sometimes I feel trapped here."

"You may be my wife, but you sure as hell don't act like it."

This was going badly. "Listen Adam, I've had the first nice day in a long time. Don't you go and ruin it now."

"Ruin it, Huh? I come in after a tough day at work to find you all gussied up and humming a tune and all you can say is *don't ruin it?*"

"Well, what do you want me to say? Oh hi honey, it's so good to see you stumbling home and full of booze. Would you like another drink to settle your nerves after a tough day with the tires?" She knew she shouldn't have said that last part. It was demeaning and insulting, but with Adam half drunk, she really didn't care. He could clean himself up and do better than the Goodyear Store anyway. He could go back to college. They both could.

"You bitch – "

Mae cut him off before he could say more, "You can just shut up. I've had a nice day and I sure as hell don't need you coming into my kitchen drunk and spoiling it."

"Your kitchen? Your kitchen? Everything in here is mine or paid for by me. The house is mine too."

"Well, isn't that a nice thing to say to your wife of less than a year! You're turning into a pig, you know that?"

"The only reason I'm this way is because of you. You're nothing but a lazy, cold bitch."

"And I'm the way I am because of your drinking and abuse."

Taking a beer from the refrigerator, Adam stumbled to his chair in the living room, not bothering to turn on the TV.

Mae yelled from the kitchen, "Good Adam, that's just what you need, another beer!"

The full bottle shattered against the iron wood stove in the corner of the room sending a shower of foaming beer in all directions from floor to ceiling.

Grabbing her keys, Mae walked to the door screaming, "You can clean that up yourself, you bastard!"

Mae went for a drive and ended up sitting on the bleachers at the high school football stadium, shivering in the cool night air. High school seemed a lifetime from the distant past, yet she was a student here less than a year ago. It seemed crazy. This whole last year seemed crazy. She started to cry again, but stopped herself. Enough crying, she thought. That won't bring the baby back. That won't bring Adam's knee back. This is simply where she was in her life and she better get on with it. Tears are over with – a thing of the past. It's time to look ahead. Make up with Adam and move on. Things were said by them both that she was sure they didn't mean. Apologize and get things back on track. And while you're at it, she said to herself, get the house cleaned up and the flower seeds planted. You've spent enough time doing nothing.

Feeling stronger than she'd felt in weeks, Mae drove home. Walking through the front door, she could smell the beer before she turned the lights on. Adam was asleep in the same chair he'd been sitting in when she'd left. Four empty beer bottles lay next to him on the floor. Alright, Mae thought, I'll cut him some slack this time. Without worrying about making noise or waking Adam, she got a sponge and a bucket. After carefully picking the shards of glass from the carpet, she soaked as much of the beer up with the sponge as she could and then went to work on the walls and ceiling. She could still smell the beer, but it would dry out and fade soon enough. Next she went to the kitchen and threw out the half prepared dinner she'd been fixing when Adam had come home. She made herself a quick sandwich, flipped off the lights and went to bed.

Sometime in the middle of the night while sleeping on her side, Mae woke to hear a rustling in the bed next to her. Adam. She closed her eyes to return to sleep. But before she could drift off she felt his calloused hands sliding her night dress over her thighs and above her waist. She pushed his hands away saying groggily, "Not now. I'm sleeping."

"You've slept enough," was all he said and thrust a finger into her crotch.

Instantly awake, Mae nearly yelled, "I said not now! Leave me alone. You're still drunk. Go to sleep."

Adam's finger withdrew, but was replaced with something more substantial. Entering her abruptly he grunted, "You can sleep after."

Mae let him have his way. Lying on her side with Adam behind her, she endured his rough pounding and thrusting. She could smell the beer and booze on his breath and it nearly sickened her.

"Move, damnit!" Adam panted, but Mae remained still. He might be fucking me, Mae thought, but I won't fuck him back.

Whether it was the alcohol or something psychological, Mae didn't know, but Adam couldn't climax. He stayed hard, unfortunately, but couldn't get off. The minutes turned into more than a sore and sweaty hour. Mae covered her ears with her hands so as not to have to hear him pant and grunt over her hair and shoulders. She tried unsuccessfully to not be aware of his salty wet skin rubbing against her from her legs to her neck. *Finish, for Christ sake!* She thought. Then, as suddenly as he'd entered her, he withdrew saying, "Goddamn you. You unmoving cold bitch!" and he stumbled off to sleep on the sofa.

When Adam returned from work the next day, he arrived sheepishly holding an inexpensive bouquet of flowers. Handing them to Mae he said, "Mae, I'm so sorry about last night… and a lot of other nights too."

Mae took the flowers and placed them in a vase from a kitchen cabinet. She didn't say anything to her husband except a mumbled "Thanks," when he handed her the bouquet.

"Look Mae," Adam said, "I'll quit drinking. We can go out like we used to, have some fun."

Mae still said nothing.

"And I've been thinking, I think all you need is to get pregnant again. That's what started all this in the first place. We'll have a baby and then everything will be alright."

Mae looked at her humble husband standing in front of her. "I don't know about trying for another baby. Not just yet anyway."

"Why not?" Adam said honestly bewildered.

"Because I'm just not ready," Mae said.

Adam started to say, "But – " and Mae cut him off with "I don't want to talk about it. End of discussion."

And it was.

The week after having lunch with Joanne, Mae called her friend on the phone and arranged another lunch with her. They took a table in the restaurant at the Best Western Hotel. It was refreshing to have a little girl time and a little girl talk. Joanne was an enthusiastic talker and seemed to know everything that was going on in Mill Valley. She was also proving herself an empathetic listener when Mae explained Adam's knee injury and how it ended his football career at UT. When Mae told her about the miscarriage, Joanne reached across the table taking Mae's hand and let a few sympathetic tears run down her cheeks.

The lunch lasted over an hour. Glancing at her watch Joanne said, "I don't know where the time's gone! I have to get back to the store." She reached for her wallet in her purse, but Mae insisted on paying.

Joanne smiled at Mae, "Okay, I'll let you pay this time only if I can pay next time."

Her meaning was well received by Mae who said, "It's a deal." Then thinking a moment, asked, "Why don't we make this a weekly lunch. Say, this time every wednesday?"

"That sounds great. I'd like that, Mae."

They both left the restaurant in good spirits knowing a friendship had been rekindled.

Adam was true to his word and came home straight from work every day. He tried to be helpful around the house and kitchen, but usually managed to just get in the way. Mae appreciated his efforts but still had difficulty warming to him intimately. Adam was certainly less forceful, but Mae knew her lack of enthusiasm for sex didn't go over well. Part of the problem stemmed from Mae thinking about getting pregnant again every time Adam tried to get close. If things weren't great now, how would they be with the added responsibility of a baby? Clearly, Mae thought, things had improved, but not to where she felt comfortable enough to want to get pregnant. But was this line of thinking right? Deep inside, was she just afraid of another miscarriage? She couldn't discuss this with Adam and this was best kept from Joanne. She needed to talk it through though. Her own parents were in the middle of a move to Tampa and Mae didn't have that kind of openly honest relationship with her mother anyway. No, there was only one person to contact, one person she felt safe to speak to in Mill Valley. Dr. Foster.

She made the appointment with the receptionist under the guise of severe headaches. Dr. Foster was a kind man who listened carefully and listened well. Mae spoke of her fears of becoming pregnant again and having a child. She also discussed the struggle she'd had with her lengthy depression after the miscarriage.

When Mae paused to gather her thoughts, Dr. Foster asked, "And how are things between you and Adam?"

Mae felt stunned into silence. She knew it was Adam who was at the heart of her problem. More than any fear of miscarriage or fear of childrearing responsibilities, Mae was afraid of having a baby with a nineteen-year-old father with alcohol issues and inclinations of verbal and even physical abuse. Sure, he wasn't drinking now, but Mae knew the alcohol could begin again at any time. If this visit with Dr. Foster was going to be worth anything, Mae had to tell him everything. And so she did.

"Mae, you came all the way to my office to talk and hear my advice," Dr. Foster said "so I'll assume you want me to give it."

Mae nodded attentively.

"Never mind the pregnancy part – Mae, you're a strong and healthy young woman. You should have no problem bringing a pregnancy to full term. That shouldn't be a problem unless there are more issues concerning this than you've told me."

This time Mae shook her head.

"Okay, listen to me carefully Mae. Bringing a baby into the world isn't an easy proposition. It's expensive and stressful. For at least a year or two you'll lack for sleep and all spontaneity will go out of your life. You'll basically live for your baby. Now, don't get me wrong, starting a family is one of God's true gifts to a couple. Sure, things can be a little tough at first, but under the right conditions, a baby is a wondrous thing that brings incalculable joy. But I said *under the right conditions* this is the result. Under the wrong conditions – and by that I mean a couple with problems getting along well, financial problems, intimacy problems, drug or alcohol problems, or any number of other problems – well I think you get the picture. Under less than favorable circumstances a baby only adds stress to a marriage and can easily split a couple apart. If you are considering having a baby Mae, you better make awfully certain you and Adam have a strong relationship.

Mae sat listening.

"Something else, Mae," Dr. Foster said. "You and Adam are very young. Maybe your marriage isn't strong enough or solid enough for a baby at present. Don't feel rushed to begin a family. There's no need to make any immediate decision on this topic. Give yourselves time. As I said, babies are expensive. You might want to start a savings account now so you'll be less stressed financially when you do decide to become pregnant. You should talk to Adam about these things. Every good and successful marriage I've ever known was based on good communication."

Mae thought a moment before responding, "I agree about communication being important, but how do I tell my husband I don't trust him to not drink and to stay sober."

"I can't answer that for you. Maybe you need counseling. That can be very helpful."

"I don't think Adam would go for that."

"Well, I will advise you one thing. If you are unsure of having a baby, you shouldn't get pregnant. I can give you a prescription for birth control pills. It's a personal decision you can make right now, right here in my office." Dr. Foster looked at his watch, "I have other patients waiting, but I think I've given you all the advice I can."

Mae stood, put on her sweater and said, "I'll take the prescription."

VII

Mae's concern over getting pregnant vanished. Adam still spoke almost daily about trying for a baby, and to keep the peace and avoid the discussion that would follow if Mae resisted the idea; she pretended to acquiesce to Adam's wishes. It was easier for her to say, "I'm okay with it if I get pregnant, Adam. We'll have to let fate decide for us." These kinds of statements put an end to further talk of babies and pregnancies and cribs and parenthood, thank God. The subterfuge was subtle because it was a topic Mae never mentioned and after a while, Adam didn't much either.

She still had difficulty in the arousal department. Maybe it was that she'd never dated any other boys in school, or that Mae had no sexual experience outside of that with Adam, but she was either losing interest in having relations with him or she had already completely lost interest altogether. At least, sex became less frequent and when it was unavoidable, he was sober. Mae had read somewhere that this lack of sexual desire often arrived in later years of marriage – maybe ten or twenty years later. She didn't know how common it was for a nineteen-year-old wife nearing the end of her first year. Perhaps the feelings would return. For now, just getting over her bouts of depression was a victory of sorts. She could work on the other stuff later down the line.

The bright spot in her week, in her life actually, was lunch with Joanne on Wednesdays. Even though she didn't need to, Mae made a kind of ritual of enjoying a bubble bath on each Wednesday morning before putting on makeup and choosing a nice outfit or dress to wear to lunch. Wednesday became her connection with the world outside Grandma Kessler's farm house. Sometimes after lunch when Joanne returned to the dress shop, Mae would browse the stores in Mill Valley or even drive the twenty-three miles to the nearest mall for some shopping.

Since Mae apparently felt good enough to shop and go to lunch with Joanne, Adam suggested she return to waitressing at the Waffle House. That was the last thing Mae wanted. She'd rather be alone at home than spend her time serving breakfast all day. On one occasion after Adam had paid the monthly bills, he said, "Mae, if you'd get your old job back, these bills wouldn't take such a big chunk out of my pay."

To which Mae replied, "Well, if I'm probably going to be pregnant soon, I'd hate to get hired and then have to leave like I did last time." The unintended consequences of this flippant little lie would eventually prove life-altering for both of them.

On a Wednesday night, Adam came home from the Goodyear store after having only one measly little beer with the guys after work. Mae was still wearing the new dress she'd bought the previous week for her lunch date that day. Mae was at the sink when he walked into the kitchen, put his arms around her from behind, nuzzled her neck and said, "Well, don't you look pretty today."

Mae spun around and pushed him away. "You've been drinking! Don't even try to deny it. I can smell it on you!"

"One beer, Mae. Jesus Christ, can't I even have one crappy little beer?"

"No Adam, you can't. One *crappy little beer* leads to two and then three *crappy little beers* which leads to chasers of Jack Daniels before even more *crappy little beers* and then you coming home stinking drunk!"

Adam stood looking at his dressed-to-the-nines wife and said, "If you only knew how much of a bitch you sounded just then…" before he turned on the TV in the living room.

Mae left the kitchen and returned a moment later wearing jeans and a T-shirt. She'd also pulled her hair into a pony tail. So much for a happy end to a nice Wednesday, she thought.

The following Wednesday Joanne arrived a few minutes late at their table at the Best Western. "Sorry Mae," she said breathlessly. "This will have to be a short lunch. Mrs. Tobias – you know, she's the new choir director at church – anyway, she's coming in for a fitting and Mom's not feeling great. I think she's coming down with a cold. So I have to be there to take care of her."

"Don't worry about it Joanne," Mae said, masking her disappointment. "Just relax and try to enjoy the time you have."

"Thanks Mae, you're terrific."

They ordered lunch which Joanne nearly gulped. She kept looking at her watch every few minutes. Finally Mae said, "Joanne, for goodness sake, don't worry about lunch today – just go. I understand, really."

"Yeah, you're right. I'll get the waitress to box this. I really gotta get going."

"We'll do it again next Wednesday. Maybe if you can get some extra time we can do a little shopping after lunch."

"Sounds great," Joanne said. "I'm sure I can get the extra time. See you then."

Mae was disappointed in Joanne's early departure but she relaxed and enjoyed the rest of her lunch by herself. She even ordered a slice of cheesecake for dessert with a cup of tea. This wouldn't be a total loss.

Work ended for Adam at 5:00. If he arrived home by 5:15, Mae knew he wasn't drinking after work. Anything after about 5:40 meant he'd stopped for a few with his friends. Mae was starting to accept his drinking since she seemed to be able to do little to stop it without sounding like a bitch. If Adam wanted to drink, fine, he could. Coming home drunk was a different matter. That she found hard to tolerate. And since she wasn't working, she had little right to say how he should or shouldn't spend the money he made so long as the bills got paid on time. If she were working and they pooled their paychecks, that would be different, but it had been a long time since they were doing that.

At 6:20 Adam arrived home. Mae got to where she could gauge the amount of alcohol he'd consumed by the clock on the kitchen wall. Lunch break was at noon, so by 5:00 he was drinking on an empty stomach. Any time he got home after 6:15 meant he'd had enough time to down more than four or five beers. Beyond that he'd slur his words and be less steady on his feet. Three beers he seemed to handle alright, but when he started the Jack Daniels things went downhill fast. Tonight was one of those times.

"Did you have lunch today with Joanne?" he said walking into the kitchen.

"Oh thanks, Darling. Yes, my day was just fine. I sure hope you had a nice day too," Mae answered sarcastically.

"Did you or didn't you have lunch with Joanne?"

"Not that it's any of your business, but yes, I did."

"Don't you lie to me!"

"What in the world has gotten in to you?" Suddenly Mae was seriously confused.

"Tim Gentry from work had to go on a service call at the Best Western today. He said he saw you eating by yourself. When he told me, I ran by Suzy's shop and saw Joanne inside with some woman. So, I can add one and one and get two just like the next guy and I say you just lied to me. I wanna know what you were doing at the Best Western Hotel!"

"So that's what this is all about, huh? Now you don't trust me? Is that it?" Mae was getting angry now. "Just what the hell do you think I was doing?"

"I'm not sure I really want to know, but I can tell you this. You have no interest in me anymore. I figure maybe you have interest in someone else."

Mae started to laugh.

"Don't you laugh at me, you lying bitch!"

"I'm going to assume that's Jack Daniels doing your talking for you. I won't stand you calling me names anymore."

"Are you going to answer my question, or not?"

"I shouldn't, but I will. Just this once, I will. But you better never, and I mean never come into this house again drunk and tossing around accusations at me. I don't deserve it." Mae was fuming now and let her words out before she thought about what she was saying. "And I'll tell you something else. You're becoming a flabby, drunken pig. Your breath stinks of booze half the time and look at the gut on you now. You're becoming a pathetic slob who can't get used to the idea that he's not a football star anymore. Face it Adam, you're just a tire jockey with an embarrassing tattoo working at the Goodyear store and unless you get your shit together and go back to college or get some kind of training, that's all you're ever gonna be!" She stared at him with true hatred in her eyes.

"And to answer your insulting question, I did have lunch with Joanne, but she had to leave early because Mrs. Tobias needed a dress fitting and Suzy was sick. If you don't believe me go to the Best Western and ask to look at the bill. Then you can go over to the church and find Mrs. Tobias and see what time her fitting was scheduled for at Suzy's. If you had half a brain, you'd have already done that if you had suspicions about your wife. You make a lousy detective. Better stick with fixing flat tires. It suits you!" She pushed past him on the way out of the kitchen saying, "And you can make your own damn dinner from now on. I'm sick of waiting around for you to show up after drinking with your good-for-nothin' pals."

The alcohol had slowed Adam's brain. His response was feeble. "Yeah, maybe that's true and maybe that's not. We'll see." But Mae was already in the Toyota headed for the high school bleachers again.

VIII

It had been nine weeks since Mae had sat alone on the old high school football stadium bench seats and formulated the idea of offering guitar lessons to kids. She knew she desperately needed more in her life than keeping house, going out to lunch with Joanne and dealing with Adam. Going back to the Waffle House wasn't going to happen. Besides, she'd told Adam she might be getting pregnant and didn't want to have to quit on them again. But giving guitar lessons would bring her some extra money, get her out of the house and allow her some space from Adam.

Mae posted index cards offering kids' guitar lessons at the middle school, the grocery store and at two churches. Within three days she was taking the cards down. The responses had been quicker than she'd thought possible. Already she'd lined up five kids and that was enough. At twenty-five dollars for an hour lesson, that was perfect. Five kids, five evenings a week for an hour or so each would work out just fine. If she wanted to give more lessons all she had to do was post the cards again.

Since their blow up two months ago, Adam had been more reserved and even sullen. He fixed his own dinners and spent most evenings in front of the TV. He drank after work regularly, but not to the point of drunkenness. Most of the time he slept in one of the other bedrooms or on the couch. This was fine with Mae. Her feelings toward him had evolved from anger to ambivalence. A few times he'd brought flowers to Mae and mentioned starting a family. Mae knew his intentions were good. He was, after all, making an effort. But it was too late for that. By now she couldn't imagine going through a pregnancy and bringing a newborn into this house. Mae dismissed Adam's attempts by saying she still needed to recover from her last pregnancy. She continued taking the birth control pills for the times when sex was unavoidable.

Guitar lessons were arranged for 7:00 in the evening. This allowed Mae to have a quick dinner before leaving for a student's house. Adam rarely came home before 6:30 so she was able to avoid him most evenings. Sometimes she left the house early to sit and play her guitar for a half hour or so in a park before giving a lesson. It was good to be playing again. There were also times when she stayed longer than the hour lesson to play alongside a couple of her more accomplished students. Sometimes, just for her own satisfaction, she'd play for the parents after a lesson. She almost always drove home later in the evenings feeling refreshed and alive. Those feelings usually died the moment she walked through her own front door.

On a Sunday afternoon Adam was changing the oil in his pickup while Mae sat reading in the living room. Through the open window Mae heard Adam exclaim, "aw shit!"

Coming into the house he said, "that idiot at the auto parts store sold me the wrong damn oil filter. I gotta take this one back. I need your car."

Without looking up from her book, Mae said absently, "Keys are in my purse – on the kitchen counter."

The following Wednesday morning – lunch with Joanne Wednesday – Mae had just settled in to her hot bubble bath when she heard Adam's pickup return to the house. He must have forgotten something she thought, closing her eyes to enjoy the fragrant soak.

The tranquility was broken when the bathroom door swung open and Adam stepped next to the tub. "Get out of the tub Mae."

"Are you out of your mind?" she answered, annoyed. "You should be at work."

"Get out of the tub!"

"No, I won't get out of the tub. What's your problem?"

"You lied to me."

"Oh Christ, not this again…"

Mae stopped speaking the moment Adam held up her container of birth control pills.

"As I said, you lied to me."

"Listen Adam, I can explain that. Why don't you go to work and we can talk about this when you get home. I don't have any lessons tonight and we can straighten this out."

"I'm not going to work today. I called in sick." He stared down at Mae in the tub. Neither said a word for a few moments and then Adam exploded.

"Get out of the fucking tub! Now!"

Before Mae could respond or even move, Adam grabbed her hair in his left fist and her upper arm with his right. In an instant Mae was dragged from the tub.

She started to scream, "Get your goddamn hands off – " but the swift open-handed slap that landed on her left cheek stopped her words. The fast follow-up slap to the other cheek brought her to silent shock.

Dripping bubbling bathwater and standing on trembling legs before Adam he said, "I found these pills in your purse. You lied to me about wanting to get pregnant."

Mae tried to speak but her face was numb and her ears rang.

"What else have you been lying about? Huh, Mae? What else?" and he slapped her again. Hard. Mae fell to her knees and began to sob.

"I thought you were lying the first time I suspected something, "Adam stammered. "Now I've got proof. I know you, Mae. I know how you like to fuck – or at least how you used to like to fuck. No, I think you still like to fuck, just not with me!" He pushed her violently and Mae fell on her back, banging her head on the tile floor. The room started to go dark. She felt herself fade. She came to with Adam on top of her, pounding and thrusting with a violent force she'd never experienced before. Her back and buttocks rocked into the unyielding, hard tile floor while Adam's weight kept her from getting a full breath of air. She started to fade again, but another slap to her face brought her back. She tasted blood.

"Move for me you lying bitch, or I'll slap the shit out of you."

Mae moved as best she could, pinned under his weight. This was like a dream – no, a nightmare, she thought. A few minutes ago she was relaxing in a scented bath and now she was being raped and beaten on the floor. This can't be real. This can't be happening.

With a series of loud grunts, Adam concluded his attack. He lay heaving but otherwise motionless on top of her. He got to his feet and put his jeans and shoes on. "Get up," he said, but Mae just laid on the floor with her eyes closed.

"Get up, goddamnit!"

Mae did not move.

With incredible strength that startled Mae, even after what she'd just been through, Adam crouched down, grabbed her upper arm, and with one heave lifted Mae to a fireman's carry. Standing upright with Mae over his shoulder, he calmly walked out of the bathroom, through the kitchen and down the short flight of stairs to the root cellar. Mae tried to focus, tried to understand what was happening, tried to just figure out where she was being taken.

She was dropped to a mattress on the concrete floor. Next to it was a chair from the living room. Adam sat in the chair looking down at her. Mae felt more vulnerable than ever before in her life. She tried to cover her nakedness with her hands. Adam saw this and laughed.

"Trying to be modest, huh Mae?" Adam slapped her hands to her sides. "A little late for that, don't ya think?"

Mae tried to comprehend the last fifteen minutes of her life with no success. Her face still felt numb. When she wiped her lips with the back of her hand she saw a light smear of blood.

Adam folded one leg over the other. "Now, you're going to tell me who you've been fucking."

And so began the most horrific and transformative week of Mae's twenty-year-old life.

TWENTY

"I don't know about you Tom, but I need some more coffee," Mae said as she walked to the kitchen and refilled the French press with grounds. She ran water in the kettle and said, "I'll be right back."

"You know Mae," Tom called to her, "You really needn't go on with this. I believe I've gained a full understanding from what you've already related."

"That's nice of you, but I want you to hear the rest. I owe that to you."

"You don't owe me anything."

"But I do."

Mae filled the press with boiling water. "This will only take a couple minutes. Can I get you anything else? Something to eat?"

"No, I'm good for now," he said. Then looking at his watch, "It's going on 6:00. Play your cards right and I might just take you to breakfast."

Mae returned with the coffee mugs. Forcing a sleep-deprived smile, she said sarcastically, "but Tom, what would the locals think if we showed up together for breakfast at the crack of dawn?"

"Probably that I'm one lucky guy."

"You're sweet, but you may not think that when I finish my story."

"I doubt there's much you could say that would make me think differently."

"Don't be so sure," she said. Tom noticed the serious tone she'd once again taken.

Mae took a sip of the steaming brew. She put the mug down on a wood coaster on the table in front of them. "Here goes," she said.

"So Adam left me alone in the cellar. As I said, there were no windows – just a couple hanging light bulbs, a few shelves of canned preserves, the mattress from one of the other bedrooms and a chair. Naturally I tried the door, but it was a thick, heavy thing that bolted from the outside. Remember, I was wet and naked and probably still in some shock. I recall feeling so cold I couldn't stop shivering. I know I laid on the mattress and must have fallen asleep because the next thing I knew Adam was back. I'd lost track of time. I didn't know if it was day or night or even what day of the week it was. Adam sat in the chair just looking at me for the longest time. I remember how calm and in control he acted while I was shivering and scared out of my mind.

"He said something like, 'Are you ready to tell me who your boyfriend is?'" I don't know exactly what I said, but I told him there was no other boyfriend. That was the last thing on my mind. I said I was just giving guitar lessons. He said he didn't believe me. He called me all sorts of horrible names and accused me of being a slut and a whore. Tom, he was completely off his rocker."

"Really, Mae, you don't need to continue with this. I understand –"

"No, you don't understand, but thank you for being so considerate. I'll finish the story.

"Without going into a lot of details that frankly, I'd just as soon put out of my mind, suffice it to say Adam told me he'd cancelled my guitar lessons and called Joanne saying I had to go out of town unexpectedly. He said nobody would come looking for me. He also refused to believe anything I said about not having a boyfriend. Before he left he raped me again and beat me with his belt."

Tom interrupted, "Jesus Mae – "

"No, let me go on. Please Tom. I need to get through this and it's important to me that you hear all of it."

Tom took a sip of his coffee and nodded.

"So, again Adam left. I remember I had welts all over my legs and back. There was no escape. Every time he whipped me he'd ask who I'd been with and every time I said no one he'd whip me again.

"Next time he came down to the cellar he brought a pair of high heels and a thin shawl he found in my closet. He made me put the heels on and wrap the shawl around my neck. He told me to dance for him. I thought he was crazy and I told him so. When he removed his belt again I danced. He gave me instructions on how to move, what to show. I'm sure you get the picture. I did what he wanted and when I had him excited enough he raped me again.

"Each time he did this, I tried to resist, but that only increased his, shall we say, efforts. He seemed to get off on my struggling and screaming."

Mae paused to collect her thoughts and drink some coffee. "You know Tom, it's a funny thing. When Adam and I were in high school and later just married, sex was new and exciting. I'd do anything to please him and he'd do the same for me. Even things we might have once thought uncomfortable or unclean became pleasurable because we each thought we were doing things the other wanted. I got as much satisfaction getting him off as I did when I was being made to feel satisfied. Lovemaking was fun and new and, well, it was just wonderful to share. And now, here in that goddamn cold and damp cellar, what we'd once enjoyed together became a physical assault – a demeaning, debasing, despicable play in which I was being forced to act. It was a good thing Adam brought down a bucket of water and another empty one for me to use because I vomited after every visit.

"Every time he returned, and keep in mind, I don't know whether it was once a day or twice a day, morning or night or in between, he'd ask me who I'd been seeing. It went worse for me each time I denied his accusations. He made me do things, and did things to me that I wish I could erase from my memory, but I can't.

"Then one day he came down the stairs with a cat. A solid gray cat. He told me it was a gift – something to keep me company while he was away. He left me a litter box and some cat food. I named the cat Smoky and I think he was the only thing that kept me from going insane.

"Adam returned a few times over the next days – I assume they were days. Time went by slowly. He made me sing and dance or pose or do things to my self while he watched. I was beyond humiliation. I think my performances were worse than the rapes. I had to pretend I was enjoying getting him excited – that I wanted him. I assure you, that was not an easy task.

"Then he returned with a kitchen knife. I didn't know what he had planned, but any way I tried to think about it brought me to the same conclusion – that things were turning from bad to worse – much, much worse. Adam sat in the chair and Smoky jumped onto his lap. He sat there holding the knife and stroking the cat. Then he asked me for the thousandth time who I'd been seeing – who I'd been fucking, as he put it. I remember falling to my knees crying, begging him to believe me that there was no one, that I'd been faithful. He ordered me to stand and stop crying. I did this as best I could. Then he said, 'I'll ask you one more time. Who have you been fucking?' Out of desperation I blurted out the first name I could think of – some guy from high school. I didn't know what might happen next. I was just glad Adam and his knife had left. But he returned a short time later and took up the same position as before. Again, the cat jumped in his lap. Adam had the knife. He said he checked the name I gave him. He must have remembered the guy. He said he found out he'd moved to California after graduating and was going to college there. I remember him smiling at me with a smug look of satisfaction on his face, as if he'd just solved the world's toughest mystery. He said he'd teach me not to lie to him and with one stroke cut off the last four inches of Smoky's tail. The cat screamed and ran to a corner of the cellar. Adam got up and said, 'I'm going to give you a few minutes to think things through. When I come back I want answers – the truth – or I'll carve that cat up an inch at a time until you do. And after I'm done with him, I'll start on you. And when I'm done, believe me, nobody will ever want to fuck you again.'"

Mae grabbed a tissue from her pocket and wiped her eyes. "Sorry, this isn't easy."

Tom started to say something but Mae held up her hand.

"Not 'till I'm finished. Then you can speak."

Again, Tom nodded.

"I was sure this would be my last chance to do anything. I was living off Grandma Kessler's preserves and I thought of breaking one of her jars and using a piece of glass as a weapon, but that probably wouldn't do much. Adam was big and strong. I'd be lucky to put a scratch on him and even if I did, God only knows what he might do to me. Everything I'd said until now hadn't worked. Crying and begging and pleading did nothing but egg him on. I believe it made him feel more dominant and commanding. I formulated a plan just as Adam was returning. I'd try something totally different, something to throw him off guard.

"He sat in the chair with the knife and said, 'Well?' I stood up and put on the heels I know turned him on. I started softly singing a song and dancing around the mattress and then his chair. I forced a smile on my face. I could tell he was interested. I kept dancing and swaying and said in as sexy a voice as I could muster that he was right, that I'd been a bad girl, but that I'd learned my lesson, that I loved only him, wanted only him. I said nobody could satisfy me like he could and on and on. You get the picture. I teased him and talked to him. When he'd reach for me I'd back away and say, 'not just yet.' I strung him along like this until I was sure he was aroused. I made myself kiss him. He lifted his hand – the hand without the knife – to touch me, but I gently pushed his hand away saying now it was my turn to please him as he'd been pleasing me. Believe me, it was all I could do to not choke on those words."

Mae took another sip from her mug and said, "look Tom, there's no other way to go on than to be blunt about what I did next. So, just be forewarned." She put the mug down, took an audible deep breath and continued.

"I told him to stand, which he did. I got on my knees and undid his belt – the same belt he'd beaten me with I might add – and pulled down his pants and boxers. I fondled him and then took him into my mouth. I looked up and his eyes were closed. I pushed him back and he sat in the chair with me between his legs. I stroked him with my hand and took a testicle into my mouth. It was now or never. This was my chance, I think my only chance, and I took it. With all my might I bit down and crushed him between my teeth."

Mae looked at Tom who forced himself to remain expressionless.

"I remember hearing a god-awful scream, like a woman's scream, when I bit down. His hands flew to his crotch and the tip of the knife slit me here," Mae pointed to the threadlike scar running down from the corner of her left eye to the top of her cheek.

Tom said, "I never noticed that before."

Mae said, "I see it every time I look in a mirror, every time I put on makeup or brush my hair."

"I'm just curious," Tom said, "I assume you told all this to Joseph?"

"Not all of it. He got the abbreviated version, the condensed version. I wanted you to hear everything."

Another sip of coffee and she plowed on, "I didn't even feel any pain. Thank God the knife was sharp and made a clean cut. He continued howling and holding his crotch. He wasn't aware he'd dropped the knife. But I was.

"I picked it up and stabbed it into his inner thigh. I remember feeling the tip embed in bone. Adam just kept screaming. It was deafening. I jumped up, grabbed the cat and ran up the stairs, shutting and locking the door behind me. I don't remember calling 911, but I did, and then ran from the house.

"It must have been a few minutes later when a sheriff's car drove up to me. I wasn't even aware that I was still naked. I was running down the road away from the house, still holding on to the cat. Blood was streaming down my face. The sheriff and his deputy got me calmed down and wrapped in a blanket. Smoky ran off. I never saw him again. Riding in the back of the car to the hospital I told them what had happened to me. I was nude, covered in bruises and welts and streaming blood. They believed me.

"I woke up some time later in a hospital bed and found that a week of my life had passed in that cellar. The doctor said the sheriff wanted to speak to me again and I said that was okay. I was up to it. He asked me some questions that I don't recall now and I finally asked him if they'd brought Adam to the hospital too. Why he answered the way he did, I still don't know. Maybe he thought it was something I'd want to hear, but he said, no they didn't bring Adam to the hospital. They brought him to the morgue.

"The morgue? This didn't make sense. I told him I stabbed Adam in the leg so I could run away without him following me. I said I didn't try to stab him in the chest or neck, that I didn't try to kill him. And the sheriff said I may not have tried to kill him, but I sure as hell had. He said I stabbed him right through his femoral artery, that he probably bled out in less than a minute. Then he said, and I'll never forget this or the way he said it, 'for what it's worth ma'am, I think the son-of-a-bitch got exactly what he deserved. Good for you.'

"They called in a pretty skilled plastic surgeon who closed my cut without leaving much of a scar. An inch different and I'd have lost my eye. Later there was an inquest and no charges were filed against me.

"The newspapers had a field day with this one. All over Tennessee were headlines like, *Homecoming Queen Slays King; High School Sweetheart Dies in Sex Dungeon;* they even used the last line from King Kong: *Beauty Kills the Beast!*" It was unbelievably awful. When word leaked from the coroner's report that Adam had a crushed testicle, well, you can imagine the jokes and insinuations. I was both a heroine and a killer-whore. The name *Ball Biter* got started somewhere and stuck. That's how I was known. When I called my parents who were too busy doing nothing at their new retirement home in Florida to come up to see me, all they could say was that they were glad they'd moved before this scandal hit. Nice, huh?

"I tried to get together with my dear friend Joanne, but she told me on the phone it wouldn't be good for her reputation to be friends with me anymore. That's when I called the people who'd bought the rest of Grandma Kessler's land and made a deal to sell the house and remaining two acres. Part of the deal required them to bulldoze the house. I got that in writing.

"So, I took what little I had and drove back to the University of Tennessee. I went by my maiden name Holland and took jobs waiting tables and occasionally singing. I gave some guitar lessons too. It took me almost six years, but I got my degree in accounting and took a bunch of extra courses in english, history, psychology, anthropology, you name it, just so I wouldn't end up ignorant like about everybody else where I grew up."

Mae picked up her coffee mug, looked inside and put it back down on the coaster. "And now there's only one final part to relate. And of everything I've already told you, this I actually have come to grips with. It took me a while, but I'm okay with it. More than okay, actually." She took another deep breath and continued, "A few weeks after moving to Knoxville, I began to feel sick. I knew what it was immediately and I had an abortion. And Tom, until that moment I didn't even agree with the whole concept of abortion. But a child conceived in that kind of cruelty and violence and fathered by a…" Mae paused a few seconds thinking and said, "by a man with such a broken spirit – well, no child like that should ever be brought into this world."

Mae looked directly at Tom, almost challengingly. Tom made no comment and Mae concluded, "This part I've told to no one but you. And I won't ever make mention of it again."

Tom nodded in silent agreement.

"After college I got my first job as an accountant in a hardware chain based in Nashville. Some caring individual in the office did an online search and before I knew it, I wasn't Mae Holland anymore – I was *The Ball Biter.* I was fired for some kind of trumped up reason before I had the chance to quit. That's when I legally changed my name to Mae Hollis and some years and a lot of miles later here I am."

Tom still sat expressionless on the sofa. He picked up his mug and drained the last of the time-cooled coffee from the bottom. Mae did the same and turned to him.

"Still want to take someone like me to breakfast? If you don't, I completely understand."

Tom stood and looked at his watch again. "Mae, I'd be honored to take you to breakfast or any other place you desire."

They entered the Lunden Diner – *open twenty-four-seven* – the sign read. A tired looking middle-aged waitress greeted them and said, "The place is yours – choose your seats."

Tom led the way to a booth at the far end of the restaurant. After ordering the special *pancakes for two,* Tom said, "Mae, I have to tell you that I think you are even more remarkable than I'd previously thought. You're strength and resilience inspires me."

"Did you practice those lines on the drive here?" she chided him.

"No, I'm serious."

"Well, thank you, but I think you missed a few important points of what I told you."

"Actually, I think I missed very little."

"Didn't you miss the point about the young wife who refused to be loving and supporting of her young husband – the same husband who through no fault of his own had all his dreams and future plans blow up in his face in one afternoon?"

Tom said nothing.

"Didn't you miss the point about the self-centered little bratty wife who perhaps drove her hard working husband to drink and then gave him nothing but grief about it? How about the point about the beautiful and sexy newlywed wife who denied any intimacy with her humbled and embarrassed newlywed husband – the same one who lied to him about wanting to start a family while secretly taking birth control pills? Didn't you miss that point, Tom?" Mae seemed almost angry with him.

"No Mae, actually like I said, I missed very little if anything. What you pointed out to me just now was perfectly obvious throughout your rendition of the past. I like to think my powers of concentration and perception are keen enough to grasp the underlying nuances of the storyline."

"Okay Professor Sloan, then I take it you simply refuse to be any kind of judgmental."

"Quite the contrary. I listened and formed my own judgments."

"Care to share your verdicts?"

Tom took a bite of pancake, chewed for a moment, swallowed and put down his fork.

"I'd be glad to. First, I see two young people with no experience behind them except that of the surreal world of high school, foolish enough to get married. And I'll add that the two sets of approving parents should have been horse-whipped for allowing or even encouraging such a union at that ridiculously immature time in their lives."

Now it was Mae who sat expressionless saying nothing.

Further, I disregard such terms and expressions as "self-centered, humbled, denied any intimacy", etc. etc. etc. ad nauseum! Mae, let me remind you I've taught eighteen and nineteen-year-olds in numerous classes for years. Believe me, I know from whence I speak. People at that age are largely *children* struggling to find *themselves*, much less successfully sharing in something so complex as marriage. Who you were then is not who you are now, Mae. Maybe you are who you were at thirty-five or possibly thirty, but not who you were leaving high school. I see you in the present and I see a woman who is sensitive and caring enough to blame herself twenty-something years later for her tormentor's misguided and clearly criminal behavior. I see a strong woman who has rebounded from a trauma that many – nay – most women could never come to grips with to any degree. Yes, I accept you are still deeply troubled by your past – and that I also believe is because it will take more than you dealing with such a secret alone and by yourself. You have punished yourself over this for years. You've become your own judge and jury who have found you guilty for a situation that got out of control and sentenced you to a state of self-loathing and incompleteness."

"So what do you prescribe, Doctor Sloan?"

"I suggest to you that you have done your time and paid for any sins you may think you have committed. I suggest that you leave the past in the past. I suggest that you allow others into your life, allow others to know you, others to love you."

Mae put her own fork down. "I don't want to allow *others* into my life, or *others* to know me, or *others* to love me."

Tom was about to speak, but Mae hushed him and continued, "I don't want *others,* Tom, because I only want *you.*"

AFTERWORD

SUNDAY – FIVE WEEKS LATER

Mae had donated her old Taurus to the reservation and replaced it with the gleaming white Ford SUV parked off a little used dirt road in the desert. Close by, she and Tom had spread their blanket.

Cutting the last of a particularly good wedge of smoked Gouda, Tom speared a piece of the cheese with the tip of his Ruana knife and offered it to Mae. She sipped some Chablis and plucked the Gouda from the extended blade.

"Well," she said, "I guess this will be our last Desert Sunday."

"For now, anyway – yes. Who knows about the future though."

"Think you'd ever want to come back here?"

"Probably not right here, but maybe somewhere in Arizona. I'm not thinking that far ahead."

He offered Mae another piece of cheese but she shook her head declining the offer and said, "Tomorrow's the big day. Are you all packed?"

"Yes. I didn't arrive here with much so there's not much to organize. How about you?"

"I really don't have all that much either, but everything is boxed and ready to go."

"Good."

"Gonna miss the Boxster?" Mae asked.

"Sure, it was a great car, but where we're going I think a Jeep would suite me better. I'll have a good look at them when we get to Montana."

Mae finished her wine and rolled on her back. She closed her eyes and let the sun shine on her face. "I'll miss these warm days."

"There will be others. Instead of Desert Sundays we'll have Montana Sundays."

"Mmm, that has a nice sound to it," Mae thought a moment and said, "I still can't get over Joseph leaving me his ranch. I mean, how many healthy and single twenty-nine-year-old men bother to make out a will?"

"I know," Tom said thoughtfully. "It's as if he knew intuitively that his time was running out. Maybe it was a premonition or some sort of vision. Something must have influenced him to do it."

"Lately I've been thinking how unlikely all this is. I mean, Joseph coming here from Montana, me breaking down outside Lunden and settling here, and then you dropping in from outer space like you did."

"Now hold it right there, Mae. New York is not exactly *outer space*."

They both laughed and Mae said, "Well, around here it sure is," and they laughed again..

Becoming serious, Tom said, "I remember Joseph saying to me once that some people come into our lives as teachers – to enlighten us – and some people come into our lives as students – for us to enlighten." He looked at Mae who still had her eyes closed but was listening intently. "I think that holds true for the three of us in particular."

"I do too," Mae said. "And I feel fortunate that I was able to enlighten you and Joseph, at least to the extent that you both were able to grasp the lessons I could offer."

Tom chuckled. "It's always good being able to have a serious discussion with you Mae."

"I'm always here to help."

Tom glanced over and saw the grin on her face. It was good to see her happy, he thought.

"What do you say? Time to wrap this up? We've got a lot of miles ahead of us tomorrow."

"I guess so. Monday it'll just be us two killers on the road fleeing to Montana."

Again serious, Tom said, "I know you were only joking Mae, but I don't see it exactly that way. You and I are no more killers than Jake was a killer because he came back alive from Vietnam; or Joseph was a killer because he hunted game for food; or that coyote we saw earlier was a killer. They were just survivors and that's the difference. Roger was a killer and I believe Adam would have been a killer. You and I are merely survivors and sometimes survival requires extreme measures. But that's part of the system that's been grinding away for millennia."

Tom got up and began putting away the wine bottle and the other picnic items. Mae stood and stretched. "I think you are good for me Tom Sloan," she said.

Tom faced her and Mae stepped closer to him, putting her arms around his neck. He pulled her close. There was no hesitation in her strong embrace. And she did not pull away.

Above, floating on warm thermal air currents and silhouetted against the clear azure sky, two ravens croaked and called as they circled and dodged together playfully. They folded their wings and spiraled, then tumbled and circled some more, sparing and feinting with each other before they flew out of sight to the north.

About The Author

William Goodman resides with his wife, Marion, in Bozeman, Montana and part of the winter months in Cave Creek, Arizona. An experienced outdoorsman, he is equally at home in the Rocky Mountains as in the Sonoran Desert. Both of their sons live in Montana.

Contact William Goodman at goodman.williamt@gmail.com

Made in the USA
San Bernardino, CA
08 July 2014